Rebecca Yarros is the No. 1 *Sunday Times*, *New York Times*, *USA Today* and *Wall Street Journal* bestselling author of over fifteen novels including *Fourth Wing* and *Iron Flame*. She loves military heroes and has been blissfully married to hers for over twenty years.

She's the mother of six children and is currently surviving the teenage years with two of her four hockey-playing sons. When she's not writing, you can find her at the hockey rink or sneaking in some guitar time while guzzling coffee. She and her family live in Colorado with their stubborn English bulldogs, two feisty chinchillas and a Maine Coon cat named Artemis, who rules them all.

Having fostered then adopted their youngest daughter, Rebecca is passionate about helping children in the foster system through her nonprofit, One October, which she co-founded with her husband in 2019. To learn more about their mission to better the lives of kids in foster care, visit www.oneoctober.org.

T0349252

Also by Rebecca Yarros

Empyrean
Fourth Wing
Iron Flame

Flight & Glory
Full Measures
Eyes Turned Skyward
Beyond What Is Given
Hallowed Ground
The Reality of Everything

Renegades
Wilder
Nova
Rebel

Legacy
Point of Origin (Novella)
Ignite (Novella)
Reason to Believe

Muses and Melodies

A Little Too Close

REBEL

REBECCA YARROS

NO.1 *SUNDAY TIMES* BESTSELLING AUTHOR

PIATKUS

PIATKUS

First published in the United States in 2017 by Embrace,
an imprint of Entangled Publishing, LLC
First published in Great Britain in 2024 by Piatkus

1 3 5 7 9 10 8 6 4 2

A CIP catalogue record for this book
is available from the British Library.

ISBN: 978-0-349-44259-4

Printed and bound in Great Britain by Clays Ltd, Elcograf S.p.A.

Papers used by Piatkus are from well-managed forests
and other responsible sources.

FSC
www.fsc.org

MIX
Paper | Supporting
responsible forestry
FSC® C104740

Piatkus
An imprint of
Little, Brown Book Group
Carmelite House
50 Victoria Embankment
London EC4Y 0DZ

An Hachette UK Company
www.hachette.co.uk

www.littlebrown.co.uk

To Emily Lynn, my own little Rebel, my inspiration, my favorite wedding present, my OTH binge-watching partner, my friend, and most importantly: my daughter. Never doubt that you are the change the world needs.

Chapter One

LAS VEGAS

That kid was still staring.

I stood in the lobby of the Bellagio, scanning through my text messages, blatantly ignoring most of them, but when I looked up, the gangly, mid-teenage boy was still gawking. The kid was wearing a Fox Motocross hat and a shirt from the Nitro Circus World Games, and judging by the way he was glancing from me to his phone and back again, he knew who I was.

Luckily, my phone went off, making it easy to ignore the fact that he was probably tweeting out my location right now. *Great.*

Little John: ARRANGEMENTS ARE MADE.

Penna: THANK YOU. OUT FRONT IN FIFTEEN?

Little John: I STILL THINK THIS IS A SHIT IDEA.

Penna: I'LL BE SURE TO NOTE THAT.

I slid my phone into the back pocket of my jeans as the kid headed in my direction, glancing to see where his parents were in the check-in process.

"Excuse me?" His voice cracked.

"What's up?" I asked with a smile.

"I know this is probably stupid, but are you…Rebel?"

Busted.

"Sure am." I forced the muscles in my face to maintain the curve to my lips.

The kid's eyes went wide, and my smile turned genuine. "I love you." He turned ten shades of red. "I mean, I love watching you. Oh crap. I'm not a stalker or anything."

Laughter gently shook my shoulders. "Don't worry. I absolutely knew what you meant."

A couple selfies later, the kid was on cloud nine.

"Do me a favor?" I asked him as I signed his hat.

"Anything."

"Can you wait a couple hours until you post that on social media? It's really important." I knew the kid might do it anyway, but I felt better having a promise.

"Yeah. Sure. No problem!" He gave me an enthusiastic head nod.

"Thanks." I handed him back the hat as his parents approached.

I had already turned to walk toward the bar when he called out.

"Rebel, does this mean you're back?"

"We're about to find out," I told him just before I slipped out of view.

It always floored me when I was recognized in public, that we'd somehow gotten famous enough for that stuff, but this time felt different. Maybe it was because I was off on my own for the first time—without Pax, or Landon, or Nick… or Brooke. Maybe it was because I hadn't participated in a Renegade stunt in the last three months.

No. That wasn't it. It was because the kid managed to know me when I was having trouble recognizing myself anymore.

Rebel. I'd earned the nickname early, seeing as I never conformed to the societal norms my parents expected for a little girl. Motocross bikes, snowboards, parachutes, bungee lines, those became my dollhouses. The X Games took the place of cotillion. I bucked every trend, and gold-medaled in the Whip, which, up until me, had been a guy-only event. Instead of joining the Junior League, I gave in to my addiction for adrenaline and extreme sports, founding the Renegades with three of my closest friends who became my brothers. The number one way to get me to do something was to tell me that I couldn't. I rebelled.

But this time was different.

This time, I was rebelling against my friends—going off book.

The noise from the casino assaulted my ears as I headed toward the bar where Patrick said he'd meet me. My flowy tank top and skinny jeans paired with black Vans weren't exactly the norm in the bar, but I was used to sticking out.

A quick scan of the room told me Patrick wasn't here yet, so I headed toward the bar, leaning against its granite top.

"Can I help you?" the bartender asked.

"Ice water with lemon, please," I ordered, sliding into the chair.

"Coming right up," she said and left to fill the order.

"Living dangerously?" A deep, slightly accented voice asked from next to me.

I turned toward him and nearly sucked in my breath reflexively. *What a killer smile.* The guy was gorgeous in a can't-help-but-stare kind of way, with thick black hair cut military short, deep, chocolate-brown eyes, tanned skin, and a grin that had me leaning against the bar in hope that it would catch the drool no doubt pouring from my mouth. Dimples and... *Oh my fucking arm porn.* The sleeves of his dress shirt were rolled up, hinting at the tantalizing lines of his bicep. My stomach clenched, the first physical reaction I'd had to spotting a hot guy in *years.*

He cocked an eyebrow at me, that smile turning sexy, deadly—he was more than aware of his impact on me, but it came across as playful instead of the cocky, sleazy way I was used to. I let loose a grin of my own and shook my head at myself. I was constantly surrounded by hot, scrumptious, defined men, and here I was losing my shit over a stranger in a bar.

A stranger who didn't know me, what I did, or what had happened to me in the last three months.

"I'm Cruz," he said, turning on his barstool to face me fully.

"I'm Pen—Penelope." My full name sounded odd, since I always went by Penna. But I wasn't Penna tonight. Or Rebel. Hell, I didn't know who I was.

"Penelope," he repeated, caressing my name with his accent.

Never mind, it sounds delicious when he says it. What was that? Spanish? Not quite, but it was just as sexy.

"You're not drinking tonight?" he asked, running his thumb down his still-full glass. No wedding ring.

I thanked the bartender and put a five on the bar as she handed me my lemon water, then turned back to Cruz. "Nope. Need a clear head."

One of his black eyebrows rose. "Underage?"

"Wouldn't you like to know?" *Are you flirting?* I didn't flirt. Ever. Maybe for the cameras and the crowds, but never on a personal level.

"I would," he said, leaning forward.

I met him halfway, whispering in his ear, "I'm jailbait and only here to get you into massive trouble." God, he smelled good—like warm, expensive cologne…and something I couldn't put my finger on.

His brows knit, like he was trying to figure out if I was kidding or not. Finally I laughed, the sound bright and unburdened. "Just kidding. I'm twenty-one. I'll actually be twenty-two next month."

"Thank God." The look in his eyes sent every hormone that had lain dormant in my body into overdrive. I took another sip of my water, hoping the temperature would cool down the parts of me that had no business heating up right now.

Before I could throw myself any deeper down the rabbit's hole, I felt a hard smack to my ass. *Oh, hell no.*

I spun, sending my elbow into the gut of the guy behind me, then finished the turn, putting my hand to his throat as I pinned him against the bar.

Fucking Patrick.

"Relax, Rebel. Just wanted to keep you on your toes," he said with a slick grin, putting his hands in the air.

"Keep your fucking hands to yourself, or the next time you touch my ass, you'll pull back bloody stumps."

He gave me a look of mock surprise. "Man, is that any language for a lady?"

"Shut up, Pat. You never would have pulled that if Pax and Landon were here." I eased up off his throat and took my barstool, more than aware that I probably looked psycho to Cruz.

Patrick shot me another smile and took the stool next to mine, motioning to the TV above the bar, where ESPN was showing the highlight reel from today's competition at the X

Games. "Well, they're not, which is why you called me."

"I called you because you're the only Renegade not halfway around the world, or in Aspen, and I need someone I can trust." My gaze flickered to Cruz, who had turned back to his friends.

All for the best. Not like anything was going to happen there, anyway.

"Yeah, well, the summer games are more my thing," Patrick said, pulling my attention back to him. He was pretty average for a Renegade. Excellent athlete, but not the best. Good-looking, but not...well, Cruz. He leaned toward me, his breath hot in my face. "And here I was hoping that you just wanted to see me alone."

I blinked and pulled back. There was no way. Was there?

"Have you been drinking?" I asked, hoping I was wrong. Sure, Renegades were reckless, dangerous even, but there was one line we never crossed—we *never* mixed stunts with substances. That crap would get you killed.

He shrugged. "I had a few. Nothing to worry about. I can still jump."

"No, you can't." I looked away, watching my plans melt faster than the ice in my glass.

"What are you talking about? I can."

My gaze swung to his. "No. You. Can. Not. Not something this dangerous." What was I going to do? Abandon it? Wait and call in backup? Admit that I couldn't handle it on my own?

His stare turned mean. "Who the hell are you to decide that?"

My thoughts stilled as icy anger swept through me. "I'm an Original. This is my stunt. My equipment, and I'm telling you that you're not on it anymore."

He scoffed, pushing off the barstool. "Fuck you, Penna. One day someone is going to knock you off that pretty little pedestal you think you stand on. Everyone knows you're broken. Figure your shit out by yourself. I'm gone."

He walked away without a backward glance, and I suddenly wished my glass was full of vodka instead of water. He was right about one thing—I was broken. That wasn't something I admitted lightly, but when my best friends were currently partying in Aspen, celebrating their newly won X Games medals, and I was holed up in Vegas...well, I was broken.

I should have been there—competing with and against them. Rebel would have been. She was tough, smart, aware of her skills and worth. But I'd somehow left Rebel on the floor of the arena in Dubai, crushed under the weight of a motocross bike and a stadium light her own sister had sent crashing down.

For the last three months, I'd felt like plain ol' Penna, and no matter what I did, I couldn't rouse Rebel, couldn't get her to stand up and take notice that I was withering away.

The doctors had cleared my leg a month ago—just before Christmas—but I'd given every excuse not to get on a bike, a snowmobile, anything that put me back in the seat as one of the Original Renegades. I was out of shape from the months I'd been in a cast, but it wasn't just my body that needed the rehab. My head was clouded—I couldn't focus, and my heart was broken. I missed the one person I wasn't allowed to— Brooke.

Tonight was supposed to be my first step back into badassery. *So much for that plan. You can't do it solo.* Breaking that Renegade rule was just as bad as the substance one. We were clean, sober, and used the buddy system when it came to stunts.

"You okay over there?" Cruz's voice cut through my self-pity party.

"Yeah," I assured him, unable to force a smile. "My plans

for the evening just drastically changed."

"For the better, if you're referring to the ass-grabbing asshat."

"Saw that, did you?" I asked, thankful that ESPN had switched over to hockey highlights.

"Yeah. I would have jumped to defend your honor, but it was pretty clear that you were completely capable of handling it." He saluted me with his glass but put it back down without drinking.

"Thank you." Being surrounded by guys like Landon and Pax, it wasn't often that I got to fight my own battles. It was oddly nice to be seen as strong and empowered.

A wedding party came through the door, the bride dressed in a strapless white confection that contrasted with her mocha-colored skin gorgeously. She leaned over the bar next to me, and when the bartender didn't immediately appear, she whistled.

My kind of girl.

"I need some club soda. My friend trashed her dress," she ordered.

"So what are you doing with your night now that your other plans have collapsed?" Cruz asked.

I glanced at my phone. Little John was waiting out front.

"I'm not sure." What *was* I going to do? That was the billion-dollar question.

"We don't have much planned," he said, nodding his head toward his friends, "but I'd be more than happy to have you hang with us. Or you and I can sit here a little longer and not drink," he added with another heart-stopping smile.

Before I could answer, the guys at the bar called him. "Think about it," he said, and turned back to his friends.

"Girl, I would more than think about that. I would ride that train," the bride said.

I nearly spit out my water. "I'm sorry?"

"You're not, but you will be if you don't jump that." She gave Cruz a once-over.

A blonde came over, a red splotch on her pale green dress. "I can't believe I did this," she said with a southern accent.

"Don't stress. Pictures are done, and all that's left is the party," the bride assured her. "Besides, it wouldn't be us if stuff didn't go wrong."

"Did you get something?" a redhead asked, joining them.

"Here it is." The bartender handed a small bottle over the bar.

The girl signed a bill for the club soda. "Thanks. Ember, you got that?"

"Yeah, we're good," the redhead said, blotting the blonde's dress.

The bride turned, leaning back against the bar. "So are you going to take him up on it?" she asked me, nodding toward Cruz.

"I...uhh...don't know."

"Well, you should. The last time someone looked at me like that...well, let's just say he climbed up onto a bar for me, and I ended up marrying him," she said with a grin in the direction of the door.

My phone *ding*ed as three guys approached.

Little John: HEY, ARE YOU COMING OR WHAT? YOUR WINDOW IS CLOSING.

I swallowed, my brain going through every possible scenario. What if I did it by myself? Landon and Pax would be pissed, but it wasn't like they weren't already going to freak out about me doing this without them. What if I cancelled? Would I ever get up the nerve to get back in the game? I'd never been a toe-in-the-water kind of girl. I was a dive-headfirst-and-see-what's-at-the-bottom girl.

"Seriously, take him up on it," the bride urged as a huge,

hulking guy in a tux swept her up over his shoulder.

"Talk time is over," he said with a smile. "Josh, get the door?"

"Go for it!" the bride stage-whispered with a grin as she was carted away.

"My pleasure," another guy called out, opening the door as the six of them left.

I wiped the condensation off my glass with my thumb and snuck a few glances at where Cruz's drink remained untouched. *Maybe...* It was insane, but so was what I was about to do.

"Well, what do you say?" Cruz asked, turning toward me as his friends all stood, preparing to leave.

Jump. It's what you're good at.

"How familiar are you with parachutes?"

His eyebrows shot up. "I'd bet I'm more familiar than you are."

"That's a bet you'd lose," I said with a smile I couldn't contain. My stomach clenched every time his eyes met mine, but I'd never felt better.

"Somehow that does not surprise me," he said slowly.

"Cruz, you ready?" one of the guys asked.

He tilted his head at me in question.

"I've got a better idea," I said quietly.

"Lay it on me."

"Want to do something highly dangerous with me?" I held my breath while he didn't just look at me, but *saw* me. In those few heartbeats, I felt naked even though his eyes didn't leave my face. Every instinct told me to look away, but his eyes were made for drowning in, and I was already going under.

"Any other details?"

"Nope. You're in or you're out," I said with more bravado than I felt.

"Cruz?" his friend prodded.

I watched the debate silently play out in his eyes before he nodded slowly. "You guys go ahead. I'll meet up with you later," he said without breaking eye contact with me.

My heart leaped, my pulse picking up to a gallop. *Holy shit, I'm really doing this.* God, I hoped he wasn't lying—that he was experienced. What were the odds I'd end up sitting next to someone in a bar who was capable of this?

Fate, my heart whispered.

Shut the hell up, my brain answered.

I didn't get gooey over guys. Gooey made you soft, made you weak.

"Shall we?" he asked, standing as his friends left.

My feet hit the ground. Whoa. Even at my five-eight height, he still had a good four inches on me, and that *body*. The guy was built, probably even more so than Pax, which was hard to accomplish, and the rippling of those very cut arm muscles told me that the rest of him was probably just as defined.

We made our way to the front of the hotel where Little John waited, our strides evenly matched.

"In all fairness to you, this might be slightly illegal," I admitted, leading him to where Little John waited outside.

"Aren't you just full of surprises?" he said quietly as he held the door open for me.

"You have no idea."

I was even surprising the hell out of myself tonight.

Chapter Two

CRUZ

LAS VEGAS

My eyes strayed to her ass as she folded herself into the dark black sedan that waited for us outside the Bellagio. I prided myself on not being a misogynistic asshole, but it was right *there*, all perfectly round and grabbable, encased in those jeans that looked like they'd been stitched with only her body in mind.

"You coming?" she asked from inside the car, slipping into a leather jacket.

Well, this was either the beginning of an epic story or a horror movie. Either way, I was committed.

I slid onto the leather seat, and we were off before I had even clicked my seat belt. A large, bald man glanced back from behind the wheel before turning onto the strip.

"You're not Patrick."

"I am not Patrick," I confirmed as the guy's eyes widened.

Was he her driver? Her bodyguard? *Please don't be a jealous boyfriend.*

"Let's go," Penelope said, looking out the window. "Patrick was drunk, so I had to lose him."

"Are you kidding me?" the guy roared.

"Nope. There was zero chance I was putting him in a rig like that."

The guy's fingers tapped on the wheel while we waited for a light to turn. "Shit. Okay, well, who is this guy?"

"Little John, this is Cruz. Cruz, this is Little John. He's our stunt manager and a really close friend," Penelope explained.

Little John. Like Robin Hood?

"Okay," I said, trying to go with the flow. Stunt manager... damn, who was this girl?

"And what qualifies him to pull this off? Or did you grab the first good-looking guy from the lobby?"

"It was the bar, actually," I corrected him as we began driving again, turning down a side street.

"Fuck my life, Penna. What the hell are you thinking? You can't just throw some stranger into a rig and expect shit to go right. Pax and Landon are going to freak out."

"They are not my problem," Penelope answered, but her hand flexed on her thigh.

Maybe those are the jealous boyfriends.

"Right. They're mine. And so is this guy"—he thumbed in my direction with his free hand—"when you get him killed."

"He said he can jump," she argued.

"Oh really?" Little John snapped as we pulled up outside the back of the Linq Casino and Hotel. "Like what? A few tandem jumps with his buddy to cross off his bucket list? You can get him seriously hurt, Penna."

Okay, that's enough.

"Look, I have no clue what we're doing, or who you are, but I have nearly a hundred jumps with the 82nd Airborne. I'm not exactly a rookie here."

That earned me a surprised look from both of them, but I far more enjoyed seeing Penelope's blue eyes widen. She struck me as the kind of girl who was hard to impress.

"You're in the military?" Little John asked.

"I did my three years and got out," I answered.

"Thank you for your service," Penelope said in a soft voice. "Now I feel bad for giving you shit about jumping." Her nose crinkled in the cutest way.

"Don't worry about it. Now are we just going to sit here all night? Because I remember a beautiful girl promising me something dangerous and a touch illegal."

"A touch?" Little John snapped at Penelope. "Did you tell him *anything*?"

"Look, it was kind of an impetuous decision."

"You? Impetuous? Never," he said sarcastically.

"Quit being an ass. Are we cleared to go?"

He muttered something that sounded like, "they're going to fucking kill me," and then opened his door. We followed suit, meeting at the trunk, where Little John handed us two packs, harnesses and helmets attached. Apparently we were jumping off something, and given that there wasn't an airport in sight, we had to be BASE jumping…which was illegal as shit.

"Still want to do this?" Penelope asked, slinging her rig over one shoulder and threading her nearly waist-long blond hair through the back of a baseball cap. For being so slight, she handled that pack like it weighed absolutely nothing.

"Since I don't know exactly what we're doing, that's kind of an unfair question." I took the black cap she offered and slipped it on.

She pointed up, and I followed the direction of her finger to see the High Roller, the tallest Ferris wheel in the world. "Are you kidding? That thing…"

"It's five hundred and fifty feet at the top," she supplied, already following Little John toward the back of the building. We passed under the giant metal platform where passengers boarded the ride, and my mind spun a hell of a lot faster than that Ferris wheel. "You don't have to do it if you're scared," she tossed over her shoulder.

Like I was scared? The jump itself didn't bother me. The repercussions of being caught? That could fuck up everything I'd been working for the last eight years. As gorgeous, enchanting, and utterly intoxicating as this girl was, I couldn't throw away everything over an illegal jump.

She turned, holding the door open for me. "If we get caught, which we won't, the biggest penalty we'll face will probably be trespassing, which is a slap-on-the-wrist misdemeanor. Look, you don't even have to do it. You can leave now, or you can ride up with me and ride back down, or you can jump."

She stared up at me, every inch of her body language screaming that she didn't care what I did. She was going to do whatever she wanted. But her eyes told a different story. There was something damaged there, a desperate plea that tapped into my soul in a way I'd thought I was immune to.

Man, was I wrong.

She wasn't a damsel. She *was* in distress, but she wasn't going to say a word about it, and that set off every alarm bell in my brain and engaged that sense of chivalry Grandma had busted her ass to instill in me.

Shit. Double shit. Fuck.

I wasn't reckless by nature—far from it. I played life like the chess game it was, more than aware of the consequences of my actions seven moves from now. Maybe it was knowing that I was leaving tomorrow for the next few months, or I could have lied and told myself it was for the thrill. It wasn't. It was for her—this phenom of a woman I'd met barely an hour ago.

A misdemeanor would be a pain in the ass but wouldn't shred my plans like a felony. *Holy shit, you're seriously debating the seriousness of different charges?*

"I'll ride with you," I told her.

The relief in her smile sent a wave of warmth through me. *Good decision for her. Bad decision for you.*

I told the devil on my shoulder to shut the hell up and followed them into the darkened hallway. We entered at the head of the ticket line, where no one waited, as if the line had momentarily paused.

"I took care of everything," Little John told Penna. "We're already past the bag check, so they won't see the chutes. These are your tickets. Make sure yours is on top. The attendant marked it. He'll bypass the security on your pod, and the rest is up to you. I'll be parked right out back. When you land, ditch the chutes—you're worth more than they are."

"Got it," Penelope said, taking the tickets.

"Are you sure about this?" Little John asked her.

"No," she answered, and my gaze snapped to where she shook her head at him. "But if I want to be *me* again, this is what I have to do. There's no toe-dipping, no easing my way back in for the documentary. Either I pull this off, or I don't deserve to be a Renegade."

"That's bullshit."

"That's the truth." She leaned up and kissed his cheek. "Thank you. I know what this cost you with them. I'll see you at the bottom."

"Just be safe, and you know…don't get him killed, either." He pivoted and left us standing inside the doors that led out to the platform.

Noise coming up the hallway told me that the line was reforming and heading our way. "Let's go," I said, placing my hand lightly on her lower back to guide her through the door. It wasn't anything I hadn't done on a date, but simply touching the small of her back sent a wake-up message to my dick.

Down boy. There's no time for that. I promptly removed my hand.

What the hell am I doing? I asked myself that the entire time we approached the attendant, watching him load the pod directly ahead of ours with at least ten people.

Penelope handed our ticket to the attendant, whose eyes widened slightly at the mark in the corner. He nodded, guiding us into the transparent pod that would easily fit twenty or more people. "You'll note that the exit door is on the opposite side," he told us. "It's about a half-hour ride total, so enjoy. Welcome to the High Roller."

We stepped over the six-inch gap that separated the platform from the pod, and the attendant closed the door, ensconcing us in a darkened, purple-lit sphere. Rocking was nonexistent as we started our ascent.

The television monitors immediately started babbling about the stats of the Ferris wheel. A few quick button-pushes and they were silenced. I put the pack on the floor as Penelope did the same, and then we both stood at the windows, watching the lights of Vegas above us. Soon they'd be beneath us.

"I owe you an explanation," she said softly, catching me off guard.

"I'd like one, but I made my choice. You don't owe me anything." Our shoulders brushed, and that same electricity I'd felt earlier hit me. I didn't even know who this girl was, but we had some insane chemistry.

"I've never done this before."

"Which part? The BASE jump? The illegal factor? Or asking a random stranger if he'd like to break the law with you?" My lips turned up at the utter absurdity of the situation.

She laughed softly, a gorgeous, light sound that made me instantly want to hear it again. "I've never picked up a guy. Let alone a guy in a bar. Add to it that I then asked if you wanted to risk your life with a stranger, and it's been an evening of firsts."

"Really? Man, this just happened to me last week in Seattle," I joked.

That earned me a breathtaking smile and another light laugh. God, the girl was truly a masterpiece. Her face had classic, almost Grecian, features with high cheekbones, a pert nose, and a mouth that begged to be sampled. Those eyes, though—light blue with darker flecks that had me staring way longer than necessary.

"How old are you, anyway?" she asked.

"Twenty-seven. Worried I'm underage?"

"Nawh, just making sure you couldn't join AARP."

"Ouch," I laughed.

Her eyes focused on the buildings as we passed floors, slowly rising into the Vegas skyline. "I can't believe I did this." Her phone *ding*ed and then *ding*ed again before she could get it out of her pocket. "Shit," she muttered, scanning over the text messages.

"Issues?"

She thumbed over the messages as another one came in. "Pax. Leah. Pax. Landon. Rachel. Nick. Shit. They know I'm here."

Panic crept into her eyes, and her teeth worried her lower lip.

I checked my watch. "Okay, we have about ten minutes until we hit the peak."

"Right," she said, still reading the messages.

"And chances are I'm never going to see you again once we land."

She looked up at me. "*We* land?"

"*If* I jump with you," I clarified. "Point is, you're up here with someone you just met in a bar an hour ago, when you clearly have people who care about you. It's none of my business, but there's something missing in this equation."

She glanced at me and then to the skyline, turning off her phone and slipping it into her back pocket. "You don't know the first thing about me."

"And maybe that's why I can say that to you." Was I really going to have to jump with this girl to get her to open up? Something was eating away at her, and it was obvious she wasn't going to reach out to anyone from those mysterious text messages. I looked back toward the pack on the floor. "How did you stow the lines?" If I was even going to consider jumping off this Ferris wheel, I needed to know there was an actual parachute in there.

"Classic figure-eight pattern."

"No primary stow?"

"And no slider." She shrugged.

"Wait. No slider, *and* no primary stow?"

"Taking off the slider gives us a faster open time, and with five hundred and fifty feet—"

"We need those seconds," I deduced. We'd be falling for only a few seconds as it was. If Little John was there at the landing, if we could lose the chutes, if the hats had helped us avoid the cameras…*we might not get caught.*

"And the stow would just add another unnecessary step in deployment," Penelope finished.

"You're really good at this, aren't you?"

A corner of her mouth lifted. "I'm a very well-paid extreme athlete. Or…I used to be, anyway." She ended on a near whisper.

"And you're not now?" She shot me a look, and I raised my hands. "Hey, I have one night, just a few minutes in this eternity of ours, to try to understand you." *To try to help you.*

"Do you have to understand everyone?"

"Yes. I have a slight control issue." *And a hero complex,*

according to my grandmother.

I felt her gaze on me but kept mine on the skyline, which we were slowly, finally rising above.

"I got hurt a few months ago," she said, crossing her arms under her breasts.

With supreme effort, I kept my mouth shut. She needed someone to listen, not talk. My effort was rewarded when she sighed and continued.

"My group—the other athletes—we're more like family than friends. One of my really good friends, Nick, was paralyzed working on a new trick, and my sister…she loved him, and when he shut everyone out, she broke. We've been shooting this documentary, mostly to get Nick a name in stunt design, and things went wrong from the start. Equipment was tampered with, people got hurt, Leah almost died," she whispered. Shaking it off, she sucked in a breath. "Brooke— my sister—she was trying to hurt Pax, but I was the one she got instead, thank God. Crushed my leg." She rolled her ankle. "I've been cleared for a month now to get back in the saddle, but instead of being excited, I asked for an air cast. I *asked* to be sidelined."

"Is that why you're not with your friends?"

"They're in Aspen for the X Games. I wanted to get on the plane with them, but I just couldn't watch and wonder if I'd ever have the balls to do it again. I had to find out, and if I'd let them know, they would have coddled me, told me to ease my way back in."

"You're not an ease-in kind of girl?"

She rolled her eyes at the double meaning I hadn't intended, and I laughed. Apparently my subconscious had ideas of its own, which was understandable, seeing as how her entire body screamed hot, keep-you-coming-until-dawn sex. But it wasn't the curves of her body that got me on this Ferris wheel in what was potentially the most reckless choice of my life—it was the broken look in her eyes that peeked out when she let her guard down.

"I'm a jump-in-with-both-feet-and-then-measure-the-depth-later kind of girl," she said. "Ever since I sat on Pax's first motocross bike and then demanded my own, I've never feared flying, or the fall. If I can do this, then maybe that girl is still in here." She tapped her chest. "If I can do this, I'm one step closer to looking at my bike without my stomach turning over."

I already knew that if that girl wasn't still there, she wouldn't be standing here with me. She'd still be on the ground. But I wasn't the one who needed to be convinced—she was.

I nodded to myself and took a deep breath. *Looks like you're jumping.*

"You've got some good lawyers to get us out of this, right, extreme-athlete girl?" I asked, reaching for the pack.

"The best," she promised. "Besides, like I said, it's a misdemeanor, and they're not going to catch us anyway."

"How sure of that are you?" I asked, examining my pack. I wish I'd had room to roll it out and repack it for my peace of mind. *Leap or don't, but no easing-in, remember? Trust her or don't. Help her or sit the fuck down.*

"A nice bottle of champagne certain," she said with a smile that stole the air from my lungs.

"I'll hold you to that." A few snaps later and I was in the harness, tightening the straps and adjusting the helmet. I rolled down my sleeves to protect my arms the best I could.

The pod rose above most of the casinos around us. "It's gorgeous," she said reverently. Her gaze swept the skyline, her lips parted as she braced her hands lightly against the glass.

"Yeah. Beautiful view." I never once took my eyes from her.

She noticed, glancing my way and blushing.

"It's about time." She pointed to the television monitor that showed we were only a minute from the zenith of the rotation.

She headed for the opposite side of the pod, opening the door with a lot less effort than I'd imagined it would take. I quickly wiped her fingerprints off the glass with my sleeve.

The breeze swept in, the January air clearing my head as I stepped to the open doorway next to Penelope to look down over the nearly empty parking lot.

"You have to clear that tree," she said, pointing.

"You need to watch that lamppost."

"God, I love this feeling," she whispered, as if she hadn't meant to say the thought aloud.

"The rush?" I guessed.

"The anticipation. The war that silently rages in my body between what I want it to do and what it knows isn't safe. The way my stomach tightens and my heart starts to race. The moment the decision is still mine."

I knew the exact moment she was describing because I'd lived it—I was in it now. It was the moment you stood on the edge of epic and decided to topple over.

She looked up, snapping her static line hook to the steel rod above the doorframe. I did the same and then stood back, checking the monitor for our location. "It's time."

She moved her toes to the very edge of the pod, her black Vans standing out against the metal plate. Then she closed her eyes and lifted her face to the sky, pure joy washing over her features.

Enchanting. That girl she was seeking was closer to her surface than she realized.

"See you at the bottom," she said over her shoulder with a thousand-megawatt smile and jumped.

She was fucking fearless, and even if I hadn't been wearing a parachute, I might have jumped just to stay close to her—

she was that magnetic.

"Go to Vegas, they said. It will be fun, they said," I muttered.

I counted two full seconds, watching her chute deploy, then stepped out into nothing.

Chapter Three

LAS VEGAS

Holy shit. You did it.

Adrenaline pumped through my veins, heightening the rush of euphoria that flooded all of my senses. I did it. I was still me.

Maybe I was damaged, a little broken, but I was still *me*. As long as I had this, everything else made sense. Even if I couldn't pull it off in front of the cameras, or hit the ramps with the other Renegades, I had this moment.

The ground rushed toward me, the parachute slowing my descent, but not enough to make it an easy landing. I cleared the lamppost, passed the tree, and lined up with the parking lot where Little John waited. Then I bent my knees and met the asphalt at a run as the Earth welcomed me home.

I spun, immediately checking for Cruz, and nearly sagged in relief as he landed about twenty feet to my right.

Our eyes locked in the dim lighting, something tangible but indescribable passing between us.

Then the moment was over, and I was scurrying to gather up the chute before security got here. There was no way we'd gone unnoticed.

"Ditch the chute!" Cruz yelled as he ran toward me, already having cut his loose.

Little John whipped the car around, squealing to a halt right in front of us.

"I can get it!" I said, gathering the fabric in my arms.

Cruz turned me in his arms and unclicked the harness from the chute. "We have to go. Ditch. The. Chute."

He didn't raise his voice, but he didn't leave room for argument, either. "Okay," I said, like he hadn't already made the decision for me. He was right; the chutes didn't matter. They had no identifying marks and couldn't be traced back to us.

He took my hand and pulled me toward the car, yanking open the door. I dove into the backseat, scooting behind Little John as Cruz slid in next to me.

"Go!" I yelled as the door slammed shut.

Little John took off, tearing through the parking lot in the opposite direction of our hotel. Cruz's jaw was locked, the muscles flexing as he turned to look behind us. "You're in the clear so far," he told Little John.

"Good, good," Little John muttered.

We rode in silence, coming down from the adrenaline high as we kept a lookout. About five minutes later, Little John drove into a residential neighborhood and pulled over. "One minute," he said, hopping out.

"Wow," I said, unable to think of another word to sum up what that had been.

"Pretty much," Cruz said, unclipping his helmet and running his hand over his hair.

Little John climbed back in. "Okay, license plate is back on, and we're heading to the hotel. How do you feel?"

My lips curved. "Rebellious."

"Thank God," Little John said, smacking the steering wheel. "If that brought you back, then it was all worth it."

"Yeah," I said quietly. Did it bring me back? I felt like me—the rush was the same, the feeling that I'd just beaten not only the odds but my own expectations. But was I ready to be back in the real game? Riding my bike? Filming?

"Bobby is going to shit bricks that you didn't film that."

"It was for me, not the documentary. The world already saw me self-destruct once this year, and I let him use it. This was mine."

"And your contract?" he asked as we pulled into the entrance of the Bellagio.

"My contract says that I'll let him film every extreme sport I take part in that's sponsored by the Renegades. Which…this wasn't."

"Either way, I'm looking forward to a phone call."

I leaned forward, hugging him against the seat. "Thank you. I know this was not what you wanted for me, and I'm seriously grateful."

He patted my hand, then squeezed. "I'd move mountains for you, Penna."

"Does that include letting me sleep in tomorrow?"

He laughed. "Hell no. Flight is at noon. I'll be at your room by eight, and you'd better be ready to go."

"Fine." I kissed his cheek as he pulled up to the door and put the car in park. "See you in the morning!"

Cruz held the door open for me, and I slid out. He was tense, his eyes focused anywhere but on me. His hand rested on my lower back as we walked through the doors, and I didn't shake him off. Instead, I savored the touch, wishing I could lean into him.

How ironic; I'd finally found a guy I felt inexplicably drawn to, and I had only another thirty seconds with him.

We made it to the elevators in silence, ignoring the hustle of the casino, and the doors shut, leaving us inside in a tension-filled silence. What do you say to a stranger who just pulled off a highly illegal BASE jump with you? What was I supposed to say about the hum in my blood, the way his scent made me want to snuggle closer?

What the hell was wrong with me?

"So…" My voice faded out, trying to think of something to say as we tapped the buttons for our floors.

"You're insane," Cruz said, finally turning to me, those delicious, melty eyes swallowing me whole. "You know that, right? Crazy hot—no, exquisitely beautiful—smart, strong, and incredibly magnetic, but a little fucking nuts."

"Yes," I whispered as the elevator rose.

He blinked a few times as his smile came and went, shaking his head like he couldn't believe I'd admitted to it. How could I not? I wasn't sure anyone could do what Renegades did and not lose a piece of their sanity.

I'd been questioning mine more and more lately.

"I've never met anyone quite like you," he said softly as we approached his floor. I had maybe another five seconds with him before he was gone.

"That's because there's no one like me," I said honestly. "I can say with 100 percent certainty that I'm an Original." I cracked a smile at my own little pun that he couldn't possibly understand.

The elevator *ding*ed when we arrived at his floor. Time was up.

"That, you are."

My stomach tightened as he stepped toward the elevator doors as they opened, revealing a long hallway.

I would never see him again.

What if I never felt this kind of connection with anyone else? What if he was the one guy I was capable of feeling something with? What if I was about to miss out on something that was truly once-in-a-lifetime because I was ironically scared to jump?

What if was unacceptable.

His hand reached for the door, holding it open, and he looked over his shoulder at me. "Thank you for tonight. I'll never forget it."

Neither would I…and I wasn't ready for it to be over.

"Have you ever stayed in a penthouse suite here?" I asked before my brain could stop my mouth.

"I can't say that I have," he replied, his eyes darkening as his gaze moved to my lips.

Oh my God, I'm going to do it. My stomach knotted worse than before the last X Games.

"Want to? I mean, I do owe you champagne." Hopefully my shaky voice came out breathless and seductive.

The lines of his back tensed.

"I promise it's mine. All legal, and I won't even make you jump out of it."

He turned slowly to face me, his hand still blocking the elevator doors from closing. The longer he stared at me, the faster my blood rushed, quickening my belly, turning my thighs almost liquid. How could a simple look turn me on so fast, so completely?

"Penelope…" He said my name like a half plea, half prayer.

"I know what I'm asking," I assured him. All I'd have is this one night with him, and tomorrow he'd be a memory, but it was better than wondering *what if.*

"Are you sure about that?" He stalked forward, the elevator doors closing behind his broad shoulders. My pulse leaped as he filled my vision, my thoughts centering on what his skin would feel like under my fingertips.

I nodded, and he shook his head.

"I need the word." His breath was sweet as he leaned down, his lips merely inches from mine as the elevator rose again.

God, I could barely think with him this close. He watched me expectantly, with more than a hint of hunger in his eyes. Usually I'd shut a guy down at this point, but this was nothing I'd ever experienced before. Cruz's blatant desire made me feel powerful, intrigued, and turned on—humming with sweet electricity.

He didn't just want me as a trophy—he didn't even know who I was.

He just wanted *me*.

"Yes," I finally said, the word giving my consent not just to him but to myself. I was free to let go for once in my life— damn the consequences.

His mouth brushed over mine, sweetly, as though he was physically asking for the permission I'd already verbally given him. Our lips met in a soft caress that had me on my toes, leaning up for more. It was a kiss that sent awareness rushing down my limbs, waking each of my nerve endings. It was the first chapter of a romance novel, a bewitching introduction that had me hungry to turn the next page, already hooked on his taste.

He pulled back with a smile, his gaze skimming over my face in a way that made me feel like a work of art. Before he could say anything, the elevator *ding*ed, announcing that we'd reached my floor.

I took his hand and led him down the immaculately decorated hallway a short distance to my door. My hand shook slightly as I took the key from my back pocket, and I missed the lock, just skimming the side. *So much for being a badass in charge of my sexuality.*

Cruz's hand covered mine, strong and warm, as he leaned against me slightly, his lips caressing the shell of my ear. "You are under no obligation to open that door or to invite me inside, Penelope."

God, I loved the way he said my name. I barely suppressed a shiver from the chills that swept down my spine. With a quick, sure motion, I unlocked the door.

As soon as the light flashed green, I turned the handle and stepped inside the suite, looking back over my shoulder at the beautiful man who stood at the threshold. "Do you need an invitation?" I asked.

"Yes," he said, bracing his hands on the doorframe like he had to hold himself back.

This was it. Was I really going to invite a stranger into my suite? Into my…bed? *You never know someone until you jump with them.* How many times had I said that to new Renegades?

Cruz waited there, radiating raw sexual energy, watching me decide, his eyes an intense combination of desire and patience. Something told me he'd be the same in bed—unhurried, thorough, and utterly consuming.

For the first time in my life, I wanted to be devoured.

"Come in," I said softly.

He pushed off the doorframe, and in three strides, I was in his arms. One of his hands gripped my waist as the other cradled my face. The door shut behind him at the same moment his mouth met mine.

This kiss wasn't the light caress our first had been. His tongue ran across my lower lip, and with the gentle pressure of his thumb under that lip, I opened for him. His tongue slid inside, hot and insistent, rubbing mine with an expertise that had me gripping his shirt within the first few seconds.

He backed me up until my ass hit the table behind the sofa, a vase falling to the floor with an anticlimactic thud. I felt his smile against my mouth, and mine echoed it for about a millisecond before he reclaimed my mouth, his hand sliding to tunnel through my hair. He changed the angle, kissing me deeper, until my entire world narrowed to the feel of his mouth on mine, the electric current coursing through me, and my mindless need to get closer to him.

He kissed me and kissed me some more, never pushing, but taking everything I offered. His taste was maddening, as dark and rich as his scent. My fingers drifted over the hard muscles of his pecs until I looped my arms around his neck, my breasts pushing against his chest as he pulled me closer.

I wanted more—needed more of this sweet burn that had ignited in my belly, this clawing desperation to feel his skin against mine. My nipples tightened, making me hyperaware of every brush of fabric against them. "Bedroom," I whispered.

"Where?" he asked, gently taking my earlobe between his teeth.

Holy. Shit. That felt amazing.

"Down that hall." I motioned with my head, unwilling to let go of him.

He lifted me by my ass, the motion effortless and all the sexier for it. My legs wrapped around his waist as his mouth returned to mine, and he carried me down the hallway toward the bedroom. The curtains were open, the lights from the strip softening the angles of his face as he laid me on the soft bedspread. Cruz was gorgeous, elementally, perfectly hot—primal, even—but seeing him above me took him to another level.

His mouth slid down my jawline, my breath hitching with every kiss he put to my throat. I gasped as he sucked lightly on a sensitive bit of skin, my fingers raking through his dark, thick hair to hold him to me.

I felt drunk, intoxicated by his mouth, his scent, his weight, as he settled between my thighs. In that instant, I understood the hype of sex, the drive for this intense pleasure that was overwhelming all my senses. The few meager kisses I'd had before were nothing compared to this. Kissing Cruz made me feel borderline insane—every ounce of logic fled as he kissed my collarbone, and I became a creature of pure physical need.

Skin. I wanted his skin against mine, wanted to run my fingers along the lines of the muscles his shirt more than hinted at. I tugged at the fabric of his shirt, and he sat up on his knees as my legs fell off his hips, my thighs open. A smile ghosted his lips as he reached behind his head and pulled the shirt off in a seamless move.

My breath abandoned me as I took in the sheer perfection of his torso. I was used to ripped guys, but Cruz was the most perfect specimen of man I'd ever seen. I reached for him, my fingers skimming over the deep indentations of his washboard abs, exploring the ropes of muscles that defined his torso. An Airborne tattoo stood out against the curve of his bicep, but the rest of him was unmarked—just yards of tan, velvet skin that my mouth was eager to taste.

"You…" I shook my head when I couldn't find the words, my tongue swiping over my kiss-swollen lips. "You're incredible."

"I was thinking the same thing about you," he said, running his hand between my breasts but never touching the rigid peaks. "Except maybe a little dirtier."

My fingers wrapped around the silver chain he wore around his neck, a medallion fitting neatly into my palm as I pulled him back down to me. He lowered his weight slowly, dipping to tug at my lower lip with his teeth.

"How much dirtier?" I asked, my breath coming in near pants.

"Filthy," he said against my neck, moving down to my neckline.

I was going to lose it if he didn't touch me soon.

As his hands skimmed my rib cage, I arched up, and as if he read my mind, he palmed one of my breasts. I whimpered as his thumb rubbed over my nipple, the sensation tightening the bud but seeming to soften me everywhere else. My hips rocked against his, and he hissed as I felt him, long and hard where our bodies met, separated by only a few layers of fabric.

God, I *wanted*, and though the feeling was new to me, I welcomed it like I did every new experience—with eagerness. I was twenty-one years old, and if this was the only time I'd ever feel this kind of desire, then I was going to grasp it for as long as I could.

"Cruz," I moaned as he set his mouth to my breast, his teeth raking me through the fabric of my shirt and bra. The friction was exquisite, and though he hadn't so much as touched me beneath my waist, that's exactly where the sensation gathered, making my hands fist in his hair as a glorious restlessness took over. "Please," I begged, arching my hips to rub against him.

"Say it again," he growled in a low voice that sent a wave of warmth through my thighs.

"Please," I repeated, knowing I needed more and that he could give it to me.

He rose over me until our eyes locked. "My name, Penelope. Say my name. Someone as beautiful, as intoxicating as you are never has to beg, especially not when all I want is to worship every inch of you."

Whoa. I melted with those words and the raging desire I saw in those brown eyes. He made me feel sexy, like some kind of powerful siren. My lips caressed his lightly, pulling back to keep the smallest space possible between us. "Cruz," I whispered.

A low sound rumbled from his chest as he took my mouth, claiming it with his tongue the same way I wanted him to take my body, with sure, powerful strokes that drew out every ounce of pleasure he could.

My hips rocked again, seeking some kind of pressure to appease the need that spiraled tight within me. He flicked open the button of my jeans, and then rested his forehead against mine, our breaths mingling as he paused.

"Yes," I told him, knowing he wanted the word. "Touch me."

His hand slid into my open jeans, his fingers rubbing over the blue lace thong I wore. I'd never been so thankful to have a pretty underwear fetish.

Then all thoughts ceased as he swept the fabric to the side and ran his fingers along my seam. His mouth settled over mine, kissing me breathless as his thumb delved, brushing over my clit.

I broke the kiss with a gasp as pleasure radiated through me in a burst.

"Penelope." He said my name like a revelation, in wonder, in reverence, stripping away every defense, every layer I'd carefully constructed. In that moment, I wasn't Penna. I wasn't Rebel. I was Cruz's Penelope, and that was…*everything*. Our gazes locked, and I'd never felt such an intense connection to another human being in my life.

My hands slid to his shoulders, my nails biting into his skin as he stroked me, bringing out a feverish, all-consuming need to—

Bam. Bam. Bam.

There was a pounding at the door of the suite.

We both froze. "Expecting someone?" he asked, his breath controlled, but his eyes wild.

I shook my head. "No, but it could be Little John making sure I'm okay. Give me a second."

I cursed the overprotective nature of my friends as Cruz rolled off me. Funny, we were no longer physically touching, but I still felt that same connection as if we were.

He watched me hungrily as I buttoned my jeans and zipped them closed. Little John would freak if he saw that I'd brought a stranger back to my room. Then again, right now Cruz felt like anything but a stranger.

I leaned over, kissing him deeply and savoring his taste, the stroke of his tongue, the caress of his lips.

The banging started at the door again. "Damn it," I cursed. "Just a second," I promised Cruz and walked out of the bedroom, closing the door behind me and hoping my hair wasn't a giveaway to what I'd been doing.

"I'm coming," I called out as the banging came again. Someone had better be dead for this interruption, or they were about to be.

I yanked open my door to see the concierge standing there, a look of panic on his pinched features. "Miss Carstairs, I'm so sorry, but these gentlemen—"

Two police officers pushed past him, their blue uniforms sobering me instantly. "Penelope Carstairs?" they asked.

"Yes?" My stomach tightened in knots of nausea.

"We're going to need you to come with us to answer some questions," the shorter of the two said, spinning me quickly and yanking my arms behind my back.

Fuck. My. Life.

"Ow!" I said quietly, hoping that Cruz wouldn't hear— that he wouldn't come looking. If they knew I was the one who'd BASE jumped from the High Roller, they'd be after him, too. "What is this pertaining to?"

The cuffs were cold against my wrists as the short one pulled me through the door. "Where can we find your jumping partner?" he asked, ignoring my question and answering it all in the same breath.

I shrugged. "I don't know which room he's staying in. I only met him in the bar."

He narrowed his eyes in suspicion, and I smiled at him. I'd

learned early the best way to lie was to tell the truth as much as possible.

"So you admit to criminal trespass?"

I kept my smile sweet. "I admit that I'd like to call my lawyer."

So much for stepping out on my own. Pax and Landon were going to kill me for this one. Then again, there really wasn't such a thing as bad publicity when it came to stunts.

The cop shook his head at me, disgust evident in the set of his mouth, and walked me out of the room, heading toward the elevator. His radio went off with a few calls as we descended to the ground floor, but I tuned them all out, my mind racing, praying they didn't find Cruz.

Which lawyer did I want to call? Not Daddy's. He had his hands full with all things Brooke-related.

My thoughts were interrupted by the *ding* of the elevator doors. We walked out onto the crowded casino floor, and I was thankful that in Vegas a girl being led away by the cops wasn't too uncommon an occurrence.

I ducked my head just in case I was recognized, and the cop led me through the very door where Little John had dropped me off, less than an hour ago. They'd found me unbelievably fast.

Another cop waited next to one of two patrol cars, and he opened the door as I approached, a wry grin in place. "Well, Miss Carstairs," he said as he gently guided my head so I didn't hit it as I was put into the backseat. "The next time you want to pull an illegal trick like that, you might want to make sure your location wasn't tweeted out by an overzealous fan."

The kid in the lobby. Shit. Shit. Shit. *Shit.*

He slammed the door, and I was alone in the patrol car briefly before they both took the front seats. Well, this was going to be a long night, and one I was never going to live down once Pax and Landon found out.

I wasn't worried too much about the legality. I'd no doubt pay a fine, but it wasn't like I couldn't afford it. But shit, I was going to have to call Brandon—Wilder's pain-in-the-ass, overly suited brother who got us out of crap like this when we screwed up.

Or maybe not. Maybe I could handle it on my own.

We pulled away from the Bellagio, but my head snapped back as another officer came through the door. My neck strained, trying to keep them in sight as we turned, but it was impossible.

No, oh no. Now I wasn't worried, I was terrified.

I was going to have to call Brandon.

They had Cruz in handcuffs, too.

Chapter Four

LAS VEGAS

My knee bounced under the cold, metallic table of the interrogation room while my hands, still cuffed, rested on the smooth surface. The lack of a clock in the small room made it impossible to gauge how long I'd been in here, but considering the fact that I was hungry, I had to guess it had been hours.

Hours since I'd pulled my shirt on and gone into the hallway to see what was taking Penelope so long. Hours since I'd been shoved against a wall like I was some kind of threat and had my hands cuffed behind my back. Hours since they had dragged me down to this station, put me into this room, and promptly forgotten about me.

No phone call.

No bathroom in sight.

No information about where Penelope was.

Penelope. I tried to keep my mind from wandering to

her—it would only drive me crazy when there was nothing I could do to help her from here, but she was on my brain every other minute.

Hopefully she was okay. Hopefully she wasn't scared. The woman had a backbone of steel—I'd known that in the first moment I set eyes on her—but there was also something fragile about her, like all that armor she wore was held together by only a fraying string.

What the hell had I been thinking? For fuck's sake, I was due to fly out of Vegas in what had been less than twenty-four hours. Had the last couple of hours cost me what I'd been working my entire adult life for?

I'd been so damned stupid to jump off that thing with her.

But she'd needed someone, and I could admit that I'd wanted to be that someone.

Besides, holding her? Touching her? Feeling every soft curve of her flawless body against mine? Worth it. I'd never felt that kind of chemistry with someone before, and with Penelope I'd been a moth drawn to the flame she was—wild, beautiful, and hypnotically irresistible.

My gaze drifted to the mirrored wall. I'd watched enough *Law & Order* to know there was a good chance cops were on the other side of that glass, watching me. For the first time since meeting her, I was glad I didn't know Penelope's last name. I couldn't give them any more information to use against her than what they already had. How the hell had they found us?

The doorknob turned and immediately had my full attention. First an officer came in and wordlessly unlocked my cuffs, removing the metal from my wrists. As he left, two men walked in, both dressed in tailored suits. The older, short, heavyset one held a file while the taller one behind him obviously held the power. He crossed his arms and leaned back against the wall, watching me in a way that I recognized all too well from my years in the military—he was analyzing every one of my details. That smirk he wore told me he wasn't too impressed. He looked equal to me in the age department, but he was definitely winning in the asshole category.

The chair in front of me squeaked as the older one scraped the legs on the linoleum floor before sitting in it. He swallowed nervously, adjusted his glasses, and slid a paper and pen toward me.

"Mr. Delgado," he said, "if you'll sign that, I will officially be your attorney, and anything we discuss will be privileged."

I blinked. "I haven't had a phone call."

"You won't need one. They're not booking you or pressing charges," the younger one answered. "But that deal sticks only on two conditions. The first is you sign that paper to secure Mr. Schur here as your attorney."

Who the hell were these people? I read the simple document that was exactly as he said, but hesitated at signing it. "Are you a public defender?"

Mr. Schur scoffed. "Hardly."

Given the threads he wore, I believed him. "Then why represent me?"

"Because it's what Penelope wants," the younger one answered, his tone low.

"Is she okay? Where is she?"

The man's eyes narrowed slightly. "She's fine, and she's outside, waiting for us to finish up here so she can catch her flight."

"No charges against her, either?" There was zero chance in hell I was taking any kind of deal to walk away if she was going to be punished.

The corners of his mouth tugged upward, but it wasn't quite a smile. "No charges for her, either," he assured me in a softer tone.

I swallowed, weighing my options, and decided to trust Penelope, scrawling my name across the line that read: client.

That was twice tonight that I'd put my life in her hands.

Mr. Schur visibly relaxed across the table from me. "Okay, now that's taken care of, if you'll simply sign this nondisclosure agreement, you can be on your way. No charges. No mug shot. No record of this ever having happened."

"Nondisclosure?" I asked, reading over the document. "Why?"

"Because while Penelope *wants* you clear of any implication of wrongdoing, this is what she *needs*," the younger one answered, still leaning against the wall.

"And who exactly are you?" I asked.

"The one who ends up fixing everything they inevitably fuck up." He let loose a rough sigh.

"They?"

"Sign the paper, Mr. Delgado."

My eyes narrowed at him. "How do you know my name? I never told Penelope."

"You told the officers when they brought you here, and the moment Penna demanded your freedom, you became my business. So let me fix this shitstorm. Sign the paper, and you get to leave."

"Penelope is outside?"

"Only until we're done here. Don't expect to ever see her again."

Who the hell was this guy to her? A brother? A friend? A...lover? I swallowed the flash of rage that came with that thought. There was no use going primal over a woman I was never going to get to see again.

So why did I have a quick fantasy of bashing his pretty little face into the wall?

"Look, Mr. Delgado. You can sign that paper and show up at UCLA on Monday like you're supposed to, or you can get booked on trespassing charges, which I'm sure the university wouldn't be too happy about. What is it going to be?" He arched a superior eyebrow at me.

He might have more money than I did—scratch that, of course he did—but he was in no way superior. I had two college degrees and a chest full of medals at home to prove it.

As much as I hated it, he was right. I needed to sign the paper. It promised that any of the events that transpired tonight would never be made public.

"Her name isn't on here," I said.

"No, it isn't," Mr. Schur said.

"I don't even get to know her last name?" I asked as I signed the damn thing.

The guy reached over Mr. Schur and snatched the paper from the table. "Thank you." He turned, striding out of the room with Mr. Schur hot on his heels.

I pushed away from the table and headed after them, half expecting the cops to grab me and tell me there had been a mistake. They were already through the door that led to where the cops had brought me in, and I broke into a run to catch them. I needed to see Penelope, to know she was okay. To at least have a way to check on her…to have the slightest chance to see her again.

"Hey!" I called out once I saw him in the waiting room, realizing I still had no idea what the hell the guy's name was.

He turned, his hand on the door that led outside. "Yes?"

"What's her last name?" I asked, needing to know.

He held the door, and Mr. Schur walked out.

My chest tightened with a desperation I hadn't felt since I'd last been deployed. "Please," I said softly, hating that I had to ask him for anything.

The guy shook his head. "Sorry. No glass slipper, either." He shot me a cocky smirk that I wanted to immediately rip off his face, and then left.

I ran to the door, but by the time I swung it open, I caught only the taillights of a stretch limo that Penelope was in. I knew it in my bones.

That one glimpse told me what I'd already known.

That girl had been way out of my league.

Chapter Five

"Miss Carstairs." Mr. Schur nodded politely at me as he slid into the limo, scooting down the long side seat toward the driver.

"Mr. Schur," I acknowledged, well aware that I was definitely not his favorite person on the planet. "Is he okay?" I asked Brandon as he stepped into the limo, taking the empty seat next to me.

"We're ready to go," Mr. Schur said to the limo driver.

"He signed," Brandon said, as if that ended the conversation.

"But is he okay?" I repeated as the limo pulled out of the LVPD station. "It's been hours since we were brought in."

He shot me a withering glance, which I gave right back. I'd known Brandon for my entire life; I wasn't taking his shit.

"I was airborne from L.A. within an hour of you calling,

legal counsel in tow. I'm really not sure what else I could have done to get you out of there faster."

"That's not what I mean," I said, properly chastised. "Thank you for coming so quickly—for coming at all."

"Of course I came. You're the closest thing I have to a little sister. That doesn't mean I'm not extremely pissed off at you right now."

"I know." I counted three breaths before I couldn't wait another second. "But seriously, is he okay? Cruz?"

Brandon's sigh could have propelled the U.S. sailing team. "Yes, the guy you illegally BASE jumped with is fine. You know, the one you took to bed before you even knew his last name? That one? He's great."

"You don't get to give me shit over that, Brandon. Not when your list of one-night stands is half the population of L.A."

My stomach sickened as we turned in the direction of the airport instead of back to the hotel. "My things—"

"Are already aboard the plane. If we take off in the next hour, we can get you back to L.A. and on the flight to Tokyo with the other Renegades. Or did you forget that you're due back in class in less than twenty-four hours?"

"You already got my stuff?" I asked, pushing away the knowledge that in less than a day, I'd be back aboard the *Athena*, traveling the world, taking classes, filming a documentary that I wasn't sure I should be a part of anymore.

"Yes, between making a generous contract offer to the owner of the property you violated, assuring there would be no charges, and making a donation into the account of the very savvy reporter who managed to get ahold of the cops' one camera shot that got a decent angle of you getting on the High Roller, I sent someone to your hotel room to pack you up and check you out." He took out his cell phone and started returning texts.

"Efficient," I said slowly. I was grateful, but he'd also just taken my last chance to see Cruz. An ache I didn't know how to process bloomed in my chest, and I rubbed just over my sternum, as if that would soothe it. *You knew him for a couple hours; stop acting like a sap.*

"Paxton says we have more than enough time to get you to LAX for their flight in a few hours."

Paxton. Landon. *Damn it.* I'd have to explain, and I didn't have the words they would want. "You know, I have to swing by my place in L.A. to grab my bag, so maybe—"

"You were in the States for all of seven days; how much luggage did you bring?" He arched an eyebrow at me.

"Enough that I don't want to leave it at home," I shot back, feeling every bit the petulant toddler he'd known me as at one point.

"They can hold the flight. Benefit of them taking the Wilder Enterprises jet," he said as he flipped another screen on his phone.

"Brandon," I said quietly, and his eyes jerked to mine. "Please. I can't see them yet. Just tell them I'm taking a later commercial flight. I'll be back in time for class."

He made a few finger swipes and lifted the phone to his ear. "Cynthia. Yes, I know it's three a.m."

Guilt slammed into me. Once again, I was making someone else's life difficult because I couldn't get my shit together.

"I also know how much I pay you," Brandon said with an eye roll. "Right. If you could please book Penelope Carstairs on a six p.m. flight to Tokyo out of LAX? Yes, that Penelope. Perfect, thank you." He hung up and went into his emails. It was hard to believe he shared any genes with his reckless brother. The two couldn't be any more different.

Within a half hour, we boarded the private jet that bore the Wilder insignia, and I buckled into a soft leather chair across from Brandon as he finished up another business call—this one in French.

For the first time in my life, I dreaded takeoff. I didn't want to go back to the ship, back to the stunts, back to the friends my ignorance had nearly gotten killed. I didn't want to go back to the puzzle where I used to fit perfectly, knowing my edges had totally changed shape. I wasn't sure I fit anymore.

But for just a few moments tonight, I'd fit with *him*. There had been no pressure, no expectations to live up to, no assumptions. I had simply been *me*, broken pieces and all, and it had been enough.

"Will you at least tell me his last name?" I asked Brandon. That was all I needed to find him on social media.

Brandon looked away to the strip as we rose above Vegas. "No, I won't."

"You don't have to protect me, Brandon. I'm a big girl."

His glacial eyes cut through me. "It's not for your protection. It's for his. You're not yourself. Let it go."

I managed to sit up straighter even though it felt like I'd been punched in the stomach. Brandon was right. In a matter of hours, I'd convinced a gorgeous, phenomenal stranger to illegally BASE jump, and then took him back to my hotel room where he'd been hauled down to the police station. It had been out of character even on my wildest day. I'd been reckless, and if not for Brandon, Cruz would have had to pay the price.

Yeah. It was best that I didn't know his name, couldn't search him out.

That didn't mean I didn't want to, though.

• • •

"So you got that cast off," the Abercrombie model in the elevator with me said in a slow, southern drawl.

"Yep," I said, keeping my eyes on the numbers that told me what floor we were on.

"Well, let me know if you feel like…working it out, Rebel."

My fist clenched on the handle of my suitcase. I'd been back on board the *Athena* for all of twenty minutes and I was already being hit on by horny frat boys. *Great.*

With a *ding*, the doors opened on my floor.

"Will do," I said with a sarcastic, bitchy smile and a little nose wrinkle as I stepped out of the elevator. "Not a fucking chance," I muttered under my breath as I pulled my luggage behind me down the narrow hallway toward our suite. The ship rocked gently as we pulled out of Yokohama Port. I'd procrastinated at the Tokyo airport for so long that I'd nearly missed the boat. Hell, I almost wished I had. My sense of foreboding grew with every step I took, but eventually I unlocked our corner suite with a swipe of my key card.

The marble entryway welcomed me home. Sure, the Renegade suites were over the top, but so were we. "Honey, I'm home," I called out, detouring from the hallway into my bedroom.

It looked exactly as it had when I left here over a week ago—down to my discarded bra on the armchair. Neat had never been one of my virtues, and I never let Hugo clean up after me. Hugo was assigned to our cabin for his work-study program, kind of like how Leah was Pax's tutor for hers. It still felt weird to have him always waiting on us, though. I tossed my suitcase onto the bed and stared out the sliding glass door that led to my balcony, watching the skyline grow smaller.

A noise in my doorway made me turn around.

"Here you are! We were so worried," Leah said, concern radiating from her whiskey-colored eyes. Pax's girlfriend was one of my favorite people—warm, wicked smart, and genuinely kind.

"Worried you were going to miss margaritas!" Rachel called from down the hallway.

I smiled, shaking my head as I looped my arm around Leah's shoulder and led us down the hall to the living room. Rachel—a five-foot nothing, black-and-purple-haired spitfire—was on her tiptoes, pouring tequila into a margarita machine that boasted some Jimmy Buffet lyrics on the side. "Really?" I asked.

Rachel grinned at me over her shoulder. "They'll be ready after seminar."

"Shit, we have class today?"

"It's just seminar class since we officially start third term today," Leah assured me. No doubt she'd already decided her end-of-year thesis topic and probably had it started by now.

"Which one are you in?" I asked.

"Latin American History," she answered as Rachel climbed off the counter, her margarita mission complete.

"Oh, good, I think I'm in that one, too," I said.

"You are," she assured me. "Actually, we all are. You, me, Rachel, Pax, and Landon. One big happy family!" She grinned, radiating the kind of happiness that I envied, and I couldn't help but echo her smile. She'd been through so much, losing her high school boyfriend in a horrific car accident that had nearly killed her, too, but her injuries healed, scars formed, and she'd conquered her fears with the kind of grace I could only hope to find.

"Speaking of the twosome..." Rachel gestured to the sliding glass door at the back of our suite, which was currently being opened by my two oldest friends, who were also the last two people I wanted to see.

Pax looked pissed until his gaze found Leah, and then he instantly softened. He was solidly built with muscles he'd honed for motocross, but he turned into a giant teddy bear for his tutor/girlfriend. He hugged her as Landon made his way across the room to me, all six foot four of Hemsworth-looking snowboarder folding down to kiss Rachel first. Apparently those two had finally worked their shit out.

Then he wrapped his arms around me and pulled me to his familiar chest. He smelled like summers at the skate park, like cedar, and safety, and friendship. I sagged against him, and he held me tighter. "I was so worried, Pen. When you didn't show in Aspen…"

"I know, and I'm sorry," I told him.

"What the fuck happened?" Pax semi-shouted.

"And that, Leah, is our cue to leave," Rachel said, tugging Leah out the sliding door as Landon let me go.

"Traitors!" I called out.

Leah threw back a look of apology before Rachel pulled her out of sight. The sound of the door shutting reminded me of taking a road trip with my parents when they were pissed at me. That locked door meant there was no getting out, and I'd have to sit there and digest whatever tirade they deemed worthy.

At least then, I'd had Brooke.

"Don't yell at her," Landon warned.

"Penna doesn't need you to defend her," Pax snapped, his arms folded in front of his Fall Out Boy shirt.

"He's right. I don't," I told Landon. "I'm sorry I didn't come to Aspen. I just…couldn't," I admitted.

"Oh, but you could BASE jump off the goddamned High Roller in Vegas?" Pax seethed. "Jesus, Penna, with a stranger, nonetheless? You could have been killed at that height, let alone the legal ramifications."

"Brandon," I growled, my eyes on the ceiling.

"What the hell does he have to do with it?" Pax asked.

"He didn't tell you…?" My eyes darted between my best friends.

Landon shook his head.

"Well, shit," I said, walking between the boys to take a seat on the couch. Landon sat between me and where Pax stood, no doubt playing the barrier.

"There was a YouTube video," Landon told me. "Put that together with the tweet from some kid at your hotel, and what Patrick said—"

"Patrick? Did he tell you that he smacked my ass like I'm some rally girl? Or that he was going to jump with me totally and completely wasted?" To hell with that guy.

"He what?" Pax flat-out yelled.

"Oh, he left that out, I see. Yes, I planned a jump with Patrick, and when he showed up drunk, I took the guy at the bar"—they both sputtered—"who had jump experience in the army. Okay, it wasn't a brilliant idea, and it could have turned out *really* bad, but the jump…" I trailed off, and a smile tugged at my lips. "It was amazing, guys. The lights, the distance, the rush. It was all perfect…you know, until the cops realized it was me."

"They what?" Landon's jaw dropped.

"Oh yeah." I studied the immaculately clean coffee table. "Cops showed up at my room, I called Brandon, he fixed everything"—*for both of us*—"and I hopped a flight back here. See, everything worked out."

"Penna," Pax said gently and waited until I looked up to meet his eyes. "You called Brandon? Not me? Not Landon? Not Nick?" The hurt in his eyes made me swallow whatever snarky comment I'd been prepared with.

"You guys were celebrating your X Games medals, and…"

"Say it," Landon urged.

"And I didn't want you there, looking down on me, judging what I'd done."

The only sound was the gentle whir of the slushy-style margarita machine as they processed what I'd said.

"You should have been with us," Pax finally said.

"Maybe. But I didn't feel that way. I had to do that jump alone, guys. I had to prove to myself that I had what it took to step off that platform—that under this hot mess, there's a tiny bit of me left."

"And?" Pax asked.

I searched my heart, hoping the answer would miraculously appear. "And I'm not sure. I did the jump, but something's changed. I've changed."

"Do you want some time off?" Landon asked. "I don't mean downtime here. I mean…" He took a deep breath. "Do you want to go back to L.A. while we finish the documentary?"

"No," Pax interrupted.

"Shut up, Pax," Landon snapped. "I told you she needed time."

"I can speak for myself," I said, my tone softer than my words. "Yes, I want to go home. No, I don't want to be here. But I'm scared if I leave now I won't come back."

"We'll be home in three months—" Landon said.

"No, I mean to the Renegades at all." There. I said it, but the knot in my chest that had been there since the accident didn't dissipate. Instead it wound tighter.

"Fuck that. You're an Original. It's been the three of us since we were in diapers. We built the Renegades from nothing, and we don't work without you."

"I think the last two podium trips just disproved that theory," I replied with a wry smile.

"As individuals, sure," Pax argued, "but we are the Renegades. Before the movie, the stunts, the publicity, the sponsors, it's *us*. We. Are. The Renegades."

"Maybe I'm not!" I cried. "Maybe…maybe I should go." Everything felt so topsy-turvy, like one of those paintings where the stairs were the ceiling and the ceiling was the wall. Nothing was right.

Landon pulled me in to his side, and Pax fell from his chair, hitting his knees in front of me. "Penelope Carstairs. I don't care if you never do another stunt, you're still one of us. We will wait as long as you need, and we will accept whatever decision you make. You two are my best friends, and I promise we'll work through this. Just…please stay. Please give us the chance to be here for you the way you've always shown up for us."

These two, the family we'd built, had been the only thing I'd ever been certain of. Nick had come along, Brooke had held me steady, and my future had been so obvious the moment I touched a motocross bike. But then Nick was paralyzed, and Brooke became the most reckless of all, and everything fell to shit.

The door slid open behind us. "Hey, I hate to interrupt, but we'll be late for seminar if we don't go," Leah called out.

"Penna?" Landon asked.

"I'm here, right?" I faked a smile, and the look in Pax's eyes said he knew the difference. "Let's get to class. We'll figure this out later."

Pax's jaw flexed, and Landon's arm tightened around me, but they both agreed. This conversation was bigger than the ten minutes we'd given it. Hell, it was bigger than ten hours, and the problem was, now I'd admitted that I wanted to go home. By saying it aloud, I'd given the words power, and they chipped away another layer of my Rebel veneer.

I quickly changed, needing to get the airplane smell off me. A pair of skinny jeans, my Wonder Woman tee, and Vans later, I pulled my hair into a loose knot on the top of my head and blew the stray strands from my face. It wasn't like I had anyone to impress so this morning's—or yesterday's… whatever—makeup would do.

Ten minutes later, the Renegades had claimed the center chunk of the class, Landon and Pax flanking me like they were scared I would run at any moment. I pulled my notebook and purple pen from my backpack, placing them on the desk in front of me as Pax stared out of the floor-to-ceiling windows in front of us that showed nothing but open sea.

Would Cruz have liked it here? Was he more of a mountain guy or an ocean guy? Or both?

"—so she ended up leaving," I heard Leah say from behind Paxton, disrupting thoughts I had no business having.

I turned in my seat. "What are you talking about?"

"Oh, our teacher from last term for Cultures of the Pacific. Dr. Messina," Rachel said. "I guess she was supposed to teach this class, too."

"I noticed the change on my schedule this morning." Leah nodded.

"I didn't have her last term, but I did for first," I said. "Is she gone?"

"I guess she was homesick or something," Rachel shrugged.

"New term. New teacher," I said, turning back to my notebook. I started to doodle, concentrating on the purple streaks as I sketched out a rough version of the High Roller. The purple almost matched the lights from the Ferris wheel.

God, he'd looked gorgeous in that light—strong, sure, confident, and in total control even though he was in a situation where there wasn't such a thing.

The door opened and shut, and I knew I'd have to put my pen down and rejoin real life. I yawned as jet lag caught up with me. I was in desperate need of some real sleep, or some real caffeine.

"Welcome to Latin American History."

At that deep, lightly accented voice, my pen fell to the paper, as useless as my brain.

"This class will also serve as your Study At Sea seminar, which means I have the joy of getting to know each of you very well over the next three months since you'll be writing a thirty-page thesis for me."

The class groaned, and I slowly dragged my eyes from the paper, past the neck of the red-haired boy in front of me, to the man who stood at the head of our class, casually leaning against his desk. I took in the way his pants hugged his hips, the contrast of his rolled white button-down against his tanned skin, and the loose green tie at his throat. My gaze caught on his lips, the strong line of his nose and cheekbones, to the melty chocolate eyes that were focused on the other side of the room as he addressed the students there. His hair looked like he'd run his hands through it more than a few times, and his teeth flashed white when he grinned, those panty-dissolving dimples appearing.

My heart stopped beating and my breath froze in my lungs, as if the slightest motion would make him disappear. A rush of heat flushed my skin, and the knot in my chest loosened, unraveling as surely as my body had the last time I'd seen him.

"So let's get started, shall we? I just flew in from the States today, but I'll be sure to learn all of your names by the end of the week. Now if you'll let me have this moment, I've been waiting eight years to say it— My name is Dr. Delgado."

Two thoughts slammed into me simultaneously.

One—*Delgado*. At least now I knew his last name.

Two—Holy. Fucking. Shit. Cruz was my professor.

Chapter Six

AT SEA

Dr. Delgado. After all these years of working my ass off, I finally got to say it to a class full of students. Sure, I was here only because Dr. Messina had been my mentor last year at UCLA, but I'd take it. I was a college professor…as long as I didn't fuck it up.

Vegas had almost destroyed this chance for me, but damn if I hadn't thought about *her* every five minutes, anyway. Penelope wasn't the kind of girl you just forgot.

I did my best to meet each of my students' eyes as I swept the room from right to left, making sure I saw all of them—acknowledged them as individuals. "We have a little over a week while we cross the Pacific and head down the coast, and then I'll expect you on 90 percent of my shore excursions for class." I looked to the next row, where a guy who seemed weirdly familiar caught me off guard for a breath. Then, a knot of blond hair grabbed my attention, and my gaze flickered over. "I know you have other classes, but—"

No. Fucking. Way.

Sitting in my class, her mouth slightly agape—those gorgeous, soft lips parted—with wide, crystal-blue eyes, was Penelope.

My Penelope.

I locked that thought down tight.

She was here. On this ship. In my classroom. I didn't have to search Facebook for every Penelope with blond hair. I didn't have to hunt down Brandon Wilder—I'd at least gotten that information from the cops—and beg him to tell me where to find my Cinderella.

She was sitting right in front of me.

A kid coughed, and I blinked. *Damn it.* I was standing in front of my first college class, staring at a *student.*

"Right," I said, looking down at the industrial-grade carpet beneath my feet to keep my eyes the hell off Penelope. I shook my head, got my shit together in the span of a heartbeat, and looked back up. If I could handle a year in a forward operating base on the Afghanistan/Pakistan border, I could deal with this.

I raised my head and continued meeting every student's gaze. Well, every student but one. "Sorry. Like I was saying, I expect you on 90 percent of my shore excursions. Your theses are no joke, and you'll want to draw on every experience I can give you."

My attention strayed to Penelope's stunned stare, her head tilted like she couldn't believe I was here. Her face said everything I felt.

I ripped my gaze away, turning back to my desk where I'd left a folder of syllabi. *Get control, or you'll ruin everything.*

Papers in hand, I walked to the head of each row, handing them a stack to pass to the students behind them. "This is your syllabus for the term," I said, leaning back against my desk and keeping my eyes on anyone but Penelope. "When thinking about your thesis topic, which—if you look at your syllabus—is due March fifteenth, which coincides with—"

"Peru," one young lady called out from the right side of the classroom.

"Peru," I agreed. "Topics I think would be of interest would be on the intersection of culture and history—how events shape the people who shape their nation and vice versa. You'll find a wealth of opportunity to immerse yourself in the rich history of Latin America this term. Since assigning your reading and handing out your syllabus was all I had planned for you today, are there any questions?" I paused, and when no hands went into the air, dismissed the class, reminding them that my office hours and email address were on the back sheet of the synopsis.

I busied myself with stacking my papers, praying Penelope wouldn't stop as the class filed out. When the door shut and I was left alone in blissful silence, I sat back against the desk, rubbing the heels of my hands over my eyes.

This will be okay. I could ignore her, pretend that I didn't know the rebellious spirit behind those blue eyes, or the way her kiss tasted like the sweetest kind of sin, or how she felt beneath those jeans.

Shit, this was wrong. I couldn't even think of her like that anymore. She was somehow halfway across the world with me and now my student. That was it. Student.

Wait, that meant…

My fingers flew through the contents of the manila folder on the desk, then ran down the list of names until I found hers. "Penelope Carstairs," I said softly, testing the weight of it on my tongue.

My stomach clenched as my surprise gave way to something darker. How the hell was this possible? How was it that I'd found this extraordinary woman again only to have her completely off-limits?

"This will be okay." I repeated the lie quietly. I'd spent only a handful of hours with her; it wasn't like we had a history.

You had a connection.

So what, we shared a few kisses. We hadn't had sex, so that line hadn't been crossed, right? I wasn't in love with her. Hell, I barely knew her. We just happened to have some chemistry.

Chemistry hot enough to sear off your nerve endings.

And my common sense.

I scanned the rest of the class roster, my eyes catching on another last name. Well, wasn't that just peachy? Maybe she hadn't been *my* Penelope after all.

The door opened, and I turned to see the very woman who'd haunted me these last forty-eight hours. She took in the room, and once she saw that we were alone, she closed the door behind her, tugging her bottom lip between her teeth.

I knew exactly how soft that lower lip was, the way she liked to have it sucked on lightly.

Student. She's a student.

"Miss Carstairs," I said softly. Damn, that came out way more intimate than I intended.

"Dr. Delgado."

Fuck, that sounded even better coming out of her mouth than it had mine.

She examined the floor, the ceiling, each of the walls, and the window before finally letting herself look at me.

Moments passed in silence as we simply stood there watching each other. I hadn't imagined our intense connection. It was real. It was electric, and it was now dangerous to everything I'd been working for. I was so fucked, and not in the good way. "Penelope," I whispered, allowing myself the simple pleasure.

"Cruz," she replied with a shy smile. As she took a step

toward me, I backed away, rounding the desk to keep it between us.

"You stay over there. I'll stay over here," I said.

She simply arched an eyebrow at me.

I swallowed. "I'm your teacher. You are my student."

"This is really fucked up," she said, running her hands over her face. I wanted to pull them back, to make her look at me with those ocean blue eyes so I could fix everything that was wrong.

But there was no fixing this.

There were so many questions I wanted to ask her. How she was here. Where she was really from. What she'd been doing in Vegas in the first place. "Is Paxton Wilder your boyfriend?"

Shiiiiiit, that was *not* what I meant to ask.

"My teacher wouldn't care," she answered with a smile that knocked the wind from my lungs. She was too damn beautiful for my peace of mind.

"Okay, well, for the next five minutes, let's just pretend that I'm…not. Then we'll begin our official roles," I offered. That had to be the best plan, right? If not, the questions were going to drive me mad.

"So, Cruz cares, but not Dr. Delgado?" Penelope asked with an incredibly sexy smirk.

"Something like that," I admitted. *Hell yes, I cared.*

"Pax is pretty much my brother. So is Brandon. That's why I called him to get us out of the Vegas situation. He has more than a little experience cleaning up the messes we make."

"You do that a lot?"

"Get arrested? Or make messes?"

"Both? Either?" I backed up another step, trying to put more distance between us. Not that it mattered. The very air between us was electrified.

She shrugged. "Pax got arrested in Madagascar, but that's

a long story." As if remembering whatever happened, her face fell. "But yeah, we make messes. It's kind of what we do."

"You meet strangers in bars, take them BASE jumping, and then—"

"No, and definitely no! I've never done either of those things before. Besides, what are you, the youngest professor in the history of...?" Her hands gestured wildly. "Well... history?"

"Smooth," I laughed. "I graduated high school at seventeen with enough AP classes to put me as a sophomore in college, joined the army, and took classes through their program every day of my three years of service. I graduated with my bachelor's degree right after I got out at twenty, spent two years on my master's, and then went straight into a PhD program. I actually just defended my dissertation over break. Dr. Messina was my advisor and asked if I would fill in for the last three months because she couldn't stay, and I was free until fall. I was only in Vegas to say good-bye to my friends before flying out."

"But you're so young...and hot. Did I mention hot? And a really good kisser."

I ignored the way my dick jumped and told my brain to get the images of her under me off replay. "Penelope, I'm your teacher."

"Not for these five minutes, you're not, remember?" She folded her arms under her perfect breasts and arched an eyebrow.

Damn, the woman could dish it out.

"Right."

Tension grew between us, an almost palpable presence.

"What do we do?" she asked softly, losing that sharp edge that had hooked me in Vegas and revealing the vulnerable center of her that had reeled me in.

"There's nothing to be done," I answered, my voice

dropping. "I'm your teacher. You're my student for the next three months."

"And after that?"

"You'll go home, and I'll head off to the East Coast. I have a job lined up there already."

Her gaze dropped to the desk, and I hated the way her eyes closed slowly.

"Okay, well, what if I take a different seminar class?"

"Penelope."

She swallowed.

"Look at me." My voice was so soft it was nearly a whisper.

Her eyes rose slowly until those Caribbean blue orbs landed on me, nearly killing my resolve on what I had to say next.

"It wouldn't matter. You're still a student, and I'm still a teacher who can't afford to lose his first job because he has…" Shit, I couldn't think of the words. Because there were none. We weren't a one-night stand, since we hadn't gotten the night. *God, I wish we'd gotten the night.* We weren't together in any sense of the word, and yet we'd experienced something intense and meaningful. I knew in my bones that she'd felt it, too. She lifted that brow again, challenging me to find the words. "Fine. Because I have a connection with a student."

She blinked quickly and nodded. "Right. Of course you're right. Besides, I need this history credit to graduate, and it's not like there's another history class being given right now. Small ship."

"Small ship," I agreed, realizing with those words how hard it was going to be. She'd be everywhere—in my class, in the halls, in the cafeteria, in my head, but never in my bed. She was, as of this moment, untouchable.

"Do you want me to drop the class?"

I shook my head. "There's no reason to punish you, especially if you need the credit to graduate. It's not like either of us knew."

"But won't you get in trouble?"

The worry in her eyes and the way a little line appeared between her brows nearly made me reconsider. It didn't matter that we'd only shared a few hours together, I cared about this girl—this woman—and I knew she cared, too.

"I think as long as we keep our past…discreet, we'll be fine. I can't afford to lose this job." *Or my only chance to get to Elisa.*

"By discreet, you mean secret." Her gaze flickered toward the clock. Our five minutes were nearly up.

"Only if you agree. I'd never ask you to lie for me." *No matter what it could potentially cost me.*

"Of course I'll keep it a secret. I don't want you to lose your job. Like you said, it's not like we knew." She shook her head and huffed out an exasperated sigh. "God, I wish we still didn't know."

"Penelope," I whispered, as if the slice of pain through my chest cut off my vocal cords.

"I know. I should be going."

"Wait. I have thirty more seconds." It was out of my mouth before I could think better of it. "I just wish I had something better to say to fill it."

"You don't have to say anything," she responded.

We stood there, our eyes locked, listening to the metronome-like ticking of the seconds on the clock. The desk still sat between us, a proactive no-man's land, but damn if it didn't feel like she was still in my arms back in Vegas. My fingers twitched, remembering the silk of her skin. This was madness. Utter and complete insanity.

"Time's up," she said, stepping back from the desk. "Dr. Delgado."

I inclined my head. "Miss Carstairs."

"I'm sure I'll see you around. Small ship, remember?" She

forced a smile and walked out without waiting for a response.

"Small ship," I said to my empty classroom.

. . .

"So are you finding everything you need?" Lindsay asked as we got off the elevator on the ninth deck.

The blond teacher, who looked to be only a few years older than I was, had been kind enough to show me to my room, which was right down the hall from hers, when I'd come aboard this morning. She was pretty, with an average face and figure…or maybe she was beautiful but Penelope had simply upped my standards to impossibly high.

"I think so," I answered. "So far I've found my bedroom, the bathroom, and my classroom."

"How do you like the suite?" she asked as we neared the door at the end of the long hallway.

"It's really nice. And I like the other teacher I share it with. Westwick?"

She nodded. "He's not too bad."

"Do all of the teachers have suites?" I asked, trying to think of something to say that wasn't *hey, I'd like some alone time to think about what the fuck just happened with Penelope.*

"Yep. Suites are all for the teachers, except for the ones on deck ten. Those belong to Paxton Wilder and his crew of daredevils, since he owns the ship and all. They're reasonably good kids when they're not terrorizing the ship with their stunts. Just a few months ago they seriously parasailed behind the boat!"

Wilder, a twenty-two-year-old, owned the ship. Daredevils. *Penelope.* My mind raced, taking in all the information possible.

"Is that so?" I asked.

"It is!" Her forehead crinkled. "Oh my God, listen to me

ramble. I bet you'd like to kick that jet lag, huh?"

"Sounds about right," I said, forcing a quick smile.

"Well, how about I show you the dining hall later?" she asked, resting her hand on my forearm.

Hell no.

I moved toward my door, my key ready, naturally breaking the contact. "That actually sounds perfect. How about we grab some of the other staff? I wouldn't mind making a few friends."

Her smile lost a little of its brightness, but she nodded. "Yeah, absolutely. Six work for you?"

"Sure," I answered. An awkwardly spaced good-bye later, I was through my suite door and finally alone. I walked directly to my bedroom, which was the first on the right, and tossed my leather bag onto the bed, where my suitcase was open and in disarray from my hectic search for class-ready clothes.

I took out the file I'd made up for Elisa and opened it to her photo. It was the latest one she'd sent me. Her eyes were too familiar, her smile one I'd seen thousands of times… God, she looked just like *her.* I clipped the photo back on top of the ones I couldn't stand to see ever again—the ones she'd documented of her bruises, the scars from where she'd had pins placed in her arm from the last time he broke it.

Never again, I promised myself. But every day she stayed with him was a day too long, a day full of the possibility that she wouldn't make it out of there alive. There were too many days between now and when I could get to her, but I was on my way. I closed the file and slid it into the bottom drawer of my nightstand.

I bypassed my uncharacteristic mess and went onto the balcony, which was private to my room. Leaning on the white railing, I took in the full-ocean view, letting the breeze relax me. I decided this one spot would be my refuge, where I could absorb some much-needed quiet.

"Like you weren't checking out his ass."

I heard the feminine voice above me and almost laughed. So much for quiet. Then again, I was on a cruise ship full of college kids. The only quiet I was going to find would likely be in my bedroom. I turned to walk inside, shaking my head.

"Nope. I most definitely was not."

I stopped mid-stride. I knew that voice.

"Oh, shut the hell up. Even Leah was ogling, and she's practically married to Wilder. I'm with Landon, and you are the lone single gal who can give us her completely unbiased opinion on the level of hotness of our newest professor."

Holy shit. They were talking about me.

I should have gone inside. I should have shut the door, worked on unpacking, and then headed for the gym.

But I couldn't seem to move my damn feet.

"He's okay," she answered.

"Penna, you're such a liar!"

My eyes shut slowly, knowing I'd correctly guessed the owner of that sweet voice.

"I am not. Maybe he's just not my type. Maybe I go for lanky blond guys and not…"

"Not guys who look like they don't have a spare ounce of fat on them and desperately need their ties pulled so they come in for a kiss? I wonder what his first name is. I bet it's something delicious."

"He's a teacher, so it's *Doctor*," Penelope snapped.

"Quit teasing her, Rachel."

My feet finally started working, but instead of heading inside, I went back to leaning on the railing.

"Fine. Sorry, Penna. I just think that maybe you need to get out a little more. You know Alex has been bugging Landon to hook you two up."

My stomach clenched, despite my brain telling it to knock

that shit off.

"Yeah, not happening," Penelope answered.

I refused to believe that my stomach would react by relaxing, but it did.

"Yeah, well, just think about it. Leah, you coming?"

"Absolutely. We'll catch you at dinner, Penna."

I heard the sliding door shut above me and looked up to see Penelope leaned out over her railing, too, blond hair now loose and blowing in the wind, completely oblivious to the fact that I was just beneath her. I bit back every instinct to call out to her, walked into my room, and shut the door.

She was no longer the enchanting, gorgeous, thrilling, dangerously damaged girl I connected with in Vegas. She was a student.

And she was right.

This ship was fucking small.

Chapter Seven

AT SEA

When shit went wrong in my life, I always headed here. Well, not *here*, on the *Athena,* but to the garage, to my bike. So naturally, knees tucked to my chest, I sat on the vinyl floor ten feet away from Elizabeth. Damn skippy, she was a girl. The RM125's curves were hard, like mine, her motor powerful, and she was capable of so many amazing things with the right rider.

I just wasn't sure I was the right rider anymore.

How the hell had I gotten into this big of a mess? How could the only man I've had a connection with in my entire life be the only guy I couldn't get near?

My fucking professor.

Not fucking, remember?

God, how was I going to sit in class, watching him? Listening to that sexy-as-hell voice? Looking at those heaven-sent dimples and squeezable ass? Remembering…

Nope.

I shoved the thoughts, memories, and all the yearning in my stupid heart into a neat little emotional box. Then I shut it, locked it, poured some concrete shoes for it, and tossed the damn thing overboard.

There was enough crap in my head without adding him to it right now.

There wasn't a time I could really remember that I wasn't in love with racing, with tricks, with feeling the power and freedom that came with freestyle motocross. Until now.

But who was I without her? Without the person I was when I rode her? Sure, I'd proved there was a little Rebel left in me by jumping off the High Roller, but she'd hidden in the darkest nooks of my soul the moment I'd come into our onboard mechanic shop.

"I guess I win the bet," Landon said, sitting next to me and mirroring my posture. His was for comfort, while mine felt like self-defense. Moments like this were why I'd always be the tiniest fraction closer to Landon. When I was at my worst, Pax would always lift me up, but Landon was willing to come down to my level and walk out of it with me.

"What bet was that?" I asked, leaning my chin on my knees. The chill had long since seeped into my shorts, but I couldn't find the energy to move, refusing to get closer to Elizabeth, but not ready to admit defeat.

"I bet Pax that you'd be here."

"Intuition?"

A small smile played at his mouth. "I'm dating your roommate."

"Ah, you cheated," I answered, unable to hold back a small grin.

"Guilty. We have a production meeting in ten minutes."

He said it without expectation or condescension, which

tightened my heart in a way neither of those two could have. "You want me to come."

"I want you to want to come."

My eyes fixed on one of the hot-pink strips of molding on Elizabeth. "I want to want a lot of things." I wanted to ride my bike, to let go of everything that weighed me to the earth and fly with her, to gain that sweet solace I'd always found refuge in.

"I get that."

"How is it that I can jump off a Ferris wheel, but I can't swing a leg over my own bike? How can I be that broken?"

"You weren't on a Ferris wheel when the light came crashing down. You were on Pax's bike. You were doing what you love, and then Brooke twisted it into something evil that it had never been for any of us."

My gaze shot to his. "Landon—"

"What? I can say her name, too. She is your sister, but she's my friend. And I say 'is,' because there's every chance that after she gets the help she needs, she'll be our Brooke again. I was there. I should have caught on, but we all missed it. I was the one who got to you first, who saw the wreckage of your leg. You can shut us all out if you want, but don't think for a second that you're alone in this."

"You've forgiven her?"

"I don't know. I'd like to think that I'm a big enough person that I can. Right now, it's still very real and very raw."

"I don't know if I can. I still can't resolve my Brooke, my best friend, my sister, with the lunatic who sabotaged the stadium light and nearly killed me. Nearly killed Leah."

He stood. "That's a choice you're going to have to make. The same as getting back on that bike. And it's not something you have to choose right now. But you could start by coming to a production meeting, not because we need you but because you know that eventually you'll *want* to."

When he reached out his hand for mine, I took it.

I had to start somewhere.

• • •

"Wait up!" Leah called, and I slowed my pace to accommodate her much shorter stride. "Man, you walk fast. Then again, if I had those legs, I'd walk fast, too," she joked, catching me mid-hallway. "Ready for another class with Dr. Delicious?"

It was our fourth day at sea. Other than a quick refueling stop in the north of Japan, we'd been shipbound. Thankfully I'd been successful in avoiding Cruz—*Dr. Delgado*, I reminded myself—all four of those days.

That didn't mean I'd avoided the gossip.

He'd pretty much turned the head of every girl on this ship, not that I could blame any of them. He'd turned my head, too.

"Delgado," I corrected her, shuffling my books as we turned the corner toward Cruz's classroom.

"Right, *Del*gado, *Del*icious…get it?" she asked with a grin.

"Yeah, totally." I forced a smile.

"So did you guys think of a place for the last live expo? Pax won't stop stressing about it."

"Not yet." We'd spent at least two hours out of each day crouched over a map, trying to figure out where we could host the last live expo before the ship docked in L.A. The plan had been Miami, until the space we needed booked out. Even Pax's money couldn't get the other event to budge.

"You guys will figure it out."

Figuring out where to host the expo was the least of my issues. Whether or not I would perform, that was the cause of a constant state of nausea. After all, it was my turn to wow everyone. Pax had pulled off the first triple-front flip in Dubai,

Landon had nearly been killed by an avalanche in Nepal, and now the spotlight was on me.

"Penna!" Bobby's voice carried down the hall, and I cringed. The last thing I wanted to deal with was a production issue.

"I'll meet you in class?" Leah suggested with raised eyebrows. She'd stay if I wanted her to, knowing Pax would have Bobby delete any footage of her she wanted him to.

"I'll be fine." I declined her offer of protection and turned to see our very frantic, caffeine-jittery producer tugging on his baseball cap.

"Rebel. Thank God."

I glanced over his shoulder and, seeing the camera, put on the smile I was obligated to wear. Because I loved Nick like a brother, and this documentary was for him. "What's up?"

"You haven't been at the nightclub since you've been back…"

"Right." I tilted my head in obvious challenge. *Shit.* The last thing I wanted to do was haul my library books down to the club. It wasn't like I was picking up guys—the whole party aspect of this documentary had always been carried by Landon and Pax.

"I just wanted to make sure you'd be at the whiteout party tomorrow night for the International Date Line crossing?" He matched my head tilt. Asshole.

"Yep, I'll be there," I said and turned to go to class.

"Preferably in something that shows a little midriff?"

Oh. Hell. No.

I spun back. "You had better be fucking kidding me, Bobby."

He threw up his hands. "Totally was. Just wanted to see if you were still in there, *Rebel*."

I gave him a one-fingered salute and walked away. "The things I do for you, Nick," I mumbled to our missing Original as if he could hear me. Passing a few loitering students outside the door, I made my way into the classroom and took my seat between Pax and Landon.

"It's like a fashion show in here today," Leah whispered, leaning over from where she sat behind Pax.

I took a quick look around, my eyebrows rising. She was right. For a crew that had fallen into leggings and sweats after the first few months on board, the girls in our class were dressed in real clothes. Skinny jeans, trendy tops, hell, one girl was even in ankle boots. I, however, had still gone the comfy route with super soft black leggings, my pink and gray Fox motocross fitted hoodie, and Vans.

"It's got to be for Dr. Delicious," Rachel answered.

"Oh my God. You, too?" I groaned.

"Seriously?" Landon said, giving his girlfriend a WTF face.

She shrugged. "Don't be jealous. My eyes are straight forward. I'm just saying that with the two of you on the monogamy train"—she waggled her finger between Pax and Landon—"there's a new thoroughbred in the stable."

"A horse?" Pax snorted. "Nice."

"A freaking thoroughbred," Leah muttered.

He turned in his seat, and I barely had time to look away before he was kissing Leah like he needed to remind her that she was spoken for. Blocking my peripheral vision, I rolled my eyes.

For the love of God, the girls all had makeup on, too, hair done like they were ready to hit up the club. Maybe if I'd been trying to attract Cruz, I would have bothered to do more with my hair than pile it on my head, or tossed on more makeup than a coat of mascara. Was that girl in the second row seriously applying more lip gloss? She'd be able to signal other ships with the sun if she kept that up.

"He's a teacher," I seethed quietly, shaking my head as I

took out my books and set them on my desk. Maybe if I kept my head down the entire class, I'd make it through without embarrassing myself. After all, he set the rules—with good reason—and the least I could do was abide by them. He was a teacher; I was a student. That was it. I could sit through his class with no issue as long as I remembered that.

"Good afternoon, class," Cruz said as he walked in.

Like a magnet, my head popped up, and my eyes found him.

Unh. He was in jeans today with a pale blue, rolled-sleeve button-down shirt, his tie a deeper shade of blue. He'd grown a full, dark scruff that clung to his jaw in the short four days since I'd started carefully avoiding him, and his hair was in a styled disarray. The breath left my lungs in a *whoosh* as our eyes locked for an electric second, and I forced mine back down toward my paper. I wanted to tug at that tie like Rachel had suggested, to pull him in to my kiss, to feel his hands on my body, to hear his words soothing the ragged edges of my soul.

It hadn't just been a physical connection between us. I could have walked away from that. It was the way he saw through the Rebel shell to *me*, the way I felt inexplicably safe and yet challenged in those few hours with him. Somehow Cruz cut through the bullshit and expected me to do the same.

He moved to the farthest seat at the front of the room, a bowl and a piece of paper in his hands. "First things first. Take a number from the bowl, and then write your name next to the corresponding number. Make sure to keep your number so someone else doesn't accidentally draw it. You'll be turning in a lot of papers in this class in preparation for your seminar thesis, which is due the day before we dock in Miami. That's only two days after our last shore excursion in Cuba."

The way his accent changed the word *Cuba* had me gripping my pencil tighter. How the hell did they let someone so naturally sexy teach? Just his voice was enough to have me crossing and uncrossing my legs. *Subtle, Penna.* Wasn't there a rule against hot teachers somewhere?

"So that I can grade you each without judgment as the term continues, you'll write only your number on the first page of each paper, then flip that page over when you turn it in. This will be our routine for each assignment."

His gaze flickered toward mine and then ripped away as he cleared his throat. He'd found a way to grade me fairly, to assure that he wouldn't favor me—or punish me—for our history. If you could call our few hours *history*. It sure as hell felt more like the present for me.

He didn't waste time, immediately launching into the reading we'd been assigned on the Aztec and Mayan cultures.

I kept my eyes glued to the text and my notes for the rest of class, knowing that was far safer than watching Cruz.

Okay, so maybe this was going to be tougher than I originally thought.

Six hours later, he was still in my head as I put my water bottle on the console of the treadmill in the deserted gym. The machines faced the ocean, which was a fabulous view to run to when it was still light enough to see the vast blue water. We were way out at sea, no land anywhere in sight, which happened to be my favorite part of this worldwide adventure. The days when we were isolated from the rest of the world. No stunts. No touristing. No phone calls. No external emails. Just sweet, blissful isolation.

Not that anyone had really tried to contact me since I'd come back to the *Athena*. Mom and Dad were busy with Brooke, and everyone else I loved besides Nick was on board. I'd even been ducking his emails about ramp design, since I had no idea if I'd need anything special for the final expo. Or if I'd even ride in the final expo.

I was mid calf stretch when Cruz walked in, his focus on

his phone. He was in shorts and a tight Under Armour tank, and I suddenly felt very exposed in my running capris and sports bra.

"Dr. Delgado," I said so I wouldn't surprise him.

His focus snapped to me, and a slight smile tugged at his lips before he straightened them. "Miss Carstairs. Getting ready to run?"

"Nawh. I just like to come up here and stretch on the treadmill sometimes."

"Nice," he said with a full-on grin. "I figured now was the best time to get some miles in without a crowd in here." He claimed the machine next to mine. "At least the music works," he said, nodding toward his phone. "No music for you?"

I shook my head. "Nope. Running for me is like sitting at the bottom of a swimming pool. I do it to drown out the noise, not let more in."

"Want to tell me what you're drowning?" He watched me thoughtfully, and in that moment it didn't feel like we were in the northern Pacific Ocean. The tense understanding between us felt like Vegas…and more.

How long would this awareness last between us? Would it fade over the next few weeks? At least enough to make the term a little more bearable?

"As my teacher?"

The muscles in his bicep moved, rippling his Airborne tattoo as he reached for the treadmill's panel, turning it on. A scar next to the parachute of his tattoo caught my eye. It was a burn mark, the width of my thumb, in a perfect circle. I quickly looked away. Cruz and his scars were none of my business.

"As…someone who worries about you."

"Just worry about keeping up," I deflected, and started the treadmill. My feet found the rhythm as his did beside me.

"I've been running since before you were born," he joked.

"Come on, you're not that much older than me. What? Five, six years? That's nothing."

He laughed, the sound deep and goose-bump-inducing. "That's everything right now. And yeah, I was running by five. I had to where I grew up."

"Where was that?" We bumped up the speed after the first quarter mile.

"Cuba."

Do not groan. That word is not sexy.

"Wow. How did you…?" I waved in his direction, keeping my pace steady. It was nice to be able to hold a conversation comfortably at this pace. Maybe I wasn't as out of shape as I originally thought.

"I'll make you a deal, Penelope. I'll answer one question for every one you do."

I didn't savor the way he said my name. Not. One. Bit.

Liar.

"Deal."

I admired his posture, of all things, the upright way he carried himself as he effortlessly moved his body on the treadmill. Sure, I'd always been drawn to athletes, but Cruz didn't fit into any category I'd ever known.

"I came to the U.S. with my mother and grandmother. My grandmother signed her consent for me to join the military right after graduation, even though she was pissed about it. Those three years didn't just get me a bachelor's degree, they gave me citizenship."

"Wow. And I thought I was driven."

"You want something bad enough, you'll find every opportunity to get it," he said, looking over at me for a moment.

"So why didn't your mom sign for you?" I hit the button to increase my speed, and he matched me as if we were running outside.

"Nope. I get a question."

"Fine." I sighed as hard as I could while at a 6.0 speed. My legs were surprisingly steady, as if my muscles remembered what my heart hadn't—my body was honed for exertion, to be pushed to the max. Three months in a cast hadn't changed that.

"What thoughts are you drowning out right now?"

"Too many. They all come crashing in without any form or order." I glanced over to see that, as usual, he was patient, content to wait for my answer. "I'm worried that we won't find a good place to have the last live expo. Miami fell through, so now we're kind of floundering." Crap, I was getting a little short of breath to carry this conversation. Maybe my leg was good to go, but my endurance was shitty. "We need it…to be spectacular… a truly once-in-a-lifetime…kind of event…and that's hard…to do when the venue…you've planned on for the last year…screws you."

Yup. I needed to hit the gym more.

"You could do it in Cuba," Cruz suggested. "It's legal now. Complicated, but doable. Just a thought, of course."

A good one. Wicked complicated, that was true, but it would be amazing to be the first show on our level done in Cuba.

"My turn?" I asked, knowing that even though we'd only run fifteen minutes, I was about done.

"Go for it."

Damn, and he was still going steady and strong, barely a sweat broken. Did his lips taste like a slight sheen of sweat? A hint of salt? Or were they as decadent as they had been in Vegas? *Knock it off, Penna.*

"Why didn't your mom sign for you?"

"She'd already gone back to Cuba. She was in the States with us for only about a year before she returned to my father."

"Oh," I said, hearing the darker undertones of what he hadn't said. She'd left him. As peeved as I was at my mom for being rather Brooke-centric right now, she'd never abandoned me.

"One more thought that's got you running?" he asked.

"My sister," I answered, my breathing becoming even more labored.

"The anger?"

"No. Don't get me wrong. I know what she did, but she won't speak to me. Won't come to the phone when I call, even. I've resorted to writing her letters, not even about all this, but just…"

"You miss her."

"I miss her."

"That's okay. You know that, right?"

"It's like she's two completely different people." I slowed the treadmill, knowing I was done. I was going to have to work myself back up to the stamina I had before the accident, but Cruz kept going, his pace gloriously steady.

"In some ways, Penelope, we all are." He kept his eyes locked on the window ahead of him as I came to a standstill.

It would have been so easy to fall for him under any other circumstances, as easy and natural as breathing. But nothing was ever easy for me. Not anymore. Maybe that was my true punishment for my part in Brooke's madness.

I wiped down the equipment in relative silence, his last words echoing through me. I was two different people, too—Penna, who followed rules and wore pretty dresses to cotillion when her mother asked, and Rebel, who broke them all.

But with Cruz, I was a third—Penelope, a curious combination of both, and I was loathe to let that realization slip away.

Grabbing my water bottle, I paused at the door to the gym. "Cruz?" I called out his first name just because I could—

it was safe here in our tiny haven.

"Penelope?" he called back, meeting my gaze in the reflection of the window.

"It's usually quiet here this hour. It's a good time to run. My favorite time, actually."

Eyes locked, his jaw flexed. "Maybe I'll see you here, then," he finally said.

My heart leaped, and I bit back a smile. "Maybe you will."

I heard him increase his speed as I found the strength to walk away from him and the momentary respite he always seemed to give me.

Chapter Eight

PENNA

At Sea

"Are you almost ready?" Rachel called from the hallway as I threw on a final coat of mascara.

"One second," I promised, racing barefoot from our bathroom to my bedroom where my silver sparkle heels were waiting.

"You know, I'm not usually a body-envy kind of girl," Rachel said as she leaned against my doorframe watching me finish, "but, holy shit, you look phenomenal in that."

"You're just saying that because it's my birthday." I slipped my feet into the strappy heels and fastened the buckles.

"Nope. I feel zero need to conform to social norms like being nice on a birthday." She half shrugged, lifting the bare shoulder of her asymmetrical white cocktail dress. With fresh purple streaks in her chin-length black bob, she looked ultra-modern and chic.

"Truth," I acknowledged as I pointed at her.

"Now can we go? We're already twenty minutes late."

"You care about the societal norm of being on time?" I smoothed the lines of my form-fitted, white spaghetti-strap dress. It fell just beneath my knees but boasted a slit that rose dangerously high on my left thigh. I'd left my hair down in a riot of beach waves and been extra careful with my makeup. I told myself that it was for the cameras, to fulfill my contractual obligations, but Cruz might be there, and he'd never seen my hair down.

He's your professor, I reminded myself for the hundredth time.

"No, but I do care about seeing my hot-ass boyfriend decked out in white from head to toe."

"Good point." We walked out of the suite to find an empty hallway. Guess we really were that late. "They didn't plan anything, right?"

Rachel looked at the ceiling, then the walls, as we made our way to the elevator.

"Rachel."

"There might be a cake."

"A cake. Okay. I can handle a cake." I nodded to myself as we reached the elevator bay, and Rachel hit the down button. So far, I'd managed to keep the day pretty quiet. It wasn't like I felt like celebrating. After all, Brooke had been with me for every birthday I could remember, and well…she was gone.

The elevator opened and we got in, then picked up two guys from deck eight on our way to the lobby.

"God *damn*," one of them said, not realizing I could see him checking out my ass in the reflection of the elevator door, or not caring, which was equally disgusting. "You're that Renegade girl, right?"

"That's me," I said, watching the floors tick by and praying for patience. If I went around decking every guy who had the nerve to look at my ass we'd never keep a sponsor.

"So why do they call you Rebel, anyway?" he asked.

The doors opened. *Thank you, God.*

"For a lot of reasons." I looked over my shoulder at the overgrown frat boy in a white polo. "None of which you could even dream of handling."

We walked onto the small landing and looked out over the massive party in the atrium.

"Bitch," the guy muttered as he walked by.

Rachel spun toward him, and I grabbed her wrist, holding her in place. The last thing we needed was a section of the documentary dedicated to assault charges when Rachel kicked his ass.

"Maybe, but certainly not *your* bitch," I called out as he walked down the stairs.

"Asshole," Rachel seethed and turned back to the railing with me to look out over the crowd.

"They usually are."

Guys scoped me out regularly, wanting to bag the "girl Renegade," or worse, use me to get closer to Pax or Landon. I wasn't Penna to them, just Rebel—a piece of ass and a trophy to brag about. When they realized I wasn't interested and they couldn't convince me otherwise, I immediately became a bitch or a lesbian to them. It happened so often that I'd become pretty much immune.

"Some party," Rachel said, her eyes roaming in search of Landon.

The atrium had been transformed in preparation for the International Date Line party. White swags of fabric draped down the support pillars that held the atrium open for ten decks, then gathered at the center. Disco balls hung, reflecting purplish lights onto the gyrating mass of college students all dressed in white beneath us. It was beautiful in a way that should have been ethereal, but instead looked downright hedonistic with the positions of some of those couples. The DJ spun from the landing of the grand staircase, the beat strong and driving.

"There he is! Let's go!"

I followed Rachel down the steps and into the crowd of white. How the hell she managed to pick Landon out of this monochromatic crowd was something I could never understand. Everyone blended together.

Was Cruz here? Did professors come as chaperones? Or maybe just to have fun themselves? I found myself scanning the crowd even though I knew I shouldn't. He hadn't been at the gym when I'd gone earlier, but changing my run time today was something I couldn't help thanks to this little soiree. I needed to run every day if I wanted my endurance back, and Bobby would have had my ass if I'd missed the party.

When the cameras started trailing us, I knew we had to be close. First term, I'd shared the three-bedroom suite with Landon and Pax, and the cameras had been everywhere but the bathrooms, allowed by the contracts we'd signed. Moving in with Rachel three months ago—where the cameras weren't allowed—had given me a modicum of privacy to recover.

We found the other Renegades in a roped-off area near the grand staircase. Two guards in white suits opened the ropes for us, and I rolled my eyes. Only Pax would create a VIP section at a college party. Landon pulled Rachel into a hug and whispered something I couldn't hear above the music, thank God. I was privy to way too much of their sex life through our thin walls as it was.

"Happy birthday, Penna!" Pax said as he swept me off my feet into a massive bear hug.

"You already said that this morning." I laughed as my oldest friend spun me in a circle.

"And I'll get to say it again tomorrow! That's the absolute beauty of having your birthday on International Date Line day. You get an automatic redo tomorrow!"

"You've been drinking," I said with a smile as he finally set me down.

"We may have opened the champagne while we were waiting for you," he admitted.

"Happy birthday!" Leah said, hugging me to her petite frame and handing me a flute of champagne.

"Thank you," I told her, gladly accepting it. Maybe if I drank enough, I'd stop looking for Cruz and find someone my own age who could hold my interest.

Fat chance.

"Penna, my dearest," Landon said as he hugged me from behind, resting his chin on my head. "Happy birthday, my favorite Rebel."

"Yeah, yeah." I waved him off, ready to be done with the birthday show. "You guys seriously needed ropes?"

"It's part of your birthday present," Pax argued, his forehead puckering as he sank into one of the three white leather couches he'd no doubt arranged to have brought down just for this.

"You need to be exclusive?" I teased.

"Where are the cameras?" he asked, tilting his head as Leah cuddled up to his side.

I glanced around the area he'd sectioned off for us, realizing they all stood on the outside of the ropes. "They can't come in?"

"Happy birthday," he said, raising his glass.

"Best present ever," I agreed and then sipped the chilled, sweet champagne. It was another concession of Pax's, pouring the sweet stuff while I knew he preferred the dry.

Those little things were never seen by the outside world, by the other students who looked over at our group while they danced. Maybe they saw us as a group of elitist friends, but we were a family, sometimes stronger than the one I had been born into.

Pax and Landon would never let me fall if they could help it. They would move heaven and earth for me, and I would do the same for them and Nick. Nick, for whom we gave up this entire year of our life, because that's what family did—took care of one another.

Maybe I couldn't ride my bike now…maybe not ever, but this was still my family.

"Cuba," I said to Pax.

He leaned forward. "Cuba?"

"For the live expo. It's never been done before, and with the new entry regulations, we can do it. There's a waiver for sporting events." I'd looked it up last night after my run with Cruz.

"Cuba," he said, drawing out the word as he thought.

"Just something to think about."

"It's a good idea. Let's look into it."

"Okay."

"What are we looking into?" Alex asked, coming to stand next to me. He was tall, lanky, with a mop of blond hair and glazed blue eyes that always made me wonder how the hell he got marijuana on board. But he was nearly as good as Landon at snowboarding, which put an equal pro in his column that almost eclipsed the con of his stonerish mannerisms.

"The live expo," I answered, looking at him. My gaze skipped right over his white tee to see Cruz leaning against the wall about twenty feet behind Alex, clearly chaperoning.

His eyes were locked on me, and I knew that look—it was the same one he'd worn just before he'd kissed me in Vegas. Teacher or not, he didn't see me as just a student. The knowledge sent a chill racing down my spine, followed by a delicious sense of awareness.

Holy shit, he looked edible. He managed to do what no other guy had pulled off at the party—make white pants sexy.

They were drawstring…all it would take would be a tiny tug on that string…

Alex said something, and I nodded absently.

I could talk to Cruz, right? No one would jump to conclusions because I spoke to my professor at a school party. Before I realized it, I'd already taken a step, but I was brought up short when he shook his head once, the movement nearly imperceptible.

My drink disappeared from my hand, and I turned to see Alex holding out his hand to me. My confusion must have come across on my face, because he looked at me like I'd lost my mind. "You said you wanted to dance?"

"Oh yeah, okay," I said, realizing I'd agreed to something when I hadn't been listening.

Pax's bouncers opened the ropes for us, and we hit the dance floor as Sia sang about cheap thrills. Alex chose a spot at the edge of the crowd that gave the cameras the best view of us, and me the best view of Cruz as he watched.

I shook my head and tried to concentrate on Alex. After all, he'd asked me to dance, not Cruz. He was my age, came from my lifestyle, and was a better fit for me in about ten thousand different ways.

As we started to move, keeping enough space between us that I was comfortable, Miss Gibson took up a place next to Cruz. She had been my math professor first term, and next to Cruz was probably the youngest professor on the ship.

He laughed at something she said, and my stomach twisted with an ugly emotion I didn't want to name. She put her hand on his arm, and I backed up until I came into contact with Alex's stomach.

His hands moved to my waist, and I moved against him as Selena Gomez took over the speakers. But as she started to sing about wanting hands on her body, I could only imagine Cruz's hands, Cruz's lips. God, I had it *bad*.

As if sensing the change, Cruz looked up, his eyes immediately narrowing as he saw me in Alex's arms. It was stupid, immature, and downright mean, but I held his gaze in open challenge and then moved even deeper into Alex. I wanted Cruz to see, to want, to be forced to admit that he wanted me, even if the rules said he couldn't have me.

I'd never given a shit about rules. They called me Rebel for a reason.

Cruz's eyes slid closed, and he swallowed hard, then forced a smile and looked back at Miss Gibson. That wretched jealousy in my belly turned sour with sadness as he led her away toward the bar.

Of course he should talk to her. Flirt with her. Hook up with her. Just like Alex was my logical choice, she would be his. I closed my eyes and concentrated on the feel of Alex's hands, steady and sure on my waist. His body, lean from years of boarding, moved against mine in rhythm with the music.

Maybe he was what I needed. Maybe he would make me forget what Cruz made me feel, or even better, teach me that I could want someone besides Cruz. Because I couldn't have him.

Before I lost my nerve, I grabbed Alex's hand and walked past the bar to the hallway of offices just off the atrium.

I opened the door and found the excursion office—where non-Renegades booked their travel, since ours was predetermined with stunts. I barely registered the look of shock on Alex's face as I shut the door behind us.

"Penna…" he said, his eyebrows sky high.

"What? You think I'm pretty, right?" I asked, looking up at him, our bodies easily a foot apart, because I couldn't bring myself to close the distance.

"Hell yeah, you're hot."

"Well, then…" I shrugged.

"Look, I'm not against hooking up with you, but I know

you don't usually…"

"Usually what? Act like a normal, single, twenty-two-year-old woman?" Every second that passed took a bite out of what I thought had been resolve to reveal the bones of jealousy-fueled stupidity.

"Well, yeah."

I leaned back against the desk, knowing he was right. Making out with Alex—or worse—wasn't going to fix the issue that I wanted someone else. It would only make me feel like shit.

"I'm sorry," I said quietly. "I really want to want you, and I know that's not something that even sounds sane."

He walked over to me and tilted my chin. "This isn't something you need to apologize for, Penna. And nothing happ—"

The door flew open behind him, and I looked around Alex, expecting to see Pax or Landon interfering as usual.

It wasn't.

My mouth dropped open as Cruz stood there, outright murder in his eyes. "What do you think you're doing?" he asked.

Alex jumped back about two feet. "Dr. Delgado! Nothing!"

"Damn right you're not. This is an office, not your closet for seven minutes in heaven. Take it to your rooms if you need to."

What, were we in seventh grade?

"Yes, sir," Alex said and looked back at me.

"I need a second to compose myself," I said honestly. The last thing I wanted to do was walk out with the guy I'd almost kissed to take my mind off the other guy.

That was an awkward moment I could do without.

"Okay, I'll see you out there," Alex said.

My eyes slid shut, and my head drooped as I heard the

door *click* softly behind them as they left.

"What the fuck was that, Penelope?" Cruz hissed.

My eyes shot to his. "I thought you left."

"What was that?" he repeated, folding his massive arms over his chest.

"That was me being horribly stupid," I admitted.

"Oh, I got that. Because it sure as hell looked to me like you were doing your damnedest to make me jealous." His eyes narrowed as he leaned against the wall farthest from me.

My face burned with heat. "That's because I was."

"Why would you do that?"

"Because I saw you talking to Miss Gibson. Because I'm stuck in junior high. I don't know." I threw my hands up in frustration. "Because you make me do stupid things like want you when I'm well aware that you don't want me."

His head snapped back like I'd slapped him.

"Don't want you? Fuck my life, Penelope. It's taken every ounce of self-restraint I have to stay away from you since we came on board, to keep my eyes off you in class. To keep from jumping from my balcony to yours when I hear your voice just above me."

"What?"

"Yeah, my room is just under yours, which means we sleep about twenty vertical feet apart. Talk about a mindfuck."

"I didn't know," I said softly, running my tongue over my lower lip in nervousness.

"Oh God, don't do that."

"Do what?"

"*That.*" He pointed toward my mouth. "Everything I told you in Vegas is still true. You're still gorgeous, still sexy as hell, still everything that draws me in like a damned magnet, but you're also everything I can't have. Don't you get that? When you pull shit like that on the dance floor, you successfully drive me batshit crazy, watching you in some guy's arms." A small laugh escaped him. "Like that kid has any idea what to do with you if he actually managed to catch you."

"And you do?"

His eyes darkened. "Don't challenge me like that."

The tension stretched between us for a quiet moment until I broke the silence. "I didn't kiss him."

"I'm well aware, because if you had, I'm not sure if I could have let him walk out of here, and that's dangerous, Penelope. *You* are dangerous to me."

"I'm sorry," I said truthfully. "Logically, I know nothing can happen between us. I get it. But I see you, and all I can think about is the way you kissed me in Vegas. The way you touched me. I can't just erase those memories, Cruz. Like I said, somehow you make me do stupid things."

"You? I make *you* do stupid things?" he nearly yelled, and I was thankful for the loud, driving beat of the music beyond the office doors. "Woman, I got into a strange car for you. Illegally BASE jumped off a Ferris wheel to stay close to you. Went to jail for you, and I make *you* do stupid things?"

He stalked forward, his movements smooth like a predator, and a low hum filled my stomach, growing stronger with every step he took.

"I let you stay in my class. Stupid. I look for every reason to run into you, while simultaneously praying you'll stay far away because I need this job. Stupid. I take one look at you in that fucking dress, and I'm so hard I'm afraid I can't hide it in a room full of students. Stupid. I can't stop thinking about the way you taste, the way you open up under me, the way your nails left little half-moons in my shoulders when I found how wet you were for me."

If he got his hands anywhere near me, he'd find out I was just as wet now. God, his words were the biggest turn-on I'd ever experienced. Next to his abs. Or his arms. Or his mouth. Crap, the man was one giant sex package begging to be unwrapped.

"Cruz," I whispered as he cupped my face with one hand, his thumb rubbing over my lower lip, while he caged me against the desk with the other.

My tongue licked across the tip of his finger, unable to help myself.

"God, Penelope. You could cost me *everything*, and yet I'm still in here with you. And this might be the worst choice of all."

His mouth met mine in a kiss that sent my senses reeling. His tongue swept in, claiming every curve he might have missed last time, until it felt like my mouth belonged to him.

One of my hands flew to his bicep while the other tangled in his hair. If all I got was this one time to kiss him, to feel like he was mine, then I was taking advantage of every second. I kissed him back with everything I had, sliding my tongue into his mouth to trace that sensitive line behind his teeth.

I felt his growl through the rumble of his chest, and he grabbed my ass with his free hand, lifting me against him. Maybe it was the strength in his arms, or his sheer size, but Cruz did something no other man had ever managed—he made me feel tiny, protected, cherished. Pure lust zipped through me, lighting my nerves on fire, knowing he was the only one who could put me out.

No one else made me want like this, or feel so desperate, electric—only Cruz.

"God, you're so damn beautiful tonight," he said against my mouth before kissing me again, this one deeper, slower, and infinitely more sensuous. It was an assault on all my senses, and he drew out every second, controlling each aspect of the caress. Never had the slow bite of my lower lip sent such shots of pure need through me, which was rivaled only by the leisurely, thorough way he tilted my head and kissed me like he had all the time in the world. In those few stolen, forbidden seconds I realized how badly I wanted them to be forever.

This was a high worth chasing. He was a risk worth taking.

My hand fisted in the fabric of his shirt as he flipped us so that he leaned against the desk with me between his outstretched legs. I rubbed against him, reveling in the power he gave over to me, the knowledge that this man had one weakness—and it was me.

His hand slid through the slit of my dress until he gripped my thigh lightly. The brush of his thumb near the line of my thong made me arch, pushing into his grip. "More," I begged.

"Your skin is so soft," he murmured as he set his mouth to my neck.

I gasped. He may as well have found my "push here for sex" button with his damned tongue.

My fingers trailed down the hard muscles of his chest. "Every time I see you like this, or in a shirt and tie, there's a part of my brain that flashes to what you look like without it," I admitted. "All gorgeous muscles and golden skin. Then I have the most ludicrous urge to strip you and lick every line of your abs. Every time I see you, Cruz. *Every* time."

"Penelope," he groaned. "You can't say things like that to me."

He took my mouth again, this time the kiss taking on an urgent tone as the beat of the music shifted outside.

He was hard against my stomach, and if he'd moved the slightest of inches, I'd finally be able to get my hands on—

Click.

Lightning quick, Cruz spun us so I was against the desk, simultaneously breaking the kiss and stepping back from me until there were a few feet between us.

"Enough with the alone time, Pennaaaaaaoly shit! Sorry, I didn't mean to interrupt."

I froze, my fingers gripping the edge of the desk as my

eyes locked with Cruz's, like maybe Rachel's voice behind him didn't actually belong to her. Maybe if we stayed just like this, she'd have T. rex vision and not really see us.

My breath was erratic, but his was steady as he closed his eyes as if he was in pain and then opened them with a new resolve.

My legs finally got the memo to move, and I walked around his still frame. "Hey, Rachel, what's up?" I forced out with a grin plastered so hard to my face that it would have cracked if touched.

Her mouth hung open. It looked like I'd accidentally managed the task no one really could—I'd shocked the hell out of Rachel. "I…um…" Her gaze flickered between us, like she couldn't quite piece together what she'd walked in on.

God, I hoped she couldn't.

"Rachel, I'm going to need just a second."

"Are you…?" she started.

Cruz turned, then moved directly to my side. "Miss Dawson, if you'd wait in the hall for a moment?"

Her eyes popped so wide I thought they might fall out. "Dr. Del…Dr. Delgado, yeah. Absolutely," she mumbled and hurried out. I saw the outline of her head through the frosted glass as she leaned back against the door.

"She won't tell anyone," I promised as Cruz put his hands behind his neck and looked at the ceiling. "It's not like she even really saw anything." When he didn't respond, I drove on. "I mean, honestly, she didn't see anything because you were over here, and I was there, so…"

His jaw flexed a couple of times as he obviously struggled. "Cruz."

"No." The word was harsh.

"I know she won't," I said, reaching for him but thinking twice about it and letting my hand fall to the side of my dress.

"Fuck," he cursed, but it wasn't directed at me, more at

himself. "You have *no* idea what just almost happened. I could lose my job. I could lose *everything*. I can't…you shouldn't… we can never…"

"At least look at me while you're rejecting me," I requested softly.

He spun, those dark eyes pinning me in place against the desk. "Rejecting you? It's pretty damn obvious that I'm incapable of rejecting you, even when it puts my entire future in jeopardy, so cut it with the self-deprecating language."

My spine straightened, and I raised my chin. "Nothing is going to happen, and even if she had seen something, Rachel won't out us. I would bet my life on her."

"So you expect me to bet *mine*?" he seethed. His shoulders dropped, and he rubbed his hands over his stubbled jaw. "I don't know her. Hell, I barely know you. There is no *us*, Penelope. There can't be. I am your professor, you are my student, and I have worked too hard to get here to let it all crumble away because I can't control my dick."

I blinked, something ugly unfurling in my belly where the warmth had been. "So it's all about your *dick*?"

"No, and that's the issue. This"—he waved his hand between us like he could see the nearly palpable connection—"can never happen again. Ever. If that means I run in the other direction when we're in a social setting, or we agree to never speak outside the classroom again, then so be it. It can't happen again, Penelope," he repeated like I was a child he needed to get through to—needed to teach.

"*You* kissed *me*, remember?" I snapped back.

"That was a mistake." His eyes dropped to my mouth, and if not for the battle in his eyes, I might have kissed him again just to prove the damn point that he wanted me—that I wasn't a mistake. "Everything between us has been one failed lapse in judgment after another, and it ends now."

"You can't end something you never started." I tore my

eyes from him, unable to look at his gorgeous face, deep brown eyes, and that mouth that was currently telling me I was all wrong for him.

"This is for the best. I'll be the adult here. This is never happening again," he repeated, like he needed to say it to himself this time.

Logically, I knew he was right, but that voice was small compared to the pissed-off one currently in control of my mouth. The clock read ten fifteen, and I laughed softly. "The good news is that it's International Date Line day, right? Or night, I guess. We'll cross the date line in a couple hours, and it will be February sixth all over again. Today never happened. *This* never happened."

I pushed past him and opened the door to find Rachel guarding it. "What the hell is going— Oh, Penna, are you okay?" Her tone changed the instant her eyes met mine.

"Sure, of course." I forced a smile. "What's up?"

Her gaze darted over my shoulder and back to me. "Remember that cake I told you about? Pax needs you on the staircase so you can make seven tiers worth of wishes."

Oh God. My birthday. The first time Brooke wouldn't stand next to me as I blew out my candles. The first time I wouldn't have her hugging me and telling me that the best thing about birthdays was knowing we'd always spend them together because boys walked away but blood stayed.

"It's your birthday?" Cruz asked from behind me.

Cruz, who didn't think I was worth the risk. Because I wasn't. You didn't spend ten years working toward a career to throw it away on the first student who crossed your path. *Seriously, you were actually the first student to meet him.* I almost laughed, but I couldn't find the energy.

I smoothed out the lines of my dress and stood straighter. "That's none of your concern, Dr. Delgado." Too much. There was too much going on. Cruz, the cake, the cameras…

I checked the end of the hallway and, sure enough, Bobby's cameramen were waiting.

"Pen—"

I shot a look over my shoulder at him. How dare he look destroyed, torn, when he'd just crumpled me up like a useless receipt from an ill-planned vacation. "You should stay in there for a few more minutes. At least until the cameras are gone."

Rachel held out her hand, and I nearly lost it at the gesture she never would have made when she came aboard three months ago—that's how far our friendship had come. I took it, composing myself and nearly crushing her hand in the process, but I knew she could handle it. Rachel was hard like I was, but strong in a way I hadn't felt in such a long time.

I gave her a single head nod, and we walked down the hallway while I got my shit together. "Nothing happened."

"Yeah, okay. Because it looked like—"

"I don't care what it looked like. Nothing happened." Apprehension slithered up my spine. What if she had seen something? What if it had been someone else? "You can't tell anyone," I whispered.

"I thought nothing happened to tell."

"Not even Landon."

"Penna…"

I shot her a look that said so many things. *Please. Help me. You owe me.*

"Fine, but we're talking about this later."

"Deal. I didn't want to celebrate my birthday," I whispered. "I told him that."

Her eyes softened. "I know. They just want to celebrate *you.*"

My face twisted as it all caught up to me, and Rachel quickly stepped in front of me and took my face in her hands.

"Say the word, and we'll walk out the back. You owe those cameras *nothing.*"

"But I owe Nick everything." Nick, who had sat with me while I hit the ramp time and again on the snowmobile, perfecting my whip until I was good enough to stand on top of an all-male podium at the X Games.

Nick who destroyed Brooke's heart and then her mind.

"Not this, you don't."

"No, I can do it." I sure as hell wasn't going to let Cruz Delgado take anything else. "I can do it," I repeated, stronger this time.

She searched my eyes for a few moments, then nodded. "Then smile pretty for the cameras, Rebel, because the whole world is watching you."

Rachel was right. Penna needed to hide. Penelope needed to scream at Cruz. Rebel needed to step forward and lock both of those needs away and smile for the documentary.

Dropping Rachel's hand, I stood taller, smiled brighter, and walked by her side through the crowd while Pax called out for me on the microphone. Then I walked up the stairs, careful not to trip, and blew out the candles on the extravagant cake Pax ordered for me, all while wishing that something, *anything*, would go right in my life.

We posed for pictures, the three Originals, while the staff cut the cake, and then I smiled until my face hurt.

I did my duty for one simple reason: I was a Renegade before anything else—because there was nothing else for me.

Chapter Nine

What the hell had I done?

At what point had I turned every ounce of my self-control over to my dick? Hell, at what point was I going to admit that my attraction to Penelope wasn't just physical?

I was so entirely fucked.

She blew out her candles, looking every ounce *X-Treme Sports Magazine*'s sexiest athlete of the year—yeah, I'd googled her—while I stood against the wall, simultaneously despising myself for what I'd just let happen and reliving every second that I'd had her mouth under mine.

It was her birthday. Her *birthday*, and I'd just hurt her. Sure, she'd responded with fire—I was learning to expect nothing less—but I'd seen the hurt in her eyes and immediately hated myself for putting it there.

God, I'd been so fucking stupid. I'd nearly let us get caught, so lost in her taste, the feel of her skin under my hands, that I didn't hear the door until it was almost too late.

What if her friend said something? Would Penelope confirm her story? Would I lose my job—lose everything I've worked for?

A couple hours later, the dateline crossed and February sixth restarted like *Groundhog Day*, I stood in my room, hands braced on my desk as I looked over the contents of the file I'd spread out on the surface.

This was why I was here. This was why I'd given ten years of my life in pursuit of an opportunity just like the one that had finally fallen into my lap last week. *This* was why nothing else mattered.

This was a chance I'd never get again, and it could work. Everything could fall into place as long as I planned carefully, executed perfectly, and kept the hell away from Penelope Carstairs for the next three months.

You can't stay away from her for a few days, and you think three months is going to happen?

I took the glossy 5x7 and stared into soft, innocent brown eyes. *She* was the reason I had to stay away from Penna. I had one chance to give her the life she deserved, the one she'd already worked so hard for. I couldn't let her end up like my mother—broken, beaten…dead.

"I'm coming, Elisa," I vowed to her.

And I never broke a promise.

• • •

The sun streamed in through the windows of my classroom the next afternoon, making it feel a hell of a lot warmer than the twenty-two degrees it was outside. We'd be pulling into Dutch Harbor, Alaska, tomorrow—our first real stop since leaving Japan six days ago.

As the class filed in, I arranged my notes, mostly to keep from looking for Penelope. Not that I needed to look for her. I'd *felt* her walk in. There was a subtle change to the air, a shift to my center of gravity.

Out of the corner of my eye, I saw her take her seat, and my fingernails bit into my palms. God, if I'd only met her a year ago, or a year from now.

Timing was a bitch.

"Happy Birthday, Penna!" the Wilder kid said, presenting her with a box.

I looked up just in time to see her say, "Seriously? I don't want one birthday and now I have two? Like yesterday wasn't bad enough."

"Just say thank you," he said, ruffling her hair like she was three.

The urge to smack his hand away from her head was immediate and overwhelming. She wasn't a child, she was a full-grown woman. *You're just pissed you can't give her a birthday present.*

Like I'd even know what to get a girl who literally had everything she could want.

"What is this?" she asked, and I blatantly stared at the key she held, forgetting about the papers in my hand.

"You have to agree to come with us tomorrow to find out."

I saw the debate play out on her face in the way her eyebrows scrunched, but then a look of yearning took over only to be consumed by a deep sigh. She was conflicted on every level a person could be, and the key seemed to be a symbol of that.

Her complicated nature was one of the things that pulled me in. Something told me whomever Penelope chose to love would never be bored.

"Dr. Delgado?" Macy Richardson called from the first

row.

"Yes, Macy?"

"Are you really leading the snowshoe expedition tomorrow? I was trying to decide on a shore excursion, and I waited until the last minute." She blinked at me, and I half expected to see words written on her eyelids like I was Indiana Jones.

"I am," I answered. "But don't feel like you have to come. You're not required to attend my excursions until we reach Mexico."

"Oh no, I'm sure it will be super fun!" She shot me a perky smile.

Great.

"I certainly hope so."

Penna looked up at me, and our eyes locked, a million unsaid things passing between us before her eyes iced over and she looked back at Wilder. "Yeah, I'll come. Nothing to lose, right?"

He grinned, and I wanted to vomit. He couldn't seem to understand that she wasn't making the choice out of want but out of anger at a situation he had nothing to do with.

"You won't regret it!" Leah, the girl behind Wilder promised.

Did they even realize what had put her on that Ferris wheel? Did they see the pain she struggled through every day with her sister, her injury, her guilt? Or did they just push her for another stunt, another appearance? If they were her friends, why weren't they taking care of her like she needed?

None of your business.

Damn, I needed to run off this frustration.

"Let's get started, shall we? Who wants to tell me what they thought of the assigned reading?"

Penelope's hand shot up, and I faked a glance down at my roster before I called on her. "Yes? Penelope?"

"It's Penna," she said, like it was some privilege to call her by the nickname her friends gave her.

Penna was the girl who put on fake smiles for her friends and those damned cameras that followed her around relentlessly. She was the outer casing that guarded the woman I knew was underneath.

That one line seemed so innocuous to everyone else in the room, but I knew the truth—she'd just shut the door on Penelope.

"Penna," I repeated dutifully.

Then I tried to feign moderate, appropriate interest as she told me her insightful interpretation of the text. Of course she'd be smart, too. The only flaw the woman had was that she was currently untouchable.

I got through class, definitely not missing the way Rachel watched me through narrowed eyes. *Yes, I'm an idiot. Yes, I took advantage of her—just not in the way you think.*

After class, dinner with Westwick and some of the other teachers, and catching up on grading from my one-hundred-level class, I headed to the gym. I made damn sure it was after Penna's preferred time and that I was alone.

Then I ran until I was too tired to regret what happened yesterday.

If I could figure out which damn part I regretted.

Chapter Ten

DUTCH HARBOR, ALASKA

"You're kidding me," I said to Pax as I stared at the fleet of brand-new snowmobiles I'd found waiting for us on a small, snow-covered field outside of Dutch Harbor.

"Whichever one you want," he said, a shit-eating grin on his face.

Snowmobiling was the one area where I was better than him, and he knew it. He wasn't just giving me a machine as a present, but the opportunity to remember why they called me Rebel in the first place. The chance to kick his ass was just an added bonus.

The longing that ached in my chest was a welcome surprise.

"What do you say, Penna?" Landon asked, slinging his arm around my shoulder.

I took in a lungful of cold, crisp Alaskan air and looked

from the vast expanse of blue sea to the mountains that rose in front of us on the small island and sighed. I wanted to forget everything for just a few minutes—Brooke, Cruz, hell, even my responsibilities as a Renegade. Maybe it was for the wrong reasons, but who cared as long as I literally put myself back in the saddle in this small way?

"I want that one," I said, pointing to a Yamaha in the center. It was lighter than some of its counterparts, and I'd be able to do more with it. I was going to have to start lifting weights again if I ever wanted to get back on my bike and hope to pull tricks.

"Rebel's back," Landon said, squeezing my shoulders before grabbing Rachel to choose her sled.

She'd been quiet since she walked in on Cruz and me in the excursion office, and I knew I owed her an explanation soon, especially since I needed her to keep quiet. Just because I was hurt and pissed as hell at Cruz didn't mean I wanted him fired, or his life destroyed for kissing me. She'd brought it up this morning, but I'd quickly shut her down, and while I'd gotten a remarkable amount of side-eye today, she wasn't pushing.

I savored the crunch of snow under my feet as I walked to my new snowmobile and swung my leg over the seat, settling in with practiced ease. The engine started with a quick turn of the key, sending vibrations through my body as the motor rumbled beneath me.

"How does it feel to be back on a snowmobile after your accident, Rebel?" Bobby asked, prompting the camera to roll in closer.

I forced a smile and pulled my goggles down over my eyes to obscure the truth. "Great! I guess now we'll find out how healed this leg is!"

"Nervous at all?" he asked.

"Nope, just anxious to get back to being me."

That was the first true thing I'd said to the cameras since I'd been smashed by that falling light.

I buckled my helmet, familiarized myself with the setup of the sled, and took off with the other Renegades, leaving the vans behind as we followed a path over the snowy hills. The motor drowned out my thoughts, the feeling peaceful, and I took the time to really take in the sights around me. The volcanic islands lent themselves to dramatic landscapes— snow-covered volcanoes masquerading as mountains that stood out in stark relief against a crystal-blue sky. We'd lucked out and arrived between storms. I wouldn't want to get stuck here when one of those suckers came in.

We rode about twenty minutes until we reached a plateau where a series of ramps had been set up.

"Welcome to your playground, Rebel," Pax said over the radios in our helmets.

My stomach clenched, at war between feelings of excitement, anticipation, and soul-crushing dread.

"You set this all up?" I asked, pulling next to him, where he had Leah on the back of his snowmobile. "It's spectacular."

"Nick took care of it. He said to tell you your favorite ramp is the one on the end over there, and that there's no pressure or planned stunt. He just wanted you to have some fun for your birthday."

"That was the last two days," I grumbled.

"Well, he wanted to build it on the boat, but we couldn't figure out a way to keep the snow from melting in the auditorium."

"Smart-ass," I muttered.

"Go have fun."

I eyed the smallest of the ramps, which was something I could—and did—do when I was barely fifteen. Maybe it was a baby step back toward being me, but it was one I knew I could take.

Driving a quick loop around the ramp, I gauged the distance and the angle of the ramp before heading back to the start of the run. If I couldn't manage something that easy, I had zero business being here. I may as well pack my bags and lick my wounds back in L.A. Besides, hadn't I just BASE jumped off a Ferris wheel?

I could handle this.

Gunning the throttle, I sped toward the ramp, feeling the familiar rush of adrenaline through my veins. My body soaked up the hormone like fuel, and I hit the ramp, bracing my weight on the rails as I catapulted up.

Midair, no outside bullshit mattered. It was just me, the snowmobile, and my ability to control the machine. There was no Brooke, no worries over unanswered letters and rejected phone calls. No parents telling me to be patient, not to ask her for the answers I so desperately needed. No Pax, Landon, or Nick expecting me to instantly be who I was before the accident. No Cruz watching me with those hypnotic eyes, telling me with his body that he wanted me while shoving me away with his words.

I was just me.

And I was enough.

Bracing my feet, I let go of the throttle and reached for the sky, my world slowing until moments of infinity lasted in each second. As gravity took hold of my body, I got control of the snowmobile, landing on the other side of the ramp as if I'd just completed the hardest trick in my repertoire.

But maybe, in digging out the pieces of Rebel that clamored to be let free from the prison I'd stuck her in, I had.

Throttling down the machine, I drove the snowmobile out of the path of any jumpers, pulling to the side of the ramp.

"How did that feel?" Pax asked, his arms open.

"Really good," I admitted, already craving the blissful quiet that had settled over my brain while in the jump. "In fact, I think I'll go again."

His eyes crinkled, the only sign of a grin when his face was covered almost completely by his helmet. "Get to it, Rebel."

With a twist of the throttle, I headed toward the run, turning as another Renegade—I think it was Alex—took the ramp. Nothing fancy, but some good air. His talent had always been big-mountain riding.

Pax, Landon, me…and Nick. We were the only ones who could handle just about everything, even though we all had our areas of expertise. Then again, we'd been risking our necks on everything that moved since we were old enough to ride tricycles.

Once Alex was clear, I studied the ramp on the end that Nick had designed for me. The height, the angles, the distance to get up to speed. It was the exact ramp we'd been working with back in Tahoe last winter before…well, everything.

I wished my cell phone was on, that I could talk to him, ask him what he really meant by building that exact ramp here, but I already knew what he'd say. *Are you a Renegade or not?*

Today I was.

My heart rate sped up, as if my body had already accepted the answer to the question my mind was fighting. I was out of shape. I hadn't been on a snowmobile all season. Muscle memory didn't make up for lack of strength.

But I'd picked the smallest, lightest snowmobile of the bunch, I was experienced, and I'd never backed down from a self-imposed challenge.

I sped away from the ramp, then turned to face it. My focus narrowed to the track in front of me that had been put down, and I let everything fade away—the cameras, the line of other Renegades watching from the sidelines. Just me and the machine.

I gunned it, speeding toward the ramp, and there it was

again—the sweet oblivion I so desperately needed. I stood, my feet locked on the bars, bracing for the ramp. The machine took the angle perfectly, and we were airborne.

My muscles screamed as I pulled the snowmobile backward into the flip. My vision turned from blue to the green of pine trees to the stark white snow as gravity took hold, pulling me back to the earth.

You're not going to make it.

The landing came into view, and it wasn't pretty. It was going to be hard—if I was able to stick it.

Barely clearing the rotation, the skids slammed into the downward slope of the ramp. My ass crashed into the seat, and my entire body jolted forward, whipping into the handlebar. *Shit, there went a rib.*

I nearly lost the machine as it tilted to the left, but I corrected, throwing both of the skids onto the snow, and slid to a stop at the end of the ramp. Barely enough common sense to overrule my joy, I managed to move the machine to the side.

My chest heaving, I hopped off the snowmobile and threw my hands in the air with a victorious shout. Then I ripped off my helmet and slid my goggles to the top of my head.

"Did you see that?" I shouted to Landon, who was running in my direction.

He didn't stop, and he didn't hug me. His hands gripped my shoulders, his hazel eyes furious as he backed me toward the line of people behind us. "What the fuck were you thinking?"

"What?" I shouted back. "Are you seriously giving me shit after I just pulled that off? I haven't done that in a year, and I just nailed it!"

"Exactly! You've barely been out of a cast for a month. I know you haven't so much as touched weights—"

"Are you suggesting that I'm out of shape?" My mouth dropped open. It was one thing to know it myself, and quite another to have Landon in my face over it.

"Hell yes, I am! Because you are! Don't expect me to treat you like some little girl, Penna, when we both know you've never stood for it in the past. I'll dish your shit right back to you. You could have killed yourself!"

"But I didn't!"

"You had *no* business trying to pull off that kind of trick after a whole whopping twenty minutes back on a snowmobile!"

"Like you had any business snowboarding at twenty-one thousand feet when you weren't nearly acclimatized for the altitude?"

"And look how that turned out! For fuck's sake, Penna!"

"I pulled it off!"

"And what if you hadn't? What if you'd broken your damned neck?"

"I don't answer to you, Landon!"

"That's bullshit! We answer to one another! We hold one another accountable! You know what happens when we don't? Nick ends up in a wheelchair."

"And Brooke drops a stadium light on me. Yeah, I'm well aware of the consequences, and I'm currently paying that price. Now stop treating me like this!"

"Like what?"

"Like a…girl!"

"News flash. You *are* a girl!"

"You damn well know what I mean, Landon Rhodes!"

"Hey guys," Pax interrupted from behind us, stepping forward to put a hand on each of our shoulders. "It's not cool when Mom and Dad fight in front of the kids, okay?"

I glanced over to where the line of Renegades watched, only to realize they weren't all Renegades. Some were the snowshoeing expedition, Cruz standing front and center, his eyes fierce and jaw locked.

Who cares what he thinks? He doesn't want you, anyway.

I ripped my eyes away and concentrated on Pax. "Are you going to light into me, too?"

"Nope," he replied. "I think Landon did a good enough job for the both of us."

Landon and I locked gazes, and he swallowed, something dark and sad washing over his face. "I can't lose you, too, Penna. None of us can."

"I'm fine," I said, this time softer.

"Yeah, physically," Pax added.

"That was rad, Rebel!" Alex said, passing by for a high five on his snowmobile.

"Thanks," I muttered. "See, he thinks it was cool," I argued after he'd passed.

"Alex is an idiot on everything except a board," Landon countered as Pax left to talk to Cruz. We'd never had a school excursion cross our path before.

"I didn't mean to scare you."

Landon shook his head. "I think you meant to scare yourself, or prove something. I'm not sure what's worse."

"I've never played it safe."

"You've never played it stupid, either." He walked off as the camera crew took his place. *Great.*

From my peripheral vision, I saw Pax gesturing toward the ramps, probably explaining the setup to Cruz. *Dr. Delgado,* I reminded myself.

"That was amazing, Rebel! What inspired you to hit up a backflip after all this time?" Bobby asked, gesturing for me to smile.

Rebel facade in place, I gave the camera a coy smile and a little shrug. "Not sure. Just wanted to shake off the dust." I gave them a wink and made my way to Pax.

But as I approached Cruz, Pax took off toward Leah. It would have been wicked obvious if I'd turned and changed directions, so I stood next to Cruz, watching Alex get ready to take my ramp.

"You seriously flipped that snowmobile," he said, his voice tight.

"Right now I'm the only woman on the planet who can," I answered without looking at him.

"And that is why they call you Rebel."

I glanced up at him, taking in his crossed arms and narrowed eyes under his black hat. "Among other reasons. I'm not very good at listening to what I'm supposed to do."

"Was Landon right? Could you have killed yourself?"

I shrugged. "Some people would say that's a possibility with every stunt."

"But you wouldn't?" he snapped.

"Not to go all Liam Neeson on you, but I have a particular set of skills that mitigates a lot of the risk." I looked down the track to see Alex take off, his motor straining under the demand of the throttle.

"But not all of it."

"Nope." There was so much I wanted to say, like how that hadn't bothered him in Vegas, but I couldn't—not in a crowd full of students, though we were pretty alone over here. "You probably need to put your snowshoes on and get back to your excursion."

"Yeah. We just saw you guys on the hike and decided to check you out."

Check me out, indeed. A corner of my mouth lifted as Alex hit the ramp.

"Not that way," Cruz muttered.

"What the hell?" Alex pulled the snowmobile into a backflip, which to the best of my knowledge, he'd never done before. He was too slow, too low, and— "He's going to hit," I whispered a full second before he came down nearly nose-first, his body flying off the snowmobile as it collided with the ground.

Alex rolled down the rest of the ramp. I took off at a run toward him, the snow slowing me down. My chest exploded in pain, and my hand gripped the side of my rib cage that had been abused when I landed.

"Throttle's stuck!" Landon yelled.

My head swung toward the noise of the whirring motor just in time to see it barreling toward me. *Holy shit.*

A bulldozer took me to the ground, rolling me under, then over, and under again as the snowmobile passed within a few feet of me—us. Cruz was on top of me, his forearms locked on either side of my head, covering me in every way he could manage.

My ribs screamed, my heart pounded, and yet every discomfort was blocked out by the concern in his eyes. "Tell me you're okay!"

"I'm fine," I forced out in a wheeze.

"Are you sure? You don't sound fine." Now those deep brown eyes were downright panicked.

"I can't breathe. You're. Really. Heavy."

"Oh shit. I'm sorry." He was off me immediately, standing quickly and pulling me up.

My arm wrapped around my injured ribs, my mind forcing the pain into a neat little box. As soon as the adrenaline faded, it was going to hurt like a bitch. The snowmobile had crashed into a snow bank and died. With that problem gone, I looked to the ramp where Alex came to a wavering stand.

"That was awesome!" he yelled, obviously not injured.

"And you think *I* was stupid?" I called out to Pax as he headed toward Alex.

He waved a finger at me but closed his mouth before he said something as equally idiotic as Alex's failed stunt.

"My first impression of you was right," Cruz said, pulling down his sunglasses so I couldn't see his eyes.

"And what was that?"

"That you're insane. You're all insane."

His words from the elevator hit me like a high-speed train. *"You're insane. You know that, right? Crazy hot—no, exquisitely beautiful—smart, strong, and incredibly magnetic, but a little fucking nuts."*

I walked away before I could say something we'd both regret, but threw a smile over my shoulder at him. "Pretty much. Welcome to the Renegades."

• • •

"Penna!" Hugo caught up to me as I waited for the elevator back on the *Athena*. In a move of mercy, Bobby had let me sneak away without a camera escort.

"Hey, Hugo!"

"Have fun out there?"

"Yeah, I actually did." I shifted my backpack, my muscles deliciously tired and my ribs more on the angry side. "You really need to come out with us one of these ports."

"Yeah, no. I love you ladies, but you—and those guys—are kind of nuts."

I laughed, feeling lighter than I had in a while. "Yeah, well, they don't call us Renegades for nothing."

"True," he answered, grinning. "Hey, you had a package come in today. I just got the notification. I'll bring it up in a little bit."

"Is it in the mail room?" I asked. "Because I seriously don't mind going to grab it. You already do enough for us."

"Nawh, I don't mind."

"Too bad. I'm going to get it. Go take that girl you've been eyeing during math out for dinner or something." I motioned toward the redhead waiting at a different elevator.

"Julie?" His head tilted like he was thinking about it.

"Yeah. Yeah, maybe that's a good idea." Then he practically ran to catch her.

"Boys." I laughed to myself as Rachel walked up. "I'm going to detour to deck six, wanna come?"

"Sure, if you're finally going to tell me what the hell I walked in on the day before yesterday," she challenged, her take-no-shit face in place. "And don't think that I didn't notice him taking you out of that snowmobile's path today."

Ah, the reckoning was finally upon me. I glanced at the students around us as we got onto the elevator. "Yeah, let's just get to the suite first."

"What are you going to do with our day in L.A.?" she asked, keeping our conversation eavesdrop-safe.

"Not sure," I said honestly. "I want to see my parents, but they're always…occupied." I knew exactly what I wanted to do, but I wasn't sure any of the other Renegades would understand or let me go alone.

"Yeah, I need to do the same. I know I just saw them before the X Games, but they'd kill me if I was in town and didn't stop by. Figured I'd load up on Cherry Coke since this boat only carries Pepsi, and pray that Landon and my dad don't kill each other during the visit."

"Yeah, good luck with that one." There was zero love lost between Landon and Rachel's dad due to some very shitty sponsorship terms that had cost them their relationship once—nearly twice.

The doors opened at our deck, and we walked out into the lobby. I winced as I adjusted my pack.

"You okay?" she asked.

"I hit my ribs on the handlebar when I landed. It's nothing, so don't give me that look."

She put her hands up, palms out. "Hey, you're a professional. If you say it's not serious, then I'll believe you."

"Thank you." We walked down the narrow hallway past

the office she'd nearly caught me kissing Cruz in, but she didn't say anything, thank God.

"Name?" the mail clerk asked as we approached the half door.

"Penelope Carstairs," I told him.

"Hey, Dr. Delgado," Rachel said.

"Rachel," he said in that gorgeously accented voice. "Penna."

It had been only a day, and I already missed the way he said Penelope.

Small ship. I cursed my luck but still glanced at him over my shoulder. It was like a law of nature—if Cruz was in the room, I looked at him. Then I craved him, missed the potential of what we could have been, and hated our circumstances. Those, too, were pretty much law since coming aboard ten days ago.

"Car…Carlson…Carstairs. Here you go," the clerk said, handing me a shoebox-sized package.

"Thanks," I said absently as I checked out the return label. *Oak Moss Grove*. I barely made it to the lobby before I ripped the packing tape down to the cardboard to open it.

The flaps came apart easily, revealing the contents, and my knees nearly gave out. "No, no, no…" I whispered, balancing the package in one arm as I sifted through it with my free hand. "They're all here."

"What's all there?" Rachel asked.

"Why? Why would she…? I don't understand." How could they all be here? There had to be some explanation—at least that's what I told myself to keep my chest from imploding. I barely fought off the urge to curl in on myself, to shrink away from the world the way she'd managed to do.

"Penna?" Rachel prodded.

I looked up, my vision blurry but clear enough to see Cruz watching me from the stairs with a look of worry in his eyes. Streaks of warmth raced down my face, and he took a couple of steps toward me before stopping himself, a letter of his own gripped in his hand.

"What's in there? Why are you crying?" Rachel asked softly.

I didn't take my eyes off Cruz. "It's every letter I've written to my sister since Dubai, since they put her in Oak Moss Grove."

His eyes softened, those massive shoulders drooping as if he felt and carried the weight of my sorrow.

"Every letter?" Rachel looked inside the box.

"I think so. And they're all unopened."

"Maybe she's not allowed to get letters?"

"No, my parents write her all the time and get responses."

"Oh."

I batted away the tears that ran down my face. "It's okay. It will be fine. Everything is fine."

I did my best to pull my shit together, knowing there could be cameras on me at any moment—even now.

Brooke wouldn't answer my calls or even open my letters. My sister, my other half. She wanted nothing to do with me, and that hurt worse than the aching in my ribs.

"Please don't tell them—Pax or Landon. They don't know that I've been writing her."

"Okay," Rachel said softly, taking the box from my hands when I began to tremble from the exertion of holding myself together, of not running to Cruz and begging him to jump off another Ferris wheel with me to make everything stop hurting.

"She betrayed them."

"She betrayed you, too," Rachel whispered.

She'd sabotaged every stunt and nearly killed Leah, then Pax, but she'd never gone after me. Even that final accident, when she'd dropped the stadium light, causing the accident that crushed my leg, she'd thought I was Pax. She'd never intentionally hurt me. Maybe that's why I couldn't stop myself from reaching out to her. But she didn't want me.

I would have traded another three months in that cast for this feeling to go away.

"But she hadn't. Not until this very moment."

Chapter Eleven

LOS ANGELES

There were few places better in the United States in February than Los Angeles. Then again, it was my home, so I was probably pretty biased.

"Are you sure you don't want to come with us?" Leah asked, holding Pax's hand as they walked down the ramp in front of me.

Disembarking was a hell of a lot faster with our VIP passes—another perk of Pax owning the ship.

"Certain," I answered. Two whole days away from their lovefest would be a welcome break. Between Pax and Leah and Landon and Rachel, it was like a nonstop Hallmark movie in our group—not that I was jealous.

Okay, maybe a little jealous.

We said our good-byes at the end of the ramp, and I promised again to get to Pax's house to practice on the ramps tomorrow. Well, they could practice, and maybe I'd work up the courage to sit on my freaking bike.

I slid in to the welcoming leather of the town car's backseat and the driver shut the door. "Where to?" he asked as we drove toward the port's exit.

"My apartment, please," I answered. "Wait!"

The car came to a screeching halt next to where Cruz was walking alone, his hiking pack over his shoulder. I rolled down the window. "What are you doing?" I asked him.

"Walking to the parking lot to get my truck," he answered with a what-the-hell-does-it-look-like-I'm-doing face.

"Your truck is parked here?"

"I had a friend park it last night. I do have friends, you know."

"I vaguely remember seeing them in the bar in Vegas," I answered before I thought better of it. "Hop in, we'll take you."

"Not a good idea."

"Oh, come on. That parking lot is at least another mile past the rest of these cruise ships. I'm offering you a ride, not a striptease. In fact, I'll promise you the opposite—I vow that my clothes will stay on."

A smile flashed across his face, those adorable dimples making a rare appearance. "You sure?"

"Get in," I said, opening the door and sliding over.

He looked over his shoulder to make sure we were alone—we were—before climbing in next to me.

"Where to, sir?" my driver asked.

"You have a driver."

"I have a service. Now tell him where your truck is, or we'll waste half our time here arguing."

"Right. I'm parked in V-19. It's a black quad-cab F-250."

"Yes, sir."

The car started to roll, and Cruz rested his head against

the headrest. "We couldn't be more different if we were from different planets."

"And yet we wound up on the same ship."

He looked over at me, those incredible eyes of his so deep that I wanted to fall in. "That, we did. So tell me, Penna." He nearly choked on my name. "What are you going to do with your break?"

"I'm going to see my sister," I told him. "You're the only one who knows."

His eyebrows shot up. "You haven't told any of your friends? Are your parents taking you?"

"Nope. I don't want to tell them about the letters, and the other Renegades…well, they wouldn't understand. I just…I need to see her. If she won't answer my phone calls or even read my letters, then I have to try this."

He didn't attempt to talk me out of it like the others would have, or argue that she betrayed us, nearly killed me, or was generally messed up in the head. He simply nodded as we pulled up next to the truck I assumed was his. "Okay, grab your bag."

"Excuse me?"

"Grab. Your. Bag. I know I have an accent, but it's not thick enough for you to have misunderstood me." His hand rested on the door handle, but he didn't open it.

"Why?"

"Because you're not going to see your sister alone. You might not be able to tell your friends what's going on. Hell, maybe you feel guilty for missing her—which is a normal human emotion—but I'm not going to let you do this on your own. So grab your bag, because I'm taking you."

"I…I have a car." Okay, that excuse sounded lame even to me.

"Right, but just for fun, let's pretend that you're not the daughter of tech-com millionaires and that you didn't pull in over a million yourself last year—"

"How did you even—" I sputtered.

"Google. Just get your bag and pretend to be normal. Get in the truck."

"You're my teacher."

His jaw flexed, the tiny muscles in the side pulsing a few times. "And you're my student. But I also happen to care about you. We're not going to cross a single fucking line," he growled, but it seemed like the order was directed more at himself. "But please, don't do this alone. Let me take you, or tell one of your friends. That Leah girl seems kind."

"She is, and I know she'd go with me, but she'd never understand." My voice dropped along with my eyes. "Brooke nearly killed her in Morocco."

"Then get in the truck, Penelope."

My gaze flew to his at the use of my full name. His expression wasn't the distant one he'd used on me the last two and a half weeks. No, he looked like the guy I'd met in Vegas, the man who had trusted me enough to jump with a chute he hadn't packed.

Guess it was my turn to jump.

"Okay."

A couple minutes and one dismissed car service later, I was belted into the passenger seat of Cruz's truck as we pulled out of the port. The soft leather interior was meticulously clean, making me wonder what his cabin looked like. I highly doubted it had clothes strewn about like mine currently did.

"Where are we headed?" He motioned toward the GPS in the dash.

"I think it's about an hour away. Is that okay?"

"Absolutely."

I plugged in the address as he hooked his phone into the dock, and then I leaned back against the seat, stealing small looks at his profile as he drove through the abominable, ceaseless traffic that was L.A. I could tell myself all I wanted that he was my teacher, but it didn't change the fact that he was the most incredibly beautiful man I'd ever seen, and for someone who spent her life surrounded by beautiful men... well, that was saying something.

"Twenty One Pilots?" I asked as his music kicked on.

"Why so surprised? I'm twenty-seven, not seventy." A corner of his mouth lifted in a smirk.

Somehow those five years between us felt as big as the Grand Canyon.

"You sure? Because I've seen your tie collection."

His mouth dropped. "Take that back."

"Nope. Just admit that you have the taste of a geriatric man in the tie department."

We pulled onto the highway, and I felt lighter with every mile he put between us and the *Athena*.

"Not fair. I had about twenty-four hours' notice before I had to pack to leave for the ship."

"So you went shopping in my grandfather's closet?" He was way too much fun to tease.

"Hardly!"

"You walked into a department store and picked out the first ten ties you saw."

He glanced at me quickly, never looking away from the road for too long. "Twelve."

"I'm sorry?" I asked, turning in my seat to full-on face him.

"I picked out the first twelve ties I saw."

"And so the truth is revealed!"

"Hey, when I was in the army, I only had one tie. It was black and matched my blues. Then I didn't have a lot of reasons for them in graduate school until student teaching, and at that point I just didn't care. What's that look for? What are you thinking?"

I tilted my head. "Just picturing you in army dress blues. My imagination approves."

"Penelope," he warned, but I didn't miss the way he fought a smile.

"I have this whole *Officer and a Gentleman* vision playing out in my head right now," I admitted.

He shook his head, his grin finally full enough to show me those sexy-as-hell dimples. "You do realize that's navy, right? Not army?"

"Who cares? Swooping in like that to carry off the woman you love? That's the stuff of legends. I can't think of any guy I know who could pull that off. Even Landon or Pax, and they're pretty swoony for those girls of theirs."

He scoffed, that grin turning into another smirk.

"What?" I asked, waiting for the next smart-ass remark out of his mouth. He didn't back down or roll over when I dished crap at him, which was one of the things I really liked about him.

"That's because you've been hanging out with boys."

"Oh really?"

"Your friends? All boys. Their little follower-Renegades? Boys. Jumping out of airplanes and flipping motorcycles doesn't make you a man. Serving something larger than yourself, sacrificing for someone you love, understanding the nature of true suffering and working to alleviate it in someone other than yourself—that's manhood."

"I have friends that definition would fit."

"No, you don't. Not fully. That's why you're still single."

My back straightened, and I crossed my arms in front of me. "Oh, that's why?"

The look he sent me could have been personally responsible for global warming. "You are a headstrong, independent, stubborn woman surrounded by a sea of boys, when what you crave—what you need—is a *man*. One who isn't going to hold you back but isn't afraid of you, either. One who knows the delicate balance between watching you fly and protecting you so you don't fall. Hell, I'm not sure any of those boys would even know what to do with you if you ever let them get their hands on you."

But you did. You do.

I shifted in my seat and forced my gaze away before either of us could say what hung in the air between us. Cruz was that kind of man.

He just couldn't be *my* man.

Now if only my libido could understand that.

"So are you sad to be leaving L.A.?" I asked, changing the subject to something safer.

"A little. It's been my home since I was nine. I'm excited for a new opportunity, but I'll definitely miss the weather."

"Why not settle in Florida, or somewhere with a bigger Cuban community? I can't imagine it was easy leaving everything behind."

"It wasn't. But we knew Miami and those communities would be the first place he'd look. We needed to blend in with our new country."

"You were running from someone." I stepped into territory I had no right to. "Maybe the person who burned your arm?"

He glanced at me briefly.

"It looked like a cigarette burn," I said quietly.

"Cigar, actually. My father is not a good man." His hands flexed on the wheel. "I thought my grandma had chartered a fishing boat for the day. That day turned into three when the motor gave out, but we made it to the Keys."

"You must have been terrified." I couldn't imagine going through that so young—or ever. It spoke of a desperation I had never tasted.

"I was never as scared on that boat as I was living every

day in his house."

"And your mother went back?"

"She did." He said it with a tone of finality that let me know the subject was closed. The last miles passed in relative quiet, until we were pulling into the long, winding drive that led to Oak Moss Grove.

"Nervous?" he asked softly as the compound came into view. It looked more like a resort than an institution…or mental rehabilitation center—whatever they were calling it.

"It's a desert out here. Look at that cactus." I absolutely ignored his question and the nausea rolling through my stomach.

"Definitely no oaks or moss in sight," he agreed, pulling into the closest open parking space.

"Right?" I nodded a little too aggressively. "Seems like false advertising."

"Penelope," he said softly, then waited until I felt strong enough to look at him. His patience—the certainty with which he always waited for me to choose—was one of his most attractive qualities. "Do you want me to come in with you?"

"Yes, please," I answered instantly. I hadn't pictured making this trip with anyone, but now that I was here with him, I couldn't imagine being here with anyone else.

I hopped down from his truck and met him at the front.

"I would have opened your door if you'd waited a second," he told me.

"I can get my own door," I argued as we walked up the wide concrete steps to the front of the reception building.

"Chivalry isn't misogyny," he rebutted.

"Touché," I said, and gave him a thankful smile as he held open the door to the facility. His hand rested on the small of my back for the barest of seconds, and I nearly leaned in to it just to see if I could feel it again.

We waited at the desk until a petite woman who looked to be in her forties appeared. Her brown eyes were kind and her smile warm as she asked what she could do for us.

"I'm here to visit my sister," I said, my voice a lot stronger than my stomach.

"Name?"

"Brooke Carstairs. I'm Penelope Carstairs." I produced my ID from my back pocket.

"Of course. Right this way. I'll let her know that you're here." She shot a look at Cruz. "It's family only."

"He's my fiancé," I answered immediately.

God bless the man, he didn't so much as flinch. He wrapped his arm around my waist, tucking me into his body with a familiarity that gave my lie a little credence.

The nurse looked pointedly at my bare left hand.

"I told her to leave it at home," Cruz said, his voice soft and soothing. "Brooke doesn't know yet, and we wanted to make sure she was at the right point in her recovery before we told her."

His lie was so smooth that I nearly believed it.

The nurse visibly melted. "Of course. How considerate. Congratulations to you both. If you'll follow me?"

She led us through a door and down a wide, lushly decorated hallway. My parents were paying a fortune for Brooke to be here if the art was any indication. "How did you meet?" she asked as she ushered us into a room marked "Visitation Two." It was set up like a home-style living room with brown leather couches, bookshelves filled to the brim, and cozy lighting.

"In a bar in Las Vegas," I answered absently.

"I saw her take out a guy for grabbing her, and I simply had to know her," Cruz added, gazing at me adoringly. "She keeps me on my toes."

How badly I wanted to slip into the lie, to believe that we

were in a relationship—that I had him in my corner, backing me, sheltering me, lifting me when I couldn't find a way to stand, and to be able to do the same for him.

"Well, you're just adorable," she said with a scrunch of her nose. "I'll be back with Brooke." She shut the door behind her, leaving Cruz and me alone.

I sank into the couch, leaning over so my head was between my knees.

"Do you need the trash can?" he asked.

"No," I said, breathing in through my nose and out through my mouth to quell the twisting in my belly.

"Want to tell me what you're thinking?"

I shook my head, lifting it. "No. Yes. No."

He took a seat next to me, his warmth radiating through the material of my jeans. "However you're feeling is okay. You're allowed to be angry with her, especially after the letters. You're allowed to hug her, to miss her, to love her. You're allowed to hate what she did, and you're allowed to forgive her. There is no wrong feeling here."

My gaze fixed on the second hand of the clock on the wall between two large windows. "The last time I saw her, I was on a stretcher. She was blurry—I was in so much pain—and I couldn't figure out why she wasn't coming in the ambulance with me. I didn't realize until later that she was the one…"

He took my hand in his—the gesture completely platonic, and yet exactly what I needed.

"I don't even know what I'm going to say to her. I just need to see her. I need to understand."

He gave my hand a gentle squeeze but didn't speak. I didn't realize until that moment exactly how badly I needed someone to listen without judgment or bias—without knowing the backstory.

The door opened, and I stood, anticipation shaking my nerves like no stunt ever had.

A tall, red-haired woman walked in. Her hair was in a perfect French twist and her white lab coat didn't have a speck of dirt on it. Her smile was kind and her eyes firm as she extended her hand. "Penna? I'm Dr. Kelley, Brooke's doctor."

"It's nice to meet you," I responded automatically, my gaze darting to the closed door. "Is Brooke on her way?"

"Why don't we have a seat?"

She took the couch across from us, and I returned to my seat. "Is there something wrong?"

"No, not entirely," she answered. "I'm so sorry to tell you this, but Brooke won't be visiting with you."

In the time it took me to blink, my body numbed. My only physical sensation registered from where Cruz took my hand. "Today?" I asked. "I'm in town only today and tomorrow. Then I won't be back in the States until May. I can come again tomorrow, if she's busy."

"Tomorrow won't work, either. She's simply not ready for a visit." Her tone was soft, placating, and yet came out like nails on a chalkboard to me.

"But she sees my parents," I said, trying desperately to understand.

"She does."

The truth slammed into me, bringing with it a shock of pain that would have laid me out if I hadn't already been sitting. "You think she's not ready to see me...because of what happened."

Never mind that we'd been sisters since infancy—that every good memory I had included her in some way. The years she'd been my best friend, my only confidant in a world where everyone wanted my secrets didn't matter to this woman. A lifetime of moments had been erased in her eyes the second that stadium light came crashing down in Dubai. To her, my relationship with my sister would always be defined by the worst day in both our lives.

She saw me as a deterrent to Brooke's recovery.

"While it's true that she's still very fragile, and we have a long road ahead of us to really untangle her issues, this was not because of anything I advised."

Wait. What?

If Dr. Kelley wasn't the reason…

"But…but I'm the reason Pax didn't press charges. I asked Brandon to work with the authorities in Dubai. I made sure she wouldn't go to jail for what she did so that she could get help. So she could come to you."

"I know."

My mind raced, trying to outrun the emotional tsunami headed toward me. Every logical explanation immediately refuted itself before I could voice it, leaving only the one I couldn't bear to hear. "I've been trying to contact her since it happened. She's refused my calls and returned my letters, and I don't know what else to do. Dr. Kelley, I just want to see my sister." My voice cracked on the last word.

"But she doesn't want to see you."

The tidal wave hit, drowning me before I even had a chance to take a breath.

Chapter Twelve

CRUZ

LOS ANGELES

I buckled Penelope's seat belt as she stared blankly ahead, taking control of her safety since she wouldn't. She'd barely said three words since Dr. Kelley had dropped that bomb and blown Penna to bits.

Her eyes had gone dead as she'd retreated inside herself. God, I wanted to battle my way through that recovery center calling out Brooke's name until she showed her damned face. Penelope deserved so much better than the shit hand she'd just been dealt.

I shut her door, walked around to my side of the truck, and climbed up, turning the key in the ignition and clicking my seat belt. "Ready?"

"I guess," she answered, her voice as flat as her eyes.

How could I take her home like this? Leave her alone when her friends had zero idea what she'd just been through?

"Where do you want me to take you?"

Her eyes darted back and forth, a look of panic growing with each second that she couldn't make up her mind. Finally, her eyes slid shut in an obvious bid to keep from crying. "I just don't care."

"Okay," I said softly, clasping her hand in mine. It was crossing the line—any physical contact between us was, really. But hell, it wasn't like I hadn't just played her fake fiancé. I couldn't see her in such obvious pain and do nothing.

I grabbed my phone and hit the first number on my speed dial.

"Hi, Grandma," I said, switching to Spanish and praying Penelope didn't know what I was saying. "I might have to miss dinner tonight."

"You will do no such thing, Cruz. Absolutely not," she lectured in rapid-fire Spanish instead of ordering me to switch to English.

I smiled, picturing her in our kitchen, surrounded by the apples we'd hand-painted my junior year in high school. "I'm not sure it can be helped."

"I haven't seen you since you rushed off weeks ago, and we never got to properly celebrate your graduation. You bring your butt home. Now."

My gaze wavered to Penelope as she stared out the window, a world full of pain in her eyes. "Okay, but I might have to bring someone with me."

"I have more than enough food."

"Of course you do. Her name is Penelope."

"Her? You're bringing a girl home? How long until you can get here?" Her voice amped up in excitement. Shit, I'd never brought a girl home to her. Truthfully, she'd been the only consistent girl in my life since I was ten.

"About an hour," I estimated.

"I'll be waiting."

"Nothing is going on between us," I said firmly, hoping she'd take the hint.

"Of course, of course. Just bring her home."

I said good-bye to my grandmother and put the truck in drive, taking an extra moment at the stop sign to really examine Penelope.

Her eyes were vague, her shoulders hunched in like she couldn't possibly take another blow. She wasn't entirely broken—but she wasn't whole, either.

"You don't speak Spanish, do you?" I asked her.

"French," she answered.

"Good. I'm going to take you somewhere, okay?"

"Yeah," she answered, still not meeting my eyes.

"Penelope," I said softly and waited for her to look at me. She finally did, those gorgeous blue eyes swimming with more than a few unshed tears. "I know it doesn't feel like it right now, but this will be okay. You will be okay."

"You're right," she answered, but my relief was short-lived. "It doesn't feel like it."

* * *

"Where are we?" she asked an hour later as we pulled up in front of my grandmother's house near Echo Park. The neighborhood had lost much of its Cuban flair over the years, but it was better than nothing, she'd always told me.

"My grandmother's house," I answered before getting out of the truck and coming around to her side. Once I'd opened her door, she slid to the ground. As if I could see inside her head, I watched her compartmentalize, tossing everything that had just happened into a small box and blinking it away for a moment.

It was the same bullshit transformation she went through when the cameras came near.

"This is where you grew up?" she asked, taking in the small house that I was sure probably fit in just her living room. It resembled a cottage, with a cobblestone path and bright green bushes that bloomed in the spring.

"Yep. We moved in when I was nine and nothing much has changed."

Her eyes skimmed over the flowers planted near the porch and the bright red shutters that stood out against the gray exterior. "I like it," she said softly, a tiny spark of life flaring in her eyes. "It looks like a real home."

That line told me more about her upbringing than Penna could have herself.

"Let's introduce you," I said, guiding her by the small of her back as we walked up the path. "A little warning, though. Grandma...she can be a little invasive. She'll probably want to know everything about you, including your credit score."

Penelope laughed, and the sound was fucking magical.

"Don't worry about me. If I can handle Christmas parties with the governor of California, I can handle your grandmother."

"You might be surprised," I said slowly.

"You don't call her Abuela," she stated.

"Was that a question?" God, I loved poking at her.

She rolled her eyes at me. "I just thought…"

"Penelope Carstairs, are you making cultural judgments about me?"

She blushed a gorgeous shade of pink, but she held my gaze, not backing down. "There is no right answer to that."

I stared her down until I couldn't help but laugh and was rewarded with a raised eyebrow. "When we moved here, Grandma banned all Spanish from the house. She told me we were in America, and we would speak English. I wasn't allowed to speak Spanish again until I was fluent in English. By then, she just liked being called Grandma. I think it made her feel like we'd done it—moved here, transformed ourselves." *Hidden.*

We walked up the stairs, and Grandma had the door open before we made it across the small porch.

"Cruz!" she exclaimed, her arms wide open.

I stepped forward, grabbing my grandmother in a tight hug and lifting her tiny five-foot-nothing, slightly rounded frame off the ground. "I missed you," I told her, closing my eyes as I took in her familiar perfume.

"Put me down!" She laughed, the lines around her eyes a little deeper than they had been last year.

"Have you grown?" I asked as I put her down. "I swear you feel taller."

"English!" She backhand swatted my chest and then pointed at me like I was ten again, learning to live in America.

"Sorry," I told Penna, who watched us with a soft smile. "I didn't even realize I'd switched over."

"No problem," she answered, waving me off.

"Grandma, this is Penelope. Penelope, this is my grandmother. She's the one who raised me, so any complaints should be filed in her direction."

"I will keep that in mind," she warned with a grin.

"Let's get you inside. You look like you need a good meal," Grandma said, ushering Penelope in the door.

The house smelled like heaven, and my eyes closed as I let out a sigh. "That smells delicious."

"*Ropa vieja,*" Grandma told me with a wink as she led Penna to the living room. "I figured you'd missed it."

"Yes, that's a yes. Need any help?"

"Don't even think about going into my kitchen," she warned with a wag of her finger. "Now, Penelope, why don't we sit and get acquainted."

They took the couch, and I settled into the recliner, hoping my feelings would do the same and calm the hell down, or at least pick a direction.

"Your home is lovely," Penelope told her, and the admiration in her eyes as they swept over the mismatched picture frames above the fireplace told me that she meant it.

"Thank you. I'm constantly told that the house is worth a small fortune if I would be willing to sell it, but I think I finally have it just the way I want it. Besides, I raised Cruz here."

"I can understand that," she said with a subtle nod, and something told me she did. She might be a little rich girl, but I was beginning to think that money was the only way she'd been spoiled. We hadn't always had a ton, but I'd been lavished with attention. There were so many different ways to be poor.

"So what do you do for a living, young lady?" Grandma's brown eyes narrowed slightly, and I knew the inquisition had begun.

"Grandma—"

"It's fine," Penna promised me. "I'm actually a senior at UCLA. I'll graduate in June after we dock in Miami."

I didn't miss the non-subtle side-eye Grandma tossed at me. "So you're on the ship with Cruz."

"I am," she agreed.

"You're a student."

"Yes, ma'am. But I also have a full-time job."

Grandma's eyebrows rose. "Good. Women need to be able to stand on their own. What do you do?"

"Well, I'm a professional athlete."

Grandma's head tilted as she openly appraised Penna's body. I almost said something, but Penna shot me a look that told me she could handle herself.

"Swimming? Track? One of those NFL girls on the sidelines with too much showing?"

Penna's eyes danced, and I wanted to kiss Grandma for bringing that out in her. "I'm actually a freestyle motocross rider. Well, mostly."

"Motocross? Motorcycles?" Grandma leaned in. God, I could have watched these two all day.

"Yes, ma'am."

"So you're a biker."

Penelope's eyes widened. "Not exactly. I mean, I'm not in a gang or anything."

"Well, you are a Renegade," I teased.

"That's not a gang," Penna snapped.

"Ignore him," Grandma ordered. "He just wants to see how far he can push you before you push back."

I laughed and was rewarded with a glare from both the women in my life. *Check yourself. Penelope is not your woman. Not now. Not ever.*

"She's on TV, Grandma. And in magazines. She does crazy, dangerous things."

"Ah, like Evel Kneival," she said with an appreciative nod.

"Yes, ma'am," Penna agreed.

"Well, isn't that something. It's good that you have a career. I'm a nurse. Been taking care of newborn babies since I was twenty-five. Gives you a purpose outside yourself. Now, I'm going to check on dinner. Cruz, why don't you give me a hand." She stood and brushed imaginary dirt from her slacks.

My eyes narrowed. "Didn't you just say to stay out of your—"

"Now, Cruz," she ordered from the doorway.

I was out of my seat instantly. "Will you be okay for a minute?" I asked Penelope.

"Yeah. Actually…" She chewed on her lower lip, and I looked away so I didn't lean down and suck it free.

"What's up?"

"You still have your phone turned on? I turned my plan off since I figured everyone I talk to is on the ship with me."

"Yeah. Did you want to borrow it?"

"I kind of want to call my parents," she whispered, her hands clasping and unclasping on her lap.

"It's yours," I said, and pulled it from my back pocket. "Code is 1202."

Her eyes widened at the trust I'd just given her as she took the phone.

"I'll be in the kitchen if you need me."

She nodded, and I left her sitting on my couch before I could question myself too much on why I'd just done that. I didn't have anything to hide from her—at least on the phone—but it was still a step that didn't need to be taken, another line crossed.

I walked into the kitchen as Grandma stirred dinner.

"Just what do you think you're doing with that one, Cruz?" she asked, never one to beat around the bush. "She's a student, right?" She'd switched to Spanish, so I did the same, knowing it was to keep Penna from accidentally overhearing.

"Yes," I said, leaning back against the tile of the counters.

"Is she *your* student?"

"Yes." There was no lying to this woman. I never had, I never would.

"Cruz." She sighed in obvious disappointment.

"I met her before I even left for the ship. It was when I went to Vegas with the guys." The kitchen was dimmer than usual, and I looked up to see one of the can light bulbs was out.

"Did you marry her?" she asked, mischief in her eyes.

"This isn't one of your soap operas, Grandma." I crossed the kitchen to the closet in the corner and pulled out a replacement bulb.

"Don't worry about that. I'll get around to it."

"Just make me a list, and I'll get it all done before I leave tomorrow," I told her, already in the process of changing the one that had gone out.

"So you didn't know she was a student?"

"Nope. I didn't realize it until I walked into my Latin History class, and there she was." Stunned. Perfect. Untouchable. And still somehow mine.

"So there's nothing going on between you two?" she asked in an exaggeratedly innocent voice.

"I'm her teacher."

"And you'd like to teach her more than history," she said, pointing her wooden spoon at me. "I'm not blind. You look at that girl like she is the first drop of sunshine you've seen after a lifetime of darkness."

"Soap operas, Grandma."

"Truth, Cruz."

"I'm not going to do anything that jeopardizes this. I have one shot—"

She spun, her eyes wide. "One shot to do what?"

Fuck my life. Why didn't I shut the hell up? I took a deep breath and prepared to be eaten alive by a woman half my weight. "The ship docks in Cuba as its last stop before Miami."

"No. I forbid it. You stay on that ship when it docks and don't you dare step foot on that island. You understand me?"

"I promised her."

"Now you promise me!" she snapped. I would have fired back, but the fear in her eyes stopped me cold.

"I can't do that. But I will promise that I will take no unnecessary risks, and I'll act only if it's safe to do so."

"I can't lose you, too," she whispered.

"You won't," I swore, hugging her.

She composed herself and stepped back. "Go tell your girl—student—that we're about to have dinner."

"Okay."

Just before I left the kitchen, she said, "And for the record, I like her."

I turned, my hands braced on either side of the doorframe. "Yeah. I do, too, which is half my problem."

Walking out of the kitchen, I saw Penna in the hallway, looking at the framed pictures that lined the space. Cringing at the thought of her staring at my awkward middle school years, I got over there quickly. "Hey, dinner is just about ready. How did the phone call with your parents go?"

"Is this your mother?" she asked, blatantly ignoring my question as she looked at one of my favorite pictures.

"Yes. That was taken right after we got here."

"Where is she now?"

"Dead. She died about ten years after this picture was taken."

"I'm so sorry," she said.

"It was a long time ago."

"These are from when you were in the army," she said, changing the subject again. I was learning that she liked to deflect anything that got too personal.

"What gave it away? The uniforms?" I leaned my shoulder against the wall and studied her as she examined every picture.

"Do you miss it?" She leaned closer at a picture of me in Afghanistan.

"Yes. Not the war, but I miss serving. This country gave me everything, and I like to give back what I can."

"Ever think about getting back in?"

"Every day," I answered honestly. "I still debate going into the reserves."

She turned and handed me my phone. "I was right."

"About what?"

The corners of her mouth lifted. It would have been so easy to lean forward and kiss her, so tempting to feel that rush I got only with her. But I'd already crossed about a dozen ethical lines with her today, and that was one I was determined to leave intact.

"Let's have some dinner," she said, walking past me.

I caught her hand. "What were you right about?"

Her gaze darted from the picture and back to me, the unmistakable flash of heat sparking there. She'd had the same look on her face in Vegas.

"You look incredible in a uniform."

She smiled at me, and my fucking heart stopped. *No, no, no. Not for you.* I let her hand go before I did something stupid like pull her closer. Like back her into my childhood bedroom and pin her to the wall so I could kiss that smile off her face.

Instead, I let her walk away, for her safety and mine.

As she went into the kitchen, I rested my head against the wall and sucked in a huge breath. In that moment, it became crystal-fucking-clear. This thing between us—whatever it was—would eventually break the self-control of a saint.

And I was no saint.

Chapter Thirteen

LOS ANGELES

"There you are!" Pax called from the super ramp. He was fully geared up, his helmet under his arm, as he talked to some of the crew. It was our second day in L.A., but my first seeing them. Cruz had taken me home after dinner with his grandmother, and I'd spent the night at my apartment, trying to simultaneously forget and remember everything about the day.

Cruz felt like a normal guy at home—not my teacher—and as much as I tried not to, I liked him. I liked his sense of humor. I liked the way he took care of little things around his grandmother's house while we were there. I liked his smile, his laugh, the way he did the dishes when we were done with dinner. I liked his effect on me just as much as it absolutely unnerved me, his ability to soothe the ache in my heart and amp up my pulse at the same time.

But then he'd dropped me at home and become Dr. Delgado again.

"Penna?" Pax said, snapping me out of my thoughts.

"Here I am," I said.

"Hey, guys. Give us a minute, okay?"

Bobby debated it for a second, but nodded. "You got it."

"How is it being back on the ranch?" I asked, motioning to the wooded area around us. Pax had bought twenty acres a few years ago and named it Renegade Ranch before decking it out with a top-of-the-line mechanic shop, a four thousand square foot house, and more ramps than I could count.

"It's nice. I'm looking forward to getting back here."

I ran my hand along the handlebar of his bike. How funny that his was the bike I was riding when it all happened, but mine was the one I couldn't touch.

"Where did you disappear to yesterday?" he asked.

I shrugged. "I needed some space."

Cruz was definitely not up for discussion, and neither was my huge failure of an attempt to see Brooke.

"I just figured that you would want to use the ramps for a day before we headed back out to sea."

"He hoped," Landon said, slinging his arm around my shoulder. He was in full gear, too, and currently glaring at Pax. "Right? You *hoped*."

"I hoped," Pax admitted. "I thought maybe being home, you would be…"

"Be what?" I asked, folding my arms across my chest.

"You."

My belly twisted, my throat closing for the barest of seconds until I could push the anger down enough to speak. "Maybe I've changed. Maybe this"—I gestured to my jeans and tank top—"is *me* now."

"You kicked ass on that snowmobile!"

"Oh, now it's okay to kick ass? Because then you were

pretty pissed that I'd dared to pull off a stunt like that."

"It was reckless," Pax snapped.

"Yeah, well, so am I."

"Get off her ass, Pax." The voice came from behind me, settling my stomach instantly.

"Nick!" I called out. Then I turned, knocking Landon's arm free, and saw Nick sitting a few feet away. His blond hair was a little longer, shaggier than when we'd seen him in Dubai, but his eyes were clearer, a sense of peace lingering there that had been missing for far too long. He had a Paul Walker surfer vibe going on.

He held his arms open, and I jumped at him, nearly smothering him in a hug. "Why don't we go for a walk?" he asked. "Well, I'll roll. You walk."

"Smart-ass," I accused, but took him up on the offer.

I saw him shake his head at Landon and Pax, and even though Pax threw up his hands, he let us walk off alone.

"What's going on with you?" he asked as we headed toward the garage.

"Nothing," I lied. "I'm fine." How the hell could I explain it to Nick, of all people?

"You know I'm paralyzed, right?" he asked as we walked in through the garage bay.

"Of course."

"Good. I just wanted to make sure you didn't think I was blind or anything. My legs don't work, but my eyes do, and you, my dear Penna, are not fine." He spun his chair around just in front of my bike.

"Do you ever miss it?" I asked.

"Every damn day." He reached out and ran his hand along the seat of my bike. "Sometimes I dream that I'm still riding. Never walking, but always riding."

"I don't know if I can ride again," I admitted quietly. "Does that make you hate me? Because I can physically but not mentally?"

He took my hand, and I looked down at him—Nick, who was always our Nitro, our fourth. The reason for the documentary, the trip…everything.

The reason Brooke lost her mind.

"You are one of the most talented riders of our generation, and no, I don't mean for a girl. I mean ever. You're strong, smart, gifted, and pretty fucking fearless, which I've always loved about you. But listen to me. If you decide not to ever get on a motorcycle again, you will still be all those things. There is more to life than riding, and if that's what you want—to step away—then you have my full support. Fuck the expectations. Fuck the documentary. You, of all people, owe me nothing."

"There are parts that I still love. That ramp you had built for me in Dutch Harbor? It was perfect. The BASE jumping, the risk, the quiet focus that conquers the noise during the stunts? I love it. But this…" I reached out for my bike but pulled my hand back at the last moment. "This feels impossible."

"You've always been good at the impossible when you want to be. And that's no pressure from me. This is your demon, and you'll choose to conquer it, or you'll choose to live with it."

"Pax doesn't see it that way."

"Pax still thinks he put me in this chair by challenging me with the triple front. He's terrified of losing you."

"Has she reached out to you?"

His eyes widened as I changed the subject.

"Brooke?"

"Brooke."

His eyes dropped, flashing with pain. "No. Look, I wasn't going to tell anyone…but I found her in bed with someone else that morning."

"What?"

He sighed, rubbing his hands over his face. "The morning I had the accident. I came home from the ranch early and found her tangled up with Patrick. I stormed out, and she begged me not to go, but I did. I came back to the ranch, and the rest is history."

What? My stomach sank while denial clawed its way up my throat, ready to scream and defend my sister. She loved Nick to an obsessive level. But that look in his eyes was open and honest, and while Nick had never lied to me in our past— Brooke certainly had.

"That's why you wouldn't see her after?" How could she do that to him? They'd been together for years, and she'd never once even hinted to me... *It wouldn't be the first time she kept something from you.*

"Yeah."

"Why didn't you tell us?"

"She's your sister, and I knew she blamed herself for the accident. It wasn't her fault, of course. I was reckless, stupid, and paid the price. But as much as I hated her for what she'd done, I didn't want you blaming her, too. Not when you needed her. I can't think of one event she didn't come to for you, or one time you were hurt and she wasn't immediately by your side. You didn't deserve to lose your sister."

I stepped into the garage bay, where I could see Pax taking the ramp, the smell of gasoline like the finest perfume and the sound of revving engines the sweetest music. Nick pulled up next to me as Pax flipped, landing perfectly on the other side.

"Every time I go to touch it, I see the light crashing. I see the roof of the arena just before I lost consciousness. I see her face, horrified by what she'd done, because she'd been aiming for Pax and got me. When I reach for that bike, I feel like I'm accepting the role I played in her descent into madness— like riding again means I don't care that I didn't see it, that I pushed it along."

"That's a hell of a burden to carry, Penna," he said softly. He didn't coddle me like Landon or push me like Pax. He simply listened.

We watched as Landon took the same ramp, his trick not as complicated as Pax's but just as flawless, and I felt a stir of longing for the throttle, the speed, the weightlessness of being airborne.

"Why don't you come back with us? I know you're not riding, but it's not the same without you, documentary or no. I'm sure Pax could work it out with the ship. You wouldn't have to take classes or anything, and my bedroom in their suite is empty."

His lips thinned, and he winced as if I'd caused him physical pain. "Just like you're not ready to get on that bike, I'm not ready to step into the light. It's one thing to design your stunts, your ramps, your gear. That's all behind the scenes. I know when the documentary premieres, I'm going to have to make a choice, but just like you, I'm sitting on that fence. The minute I step out and publicly show what's happened to me is the moment I have to admit that it's over—that there's no chance my toes will start to move again. No chance that I could show up one day at a live expo to the roar of the crowd and shock everyone with the comeback of a lifetime. Illogical, maybe, but coming out means shutting down that tiny sliver of a dream forever, and I'm just not ready."

"God, we're a pair."

"That we are."

"I miss you," I said, taking his hand.

"And I miss you all. Every day."

Pax and Landon walked toward us, and for that millisecond, it felt like it used to when it was just the four of us, our bikes, and the ramps. No sponsors. No competitions. Just four kids with busted bones, bruised and bloodied skins, and huge grins.

"I want to want to ride, if that makes any difference," I whispered.

He gave me a smile that had so many layers I couldn't possibly read them all: sadness, pride, acceptance…the list went on and on.

"It makes all the difference. And if that's what you want, you know we'll get you there. There's nothing the four of us haven't been able to accomplish when we're together."

I echoed his smile as Pax and Landon joked about something, laughing as they made their way toward us.

Nick was right. We'd always been a family—able to conquer every feat, land every trick, and generally do the impossible when we were together.

But my hope was short-lived as I realized we'd only be together another eight hours. Then it was back to the ship.

"You two good?" Pax asked, his eyes wary as he looked at me.

I forced a smile and took the first step, no matter how small it was.

"Why don't you show me that new ramp you're working on for the quad?"

Pax's smile could have lit up the world as he tucked me under his arm and walked me toward Nick's new design.

Chapter Fourteen

CRUZ

AT SEA

I had this under control.

Spending that day in L.A. with Penelope had been reckless, and I'd crossed at least a dozen ethical lines, but nothing had happened. Scratch that. Nothing *physical* had happened. So, I was perfectly in control. *Yeah, okay.*

I pounded the treadmill in the gym, facing the waters of the Pacific Ocean on the morning of our second day at sea. The water was a little choppy, but I was getting used to running while feeling like the floor was rhythmically dropping out from under me as we took the waves. Today, I'd see her in class, and I'd treat her like any other student. I could do it, because, that's right, I was fully in control. With each stride, I reminded myself just how much I had this attraction completely contained.

I hadn't taken her to my condo.

I hadn't held her hand in the car—only at Oak Moss Grove when we needed to fake the engagement.

Faking the engagement had been a complete necessity, so that didn't count.

I hadn't pulled her into my lap and held her like every one of my instincts had screamed for when Brooke wouldn't see her.

I hadn't pushed her for more about what had happened with her parents.

I hadn't rubbed her neck when she rolled her shoulders after dinner.

I sure as hell hadn't kissed her when I dropped her at her apartment, even though our past kisses had been on constant replay in my head.

So yeah, physically, I had this under control.

"Hey, Cruz," Lindsay said as she took the treadmill next to me, setting it to a walking pace.

The best part of running in the morning was that I avoided alone time with Penelope. The worst part? Lindsay was here instead. Not that I didn't like her. She was smart, funny, my own age, and if I read the signals right, which I always did, she was interested in me.

The best thing about Lindsay? She wasn't my student.

The worst? She wasn't Penelope.

"Good morning," I said, keeping a steady pace. Four miles down, two more to go.

"Busy day?"

"Nothing too bad. Two classes, and I need to work on my excursion prep, especially for Peru. That one is three days."

"Oh, I'm free at that port, and you'll need another teacher for a trip that long. Want me to pitch in?" Her eyes were hopeful, and as much as I wanted to say no—I hated even the appearance of leading a woman on—she was right. I needed another professor by school policy.

"Yeah, that sounds great. Thank you." I caught movement in the reflection of the blacked-out TV in front of me and glanced up. *Penelope.*

"Your accent…Spanish?" Lindsay asked.

She was with Landon Rhodes near the weight equipment.

"Cruz?" Lindsay prompted.

"Cuban," I answered, having to think about what the question had been.

"Really?"

Penelope looked my way and then back to Landon as she settled into the triceps machine. He adjusted her weights in a way that told me without a single word how well he knew her.

"Really," I told Lindsay, trying to stay engaged in the conversation. "I immigrated when I was nine."

"Wow. That's amazing. Any chance you want to show me around Havana when we're in port?" That hopeful look was back on her face, but this time I couldn't give her what she wanted.

"Actually, I'll be doing a class excursion the first day, and the other day I'll be off seeing some family. You're welcome on the class trip, though."

"That would be so much fun! Thank you!"

The Landon kid started doing pull-ups on the bar next to Penelope's machine, and I subconsciously counted. By the time he hit twenty-five, he had an audience of several girls on the bikes that had Penelope rolling her eyes. I hit the sixth mile and powered down the machine.

"I'm going to hit the mat for a bit. See you later?" I said to Lindsay, and her smile told me she'd taken that last part as more of an invite than a cursory nicety. *Shit.*

Retreating to the mats, which were about ten feet from where Penelope was lifting, I started with pushups, losing myself in the rhythm of the movement.

"You haven't lost too much tone, but you'll really have to

work on your biceps and delts," Landon told her.

"Yeah, I felt that when I pulled the snowmobile back. I honestly think it was pure adrenaline fueling that move."

"You were lucky. Don't give me that fucking look. You were. I know you're the best out of all of us on one of those things—hell, you're better than I am on a bike, that's not up for dispute—but you can't get back into the arena without the power to manipulate the bike. It's two hundred pounds that doesn't give a fuck what you've been through."

I made it to fifty and then hopped to my feet, my gaze locking with Penelope's as she started the machine that would work her back muscles. Her body, which she had covered in workout pants and a tank top, was perfect. She was soft everywhere I loved and toned in places that made me want to explore… *Knock that off. Student. Student. Student.*

Yeah, if I said that enough, maybe I'd actually get my damn thoughts on a leash. I walked over to the pull-up bar, which happened to be right in front of where she was working out.

"Hey, Dr. Delgado," Landon said.

"Good morning, Landon," I answered with a wave.

"Thinking about pull-ups?" he asked.

"Sure was."

"Right on. Go with the rhythm of the ship, and you'll be okay. It takes some getting used to."

"I'll keep that in mind," I said, facing the mirror so I didn't have to look out over the students who had begun to fill the gym. *Note to self: start coming earlier.*

In the reflection of the mirror, I saw Penelope arch an eyebrow at me.

Challenge accepted.

I jumped, getting a good hold on the bar, and then started my pull-ups. My muscles easily did the task—God knew I'd spent enough time in a gym for them to function at their top capacity—and I got used to the way I felt heavier in the dips of the boat, and lighter as we came back up.

Around rep twenty-two, I made the mistake of looking at Penelope as she sat at the trapezius machine. Her mouth was softly parted, her eyes locked onto my body as I sank down and lifted my weight again. Her tongue slid along her lower lip, her own weights forgotten, and I felt a second wind of energy. I could do this all day if she looked at me like that.

I hit twenty-five and kept going.

Then our eyes locked in the mirror, and I wasn't here on the ship. We were back in her hotel room, and I had her beneath me, the curves of her perfect ass in my hands, my tongue in her mouth, her whimpers in my ear.

I jerked my gaze away, knowing those thoughts would put me in a physical situation that would be made more than obvious by my gym shorts.

I hit thirty-five and dropped to the ground, rolling my shoulders in a stretch. Without looking at Penelope, I hit the mat closest to the door and started doing sit-ups, hoping that if I exerted myself enough, I'd sweat her out of my system.

I lost count of how many I did, but my stomach was borderline sore from the crunches when she walked by me.

She dropped down just low enough for me to hear her as I held myself in plank position. "Yes, yes. We all know you did more pull-ups than Landon. Yours is bigger."

I collapsed on my chest, laughing as she sashayed her ass across the gym and took up the treadmill.

God, that girl was going to be the death of me.

Chapter Fifteen

AT SEA

"I call this meeting of the Original Renegades to order," Pax said, lifting his Corona bottle.

We all clinked our longnecks and then tipped slightly toward where Nick sat on Skype next to Pax's seat at the dining room table.

"You guys do realize it's two in the morning, right? I mean, we are still in the same time zone," Nick said, running a hand over his sleep-mussed hair.

"It's the only time we can meet without Bobby knowing," Landon answered.

"So whaaaaat are we doing?" I asked as I yawned. Getting back in shape meant I was exhausted by the end of the day, let alone the middle of the night.

"While we were home, I got called in by UCLA," Pax said.

"Okay?" Landon prompted.

"There's a threat of Gabe's parents suing over what happened in Nepal."

I sat up straight, my beer forgotten on the table in front of me.

"Holy shit," Landon whispered, running his hands down his face. "I just saw him while we were home. He looked good—casts off and everything—and he sure as hell didn't say anything about this."

"It's not Gabe," Pax assured him. "His parents weren't even telling him until after we left."

"Scared we'd talk him out of it?" Nick asked.

"That's my guess. He'd never go for this shit." Landon swore.

"He signed a waiver," I said. "We all did. Hell, even Leah has a waiver on file. How the hell can they sue us?"

"They're not suing us," Pax answered quietly, opening the manila file in front of him. "They're threatening to sue UCLA for not supervising the Renegade Program, which they're saying is the cause of Gabe's injury."

"Fuck that!" Landon hissed. "Gabe got hurt because we tried to board one of the most dangerous ridgelines in the world at twenty-one thousand feet with little to no acclimatization in avalanche conditions, and guess what? An avalanche happened. We were all more than aware of the safety risks, and we chose to ride anyway. He knows that."

I crossed my flannel-pajama-clad legs under me and leaned my elbows on the table, resting my forehead on my palms. In the ten years since we'd started the Renegades as a lark in Pax's backyard to the last five where we'd become a corporation, no one had ever come after us directly. Let alone a member of our own Renegade family. It was unthinkable.

But here we were, thinking about it.

"Okay, so what's the solution?" I asked. "Brandon has one, right? If they're not coming after us, it's because Brandon shut them down before they had a chance."

"Right. Our waivers indemnify us, and it helps that we all signed an additional one specifically for Nepal. But the school is another issue. They're in agreement that we need supervision."

"Did you tell them you own this ship?" Nick questioned.

"Yeah, they weren't impressed. Not with a lawsuit being threatened. I talked to Brandon, guys. We're stuck unless we agree to a faculty member to sit in a supervisory role."

"They think we need a damned chaperone?" Landon snapped.

Pax's eyes shot up the stairs. "If you wake Leah, we're going to have words. She has a huge math test tomorrow."

I rolled my eyes, not bothering to tell him I had the same test slated for tomorrow. When it came to Leah, there was no speaking logic to Pax. "Fine. So we pick a faculty member to sign off as what? A sponsor, like we're some kind of after-school club?"

"They have to be on-site."

Landon's beer sprayed from his mouth, raining Corona all over the table in front of us. "I'm sorry, you're saying they have to go on the stunts with us? What the hell are we going to do? Strap Professor Lawson onto an ATV and tell him to hit the ramps? The guy has got to be seventy."

"Seventy-two, actually," Pax answered. He pulled a list of names and put it in front of us. "That's every teacher on this ship. I've narrowed our options down to the two most likely to say yes."

"The two youngest, I'm assuming?" Nick asked. "They've got to be able to keep up."

"The two you can find some way to partially keep happy enough to let us do whatever the hell we want, or the end of this documentary is screwed," Landon added.

Of course I knew the answer. He was over six feet tall and

two hundred and thirty pounds of carved muscle. He was in better shape than most of the Renegades and had experience jumping out of planes. He was the perfect option, and the only one I didn't want.

"Cruz," I whispered.

"What?" Pax asked.

Shit.

"Dr. Delgado. His first name is Cruz," I said, keeping my eyes open and honest. These guys were my brothers, pretty much the only siblings I had left, and if I didn't have to lie, I wasn't going to.

Pax looked down at his papers, and his eyebrows shot up. "She's right."

"How the hell do you know that?" Landon asked.

"Oh, come on. I know you guys think you're the hottest guys on the ship, but trust me, girls talk, and while you're the old-and-monogamous, he's the new hotness. Ask any woman on this ship, including your girlfriends, and she'll be able to tell you. Besides, sometimes he runs at the same time I do," I finished.

The three of them stared at me like I had three heads—like somehow in the midst of all the bikes, jumps, and stunts, they'd forgotten that I was a girl.

"Dude's in shape," Landon said with a shrug. "I've seen him in the gym, and I have no doubt he could keep up with us, or even pass us up."

If Cruz became our faculty sponsor, he'd be with us on every stunt. Every excursion. Every overnight. Between Renegade business and class, I'd never escape him. I cursed my traitorous heart, which sped up at the thought of spending so much time with him. The logical side of me knew it was the worst thing we could agree to. The sexual tension between us was heavy enough to anchor this damn ship, and if we spent that much time together, it was only a matter of time before we crossed that line again…

Or someone noticed.

"Is there anyone else we could consider?" I asked.

"Miss Gibson is the next youngest," Pax answered.

"You guys could probably charm her," I admitted, then sighed, knowing what was going to be said next.

"Yeah, but Delgado could keep up with us, and by the look of him, he might actually be down for the shit we pull," Landon added.

"He's right," Pax agreed. "I could see Miss Gibson nixing everything that's perfectly safe, just because she doesn't understand what we do."

Cruz wouldn't back down, but I couldn't tell them that. They'd ask how I knew about his military experience, or the fact that he had zero fear when we'd jumped from the High Roller. I swallowed as a lump fought for supremacy in my throat. I'd never had a secret I couldn't tell these guys, never had a problem that we couldn't all solve together, and here I was hiding the fact that I'd been trying to contact the woman who nearly destroyed us, because I missed her, and I had wildly inappropriate thoughts about the guy they wanted to bring on as our sponsor.

But I was a Renegade first.

"We ask Delgado first. He's the best choice."

"Agreed." One by one they spoke the word that sealed my fate.

• • •

The hallway on the academic deck was packed when Rachel caught up to me. "So, Landon just told me."

"Told you…?"

"About Dr. Delicious being our new sponsor?" She raised her eyebrows at me.

"Don't call him that." I looked down at my watch. Fifteen minutes until the math test I should have rested for. Instead, I'd spent my night rolling around my bed, unable to sleep, finally sitting on my deck to watch the sunrise as we pulled into the port of Cabo San Lucas. I was going to be anything but on my game for this afternoon's stunt.

She lowered her voice. "Fine. Whatever. Are you okay with that?"

"Of course. Why wouldn't I be?"

"Seriously? I haven't forgotten what I walked in on. I just gave you a little space."

"Shh!" I hushed her, knowing we were coming up on Cruz's classroom. "You walked in on nothing." *Liar.*

"Yeah, okay, and the Statue of Liberty is a knickknack. Look, if you don't want to talk to me, that's fine. I just know that you usually…"

"Talk to my sister?" I asked.

"Or the guys."

I snorted. The guys would be the last people on Earth I told about Cruz. They'd never understand, and then they'd get all protective, and crap would get really bad really fast.

I paused in the hallway, taking her hand with my free one. "I appreciate what you're saying. And if there were anything to tell, as crazy as it sounds, you'd be the person I'd come to." It surprised me how true that was, how the one person I used to hate more than anyone was the only person I knew I could trust with this if I had to.

But there was nothing to tell. Cruz had drawn that line.

"Miss Carstairs." His voice came from behind me as if I'd summoned him, and I realized that we were stopped in front of his doorway.

Rachel lifted a single eyebrow at me, and I made the "what?" face at her before turning around.

"Dr. Delgado?"

Ugh, he looked good today. Gray slacks that made his ass appear in desperate need of a grab, and a rolled black shirt with a silver tie. Did he know how to wear his shirts any other way? I kinda hoped not.

"I need to see you for a second, if you'll come in and shut the door."

"Yeah, nothing to tell," Rachel whispered over my shoulder.

"I'll meet you back at the room after class."

"Uh-huh," she said with another roll of her eyes, but she walked off.

Doing as Cruz asked, I walked into his room and closed the door behind me. "Yes, Dr. Delgado?" I asked with exaggerated innocence.

"Knock it off," he said, sitting back on his desk.

"Oh, this isn't where I tell you that I need a little extra credit and drop to my knees?" I asked playfully, leaning against the desk across from him.

"Not funny," he said, looking at me with barely leashed hunger. At least I wasn't the only sexually frustrated one in the room.

"Why did you want to see me?"

He turned and grabbed a small stack of papers. "Tell me why I should sign these."

All humor drained out of me like someone had pulled the drain on a bathtub. "The sponsorship papers?"

"Yeah."

"Damn, Pax is fast." It was only nine a.m. for crying out loud.

"Yeah, and insistent."

"What did he offer as terms?" I asked, holding my math books to my chest like a shield.

"A raise that would let me pay off my grandmother's house before we dock in Miami."

"Go figure. Pax throws money at a problem," I muttered.

"What?" he asked.

"Nothing. You take it. Hell, I'd pretty much sell my soul to pay off your grandmother's house, and I've only met the woman once."

"Wait, you want me to do this? I'll be around you all the time if I agree. You're on my class excursions, and I'd be on all your stunt trips. Is this really what you want?" His forehead puckered like he was trying to figure me out.

Good luck with that.

"No, I don't want you to," I answered.

His shoulders fell…in disappointment of losing the money? Or losing the chance to be around me?

"Do you want me to turn it down?" he clarified.

"No," I said quietly. "I don't want that, either."

"Penelope." He sighed in frustration.

"Is it just the money? Because if it's about your grandma's house, I can arrange to have that paid—"

"You will do no such thing," he snapped. "I'm well aware how much money you have. Hell, the Wilder kid throws it around without even realizing it. Do you even grasp how ludicrous it is that a twenty-two-year-old kid owns a damn cruise ship?"

I hadn't honestly. Pax's dad was preparing to step down from Wilder Enterprises, and—

"Damn, you actually think that's normal. It's like we live on two different planets."

"I just didn't want you doing this for the money, especially being around me more than you have to. I can't help what I was born into."

He put his empty hand up, palm out. "I know. I'm sorry. Just tell me what you want me to do. If you want me as your sponsor, if you need me, I'll do it."

"Do you want to do it?" I asked.

"Follow you guys around while you do impossibly cool and reckless shit? Sure, I'm down for it—as you well know. But there are other things to consider."

"Things like you…and me." *But not us.*

"Yes. We'd be together a lot."

"What does that matter? You drew a line. I'm respecting it." I shrugged like I didn't care, when it couldn't have been further from the truth. The more time I spent with him, the more I wanted.

"I didn't draw a line, school policy did. If I'm going to join on to the Renegades as your sponsor, let's make sure that's crystal clear, Penelope."

"Penna," I corrected him. "Or Rebel, your choice."

"I'm sorry?" He put the papers down and crossed his arms over his chest.

"If you are going to come into *my* world, then it's Penna or Rebel. Your Penelope doesn't exist in the Renegades. I'm Rebel, an Original, a four-time X Games medalist, one of which is in an all-male category. I don't go soft and doe-eyed for boys, because I worked too damn hard to get where I am to be a piece of ass for some guy on the circuit. If you want to take this job as our sponsor, I support you. Hell, you're the best fit for the position, honestly. But you have to realize that you don't know the girl who goes out there—you've barely gotten a glimpse of who I am."

"I know you," he challenged.

"You don't," I threw back, knowing it was partially a lie. He knew who I was in the marrow of my bones, in all the ways that really mattered, but I wasn't only the person he saw, and he was missing too much of the full puzzle to say he knew me. I shook my head, fully aware this was stupid, that we were putting ourselves and his career at risk by spending this much time together, but also realizing this would give him the means to take care of his grandmother.

"Sign the papers, Dr. Delgado," I said, moving to leave.

"That's it? That's your advice in all this? There's nothing else you have to say?"

I paused at the door and turned to him, loving and hating the way he stripped me to the barest of truths with a simple look. But I was going to have to get used to it if he was going to be with me on every stunt, every trip. I couldn't let him affect me.

A smirk played at my lips until it turned into a laugh, the irony of this situation almost too much to handle.

"Maybe one more piece of advice."

"Please, do tell me."

"Keep up."

Chapter Sixteen

CRUZ

CABO SAN LUCAS

What the hell had I gotten myself into?

Maybe it was time for a quick pro/con list.

Pros: It was beautifully warm here, and I was sitting on top of a tricked-out ATV in the middle of nowhere outside Cabo. I liked ATVs, so that was definitely a pro. There was a camera in my face—definitely a con. Oh yeah, that had been one of fifteen different waivers I'd had to sign—another con.

Penelope was ten feet away from me, wearing loose, protective pants and a tight-as-hell tank top, with her hair braided long down her back and covered with a pink bandana. She looked like a sexy, confident badass, and I wanted nothing more than to pull her in front of me on this ATV and kiss her senseless. I'd have to say that her being here was a pro.

Being this close to her constantly and knowing I couldn't touch her? Definite con.

That other girl? The one who looked at me like I was dinner—I think they called her Zoe—she was another con.

Rachel incessantly shooting me side-eye and blocking any potential path to Penelope? Another con.

"You clear on your job here?" the producer, Bobby, asked me.

"Keep up," I said, and saw Penelope smile in my peripheral vision.

"That's pretty much it," he agreed. "Don't get in the way."

"Is that what you said when that kid almost got killed in Nepal?" I questioned. "Because I can blame a lot of that foolishness on the fact that these kids are what…twenty-two? But you look like you're in your forties, so there was at least one adult who should have had better judgment on that mountain."

His eyes narrowed into tiny slits.

"I'm well aware of what these guys, and girls, are capable of. I looked them up online, and I paid attention. But if I see something that's going to get one of them killed for sure, I'll pull the plug. I'm not having one of their lives on my hands." *Especially Penelope's.*

"Just stay the hell out of the way," he grumbled and took off to harass someone else.

I knew my job. They'd almost gotten someone killed in Nepal because they were young, stupid, reckless, short-sighted, and did I mention reckless? They also were damn good at what they did, so unless I thought they were literally going to break their necks, I was keeping my mouth shut.

"Time to go!" Wilder shouted, buckling his girlfriend's helmet.

I glanced at Penelope to see that she had her own helmet fully under control. Hell, I was sure she had every element of this under control. Except maybe that snowboarder who kept eyeing her.

I don't go soft and doe-eyed for boys because I worked too damn hard to get where I am to be a piece of ass for some guy on the circuit. Her words brought me a measure of comfort that I didn't have a right to. So what if she dated these boys? She *should* date these boys. They were ten thousand times better matched for her.

But there was this loud, nearly screaming instinct that clawed through my chest, telling me that no one was better for her than I was…or would be in about a year from now.

"Renegades, let's roll!" Wilder called out with his girlfriend on the back of his ATV.

I highly doubted Penelope would ever ride someone else's ATV.

She pulled up next to me, as if she heard the direction of my thoughts, and yep, she had her own ride. "Channel six if you want everyone," she said, motioning to the radio button on the outside of my helmet.

"Noted," I said, cranking the dial.

"Want a private channel for just me?" she offered, the nervous motions of her hands at odds with the confident tone of her voice.

Temptation, thy name is Penelope.

"Someone could listen in," I said softly, wanting to accept her offer more than anything.

She glanced around us for a second and then sighed with a giant nod. "You're right, of course. God, what was I thinking? What am I thinking?"

"Pen—"

"Do you remember what I told you back on the ship?" she interrupted me.

"Keep up."

"Yeah. Do that." She slammed her visor down and took off, meeting up with Wilder at the front of the convoy, just behind the damn cameras.

I turned the radio to channel six and slipped the helmet onto my head, the voices of the other Renegades filling the small space.

"Okay, follow the leads out and don't do anything too stupid," a voice that I assumed belonged to Wilder called over the radio.

I joined in the dozen-member convoy, and we took off across the desert of the Baja peninsula, headed toward the ocean. The trail was solid as we traveled along a dried-up creek bed, the monotony of tan broken only by green cacti, yuccas, and a crystal-blue sky.

The convoy raced through the creek bed, and I had the full throttle on more than once, thankful for quick reflexes as they wove in and out of one another's paths, barely missing collisions. As the bed took a turn to the west, we rode up over the ridge, leaving the path behind, and were rewarded by a sparkling Pacific Ocean.

"Now, that's a view," Penelope said, and several of her friends agreed.

"You keeping up okay back there, Doc?" Landon called.

"If you're referring to me, then I am just fine," I answered as we raced along the sand beaches toward a set of bluffs.

"Doc, I like that," Wilder said.

"It can't be that easy," Penelope argued.

"If he wants a nickname, he's going to have to earn it," Rachel added.

"Who said I wanted a nickname?" I asked. "I'm just here to make sure no one dies."

"We're riding on a beach. Are you scared a whale might suddenly rise out of the ocean and squash us?" Penelope asked.

My jaw locked momentarily, biting back the instinct to playfully banter with her. "Knowing this crew, I wouldn't doubt it," I said.

There was muffled laughter, and then we drove even faster, the sand flying under me as the waves rushed toward us in rhythmic intervals.

Pax pulled up in front of a giant white tarp that looked to be at least thirty feet by thirty feet, and his girlfriend got off the back of his quad.

"Rebel, this one is all you," he said through the headset.

"Right." Penna turned on her quad, and I noticed for the first time a pack strapped to the back of it. "Let's get this on."

"Are you sure about this?" Landon asked as he walked over to her.

"As sure as I ever am," she answered.

A ping of foreboding hit my stomach, low and twisting.

"So Cruz," the brunette they called Zoe started, doing her best to give me a view of cleavage I had no desire to see.

"Yes?" I asked, making myself look away from Penelope before the girl caught on.

"What's that short for?" she asked, then bit her lip in an overly flirtatious move. Maybe back in college that would have gotten to me. Eh. Maybe high school. But not now. Now, I preferred a woman who didn't realize she was flirting, or who tried but was so damn cute in the attempt that it hooked me in a completely different way.

"What's what short for?" I asked, trying to clarify.

"Cruz, silly." She beamed a smile at me.

Seriously?

"It's just Cruz." My eyes flickered to Penna, who had stepped into a harness. What the hell were they doing? They'd prepped me for a simple ATV trip, and Penelope said she wasn't even getting off her ATV.

"So it's not short for something super-hot and Mexican?" Zoe asked.

I internally sighed and reminded myself that this girl was only twenty or so before looking back at her. "Actually, I'm

Cuban."

"That's even hotter!"

"You know I'm a teacher, right?" I folded my arms over my chest. The last thing I needed was a student chasing after me.

Unless that student is Penelope.

"You're not *my* teacher," she answered.

Pretty sure I was sporting a what-the-fuck face, because her smile faded really quickly.

"Leave the man alone, Zoe," Rachel said. "I think Pax needs you."

"Till later!" She blew me a kiss like I was fourteen and rode off.

"Thank you," I told Rachel as she glared over at me.

"Yeah, well, Zoe has a habit of sleeping with inappropriate men instead of dealing with her daddy issues." The petite, purple-haired girl openly evaluated me with a deep sigh. She kind of reminded me of a grenade—small but deadly when the pin was pulled. "Unlike Penelope, who stays away from guys in general."

Direct hit.

"I don't know what she's told you—"

"Nothing. She's said nothing, which is the problem. She's tighter-lipped about you than she was when Brooke…left."

"Left? Or was taken away?" I responded before my brain caught up to my mouth. *Damn it.*

"Exactly. She talks to you. Look, I'm not one to judge." She glanced over to where the Originals were gearing up. "I know more than I should about crossing boundaries."

"We're not crossing boundaries," I told her truthfully, making sure she saw it in my eyes.

Hers narrowed in contemplation.

"I'm serious."

"I can tell." Her eyes flickered to the right, and I saw a camera team approaching us. "I also see the way you look at each other and know how quickly good intentions turn to…well—" She shrugged and then plastered a smile on her face, turning to the camera crew. "Don't you guys have better things to film?"

"Whatever, Lucky Charm," the guy with the camera said. "We wanted to see how Doc is doing on his first Renegade outing."

"Considering all we've done is ride some ATVs in the desert, I'm pretty sure this won't be going on my list of most memorable events."

The hum of engines got my attention just in time to see the three Originals take off toward the bluff that rose above us, the guys each with someone on their back, but Penelope was solo. A camera crew raced off after them.

"Did you guys get stuck down here while the A crew got to follow them?" I asked, nodding toward the expedition.

"Just capturing a better angle," one of them said.

I looked from the crew to where Penelope rode with the others, making her way up the bluffs on the switchback trails. "Better angle for what?"

"You'll see. Best thing about the Renegades is they're never boring."

"I can definitely see that."

The camera crew took off, positioning themselves at the edges of the white tarp. That sinking feeling in my stomach became more pronounced. What the hell were they up to? I jumped up on top of my four-wheeler to get a little more height and cursed.

That giant white tarp had a bull's-eye painted on it.

She was going to jump off that bluff.

"Fuck."

"What's wrong?" Leah asked, coming to stand next to Rachel.

"By golly, I think he's figured it out," Rachel sang.

"They're jumping," I said in monotone.

"They're jumping," Leah agreed. "Don't worry. They're experts."

"Oh, I'm more than aware of their expertise," I said through gritted teeth. She'd be fine. It wasn't like I'd never seen her jump, and this was a hell of a lot higher than the High Roller. She'd have way more time to pull that chute.

"I think he's cranky that they didn't tell him. Seeing as he's their sponsor now," Rachel mock-whispered.

I sent the girl a look that made her smile disappear.

"You're pissed."

I didn't bother answering her. If I had known, I would have checked the height of the cliff, the weather forecast, wind speed, direction, all of it. *Like you did in Vegas?* I shut up my inner daredevil. I was the adult here, and it was my job to make sure she was safe—that they were *all* safe.

Tucking my thumbs in the pockets of my pants to keep from reaching for the throttle, I reminded myself of every single reason I couldn't drive up there and yell at her. After all, we'd done something far more dangerous a month ago.

"Why aren't you two up there?" I asked.

"I didn't want to drive his quad back down and miss the stunt. I'm not his errand girl," Rachel said with a shrug.

"I'm not a big fan of heights," Leah answered. "Besides, the view should be spectacular right here."

"No one else is jumping with them?"

"The others will go after the Originals test it. They don't stick the rookies up there—or even the more experienced Renegades—until they make sure it's safe and doable. They're actually very responsible," she finished with a hint of defensiveness in her voice.

"Oh yeah, they're regular icons of safety," I responded.

Two figures approached the edge of the bluff and looked over.

"Look! There they are!" Leah said, pointing up.

My chest expanded with a breath that didn't release as the guys ran back from the bluff's edge only to race toward it and fly off.

One. Two. Three. I counted in my head until I saw their chutes deploy, bright white against the cloudless blue sky. Only then did my breath release. Penelope hadn't jumped.

My relief turned to anxiety. Was she okay up there? Was she struggling? This wouldn't be the first time she'd jumped since her accident, so it shouldn't have been that.

Wait. I was seriously worried that the woman I was more than a little infatuated with *wasn't* jumping of the cliff? *She'll never bore you.*

Her friends unclipped their harnesses and gathered up their chutes before walking over to us, but my eyes remained firmly on the top of that bluff.

I vaguely heard them greeting their girlfriends but didn't listen in until I heard her name.

"—but there's no arguing with Penna when she's determined," Wilder said.

"She's Rebel for a reason," Landon agreed, his arm around Rachel.

"So she's jumping," I said, tearing my eyes from the bluff to stare down Wilder.

He shifted, having the awareness to look a little sheepish. "We should have told you."

"We'll talk about this later," I growled.

I didn't miss the side-eye the team gave one another, nor did I comment on it. Once she was safe, we'd have a nice little talk where I'd explain to them that this shit wasn't going to fly.

I heard the high hum, the revving of an engine.

Then Penelope rode off the cliff.

My heart stopped, the blood froze in my veins, and every muscle in my body locked up tight. She fell so fast, I didn't even count, didn't pray. I couldn't think or move.

Then her chute deployed, and she was violently jerked, but kept the ATV straight as air filled the canopy, dramatically slowing her descent.

Cheers erupted around me about the same time my lungs decided to function and my heart picked up a faster than normal rhythm.

"The chute is rigged to both her and the ATV," I said absentmindedly.

"It's her design," Wilder said with pride. "We worked on it her last day in L.A."

The day after Brooke wouldn't see her.

Did her friends even realize what she was doing? It was so plainly clear to me—using the adrenaline to soothe, the stunts to hide. She was shoving everything Penelope under the Rebel mask, and they were too fucking absorbed in their happy little relationships to see it, otherwise they would have stopped this.

She landed just outside the tarp, and the guys were off running, their arms in the air in victory. I remained on top of the ATV, able to see her smile clearly from here, but not moving. Fighting my instinct to get to her, to untangle her from the rigging, to shake her and then kiss her senseless took every ounce of my strength and concentration.

They unhooked her, and she hugged both of her friends, that mega-watt grin in place for the cameras as she did a quick interview with Bobby about the massive stunt she'd just pulled off. Solo. With zero backup, since her friends were already down here.

As the other ATVs returned and parked in a line near me, the trio walked over. Penelope looked up at me, her eyes as radiant as her smile. "What did you think?"

That I want to simultaneously throttle and fuck you.

Closing my mouth was the smartest move I could make. Pressing my lips together, I sent her a look that took that smile down to almost nothing. Then I looked past her to where Wilder stood with Landon.

"The three of you will meet with me as soon as we're back on the *Athena*."

That got their attention.

"That's right. I'm not some pushover, and I'm not an idiot, and that shit"—I pointed to the bluff—"will never fucking happen again on my watch. Not without you fully filling me in. Do you understand?"

"We were perfectly safe—" Penna started, but I couldn't look at her. Not when I was this angry, this raw from what she'd just put me through.

"Do. You. Understand?" I repeated softer, in a tone that left no room for argument.

"Dr. Delgado—" Penelope tried again.

My eyes flickered to hers just long enough to let her know she was walking in a mine field. "One change in the wind. One more second without deploying the chute. The mass of that ATV built with the speed you're traveling. One snap of a carabineer, and you would have…" I snapped my attention to the guys. "That's why you were down here. In case she didn't land it. So you'd be closer when she bled out on the sand."

"We had a medevac standing by. This isn't our first ride at the rodeo," Landon quipped.

"Just like the one who had to airlift your snowboarder friend?"

He paled.

"Tonight," I promised them in warning.

Then I walked the hell away before I did something I regretted, like pulling Penelope into my arms just to feel her heartbeat.

At the period in my life when I needed to stay put together more than anything, that woman was doing her best to unravel me one nerve at a time.

Chapter Seventeen

AT SEA

I didn't bother with putting extra effort into my hair or makeup, opting to keep it simple. It wasn't like Cruz was impressed by those kinds of things, anyway. That didn't mean I wasn't nervous. My heart galloped at an alarming rate as I turned the handle to the door of his classroom.

"One second," he said, leaned over a stack of papers.

I'd never gone for the studious types, but damn, he looked incredibly sexy with a backward baseball hat and a tight T-shirt. He looked like the Cruz I met in Vegas and not Dr. Delgado.

Then again, it wasn't exactly office hours.

I closed the door behind me, pushed the lock, and dropped the blinds to cover the window.

"What can I do— Penelope?" He startled when he realized it was me. "We're not supposed to meet for another half hour."

"I know," I said, sitting on the desk next to his stack of papers.

His eyes fixed on my ass, and I mentally high-fived myself for my choice in jeans. Snapping his gaze to mine, he sighed. "What can I do for you, Miss Carstairs?"

"You're angry with me."

He leaned back in his chair—one of those armless rolling ones—obviously putting distance between us. "We can discuss that with your friends in a half hour."

That look would be enough to shred a lesser woman, but I dished it right back. He might own me on the sexual battleground, but I would go toe-to-toe with him in every other arena. "If you were as mad at them as you are at me, that would be okay. But you're mad at *me*, and not because we didn't clear the stunt with you but because of what we are."

"And what is that?" he challenged, folding his hands in front of him like he was the most relaxed guy in the world. But those brown eyes and the deepening of his accent gave him away.

"I wish I knew."

He stared at me, stripping my emotions naked with nothing more than the arch of an eyebrow. "Me, too."

Any other time, any other place, any other situation, and I would have been in his lap, my tongue in his mouth, begging him to put his hands on me. But I wasn't really up for a second rejection at the moment, so I kept my hands and lips to myself.

"I should have told you about the stunt."

"You should have," he agreed.

"Not just because you're our sponsor but because it was overly dangerous, and you—Cruz, not Dr. Delgado—deserved to know what I was doing."

"I did," he said, his voice low and soft. "You sent Zoe to distract me."

My gaze hit my lap for a second before I found the courage to look him in the eyes again. "I did."

"You thought a pretty girl would turn my head enough to not notice the pack strapped to the back of your quad?"

"Well, now that you say it like that, it sounds pretty childish."

"It was childish."

"It also worked." Damn, that came out a shade whiny.

A smirk played at the corner of his lips. "No, it didn't. She succeeded in annoying me. Rachel pretty much warning me away from you distracted me. The camera crew asking asinine questions distracted me. But Zoe coming on to me? Not one bit."

"Oh."

"Yeah. Oh."

"I needed the time to set up the first part of the rig, and I knew you'd ask what I was doing if you paid close attention. Zoe can be very distracting. A ton of the boys like her."

"Right. A ton of the *boys,* which I'm not. Penelope, whether or not anything is actually going on between us, it's pretty damn impossible for me to look at any other woman when you're within a mile radius of me. Hell, probably while you're on the same planet."

My insides melted into a girly puddle of goo. "I don't look at other guys," I admitted.

"I'm well aware, because I can feel your eyes on me the minute you walk into a room, the same as you do mine. This"—I gestured between us—"is not for lack of want, or hell...need. If it was a matter of either of those..." His eyes slid shut.

This was dangerous. We both knew it, and yet here we were again. Magnets. Gravity. Chemical reactions. Whatever.

"I should have told you, and I'm sorry. I knew that you would try to talk me out of it. That you would think it wasn't safe—"

"It wasn't safe!" he snapped, glaring at me. "For fuck's sake! Did you do the calculations? Did you test just the ATV first against the wind before you strapped yourself to a four hundred pound piece of dead weight and threw yourself off a cliff?"

"Really, I drove it off. The velocity in the momentum sent me farther than if I had just thrown—"

His mouth crashed into mine before I realized his body had left the chair. The kiss wasn't gentle—it was a purely physical, carnal act of dominance, and I submitted. My lips opened for him, and then he was all I could taste, feel, breathe. The scrape of his scruff abraded my skin in the most delicious way as he slanted my head for a deeper kiss.

This was what I'd missed. Kissing Cruz brought me back to myself. No expectations. No stunts. No cameras. Just the one man who accepted me as I simply was.

My hands gripped the back of his neck as he pulled me forward so he was between my spread thighs. I locked my ankles around his hips, as if I could keep him there, force a submission of my own.

"Penelope," he whispered against my lips. "God, you scared me."

"I know, and I'm sorry," I told him, placing small kisses along his jaw.

He cupped my face and looked at me as ten thousand emotions crossed his face so fast I couldn't name them all.

"We shouldn't."

"I know."

"We can't." His forehead puckered as if he was in physical pain.

"I know that, too. But it doesn't mean that I don't want you. Don't want whatever this is. It just means it's that much harder."

"It's impossible." His thumb caressed my lower lip. "Impossible to be with you. Impossible to not want you. Impossible to stay the fuck away."

"So don't," I whispered.

He dropped my face and backed away like I'd burned him. "Don't say that."

"Don't say that I want you? That you're the only man my body responds to? That you're the only person who seems to know who I am under all this?"

He rested against the support pillar a good six feet away. "Do you have any idea how hard it is not to act when you say things like that?"

"As hard as it is for me to sit here and not beg you to touch me," I threw back. "What's between us isn't just physical."

"And that makes it easier? Fuck, I know that this is more. I know that this has the potential to be real. I am infatuated with far more than just your body, trust me. You're incredibly smart, driven, kind, and so big-hearted. I *like* you, and if we were back in L.A.—or hell, anywhere but on this ship, with you in my class—I would ask you out so fast that gorgeous head of yours would spin. But I have more than you could ever realize riding on this job. I can't risk it for anyone. And I can't afford to—"

That crushing feeling swept over my chest again, and I lifted my hand to my heart as if I could actually hold it together, keep it from breaking. "You can't afford to take a chance on me."

The words were selfish on my part; I knew it the moment they spewed from my mouth. Maybe I was willing to risk my heart, but he had to be willing to risk everything, and he barely knew me. It wasn't fair to ask, and yet that was all I wanted to do.

Instead of getting mad, he gently took my face in his hands. "No, not chance on you. I can't afford to involve you—"

A knock sounded at the door.

"Shit. We'll finish this talk later. Just…" He sighed, searching my eyes for something I couldn't figure out. "Just don't think that I don't want this."

He let me go and headed to the door while I got off his desk and leaned against the one in the front row instead. What the hell was he involved in?

"Gentlemen," he said, motioning Pax and Landon through the door. "I'm sorry, Miss Carstairs must have accidentally locked it when she got here."

"No problem," Pax said, handing him a manila folder as Landon shut the door behind them.

Cruz stood behind his desk, flipping through the file as Landon and Pax flanked me.

"You got here early," Landon said, a note of concern in his voice. "You could have waited for us."

"I know, but I wasn't in the mood to sit around waiting." A pang of guilt stabbed my heart. I hated keeping this from them—Cruz and my past and whatever was *not* going on right now between us.

He kissed you.

Again.

I could still taste him, feel the imprint of his lips on mine, and God help me, I wanted more. I wanted *him*, and not just sexually. That would have been easier than the direction my thoughts took—to the relationship I knew could be amazing between us.

"That's every stunt we have planned out until Miami, except the live expo," Pax said. "We never finalize those stunts until a few days prior because—"

"You're still working up to them," Cruz finished, his eyes on the plans.

"Right. Look, we're not used to answering to anyone," Pax added, rubbing the back of his neck.

"You are Renegades, after all. The name says it all," Cruz said, studying one of the papers.

"Right. We started in my backyard, and we were privately funded—"

"Your parents footed your bills."

Apparently he wasn't pulling punches tonight. Thank God I'd gotten here earlier to talk to him, or Lord only knew how much worse this could have gone.

"Not sure what difference that makes—"

"To someone like me who worked every day since he was fourteen, put himself through college, and earned even the smallest things you take for granted, it makes a great deal of difference."

"We're not a bunch of entitled assholes," Landon fired.

Cruz arched an eyebrow, ever calm. In fact, the only times I'd seen him upset were directly related to me.

"Once we got sponsors, we made our own rules. We've been on our own financially since we were all eighteen."

"I was seventeen," I said with a shrug. "Their birthdays are first."

Cruz's gaze flickered to mine, clearly not amused.

Pax cleared his throat. "Anyway. We should have told you what would happen, especially what Penna had planned."

"I'm sorry," I said softly, knowing Pax used those words too sparingly.

Cruz shut the file and sighed. "You don't *answer* to me. I'm not in charge of the Renegades, nor do I want to be. But I am responsible for you, liable for you. Which means that I expect you to act like adults, and not *entitled assholes*. I will afford you the same respect you show me, which today wasn't a whole hell of a lot."

"We thought you might freak out," Landon admitted.

"I might have, but I don't know because you didn't give me that opportunity. I would have asked you for weather reports. Wind reports. Safety standby in case something happened. I would have wanted to check your rigging, known what type of chute you were using. I definitely would have told you that she should have been on an auto-pull harness instead of letting her pull the chute. It was an unnecessary risk, which for some odd reason, you all enjoy taking when it adds nothing to the stunt. These are reasonable questions. As for freaking out…" He looked at each of the guys in turn, the darkest look in his eyes I'd ever seen. "I have seen and done things that would leave you both sobbing, hysterical messes. It's going to take a shit ton more than a poorly planned BASE jump to get me to freak out."

The urges to slap and kiss him were equal. The man turned me into a walking oxymoron.

"We have four days until we're in El Salvador. I'll meet with you the day after tomorrow at noon, if that works for you. We can address anything you have planned for the second day in port."

"We were thinking the first—"

"You'll be with me on our history excursion on the first," he told Pax, folding his arms over his chest.

"Right."

Pax was holding it together really well—I'd give him that.

"I'll see you all in class tomorrow," Cruz said, dismissing us.

Pax was ready to explode by the time we got to my suite. "What. The. Actual. Fuck. Just happened?"

We sank into the couches, Leah and Rachel each making room on theirs while I took the oversized chair, propping my leg on the settee out of recently formed habit.

"What happened?" Leah asked, cuddling into Pax.

"We got put in our place," Landon said.

"By who? Dr. Delicious?" Rachel chimed in.

"Seriously?" Landon asked, his eyes wide.

"Yeah. Sorry," she said sheepishly. "I mean, that's his nickname, right? Doc?"

"Not sure he gets a nickname," Pax growled. "What the hell does he mean *I've done things that would leave you both sobbing, hysterical messes?* Were things dangerous at UCLA?"

"He was in the army," I snapped.

Everyone slowly turned to look at me, and I cursed my inability to think before I spoke.

"How would you know that?" Landon asked.

Rachel tilted her head at me, knowing I'd just fucked up.

"He has an Airborne tattoo on his arm," I said with a forced shrug. "I saw it when we were in the gym one day. Explains his knowledge on chutes and stuff, too."

"That would make sense."

"Yeah, I thought I saw something."

"Maybe that's not all a bad thing."

They bought it. I let out the breath I'd inadvertently held. "You know, I think I'm going to get some studying in, if you guys are cool?"

Pax nodded. "Yeah. Nothing we can really do until we have his list of concerns, right?"

"Right," I said, forcing a smile. "And thank you for today. It felt great being back out there." The rush, the fall, the moment I'd wondered if the chute would work, followed by the snap and jerk of the canopy deploying…it was all part of it—why I loved being a Renegade even when I wasn't sure I could pull off the name anymore.

There was still that damned bike to deal with.

"It's just nice to have you back," Landon said.

"Yeah," I agreed quietly as I got up to leave. "Back."

I retreated to my room, closed my door, and leaned against it, a thousand emotions battling for prominence. Sure, I was pissed that Cruz felt the need to do exactly what

Landon said and put us in our place. Sure I was pissed that we had someone we were held accountable to, but not nearly as much as I hated the fact that my actions would come back on him if anything went wrong—both in stunts and whatever wasn't happening with us.

Like getting him arrested in Vegas hadn't been enough.

But stronger than the anger was a burning need in my chest that wouldn't go away. No matter how much I pushed it down, it simply came back brighter and hotter, growing every time he kissed me, every time I so much as thought about him.

It was glowing so hard I glanced in the mirror to make sure I didn't look like a damn glowworm, that my feelings about him weren't out there for everyone to see.

I wanted him—it was as simple and as overly complicated as that. I wanted what Pax and Leah had, that kind of complete devotion to each other. I wanted what Landon and Rachel had, chemistry so hot, so fated, that they couldn't stay away from the other even when they tried.

But I wanted something more—to have someone who truly knew *me*, and not just the face I put on for the rest of the world, and I had that with him.

We'd proven we were powerless to stay away from each other, even when we both knew the situation we were in made it wrong. He already knew me on a level even Pax and Landon didn't. And damn it, I *liked* him.

I wanted to be with him—the guy who slept just beneath me.

My eyes were drawn to the floor, like X-ray vision would suddenly develop and I'd be able to see if he were there or still in his classroom.

I knew the signs—hell, I'd seen them with my friends—I was heartsick. Me, Penelope Carstairs, Rebel, the girl who never let a man own her, dictate to her, or even claim her, wanted to belong to Cruz.

But what was I willing to risk for it? What was I willing to go through to be able to claim him in the same way he had already branded me?

Everything.

The answer didn't soothe me like I'd hoped—it brought that fire in my chest to a nearly painful roar, a determination that summoned up every instinct in my body to fight, to fly.

Now I just had to convince Cruz.

Chapter Eighteen

CRUZ

AT SEA

I spread the Renegade documents out on the small table in my bedroom and then put them in order of the ports. Then I pulled the last one out and read it thoroughly.

They were planning the live expo in Cuba.

Just like I'd suggested to Penelope.

I hated using her like that, but it was my only chance to get to Elisa. I trusted Penelope with my career, hell, my very life, but I couldn't risk letting her know about my plans. Even the most inadvertent slip could jeopardize everything—and Elisa's life was too steep a price to pay. Everything would have to be planned to the smallest detail, but it was possible now. I could get her out.

Firing up my laptop, I took advantage of the free wifi for teachers and sent her an email with two words. *April 24th*.

I jumped at a knock at my sliding glass balcony door.

Who the...? I sighed, already knowing the answer. *Penelope.*

I opened the door and stepped out into the night where, sure enough, the girl currently owning my dreams leaned back against my railing. Her legs were fifty-million miles long under those shorts, and her tank top hid next to nothing, but I knew she wasn't trying to be sexy—she simply was. She pushed her hair out of her face from the ocean breeze and gave me a grin that could have powered the ship.

"Hiya."

I didn't bother saying anything when I knew she could read the emotion on my face. How glad I was to see her—how I wished she wasn't here.

I held up my finger and then walked back inside my bedroom to lock the door from the other teacher I shared the suite with. Westwick barely spoke to me anyway, since he was pretty sure I was too young and inexperienced to be where I was. He was probably right, but Dr. Messina hadn't thought so, and that was all that mattered.

Then I crooked my finger at her, and she walked in, immediately looking around the room. The walls were thin, so I put on some music through my wireless speakers before I spoke. God, it was like being back in the barracks again.

"How the hell did you manage that?" I asked, motioning to the slider.

"Rope attached to my balcony. Don't worry, I wore a harness, and it's hardly the most dangerous thing I've done this week."

I flashed back to that damn ATV jump and nodded. "Which is saying something."

She shrugged, looking at the papers on my table. "It's not like you didn't know what you were getting into with me. You had a pretty accurate overview in those few hours in Vegas."

Vegas. How the hell was it possible for a word to stir my

dick? Easy. It made me think of her under me, her soft gasps, delicate moans, questing hands. As much as I tried to shut off the vision, she wasn't helping with the way she leaned over that table.

"What are you doing down here, Penelope?" I asked.

She swallowed nervously. "Who's your roommate?"

I crossed my arms at her stalling technique. "Westwick."

Her eyes widened. "You're roommates with that asshat?"

"Not a fan?"

She shook her head. "He was a jerk to Pax and Leah our first term when they missed the ship in Istanbul." A smile played at her lips. "I may have gotten him back a little, though."

"Oh?" Now my curiosity was piqued.

"I removed him from the manifest a couple times as we were coming into ports. They wouldn't let him off without a major get-the-dean hassle, and once I changed it while he was off the ship so he couldn't get back on." She shrugged.

I stifled my laugh as I pictured my uptight roommate blustering. "You hold a grudge."

"Yep."

"How do you even know how to do that?"

"Brooke did it with me the first time. She's really good at tech stuff and handles a bunch of coding with our website. Well, handled. She's way better than I am with computers, but the system on board is pretty simple."

"So you can just add people to the manifest?" A major piece of the Elisa puzzle clicked into place in my brain, landing with a mixed sense of excitement and guilt for even considering using Penelope in my plan—or carelessly risking her safety if it was discovered.

"Sure, not that it would do them any good without a ship ID, but yeah."

I mentally added another task to my to-do list and then

changed the subject to something safer. "So what has you rappelling to my balcony tonight?"

"I want you," she said as if it was the simplest truth in the universe. Then she turned around and sat on the edge of the table.

"I'm sorry?" I nearly choked. *Definitely not a safer subject.* There were different levels of sainthood. I wasn't sure turning down Penelope—if she was asking for sex—was one I was capable of.

"I. Want. You." She pronounced each word clearly, then her eyes flew wide, like she realized what had come out. "Oh my God. Not like that. I mean, yes, like that, too, but not what I was going for."

"You're going to need to clarify that." I backed the hell away from her, putting as much distance as I could between us in the small confines of my bedroom. Right now a dip in the Pacific Ocean was looking pretty good.

"Okay, you know the moment in a romantic comedy where one person goes out on a limb, and they put it all out there? Where you're holding your breath, waiting to see what the other person does? If she'll forgive him for potentially running her bookstore into the ground, or if she could really be a girl standing in front of a boy…"

"The grand gesture," I supplied, failing to stop the small grin on my face.

"Right. Whatever. This is mine."

Oh. Shit.

I tried to steel myself against whatever she was about to say. I told myself not to care that she bit her lip in nervousness, or that her breathing had accelerated. But if the last month had taught me anything, it was that nothing could prepare me for whatever Penelope did.

"I want you," she said.

"You mentioned that." *Now stop saying it before you're*

naked on my bed and I've taken this to a point we can't come back from.

"Shut up," she snapped. "This is my grand gesture. If you want one of your own you'll have to wait your turn."

"And climb the balcony on a moving cruise ship?"

"Oh, come on, that was the easy part!"

Laughter shook my shoulders until she shot me a look that said she didn't appreciate the humor of the moment. I cleared my throat and gestured for her to continue. "You want me."

"Well, you don't have to be so cocky about it."

The woman was going to be the death of me. "I can guarantee you that any way you use that phrase, I want you more." *You shouldn't have said that.*

"Not your turn, so keep your swoony phrases to yourself." She pointed at me.

I put my hands up like I was under arrest.

"Right. Okay. I want you, and I mean all of you. I can't stop thinking that what we have, what we could develop into, is extraordinary. From the moment I saw you in Vegas, I was attracted to you. I mean, come on…what's not to like? But when you listened to me on the High Roller, and then you jumped, and you put your hands on me…" She blushed the most becoming shade of pink I'd ever seen, and I fought back every urge to cross the distance between us. "Well, we know we're pretty sexually compatible, unless it wasn't…you know…for you."

I somehow found my voice. "It was very for me."

"Right," she whispered. "And I know I'm not supposed to want you like I do. I'm not supposed to think about you, dream about you, wonder what you're doing or who you're with. But I do."

She'd just spoken every thought inside my own head.

"I know you're my teacher. I know I'm your student. I

know that on an ethical level, this is wrong. But I've never felt right on any other level with anyone besides you."

My heart pounded and emotion clogged my throat. God, we were so on the same fucking page…but in different books.

"I don't do this. I don't chase boys. I don't make out with boys. I don't risk my reputation for a guy, or for some fling, and I sure as hell don't open myself up for rejection. I'm not a normal girl, and I know that. But I think that you're the only man strong enough to handle every facet of the woman I am. You're everything I want, everything I need, and I just want the chance to be what you need, too."

My eyes shut, the longing so strong that I was afraid she'd see it if she looked too closely. I was strong enough for her. I could be exactly what she needed, and we could be extraordinary.

In another time, another place, another situation.

"So I'm telling you. Look at me," she begged.

I met her level gaze, the plea in the blue depths breaking me down like nothing else could. "Penelope," I whispered.

"I'm telling you that I'll do this on your terms. If you say yes, I'll keep it a secret from everyone I know. I will climb down to your balcony. I will keep my eyes off you in class. I will avoid you in the halls…and I'll be yours when we're alone, if you'll just be mine here in this room. Please…just be mine, because this is real."

My common sense disappeared, and I was across the room before my better sense could stop me. My hands tunneled through her soft blond hair, her lower body collided with mine, and my gaze dropped to her lips. I'd never wanted to kiss a woman, or claim one, so badly in my entire life.

"There are things you don't know about me," I told her, my voice a low, gravelly mess.

"I'll learn."

But would she stay once she knew why I was really here?

"There are reasons we can't do this."

"We can find a way."

"Penelope," I whispered, leaning my forehead against hers, inhaling the citrus and strawberry scent of her hair. Everything in my body, even the very rhythm of my heart, reached for her, begged my sense of honor to give in. It would take one kiss, one word, one touch, and Penelope would be mine. Even if it was only in this room, I could end the torment we were both feeling.

But it could throw us into an even deeper hell.

One slip, and I would be fired. I'd miss my only chance to get to Elisa.

God, would Penelope get expelled? Would the media find out and drag her through the hell of public exposure?

And what kind of man agreed to keep his woman a secret—like she was something to be ashamed of?

"Say yes, Cruz," she whispered, her breath sweet and tinged with mint.

A knock on the door brought reality crashing back in.

"Delgado. Lindsay Gibson is at the door for you," Westwick said through the door. He was older by at least a decade and spent most of his time in the ship's library.

My eyes narrowed slightly. "At nine p.m.?"

"Apparently," Westwick answered, like I'd asked him.

"Give me a second," I called out, and sighed in relief when I heard him head back down the hallway.

Penelope backed away slowly, and my hands felt empty for the loss of her. "Go ahead," she whispered in challenge, tilting her head toward the door. "But whatever it is she wants to ask you at nine at night, your answer will be no."

"What makes you so certain?"

"Because you want me as badly as I want you—whether or not you're ready to admit it. And one thing I know about you is that you never settle. What did you tell me? *You want something bad enough, you'll find every opportunity to get it.* I'm offering you an opportunity. I know what you'd be risking, and that I'm wrong to even ask you to do it, but I'd never forgive myself if I never told you what I wanted—how I felt."

Take it. Just once, I could have something—someone of my own. I could grasp this lone moment of happiness and the chance to unravel the complicated nature of Penelope Carstairs.

"I have to get the door. Wait here for me?"

She gave me a sad smile. "Don't answer the question yet."

"What?"

"Don't answer yet because you haven't decided. And I'm not the kind of girl to ask twice, Cruz. I don't do vulnerable, and I'm not a masochist. If you tell me no, I won't ask again." Her chin tilted up, and I saw the fire in her that had bewitched me in the first place.

Knowing that a woman that fierce was willing to risk it all to ask in the first place nearly took me to my knees. Everything about Penelope was my undoing. It was like she'd been created specifically to torment, tease, and utterly enthrall me.

"Just wait here?" I asked again, knowing it would do me no good to order her around.

I opened the door only wide enough to slide out and found Lindsay waiting for me in the living room of our suite. She looked nervous as hell, her hands folded together as she shifted her weight from one foot to the other. She had on a green dress that flattered her shape, but nothing about her grabbed my interest. *It's hard to see a star when the full Aurora Borealis shimmers in front of you.*

Aurora. That was a good way to look at Penelope, really. You were lucky if you ever got to see her—ever-changing, colorful, impossible to guess her next move, and simply breathtaking to watch.

Maybe focus on the woman in front of you.

"Hey, Lindsay," I said. "Everything okay?"

"Yeah. Absolutely!" Oh yeah, that smile was forced. "I was wondering if you wanted to go down to the bar and maybe grab a drink with me?"

Shit. I searched deep for some desire, yearning, or simple want and came up with nothing. Why the hell couldn't I want someone like her? Someone who wouldn't get me fired?

Because she isn't Penelope.

And the truth was, I would have rather been in my room fighting with Penelope than hanging at the bar with Lindsay.

"I'm so sorry, but I was actually heading to bed," I told her.

Her face fell, and guilt settled in my stomach, low and sour. I couldn't lead her on. Even if she was the more sensible choice for me, there was no way I'd be able to focus on anyone when Penelope was near.

Because she was the only one I really wanted. It was like I'd taken a hit of whatever drug she was, and it didn't matter if I was standing in front of Lindsay—Penelope was still racing through my veins.

Shit. Shit. Double, triple, quadruple shit.

"Of course, right. It's late. What was I thinking?" She rubbed her fingers over her eyebrows.

"I really appreciate the offer. Truly. I don't have many friends here yet, and you're doing a great job of being one. Maybe we could grab some of the other faculty and have lunch tomorrow?" I did my best to let her down easily and firmly close that door.

She blinked, but she managed a shaky smile. "Yeah, that sounds great. I'll…um…just be going."

I walked her out, thanked her again, and shut the door behind her. The *click* resonated through me, like I'd shut the door on any other choice but Penelope…who wasn't really a choice.

She was an inevitability.

I opened my door to find my room was empty, but there was a note on my bed.

I told you so.

Laughter softly shook my shoulders as I tucked the note into my nightstand drawer.

If I pushed aside every ethical and contractual barrier to a relationship with Penelope, could her suggestion really work? No one ever barged in here without knocking. I had a lock on the door. Other than the off chance of someone seeing one of us pulling a Tarzan routine from the side of the ship, there was almost no way we'd get caught if we kept our relationship confined to this room.

If I had her here, knew that this was the one place we could be us, I could control my emotions outside this room. My reactions to her would be more predictable, and any tension outside would be unraveled inside—because we'd know we could have these moments.

Are you fucking insane?

Holy shit, I was justifying my need for her, actually contemplating her proposal.

I had my running shoes on before I realized what I was doing and headed to the gym so I could sweat my thoughts out of my head.

Seven miles later, she was still there.

• • •

Two days later, I was in hell.

I'd spent the morning hiking up and down the Mayan ruins of Tazumal, doing my best to keep my eyes off Penelope's ass.

But God *damn* those shorts. Sure, El Salvador was hot,

but my body temp had soared the moment she'd gotten on the bus wearing those. She'd been true to her word—keeping her attention off me unless I was lecturing on the history and importance of the Mayans and the mysterious collapse of their empire.

She'd also been ridiculously close to that Alex guy as her other friends paired off to explore the ruins on their own. I knew there was nothing going on there from Penelope's side, but his? Yeah, there was some definite interest there, and I didn't appreciate it.

I'd nearly growled when he offered her a hand up the ruins.

I'd never been a fan of someone touching what was mine.

And there's that thought again.

It was true, though. Having grown up with next to nothing in the way of material things, I took exceptional care of what I did have, and I didn't share.

Feeling this territorial over a woman was a whole new arena, though. Not that I hadn't had relationships, but none that I was willing to risk everything for, none that felt like a foregone conclusion.

"Dr. Delgado?" Casey Barros asked, blinking up at me.

"Casey? What's up?"

"Do you know how much more we'll be walking? My feet are killing me."

A quick glance at her ankle boots sent my eyebrows sky high, but I managed to control my immediate urge to roll my eyes. "You're welcome to wander for the next half hour, and then we'll walk back to the bus area."

"Oh good, I can sit." She sighed gratefully.

"Perhaps I could suggest more sensible footwear for our next excursion?"

Her cheeks tinged pink. "You're right. I just thought these were cute."

"I'm not sure the jungle really cares about cute," I replied with a grin. "And seeing as we have a three-day excursion to Machu Picchu coming up, I would definitely recommend some sturdy boots that don't have a four-inch heel."

"You're so right."

Shaking my head, I walked away from the girl to see the ruins on my own, taking the lesser-worn paths. The jungle hung thick with vines that crept over many of the structures, coupled with grass that accompanied every step up the temple, and though I knew thousands had seen the ruins before me, at some angles it almost appeared like I was discovering them for the first time.

Yes, my number one mission on this trip was Elisa. But this? The ability to see this and be here? That was a close second.

Passing by the sheltered stone sculptures, I took a moment at each to snap a few pictures and marvel at the lines carved over a thousand years ago. I spent the majority of my alone time studying the pyramid itself, taking pictures and trying to imagine it in its glory.

The mystery of human migration is what drew me to history. Wars, famine, disease, drought—all were possible reasons for an entire civilization to disappear, or more likely, pick up and move. I'd chosen Latin history for a reason—the Mayans, the Incans, the conquistadors, had all left their mark even to this modern age where sacred, ancient rituals were combined and culturally appropriated by western religion, especially in Peru, where I looked forward to taking my students. What intrigued me was watching the same patterns play out in modern society, just as those refugees who boarded rafts from Cuba or those desperate to escape Syria.

Different centuries and different cultures, but the same drive for survival.

A quick glance at my watch told me I only had another

twenty minutes or so on my own—then I'd have to round up the students—so I headed back to the small museum.

I nodded to the students who were studying the artifacts and raised an eyebrow at those who might not be putting their best foot forward.

As I curved around an exhibit, I saw Penelope standing with Alex. Logically, I knew nothing had been going on when I found them together on her birthday. Emotionally, I wanted to put a football field between them so there was zero chance of it ever happening.

I hadn't given her an answer yet, but that didn't change the fact that every molecule in my body screamed that she was mine. It wasn't a matter of want with Penelope, it was a matter of what was right and what was wrong.

Her standing with Alex? So very wrong.

Studying the art display, I listened to her laugh at something he said, and my chest wound a notch tighter. She had the right to speak to whomever she wanted, to kiss whomever she wanted, because I hadn't said yes or claimed even the smallest part of her. *But you could.* I was going to turn into a mass of knots if I didn't make a decision soon.

As Alex walked off, I turned to see Penelope studying another painting, her head tilted as she leaned in toward the art. The exhibit around us was empty, and before I let logic rule, I snagged her hand and pulled her into the nearest room, ignoring her gasp of surprise and finding the light switch before quickly shutting the door behind us.

It was a supply closet. *Way to be romantic.*

She looked up at me with wide eyes. "We could be caught!"

"There's no one out there. I looked. There's no way I'd ruin your reputation." I brushed a strand of her hair back behind her ear.

"It's not *my* reputation I'm worried about." She backed

away until she nearly touched the door.

"Yeah, well, no matter what we end up doing, there's going to be a level of risk to us both."

"What we *end up* doing? Have you thought about my question?" A spark lit her eyes, and she stalked forward. I retreated until my back hit the shelves behind me. Great, I could face down the Taliban, but I ran from a blonde in shorts and a smile.

"I've been thinking," I admitted.

"And?"

"And it's something that deserves a lot of thought. I can't just come up with an answer for you in two days."

"Right. I didn't give you a timeline."

"I just don't want you to think that I'm not…thinking."

"I know you. You're *always* thinking. Lots and lots of… thoughts. I don't expect you to take a chance on me with less than forty-eight hours of contemplation. What I asked you is big. It's huge, and it puts your career on the line. I respect that. I'm aware of what you'd be risking, and I'm patient."

A huge sigh of relief escaped, and my shoulders relaxed. "I saw you standing with Alex—"

A playful grin curved her smile. "And you got jealous." Her fingers marched up the buttons of my short-sleeved shirt.

"Penelope," I warned, even while I leaned in to her touch. "God, look at us. You made that offer two days ago, and we're already breaking it in here," I chided.

"You're breaking it in here. You pulled *me* in, remember?"

"So true. You have the innate ability to turn me into a primal caveman."

"So what are you going to do with me in the supply closet?" she asked, leaning up to run her tongue down the side of my neck.

Holy. Fucking. Shit.

I somehow managed to keep my hands to myself.

"You see, if you had agreed, then maybe I'd let you steal a kiss in here, where there's no one to see, no way we could get in trouble."

My head swam with visions of kissing her, of turning her around and backing her against the door, lifting her legs to wrap around my hips so I could feel her around me.

Not that I'd take her for the first time in a supply closet—I wasn't an asshole. No, our first time would be in a bed, where I could take the time to worship her the way she deserved.

"Maybe we'd both see it as a prelude to what would come later, when we'd be secluded in your bedroom. But either way, it would be a moment that was just us again; none of this other bullshit about roles and expectations could creep in."

Her teeth toyed with my earlobe, and my hands flew to her hips, drawing her against me. She kissed the line of my jaw and then backed away, leaving my hands empty.

"But you haven't agreed, which means this is only a meeting with my professor in a very cramped office space." She gave me a slow smile that was about to make my cargo shorts entirely too tight. "Pity," she said, then turned and walked out, shutting the door behind her.

I leaned my head back until it rested against the shelves, willing my heart to stop slamming against my ribs.

At some point I was going to have to stop letting that woman have the last word.

. . .

"So as we work toward defining your thesis, I'd like you to really open your eyes as we travel through these countries. Don't focus just on what you find lacking, though there are many more disadvantaged areas than where you're from, but on what is beautiful about the culture, what makes it unique. Yes, Casey?" I asked the girl on my right and then sat back on my desk.

We were on day two at sea of five before we'd arrive in Peru, and though this was my favorite class to teach, it was hard to keep my attention on the subject matter when Penelope sat ten feet away.

Not that she'd so much as looked at me. She was good to her word, not even making eye contact when we were in class. But it almost made it worse—made me hyperaware of where her eyes were, and where they weren't.

"Can we pick any country?" Casey asked.

"You can pick any country, any culture, any theme. Just find something that interests you enough for a paper of this magnitude."

"If we pick Cuba, will you be available for extra help since it's our last port?"

I could have sworn I heard Penelope snort, and by the look Wilder shot her, I wasn't far off the mark.

"You're right—Cuba is our last port, and that is where I'm from. But I'll be available to you all equally, no matter what your thesis choice is. You guys know my office hours, and if none of those work for you, shoot me an email. Just don't procrastinate. Your thesis topics are due in three days, when we get to Peru, and I'm not a fan of last-minute pleas for lenience. Anyone already know theirs?"

Half a dozen hands rose—about a quarter of the class.

"Good. If you want to get a jump start, you can submit them via eCampus, and I'll send you a response so you have time to rework it if you need to." The clock told me time was up. "That's it for today. If you haven't already decided, I strongly suggest you work on a draft before our next class in two days. You guys are dismissed."

I walked around my desk and busied myself with a stack of papers to keep from watching Penelope walk out. She had on black leggings today that left almost nothing to the imagination, and even though her shirt's length was adequate for the dress policy, there was enough to send my brain back to Vegas.

Damn it, everything came back to Vegas with that woman.

Would I have been so attracted to her now if we hadn't already had that night? She was beautiful, there was no denying it, but maybe if I hadn't gone to that bar, or said yes when she asked me, I could resist now. She would have been just another student. If I didn't know how stubborn she was, how driven, how reckless, how delicately damaged, I would have stood a chance. If I hadn't held her in my arms, tasted how sweet she was, seen the quiet desperation in her eyes just before the jump, we might be living a different story.

She'd be an amazingly gorgeous student.

I'd be her stoic, uninterested teacher.

And if you believe that lie there's a bridge in New York I'd like to sell you.

I was pretty damn sure that even if we'd never met then, I would still be as drawn to her now. Chemistry, fate, whatever you wanted to call it—it drew me to Penelope like the North Pole directed a compass point.

"Dr. Delgado?" Her voice brought me out of my thoughts, and I snapped my gaze up to meet her steady, blue one.

"Miss Carstairs?" I swallowed, and hoped it didn't look like I was trying to reclaim my tongue. Her hair was swept up on her head, but small, wavy tendrils had worked their way free, dusting her cheeks and shoulders. This woman was sexy without even trying for it.

"I was hoping I could run my thesis topic by you?" she asked, glancing down at my desk.

I picked up the stack of papers to keep my hands busy— and off her.

"Go ahead."

"I was thinking about immigration issues and how

they affect illegal entry into the U.S. from Latin American countries?"

That had my attention.

I looked at her until I worried the few other students lingering in the room might pick up on the electricity that flickered between us. "And this is influenced by?"

Her teeth raked her lower lip, and I feigned extreme interest in the papers in front of me for my next class.

"A friend of mine who went through a lot more than he should have to become a U.S. citizen," she said quietly. "I'm planning on examining the immigration wait times and procedures of each of the countries we visit, then comparing illegal immigration numbers based on complications, wait times, proximity, and ease of access."

Yeah, it wouldn't have mattered if I'd met her back in Vegas or not. I loved the way she looked at things—academic, stunt-related, even relationship-wise.

Except that you're the relationship, I reminded myself.

"I think that sounds like a paper I'd very much like to read," I told her.

"Excellent. I drafted it here, if you wouldn't mind looking it over before I submit it formally?" She pushed a folded piece of paper across the desk and was gone.

I fielded four more thesis topics, none of which were as defined as Penelope's, and as my next class shuffled to their seats, I opened Penelope's thesis suggestion.

Told you I could act professionally in public.
In private? Well, probably not.

I read it twice more before refolding it and putting it in a safe place so it could join its counterpart in my nightstand drawer.

We could do this.

The thought had been bouncing around in my head since

she first offered the solution, and now it screamed louder than any other for my attention.

We could be smart. Safe. It would never jeopardize my chance to get to Elisa; in fact, it would actually protect my mission here.

I couldn't stay away from Penelope any more than she could stay away from me. At some point, we would collide. Wasn't it better to set off a nuclear blast in the safety of a shelter? A controlled environment?

We were both adults, both capable of keeping a secret. She hadn't even outed me to her friends about the Ferris wheel. We could do this.

We *would* do this.

Chapter Nineteen

PENNA

PERU

"Do you have everything you need?" Rachel asked from the doorway of my bedroom as I zipped up my daypack.

"I'd better, because nothing else is fitting in there," I answered.

"I'm missing sunscreen, so I'm going to run down to the ship store if you think of anything, okay?"

"Sounds good, thanks," I told her, flipping open my laptop.

"Hey, you okay?"

I looked over the screen. "Yeah, of course. I'm actually kind of excited to have a port where we don't have a stunt to pull off. Not that I don't love it, but the break is welcome, you know?"

"Yeah. It feels like we're always moving to the next thing, going so fast that I'm scared we'll get home after this amazing trip and we'll only remember the tempo, the pressure—that kind of thing—and Landon shows zero interest in slowing down."

"Pax, either." Sometimes it seemed I was the only one who was ready for a change of pace. After six months on board the ship, I was ready for some serious recovery time, just when it was time to rev up for my portion of this documentary.

And I still hadn't decided exactly what I was going to do.

My ship-wide IM *ping*ed, and I clicked on the icon that opened the window. Cruz's name flashed at me.

"You know you can talk to me, right?" Rachel asked.

I shut the laptop, like at any moment his voice might come through the speakers, or he might pop out of the display and reveal the relationship we weren't even having. I trusted Rachel with my life, but Cruz was right—I wasn't sure I could trust her with his. She was fiercely loyal, dangerous when she or someone she loved was cornered, and there was zero chance she'd approve of the proposition I'd put in front of Cruz.

"I know," I told her, hoping she heard the sincerity in my voice.

She pressed her lips together, and I swore I could almost see her actually bite her tongue. "Okay. Well, that offer always stands. I know our past hasn't always been the smoothest—"

"I've seen sandpaper smoother," I teased. "Rachel, if there was ever something I needed to talk about, I promise I'd tell you. Right now, I'm really okay."

Lines puckered her forehead, but she finally nodded. "Okay, well, I'm going to go grab that sunscreen."

The minute I heard the door to our suite close, I opened my computer for the IM.

Cruz Delgado: MISS CARSTAIRS, IF YOU'D LIKE TO MEET TO DISCUSS YOUR THESIS, I HAVE A FREE MOMENT BEFORE WE LEAVE FOR MACHU PICCHU. I HAVE A FEW MOMENTS

OF OFFICE HOURS IN OUR PREVIOUSLY AGREED UPON
LOCATION.

His room.
This was it. Maybe.
Don't get your hopes up.
Yeah, it was far too late for that. I checked my makeup in the mirror—or lack thereof—and then headed out to my balcony. The strap was still secured to my banister railing, and I tugged it out from behind the deck chair.

I leaned over the railing, reveling in the warmth of the sun on my skin, and with the strap wrapped around one of my hands, I climbed over the railing to balance on the narrow ledge on just my tiptoes. My gaze swept left, making sure no one was watching, then I gathered the slack of the line and stepped back off my deck.

My sore arms protested as I supported my weight on the strap, and I cursed Landon's torturous training. He was demonic lately with the weights.

Hand over hand, I worked my way down until my toes touched Cruz's railing. Once I balanced on the thin strip of metal, I swung forward until I landed on his balcony. I dropped the strap and examined my reddened hands. I was going to have to buy a pair of gloves or find a better way to do that.

Too bad Pax couldn't just drill a fireman's pole between our rooms.

But that would require telling him, and he would absolutely lose his shit. Quiet wasn't exactly in Paxton's vocabulary.

So, balcony it was.

Cruz's door was open, his sheer curtains blowing inward, and his voice reached me before I had a chance to tell him I was out there.

"It's not really that long when you start to think about it, Elisa. I'll see you in a few months."

I didn't move, or even breathe—too caught up in unabashedly listening, wondering who the hell the girl was.

Don't jump to conclusions. My brain barked a warning that my heart wouldn't heed. There was another woman in his life, I just didn't know who. A girlfriend? My stomach twisted at the thought, but I quickly put it aside. Cruz wasn't the kind of man to have a woman on the side, let alone someone as inconvenient as me.

But the thought was enough to make me ready to vomit.

Knowing I'd already given him so much control over me? More vomit.

"Yeah, I wish it was sooner, too."

An aunt? A cousin? *Please God, let it be a cousin.*

I stepped into the doorframe, uncomfortable with eavesdropping, but his back was to me as he held his phone to his ear. Was that why he hadn't put his cell contract on hold like the rest of us? So he could talk to whoever Elisa was?

All awkwardness aside, I didn't want to snoop where he didn't want me, so I stepped inside and cleared my throat.

He turned quickly, his eyes narrowed for a second before he realized it was me, and then a soft smile took its place. "Hey, I'm talking to my sister. Give me just a second." He motioned to the chair that was covered with a stack of clothes, shook his head, and nodded toward the empty bed instead.

I sat on the edge of his bed—identical to mine—and sighed a pathetically huge amount of stress away. *His sister.* If anything, his announcement showed how little I really knew about him. He had an entire life off this ship, and in that regard, so did I, but here, we felt separated from the world, as if whatever burdened us had been left behind with whatever we deemed unnecessary to pack for this year.

I thought back to his grandmother's house, but I didn't

remember seeing any pictures, or anyone ever having mentioned a sister.

"Okay, I'll call you again from Buenos Aires, okay? That's in three weeks. See what you can work out by then, and call the financial aid office. I know. I love you, too. Bye, Elisa."

He hit a button on his phone and tossed it into the open pack at the foot of his dresser.

"Sorry to make you wait." His voice rumbled, low and deep.

"I don't mind."

The air in the cabin changed as if he'd hit the thermostat, or maybe it was just the temperature of my body elevating in slight degrees with every second he stared at me like that.

"Your sister?" I asked, hoping to cut the tension.

He smiled, his dimples flashing. "Elisa. Yeah. She's turning eighteen in a couple months. Just got into Harvard against pretty much every odd."

The pride in his voice melted me. He sounded like I'd felt when Brooke had been admitted to the honors program at UCLA.

"That's amazing. I guess brilliance runs in the family."

"She's pretty spectacular. Kind of a pain in my ass sometimes, but worth it."

"Most sisters are," I answered, trying to force a smile that probably came out more like a grimace. Thinking about Brooke wasn't something I wanted to do right now. "So, what did you want to talk about?"

His eyes took on a predatory gleam, his full lips tilting in a way that had me immediately restless, uncrossing my legs and shifting on the bed.

"Your proposition."

"My…proposition?" I asked, distracted by the simple movements of his body as he stalked toward me.

"Yes, Penelope," he answered as he reached for me, both

of his hands tangling through my hair to cradle the back of my head. "The one where outside this room, we're professional, courteous, and keep our eyes and hands to ourselves." He whispered the last part into my ear, his close-trimmed beard deliciously rough against my cheek.

"But in this room?" God, I hoped this was going where I thought it was. If not I was going to have a set of blue lady-balls I wouldn't be able to cure.

"In this room," he said, trailing his lips down my jawline. "Or your locked room—I'm all about equality—you belong to me."

He leaned in for a kiss, and I backed away. "And you belong to me."

"I belong to you," he agreed, his smile more than swoon-worthy as he gently pushed me back until I fell against his comforter.

"And what about when we're not in these rooms?" I asked, my heart galloping as he slid over me, bracing his weight with his knees and massive arms on either side my body.

"I'm your teacher," he said, eyebrows furrowing.

"No shit. I mean, if we only belong to each other in here, then out there, are we...you know...seeing other people?" The words rushed out of me in a stream of verbal vomit that I immediately wanted to suck back in.

No, you need to know.

His brown eyes widened, then narrowed as his gaze dropped to my parted lips. How the hell did he do that—make me feel like he was already kissing me before he so much as made contact?

"No one else. I wouldn't be able to contain myself if I saw some boy with his hands on you. We'd be found out in a millisecond."

"Is that the only reason? You're worried we'd be outed?" I raised a knee, rubbing my leg along his side in the process. I understood if it was—he was risking a hell of a lot more than I was. I might have my reputation on the line if this got out, but Cruz was risking his entire career.

"You're going to make me say it, aren't you?" he growled.

"Yep, just like you made me say yes in Vegas." I mentally high-fived myself for keeping my wits when I was under him. Everything about the man was intoxicating, from the sensual shape of his lips, to the intensity of his eyes, the heat from his perfectly-honed body—even his cologne. But I needed to know where we stood. I had to know if I had a parachute on this jump, or if I was about to head into free fall.

"You're going to be the death of me," he muttered, then looked into my eyes as if he could see my very soul—every whole and damaged piece. "There will be no one else. First off, I don't play around with women—definitely not someone I care about like I do you. Secondly, I don't want anyone else. You're the only woman who can make me crazy enough to chance this. You're the only woman I can't get out of my head or my dreams. There's no one else for me, because I'd rather have these stolen moments with you than have a normal relationship with anyone else."

Whoa.

"Normal is overrated." Well, that certainly came out all breathy.

"And you?" he asked, a flash of something running through his eyes. Vulnerability? Apprehension?

"There's no one else." I brought my hands up to cup the rough sides of his cheeks, reveling in the permission to touch him. "I've never met someone that I wanted the way I want you. No one else can even dream about competing with how you make me feel in every possible way. There's only you."

His weight came down at the same time his mouth met mine. He kissed me softly, a lingering caress that sent tingles shooting all the way to my toes.

"I need to put my hands on you." The statement came out like a plea.

"Yes," I said, knowing he'd want the words.

He glanced over at the bedside clock. "Half an hour before we have to meet for the excursion. I can do *a lot* with half an hour."

I couldn't respond—he'd reclaimed my mouth. It had been weeks since I'd tasted him, and I kissed him with every pent-up feeling I'd kept bottled under pressure, giddy that I'd never have to go that long again.

His tongue tangled with mine, slowly thrusting in a way that had my hips rolling against his as he settled into the space between my thighs.

"Penelope," he growled against my lips, one of his hands reaching down to steady my hips. With another kiss, his grip changed, the fingers digging into the thin, jungle-friendly material of my cargo pants.

"Cruz," I answered, looping my legs around his back to kick off my shoes. Thank God I hadn't put on my hiking boots yet, or that would have been as awkward as a junior-high dance.

His thumb swirled over the skin of my stomach as his mouth moved to my neck, pushing every button I never realized I had.

"I've thought about this so many times since Vegas," he admitted after a kiss to my collarbone.

Another shot of electricity raced through me.

"Me, too," I admitted, running my fingers through his thick hair, playing with where he'd let the ends on top grow out a little longer.

"Did you?" he asked, looking up at me as he ran kisses down my sternum, then hovered over a breast.

"Yes," I said, arching up to feel his mouth. I remembered exactly how that felt, his lips, his tongue, the way he could manage to take every ounce of tension in my body and spiral it tight within my belly.

"Did you remember how I kissed you? How you moaned my name?"

"Cruz."

"Did you?" he asked, letting his bottom lip catch my nipple as he lightly caressed me over my clothes.

"Yes!" I hissed, more than aware that I couldn't cry out loudly. I was happy to strip off my own clothes if it made it easier on him—and me.

"Good, because it was the only sound I've been able to hear for weeks. When you're in class asking me a question? I hear you moaning my name. When I'm watching you run, I feel the curves of your ass in my hands, rising up to meet me. When you're arguing with me, I remember how sweet you taste and envision shutting you up with my mouth, even though I know that would never work. And when you're ignoring me, doing your best to look the other way, or worse, trying to make me jealous, I remember how soft and wet you are"—he cupped me between my thighs—"here."

"Cruz." I rocked against his hand.

"I love the way you say my name." He slid up until his mouth was right next to my ear. "At some point I'm going to get you far enough away from here to hear you scream it. Multiple times."

I yanked his head back to mine and kissed my feelings into him, the desperation in my body echoed by the thrust of my tongue into his mouth, the arch of my hips.

If he could turn me on this fast with nothing but a kiss, I couldn't wait to see what else he could do. I urged him on like I did everything else in my life—with complete focus and abandon. Nothing in the world mattered outside of Cruz and the feelings that rolled through me, taking my breath with their intensity.

"If you don't touch me soon, I'll be screaming your name in a different, more frustrated way," I threatened.

Damn it, those dimples appeared.

"My Penelope is impatient, is she?" he asked with a grin.

I glared and slid backward until I was free enough to sit up. How much control did he have? What would it take to break it? With a quick pull, I had my shirt over my head. A snap later, I'd freed my breasts.

"Fuck me," he swore, his hands on his knees, his eyes going from playful to ravenous in a millisecond.

"Yes."

That did it. He was on me, over me, his fingers gently rolling one nipple while his tongue worshipped the other. That same fire within me roared to life, each tug of his mouth sending unbelievable pulses of pleasure so powerful I could almost taste them.

His hand slid down my belly to unsnap the button of my pants. *Thank you, God.* The zipper coming undone was the sweetest sound I'd ever heard next to Cruz saying my name.

He took my mouth again with deep, drugging kisses, and I only broke the sweet torture when his hand hovered just above my panty line.

"Yes," I said again, in case he missed my permission the first time. I loved that he wanted me comfortable, only willing to take it as far as I wanted, but I also wanted to know what it was like when he wasn't quite so cautious, when he felt just as wild as I did.

With a gentle bite of my lower lip, his fingers sank beneath my panties to stroke over my core, and then slipped inward until he brushed over my clit. Now the fire in my stomach burst outward, only to come right back, building higher and brighter.

"Penelope," he groaned, and I decided it was definitely the best sound I'd ever heard in my life. My name on his lips was even better than hearing it called at the X Games.

He was a bigger rush, a deeper pleasure.

I tugged at his shirt, needing to feel his skin against mine, and he obliged, taking it off with a motion that left me drooling. Then my hands were on the perfect skin of his shoulders. The man had a body that I couldn't wait to touch everywhere, explore every line, taste the softness of his skin with my mouth.

I'd always thought I was above ogling well-built guys, but I didn't think there would ever be a limit to my need to stare at Cruz.

His thumbs hooked in my belt loops, and his eyes met mine for a moment before I nodded. Hell yes, I wanted them off. I wanted him. All of him. Before he changed his mind and I never felt this way again.

He dragged my pants down at the same time as my thong, leaving me utterly, completely naked for the first time…ever. I didn't have time for awkward shyness or even self-doubt, not with the way he stared at me.

He looked at me like I was a goddess, as if the scars that I'd earned becoming Rebel didn't detract from what he found beautiful. I'd never regretted a single scar, or felt self-conscious about them, but I'd never been in bed with a man who was walking perfection, either.

"There are no words," he said, running his hand from the side of my breast to the outside of my hip. I moved with him in a ripple, the move sensual in a way I didn't realize I had in me. "I could tell you all day how beautiful you are, how absolutely fucking exquisite, but words would never compare to seeing you like this."

I might have been turned on before, but those words launched me into *all systems go*.

He lay out on top of me, the rough material of his pants wonderfully abrasive against my newly shaven legs, and kissed me soundly.

One kiss rolled into the next, his hands roaming over my curves, lighting up my nerve endings with every touch until he finally made his way back to where my body ached for him most.

He alternated kissing my neck and mouth as his fingers stroked and teased, keeping me so tightly wound that I thought I might burst at any moment. My hips jerked as he put perfect pressure against my clit, only to keep me on that tantalizing ridge I knew he could so easily push me over.

I'd never needed anything so badly in my life.

"Cruz," I pleaded, one of my hands in his hair and the other on his shoulder where I was sure my nails had left marks again.

His breathing was almost ragged as he changed his angle and slid one finger inside me.

Holy. Shit.

That felt more than incredible. I drew inward, all my muscles tightening.

"Damn, you're tight, Penelope. So small," he said, sliding his finger within me, dragging it along my inner walls as my breath hitched. Then he slipped in another finger, and though there was a burn from the stretch, it was…

That felt…felt…f…

My brain quit thinking in words.

"That's it," he whispered soothingly. "You're so beautiful like this, coming undone for me."

He pressed once more against my clit, and I didn't explode—I unraveled. He covered my mouth, and any sound I could have made, with a kiss as my body let go of everything that held it so tense and was rewoven anew.

His lips moved softly over mine, kissing me back down from the high as he gently slid his fingers free. "I can't wait to make you do that again," he told me.

I felt him hard against my thigh and smiled through my sleepy, nearly drunken haze. The man had successfully turned me inarticulate. "Me, too. I never dreamed it would feel like that," I admitted, turning to my side so I could gently palm his erection through his pants. These definitely needed to come off. I couldn't wait to see him. Touch him. Taste him. I felt like someone opened up Disney World just for me—I was the only one allowed to ride Cruz. "I think now is good."

"Wait," he said, taking my hand off him and kissing my fingers.

I pouted. "What?"

"What do you mean you'd never dreamed it would feel like that?"

"I mean, that was the most incredible, pleasurable experience of my life."

He pulled back, confusion wrinkling his perfect forehead. "But you have had orgasms before, right?"

"Sure, but nothing like that," I answered, stretching like a cat against him. I couldn't remember a time I'd ever felt this good before. "So much better than my BOB."

"Okay, I take it back. I don't need to hear about other guys right now."

"What? No, not Bob—*B.O.B.*—Battery Operated Boyfriend." I laughed. "A girl has to have something to keep her relaxed on circuit."

Cruz flipped me to my back, hovering above me with a look that told me Disney World was definitely closed. "Penelope, are you telling me that I'm the first man to give you an orgasm?"

"Yes. Doesn't that make you feel all possessive and alpha-y?"

His gaze narrowed. "How have you never…?"

I shrugged. "Not sure. I've just never let anyone touch me before."

His eyes flew wide, and he scrambled off me to stand at the end of the bed. "You've never let anyone… Holy shit, Penelope, you're a virgin?"

"Ummm. Yes?" I sat up, drawing my knees to my chest, not out of embarrassment but because it was kind of chilly now that I'd lost my six-foot-something heater.

He started pacing, his hands on his head. My gaze dropped to the massive bulge in his pants that he was obviously trying to ignore.

"Why is this an issue?"

"Why?" he sputtered. "That night in Vegas, you were going to give your virginity to a stranger?"

I arched an eyebrow. "One, it's mine to give, and two, no…I was going to give it to *you*."

He crossed his arms over his massive chest. "How?"

"I thought it would be on the bed, probably you on top since it was my first time."

"For fuck's sake. Not how was I going to take you." He shook his head. "How are you still a virgin? You're twenty-two, gorgeous as sin, so smart that you give me whiplash, you kiss like heaven, and you're a genuine badass."

"Those are reasons men want me," I said.

"Yes!" he mock-shouted, trying to keep his volume down.

"Not reasons I would want just any man."

He blinked at me, understanding dawning on his face.

A shiver ran across my skin as the breeze from the open door washed over me. Cruz sighed, taking a spare blanket from his nightstand and wrapping it around me, then he sat on the bed—as far away from me as possible.

"I'm beautiful," I said as honestly as I could. "I know it, and it's not like I did anything to deserve it. Genetics are what they are, and I figured out early that boys liked my looks. And that was before the Sexiest Athlete of the Year nonsense. But I worked really hard to build my reputation as a Renegade, and maybe I used my looks, but I never used my body."

"I never meant to insinuate—"

"I know. What I'm trying to tell you is that there's never been a guy—a man—worth risking that reputation for, worth being a piece of ass for."

"You're not a piece of ass."

I scooted over to rest my head on his shoulder. "That's why I waited for the right someone—waited for you. And once I felt what it could be like between us, I wasn't willing to let that go. If that one time in Vegas was the only time I got to feel like that, then I was grabbing on with both hands."

I felt his jaw flex as he rested the side of his head on mine. "You should have told me. I would have gone slower, wouldn't have just—"

"Nope, that was perfect. And I've never been good at slow. Once I decide what I want, I stick with it until I land that trick, or I crash and burn. In fact, if you hadn't stopped, by now this would be a moot point."

He turned and cupped my face. "I'm glad I found out."

"Me, too. And I still want it to be you." I peeked over his shoulder at the clock. "In fact we still have ten minutes…"

He scoffed and shook his head. Then he kissed me lightly, sweetly, keeping himself firmly in check, and as serene as it was, I almost loathed the kiss because I felt him lock his resolve.

"There's zero chance in hell I'm taking your virginity in a ten-minute quickie and then going on a trip where I have to basically ignore you for three straight days. Not going to happen."

Every second he stared at me knocked my ire down a notch or two…or five. "Your eyes are your best weapon. You know that, right?"

He flashed those dimples, and I groaned.

"Or maybe it's the dimples."

"You'd better get dressed so we can meet downstairs like I didn't just spend the last twenty minutes introducing you to non-battery-operated orgasms."

"But it is going to happen, right?" I almost whined, then popped my hand over my mouth. When the hell had I become this needy over something—especially sex?

Cruz laughed softly and kissed my lips again. "Yes. So much yes. All the yes. I'm going to ruin you for any man stupid enough to try to come after me." He took on a fierce expression for a moment before softening. "But not like this. When you're ready—"

"I'm ready!" I nodded.

"I'm not an airplane you can go jump out of because you want to, Penelope. There are two of us in this bed. Two of us in this relationship."

Relationship. I almost purred at the word, and then simmered the hell down. He was right. Maybe my virginity didn't really matter to me, but it apparently mattered to him, and therefore had to matter back to me. Were all relationships this complicated?

"Okay," I agreed.

"Good. It'll be worth it. The first time I take you, make love to you, it won't be where we're scared people will hear us through the walls."

"I like the sound of that."

"Me, too. Now get dressed before I lose all respect for myself now that I've become the lead in every bad porn. You're incredibly sexy wrapped up in nothing but a blanket."

I burst out laughing but hopped down and started gathering up my clothes. Then I snuck into the bathroom, knowing I could tease him with my nakedness but already feeling bad that I'd left him hard and unsatisfied. "Why a bad porn?" I asked through the door, pulling my shirt on over my bra.

"Oh, come on. I'm the older, wiser, hot professor. You're the young, wide-eyed, virginal ingénue who needs a little help after class."

I laughed as I got my pants on, then tossed open the door to lounge against it suggestively, raising my knee along the doorframe. "Well, I didn't mean to fail that exam. I was just so distracted by— Hey, you put your shirt back on."

"So did you." He pulled me close, and even though he'd just given me the best orgasm of my life, I felt that fire flare up again.

"So, you and me?" I asked softly.

"You and me," he agreed, taking my lips in a deep, soul-reaching kiss. "It's not going to be easy."

"Nothing worth it ever is."

Chapter Twenty

PERU

Ignoring Penelope as we hiked the Inca Trail was harder than it sounded. I heard her laugh, and I was immediately jealous of whomever made her do it. I saw one of her Renegades boost her up when part of the trail got steep, and I wanted to break his damn hands. I saw her smile at me when no one was looking, and it was all I could do not to kiss her stupid—consequences be damned.

Agreeing to a secret relationship hadn't contained the blast zone—it had turned me into a territorial, growling jackass.

Checking all forty-six students into the hotel in Aguas Calientes took longer than I wanted, but everyone was settled, dinner was done, the sun was set, and I finally sat at the bar with a Peruvian beer in hand. Camping would have been a better experience for the students, but the last thing I wanted to deal with was the Renegades doing stupid shit like jumping over the fire. It just wasn't practical for this size trip, so hotel it was. It was modern, clean, and had a great open-air bar with slow-spinning ceiling fans, and we were at the base of Machu Picchu, which meant tomorrow's hike would be easy compared to today's grueling expedition.

I glanced in Penelope's direction, where she sat in a curved booth, surrounded by her friends. Her hair was up and her skin had a sun-kissed glow from hiking all day. She looked beautiful, and damn if that smile didn't make me want to steal her away.

As if she felt me, our eyes locked for a precious, heated second before I studied the label on my beer. I needed to be better. Safer. Hell, I couldn't figure out how the whole group didn't already know about us, because I was pretty sure my feelings for her were etched on my face every time I looked at her.

"Man, I need one of those," Lindsay said, taking the seat next to me and blocking my view of Penelope. "You sure you want to hike up that mountain tomorrow when there's a perfectly good shuttle?" She looked at me with a desperate plea in her eyes.

"Pilsen Callao," I ordered from the bartender, then turned to Lindsay, trying not to laugh. She was exhausted and looked it—definitely not the time to poke fun. "What fun is that? Everyone wants to look back at their life and say, 'I hiked to Machu Picchu.' I have yet to meet someone who wants to say, 'I rode the bus.'"

"I'd ride the damn bus," she muttered, but perked up when her beer arrived. "Thank you," she said to the bartender, then me.

"No problem. You know, if you want, you can offer that to the students. Anyone who wants to avoid the hour-and-a-half hike in the morning can take the bus with you." It chafed me to say it, but I needed to make sure all students were capable of making it to the top, and we'd had more than a few stragglers today.

The look of relief on her face sent a pang of guilt through me. Not everyone on this trip was as in shape as the Renegades, and I needed to keep that in mind.

"You want to give them another few minutes and then do bed check?" Lindsay asked.

"Bed check? Are they in high school?" I openly laughed.

"No, but according to the State Department, Peru has one of the highest crime rates in Latin America, including kidnapping." Her wide eyes told me she wasn't backing down.

"Okay, I'll take the boys, you take the girls?" I offered.

She glanced nervously at Penelope's table. "Will you take those? I know you're their faculty advisor, and something tells me they don't listen well when they're not in class."

I looked over to where the friends were lost in conversation, no doubt hashing out the final details for the stunt the day after tomorrow.

"They're not that bad. You simply have to speak on their wavelength," I told Lindsay. When had I become protective of the Renegades?

When you claimed one of them as yours.

"Well, wavelength or not, I'll call for curfew, and then we can make the rounds?"

"Sounds like a plan." I finished my beer as Lindsay sent the students to their rooms.

I officially felt old.

"Can I ask you a question?" Lindsay asked, taking the chair next to mine again in the almost-empty bar.

"Absolutely."

"Are you seeing someone?"

I nearly spat out my beer. *Chill the fuck out, she doesn't know.* After managing to swallow, I gave her my full attention.

"Why?"

"Because you put out the just-friends vibe, and I'd rather know that you're taken—or gay—as opposed to racking my brain to think up ten different things that are wrong with me." She finished with a shrug, like my answer didn't matter.

"There is nothing wrong with you, and yes, I'm seeing someone," I said, my chest swelling with an unfamiliar emotion at being able to admit my relationship in this small way.

"Oh." Her entire posture lightened. "Well, then that makes sense. She must be something special."

Penelope's face took over my mind. Her smile, her frown, her ocean-blue eyes when she was pissed. Her reckless need to push every limit, and the fragile vulnerability she kept so tightly guarded.

"I can honestly say that there is no one in the world who compares to her." My words were soft but echoed into the deepest corners of my heart.

"Lucky girl."

"Lucky me."

We split up and headed for different floors of the hotel. After grabbing my roster, I found most of the Renegades in the hallway in various states of pajamas.

"Look, I don't care who sleeps with whom—" Whistles interrupted me, and I grinned, shaking my head at my careless use of that phrase around a bunch of college kids. "What I meant was that I don't care who is in what room, but Miss Gibson is worried about crime and kidnapping and dastardly deeds, though I can't see anyone putting up with you bunch long enough to demand a ransom. So pick a room and stay there. I'm starting at this end for bed checks."

The hallway cleared, and I went room by room, checking names off my list. The fifth door I checked was opened by Penelope. She wore drawstring pajama bottoms, a tank top, and bare feet, and yet she'd never looked sexier to me as she smiled softly. It was a look I wanted to see often, and preferably in my condo in L.A., if we made it off the ship intact.

You will.

By fall, maybe I'd see her in my apartment in Boston.

"Just Rachel and me," she said, opening the door so I could see inside.

Rachel waved from her bed, then, slipping headphones on, went back to whatever she was doing with her camera.

"I figured she'd be bunked up with Rhodes," I said to Penelope.

"She's on Penna duty," she answered. "They're not going to leave me alone until I somehow prove I'm back to normal."

"And how are you supposed to do that?"

"Probably by getting on that damn motorcycle," she answered. "We have the live expo coming up, and I still haven't so much as sat on my bike."

I leaned against her doorframe. "Are you ready?"

"I don't know, but I feel like I'll get there eventually, which is better than I felt a month ago."

"That's progress."

She looked over at Rachel, who head-bobbed with whatever music she was listening to, then whispered, "This is harder than I thought it would be."

"I know. Trust me, I know."

"I wish you could kiss me good night." That spark I loved so much lit in her eyes, and I almost cursed our arrangement.

But denying myself now so I could have her later was worth everything.

"Me, too. Though I'm not sure I'd stop at kissing you," I whispered quietly.

She stepped back into her room, door handle in hand. "Good night, Dr. Delgado."

"Miss Carstairs." I inclined my head toward her, retreating as she shut the door. This secret bullshit really, truly, purely sucked.

. . .

"Okay, everyone gather around. Let's get some actual learning done here," I told the students as we settled into an open area in Machu Picchu, head count complete.

The hike had been slightly treacherous, steep and unforgiving. Some of the paths had turned to mud due to last night's rain, but I hadn't heard a single complaint from the thirty-one students who came with me. We'd met the bus at the entrance to the site and come the rest of the way as a group.

The site itself was a damned marvel, and I couldn't wait to get through this portion of the expedition so I could explore.

"First off, make sure you're staying hydrated, and if you're feeling short of breath, don't panic. We're up here at eight thousand feet, so it's mostly the altitude."

Lindsay smiled at me, and I knew it was because she was one of the people struggling to catch her breath even though she'd arrived with the bus. I scanned the rest of the students and found Penelope with an arched eyebrow in Lindsay's direction.

Real subtle, baby. I barely contained my smile, but managed.

"Okay, welcome to today's session of Latin American history, on location, if you will. Who can tell me why Machu Picchu is so special?"

"The Inca ruled for only a hundred years, and to accomplish something like this in such a short time is amazing," Leah answered.

"Good. Yes. Archeologists believe that it had to have

been ordered by the first Incan emperor since it took about fifty years or so to build. What else?"

"It was completely abandoned, which is probably what saved it from Spanish destruction, seeing as they demolished almost every other holy Incan site during their conquest," Luke Ruiz threw out. "They never found it."

"Correct, again. Why it was abandoned continues to be a mystery. While smallpox and civil war had both already done their part to weaken the empire, there's no sign of war here. In fact, it looks like it was stopped mid-construction. What else?" I looked around the group.

"Logically, it shouldn't be here."

Her voice slid over me like warm caramel.

"Go ahead, Miss Carstairs," I prompted, daring myself to look at her as she answered. I locked down every muscle in my face, determined not to show any reaction that might give me away.

"Its location is sacred, the river beneath us, the four tallest peaks at every direction. Spiritually, militarily, culturally—it's exactly perfect for the Incans in every regard."

God, it sounded like she was talking about us, or maybe I had us on the brain so much I could twist anything she said. "You're absolutely right. But the same could be said for a hundred other sites of ruins from civilizations all over the globe."

"But this one geographically shouldn't have lasted a century, let alone six," she said.

Bingo. Her brain was as much of a turn-on as her body was—hell, even more so.

"We're surrounded on both sides by two earthquake-prone fault lines on this ridge." She pointed to both ends of the site. "But more than that, Machu Picchu gets two and a half times the amount of rain as Chicago during the rainy season, and is known for mudslides in the surrounding area. Seeing as it was built almost six hundred years ago, the site should have washed away long ago."

"Mudslides, yay," Rachel said with jazz hands.

Landon laughed and put his arm around her shoulder.

Penelope rolled her eyes.

"So if this site is perfect for what the Inca needed, and yet pretty geographically flawed, why is it still standing?" I asked Penelope.

She tilted her head, then straightened and looked around at the ruins, the sky, ground, anywhere but me. "Because they built a strong foundation."

"How?" I challenged.

She met my level gaze, a slight smile curving her lips. "They started from the ground up, terracing the mountain to hold it in place."

"So it's all in the foundation?"

She nodded. "They layered topsoil, sand, and then granite chips so that the terraces never flooded, never had a reason to give way. Then they brilliantly channeled that water through a connected system of fountains that harnessed the local spring as well as the rain, providing clean drinking water to the population."

God *damn*, I wanted to kiss her, to scream out to the world that this gorgeous, brave, smart-as-hell woman was mine. "So they turned their greatest weakness into a strength."

"Exactly."

Just like we will. She didn't need to say it; her eyes did all the talking for her.

I ripped my gaze off her before it gave me away. "Okay, who wants to tell me about the granite-cutting techniques?"

Another student answered, then another, and twenty minutes later, I'd managed to complete the entire session without looking at Penelope again. I finished up telling them about the importance of the position of the altar and the prevalence of child sacrifice in Incan culture that had been uncovered by high-altitude archaeologists in the Andes at even higher elevations than we were.

Then I reminded them of our meet-up time and set them free to wander.

I hiked the various levels of the ruins for an hour, answering questions from students, asking my own of the guide. The best part of having a two-hundred-person-a-day limit for visitors to the site was that it made it so much less crowded.

How was I lucky enough to be here? To have come from where I did—with almost no chance of survival, let alone thriving? This was a sight my grandmother would most likely never see, one that my mother never had the chance to—and never would.

But Elisa would.

She would have the life she'd worked so hard for—the one she deserved. She'd lived long enough in his shadow, under his thumb, and in two more months she'd get the freedom every woman deserved, especially one as kind and smart as my little sister.

My failure wasn't an option.

I walked carefully as I descended the carved stone steps. All it would take was one misstep and I'd fall three hundred feet down the cliff. Curving around one of the structures, I found Penelope and her friends examining the stonework on the inside of what had been a home.

"Hey, Doc," Wilder said, his arm around Leah.

"What are you guys up to?" I asked, standing on the opposite side of the room from Penelope. "Tell me you're not planning any stunts here. I'd hate to have to kick your asses."

Wilder laughed. "Nawh. We might be entitled assholes, but we're not disrespectful entitled assholes."

"Good to know," I told them. "You guys make it down to the lower terraces yet? You still have enough time before we have to head out. There's a storm coming in."

"That's what we get for visiting in the rainy season," Leah answered. "Pax, want to head down?"

"If you're asking if I'll walk you down to look at some really old walls holding up some really old terrace work, then yes," Wilder said.

One by one, they filed out, until it was just Penelope and myself.

"You should go with them," I said softly.

"There are a lot of things I should do," she retorted with a grin that nearly took me to my knees. There was something about her smile that was captivating and addictive, infusing me with the joy she felt.

"Go," I ordered softly, wishing she could stay, that I could have just a few minutes with her.

She sighed but nodded, brushing past me as she went out of the stone-enclosed house. "I can't stop thinking about your hands," she admitted softly, staring straight ahead at the skyline.

Those hands she was talking about clenched. God, the woman loved to keep me on edge. I glanced at our surroundings, making sure there were no students in earshot. "I can't stop remembering every single inch of you," I whispered across the eighteen inches that separated us. "Or thinking about how I'm going to explore those inches with my mouth the next time I get you under me."

"Cruz," she whimpered, her gaze shooting toward mine. Her breath hitched, and as much as I wanted to congratulate myself on being able to rile her with nothing but a few words, I wasn't much better off.

Virgin. She's a virgin. Slow down.

"Go meet up with your friends before we find ourselves in trouble, Penelope," I half ordered, half pleaded.

She gave me one last, searing look and then left me standing there, watching her walk away.

• • •

My phone beeped with the monotone ring that signaled an international call as I balanced it between my shoulder and ear.

Two rings later, Elisa picked up.

"Hello?"

My chest loosened, the same way it always did when I heard her voice. "Hey, I got your email, what's up?"

"Cruz! I'm so happy you called! I wasn't expecting to hear from you for another few weeks."

"Well, when I get an email from my little sister telling me it's urgent that I call, I find the time. Besides, you lucked out—we're still in Lima for one more day, so I have service." I moved the phone to my other hand and finished unpacking. We'd gotten back from Machu Picchu only a couple of hours ago, and I was due on deck in a few moments to get ready for the next stunt before we pulled out of port.

"Guess what?"

"You found a way to dig a tunnel to Miami."

"Ha. Ha. You're so very funny."

"Tell me what's up, imp." I tossed my empty daypack to the bottom of my closet. I shouldn't need it again for a month or so.

"They increased my scholarship!"

A lump grew in my throat. "Really? God, Elisa, that's amazing. How much?" I already knew I was on the hook for her tuition, but between me and loans, we'd get her through Harvard if I had to get a job with Thunder from Down Under to pay for it.

"I got a full ride," she whispered, as if saying it at full volume would somehow make it disappear.

"You what?" I sank to my bed, my knees unable to support me.

"A full ride! Tuition, room, board, all of it!"

My eyes drifted skyward, and I muttered a prayer of thanks, automatically switching to Spanish. Everything was coming together. Last year we'd thought she'd have to defer her acceptance until I could get to her next year, but here I was, here *we* were, and the pieces were starting to fit as if fate herself had designed the puzzle.

"Hey, you said English only," she chided, a smile in her voice.

"I'm just…" I shook my head. "I can't believe it. I mean, I can—you're brilliant, but just knowing that it's taken care of…I don't have words." Her tuition was paid. Her room, board, all covered.

"I guess I wrote one hell of an essay," she joked.

If I wanted to, once this trip was over, I could decide not to teach. I could go back to the army full time if I wanted, or take up underwater toenail painting. Sure, I loved teaching, but I'd always chosen my profession for this one purpose—this mission.

Grandma's house would be paid off, and Elisa's tuition was taken care of.

"What are you thinking?" she asked.

"I feel like a lot of my future just opened up," I told her honestly. We'd never had secrets between us, not from the moment she'd tracked me down seven years ago.

"I never wanted you to plan your whole future around me."

"I know, and it hasn't been a sacrifice, so don't think that it has."

"You give up too much."

"Six more weeks, and then you'll be on your way to Harvard. That's all that matters. You have a whole wide world opening to you."

"What about you? When this is over, what will you do

besides teach? Finally settle down with that girl you took to Grandmother?"

I grinned. "Grandma. Grandmother is too formal for most use. And how would you know about that?"

"She does know how to email, you know. She said her name was Penelope, and that she was beautiful, driven, smart, and strong enough to handle your idiotic ways."

"Is that what she said?" I asked, lying back on my bed. Hiking for three straight days had worn me to the bone.

"Yep. And she said that even though you swore up and down that you are just friends, you're completely—what was the word she used? Smitten."

Smitten. Infatuated. Captivated. Enchanted. Pretty much any of those descriptions worked.

"Did she tell you that she's my student?"

She was silent on the other end for a moment except for the sound of one very long sigh. "Yes. She said you were fighting it."

"Would you think less of me if I didn't fight it? If I told you I knew her before she was my student? That us being here on this ship together is either the biggest coincidence or the greatest act of fate I've ever seen?"

"I would say that if you found a glass slipper, then you put it on her foot—or whatever. You know what I'm trying to say."

"This isn't a fairy tale, Elisa."

"All love is a fairy tale if you look at it from the outside, Cruz."

"If...if something happens, and I'm caught, I'd get fired. I'd be thrown off the ship."

"Then don't get caught."

Why couldn't I see everything as simply as my sister did? Oh, right, because I wasn't seventeen and starry-eyed. "It's a really big risk."

"It's a really big reward. Look, if I wasn't involved—"

"If you weren't involved, I wouldn't be here in the first place."

"Okay, well, forgetting all that. If I wasn't in the picture, would you risk it for her? Your career? Your reputation?"

I thought about it for a second, everything Penelope and I had already been through in the five short weeks I'd known her. "I would risk my life for her. Hell, I already have."

Elisa sighed. "See? Fairy tale. Are you in love with her?"

That soft burning in my chest made its presence known, and I pushed it away. "I've been officially, and very secretly, dating her for about four days now. I think that's a little soon to be throwing that word around, imp."

"Prince Charming knew in one night."

"Prince Charming was too slow to catch Cinderella with one shoe on. I'm holding myself to a higher standard here."

"Fair enough." I heard a rustle in the background. "Crap. He's home," she whispered. "Talk again in a few weeks?"

My stomach turned queasy. *Six weeks*, I reminded myself. Then I wouldn't have the constant fear to tote around with me like a fifty-pound weight around my neck.

"Just email me with a time. Love you."

"Love you," she whispered, and hung up.

I couldn't think about what would happen next—whether or not he'd be in a good mood. If she'd hidden her Harvard paperwork well enough, every other scrap of information that could ruin our plan—or her life.

Putting the cell phone in my dresser drawer, I braced my hand on the top and looked myself in the mirror, making the same promise I had every day for the last five years.

I may have failed my mother, but I would not fail Elisa. She would live.

Chapter Twenty-One

"Wind speeds, safety measures, equipment list, and plan F, all as you requested," I said as I handed Cruz the manila envelope.

Sitting next to him in the small van that carried us from the port to the launch site was pure heaven and hell wrapped up in one delicious scent—Cruz. Even the ocean breeze coming in from the window couldn't overpower him to me.

"Plan F?" he asked, flipping through the papers.

"Well, if we don't land correctly, it's not really a plan B, it's more like a plan Fucked," Landon answered from behind us.

"I wish we had Little John. I'd feel a lot better," Leah answered. "How much longer is he in California?"

I tensed, and Cruz's eyes darted toward me. *Little John.* "He'll be back when we hit Buenos Aires," I said, trying to keep my voice level. He'd recognize Cruz, there was no doubt.

I just had to get to him before that moment happened, and then I'd beg him to keep my secret.

Our secret.

"This all looks good. Dangerous and stupid as hell, of course, but I've learned not to expect less out of you guys," Cruz said. "What kind of landing are you thinking?"

"One where we put our feet on the deck of the ship without killing ourselves," Pax called out from the third row.

"Smart-assery gets you nowhere, Wilder," Cruz said, his voice mellow and almost bored. "I'm assuming a straight on, right? Not a ninety-degree turn to approach?"

"Straight approach, no turns. Keeping the power on until we touch down for purposes of accuracy, and we'll drop the chute at landing. If we lose them, we lose them, but I'm not having someone dragged overboard," Pax answered.

"Good." He nodded as he read through the plan one last time. "I really wish you'd land on the beach, but I know you won't."

"There's zero challenge in that," I said. "No use for the cameras and nothing fun."

He shot me a look that to anyone else might look chastising, but I knew it was pure frustration. He walked a fine line between letting us do our jobs and keeping us within the parameters of what he felt was safe.

"Okay. Okay," he mumbled to himself. "Just make sure you're as on top of this landing as you can be. I'm still really not thrilled about it."

"You could do it with us," Wilder offered.

My heart skipped. "You could," I told Cruz, trying to keep the excitement out of my voice. "This was on the list you gave us, right? You know how to paraglide?"

"Sure, recreationally, but I probably have more hours than you do," he muttered, still examining the papers. He reached back with one hand and rubbed across his neck.

I caught myself just before I offered to take over the neck rub. It had been four days since we'd been alone together. Four days since he'd given me the most spectacular orgasm of my life. Four days since he'd told me that he was mine.

Mine. I'd never really thought of myself as possessive before. Boys were boys, and no boy was worth my reputation or a stunt. But knowing Cruz was actually mine made me want to tattoo my name on his damned forehead so every other woman knew he was spoken for.

"And you just happen to have an extra rig?" he asked as we took the switchbacks to the top of the bluff that Lima District sat on.

"No, we brought one for you," Wilder said, grinning ear to ear. I rolled my eyes at him in the rearview mirror, and he laughed. "Come on, once you gave us that list of everything you know how to do, didn't you think we'd con you into coming with us? You don't get an official Renegade nickname until you complete a stunt."

"Whatever shall I do?" Cruz drawled. "You brought it because you know I'm still unhappy about your landing zone, but you figure if I'm with you I won't complain."

"He's on to you, Pax." Landon laughed.

"And what about Leah?" Cruz asked. "I noticed she's not with us. She didn't want to ride tandem?"

"There was no chance I was including her in this. I'm good. Damn good, but I can't control the wind, and if a gust comes that takes me overboard, I'm not risking her," Pax answered.

"But he'd risk you," Cruz whispered so softly only I heard him.

"I risk myself," I replied. "I am just as capable, if not more so than you are, so tuck away the alpha asshole, okay?"

"You like the alpha asshole," he whispered with a smirk.

"We're here," the driver told us as we pulled up to the site. We were in the middle of a large soccer field near the edge of the bluff that would give us enough space to get a good takeoff before the plunge. It didn't hurt that we were using motorized paragliders that would allow us to fly.

I raised my face to the sun as I stepped out of the van. Being in South America in March definitely had its perks. Plus, in the next few weeks those perks would turn to ice when we hit the southernmost tip of South America. I'd take what I could get when I could get it.

Ironic how that describes your relationship, too.

"Penna?" Zoe asked, coming from the other van.

"I'll catch up," I told Landon as they headed over to where the rigs were set up, a little too close together. We'd have to space them out more before takeoff. Bobby's crew was good, but they didn't make up for Little John's absence. Even if he was the one who could fully expose me. "What's up?" I asked Zoe.

"I just wanted to say thank you for fighting for my own rig. I know the guys figured I'd go tandem, or not at all, and that you're the one who spoke up for me." Her brown eyes lacked their typical winged eyeliner and heavy makeup. She looked younger and a hell of a lot less vixenish…if that was even a word.

"Zoe, you have over a hundred hours in one of these. I checked the logs. I know your skill level. You're not here because I fought for you. You're here because you earned it. You put in the work, you're talented, and you can land a rig better than those two idiots behind you." I pointed to where Alex and one of the other Renegades, Nathan, stood. "I know you and I don't often see eye to eye, but maybe we'd be a lot closer to that if you realized you have more value in the Renegades than who you're sleeping with."

"I haven't slept with anyone since…" Her gaze wandered. "After that happened, I just wanted to stand on my own for a while. See where I really fit in."

"Since Landon. I know. That's one reason I *am* willing to stand up and fight for you, because you're finally fighting for yourself. Go strap in."

She walked past Landon without so much as glancing his way, and I blew out a sigh. That girl was all sorts of screwed in the head sometimes, but there was still hope that she'd eventually remove her head from her ass and focus more on her talent and less on her teammates. Landon had been the last in a long string of Renegades she'd worked her way through, but Rachel showing up four months ago put a prompt end to that. Landon had never stopped loving Rachel in the two years they'd been apart, and Zoe had never stood a chance. Of course she'd taken it out on him and nearly destroyed his relationship with Rachel with her pettiness, but I liked to think that change was possible for everyone.

I walked over to my rig and tied my hair into a knot to keep it clear.

"Too bad, I like it down," Cruz whispered as he walked by.

A shiver raced down my spine. That smooth, deep voice, coupled with his accent, never failed to affect me in the best ways. It was definitely on the short list for his sexiest features along with his dimples. And those eyes, and every single cut line of his abs. Screw it, the man was simply the embodiment of sex—which ironically was the one thing he was withholding.

I laid out the wing of my paraglider, which was set up right next to the one Cruz had been assigned, and checked each individual line, making sure the rig was free of any knots. Given that we were about thirty feet from the edge of the bluff, I didn't exactly have a lot of time to correct if one snagged or bunched. A bunched line meant that side would drag down the wing, and the last thing I wanted to do was spiral down the cliff edge.

I smiled for the cameras when Bobby shoved them in my

face, and explained the nature of the stunt, and then I snapped into my harness as they ran off to interview Wilder.

"Need a double check?" Cruz asked, walking over to stand in front of me.

I hiked an eyebrow at him, glancing around us as innocently as I could.

"We're set up right next to each other. If you were Wilder, I'd ask him."

"Well, aren't you polite. Go ahead and check me out," I said, lifting my arms from their sides. God, I even flirted with him when I didn't mean to.

"Happy to be of service." He pulled at my snaps, checked the lock on my carabineer, and then gently tugged at my harness, making sure it was snug.

I'd been double-checked by just about every Renegade on our team, but it had always been quick and professional, a courtesy to make sure I didn't get myself killed with loose rigging or a mistake I didn't catch.

Cruz's hands elevated my pulse, quickened my breath, and gave me flashbacks of when there were way fewer clothes between us. But even more than the physical, the way he checked me and then checked again made me feel protected, cared for in a way I never had been before.

Sure, Pax, Landon, Nick, they all loved me, cared about and for me, but there was something in Cruz's movements and blatant concern on his face that made me feel cherished.

God, I had it so bad for this beautiful man.

"Good to go?" I asked, chancing a look at him.

"Looks good," he said softly.

"Hey, need a check?" Landon asked.

"Dr. Delgado has me," I answered.

"Doc, you need a check?"

Cruz looked me over one more time and nodded. "Yeah, that would be great."

I tuned the radio in my helmet to the right channel and out of the corner of my eye watched Landon check Cruz.

Ten minutes later, every Renegade was harnessed in, and there was just enough of a breeze to pick up our wings behind us about six inches off the ground. Perfect to make sure every line was where it was supposed to be.

The engines, huge circles with one giant rotating prop, were warmed up and harnessed to our backs.

I looked to Cruz, who was examining his handheld brake system.

"Nervous over there, Doc?" I asked.

"Only about you sticking the landing." Cruz's voice filled my helmet.

I laughed, the sound brighter than I'd managed in a while. "You just worry about yourself, old man."

"Old?"

I shrugged as Paxton counted us down.

Cruz muttered something that sounded like, "I'll show you old."

There were ten of us in one giant line, and starting at the right, Paxton ran forward. His wing caught, the sail rising above him, and he took to the air, steadily climbing in altitude.

Zoe took off next, then Landon and the others until the only ones left were me, Cruz, and the cameraman Bobby had hired in L.A. to keep up with us. Apparently our GoPro footage was great, but he wanted a more professional angle for the stuff we had coming up.

"See you on deck," I said to Cruz.

Then I focused.

I ran forward, feeling the lines behind me tense, then pull as the wing caught in the breeze. Looking left, then right, I made sure both edges of the canopy were deployed equally and rising at the same rate, and as they rose above my head, my feet were no longer running—I was airborne. Shifting my weight, I sat back in the harness, crossing my feet in front of me as if I was at home watching TV.

Flying was a pure shot of nitrous to my system, making me feel ethereal and yet all too mortal at the same time. My stomach dropped deliciously as we passed over the stretch of highway that ran between the bottom of the bluff and the beach, and then we were over ocean.

"You make it okay back there, Doc?" I asked.

"Right behind you, Rebel," Cruz answered.

We followed the beach from an altitude of about five hundred feet—nothing too high considering I'd been up at about six thousand feet in one of these before, but infinitely more fun for sightseeing.

The wind deafened any other noise as the radio was as quiet as my thoughts. Once again, that blissful silence took over my brain, where nothing existed outside the moment—the stunt.

Pax broke the radio silence first. "We've got about a ten-minute flight to where the ship is in port, so have some fun. Don't do anything that will have Dr. Delgado up our asses, okay?"

A few cheers went out over the waves, and that rush I'd been waiting for hit my system. Every nerve in my body woke up, ready and waiting for whatever I decided.

I chose to go for it.

Splitting off from the group, I rose in altitude until I hit a little over a thousand feet. Then I adjusted, dipped to the right, and barrel-rolled. The ocean and sky blended into a kaleidoscope of blue as I tumbled, rolling end over end.

Adrenaline flooded my veins, the taste sweet in my mouth, and everything sharpened. This was my drug, and I was fully, wholeheartedly an addict.

Leveling out, I laughed.

"Holy. Shit." Cruz sounded purely dumbstruck.

"Still worried about me back there?" I teased him, watching Rachel fly so far beneath me that she was dipping her feet into the waves.

"A little worried about your sanity, maybe."

"What are you pulling back there?" Wilder asked.

"Just a few barrel rolls," I answered.

"Ahhhh, now that's the Rebel we know and love," he said with pure affection.

Just for fun, I rose back up and did another series, letting the world roll with me. Each dip and swing swept another layer of darkness off my heart until I felt as bright and clean as the sun above me.

The strangest yearning took hold of my heart—I wanted my bike back, needed the freedom that engine and those wheels gave me. Maybe it wasn't just the bike but the need to reclaim what I'd shoved away when Brooke had come unhinged.

"I wish you could be here," I whispered off coms to the sister who wanted nothing to do with me.

"Okay, we're coming up on approach. Remember the plan is tackle this airport-style. Everyone circles in a holding pattern so we don't clog the landing strip. Wind report says we need to come over the bridge area. Coming in from the front is more dangerous than we'd like."

The "landing strip" was the small, flat surface that covered the pool toward the front of the ship on the top deck. The production crew had built it for us to specifications, but from here it looked a hell of a lot smaller than what we'd intended.

"How is Camera Boy doing back there?" I asked.

"Camera *Man* is fine," the guy fired back, and I instantly liked him.

"Good to know. Don't die on us, okay? The legal red tape would be a bitch."

"Yeah, yeah, got it."

The ship was anchored offshore, so at least it wasn't moving, but that didn't give me any warm fuzzies considering a gust could take me into the water or I could miss entirely and smack into the side of the boat. On camera. In front of the entire universe.

No pressure or anything.

"Okay everyone, remember to lose your canopies the minute you land. The crew knows to grab them, and you, if you go with it," Pax instructed. "Nova, you want to lead us in?"

"You got it," Landon said, and headed for the landing zone as we all began to circle in a holding pattern. The wind was stronger off the shore, blowing him sideways a few times. He corrected, landing at the edge of the marked zone. His canopy flew back toward the bridge, and the crew caught it.

"One down," Rachel said.

One by one, they started to land, Rachel missing and putting down in the middle of a few deck chairs that ended up sliding with the canopy when she unsnapped.

Cruz landed perfectly, coming across the bridge deck and dropping down with impressive accuracy. He unhooked from his canopy, turning fast enough to grab the lines himself and pull it in.

Self-sufficient show-off.

If we'd had private radio channels, I would have told him as much.

With only Pax and the cameraman left in the sky with me, it was my turn. I circled until I was at the back of the ship, then came in slow. The wind was too unpredictable to come in without motorized power. I passed over the bridge, but just as I went in for a landing, a gust of wind blew me straight off course.

"Fuck."

"So ladylike," Landon said.

"Shut up," I threw back.

"Go back around," Cruz ordered.

"Yeah, that's not going to happen." Pulling a ninety degree turn, I came in from the front of the boat.

"Shit," I muttered, lifting my feet over a table in the restaurant section. "Excuse me, coming through," I said to the students in my way, who ducked, a few of the girls shrieking.

I hit the landing pad at a run, and the moment I heard the canopy hit the ground behind me, I unhooked the two locks at my waist, setting the wing free. I spun as the chute raced toward me—Pax hadn't been kidding about the wind report—and I jumped as the wing sped beneath my feet and into the waiting arms of the production staff.

Turning toward the cheering crowd that had gathered to watch us land, I met the intensely angry eyes of Cruz.

I took off my helmet and walked toward him, where he'd already removed his helmet and harness.

"Seriously?"

I shrugged. "Nailed it."

"Death. Of. Me." He punctuated every word with a finger point in my direction. "I told you to go back around."

"And I'll let you know when I take my orders from you."

His nostrils flared as his jaw flexed. "That was unreasonable."

"Do you have any idea how many times I've landed a motorized paraglider with the wind instead of against it? At least a dozen."

"On a ship? Where your landing zone is either dead on or just plain dead?"

"Did you see me go overboard? I'm more than capable of landing that, because, oh, that's right…I just *did*."

Something moved to my side, and I immediately caught on to the camera that was close enough to hear every word. *Shit.* "I'm sorry that as my faculty advisor, you're upset that I chose to land when you were against it, but being the professional I am, I gauged my ability against the wind and made my choice."

His eyes flickered toward the camera, and he sighed. "Next time let's discuss contingencies. I'd rather this not happen again on my watch."

"Noted."

The camera left as Pax came in for a landing, and I breathed a sigh of relief but didn't say anything else. There were still people all around us, and I knew that just like our kisses, the fights would have to wait until we were behind closed doors, too.

Pax landed perfectly and walked straight to Leah, the documentary crew zooming in on something I knew Pax would make them cut later.

Cruz and I moved toward the edge of the landing zone as the cameraman came in to land. He cleared the bridge with nearly no room to spare, and I cringed as his foot smacked the railing. That was going to hurt like a bitch later.

He was lined up to make contact with us, and came down steady toward the landing zone. As he met the surface at a run, another gust of wind knocked him sideways, dragging him across the deck toward the railing. Cruz broke into a run, hurdling over a table and then a set of chairs as the cameraman slammed into the side deck railing, his chute already extended over the port side.

Cruz reached him just as the cameraman's feet lifted off the ground, his massive hands slamming into the man's waist.

The chute flew free, billowing with the wind into the wild of the Pacific Ocean, while Cruz held the cameraman safely on board.

"Holy shit," Pax called out as we ran toward them.

"You okay?" I asked Cruz and the cameraman.

"Yeah."

"Good to go."

"Okay, what's your name?" I asked the cameraman, who was a shade whiter than the paint on our boat. "Because after that, I kind of feel like I need to know it."

"Victor," he said, collapsing into the nearest deck chair and putting his head between his knees.

"Well, Victor, that was close." Pax clapped him on the back. "And, Doc, I don't think I've ever seen someone move that fast. Thank you."

"No need to thank me." He nodded at Pax, shot me a look I couldn't interpret, and left.

I smiled through the interviews, talked about my choice to change up my landing instead of doing a second approach, and counted down every second until I could get out of there.

About an hour later, I walked into our suite and relaxed into the silence. Rachel had made dinner plans with Landon, and I was blissfully alone as we pulled out of Lima, the boat fairly even on the calm seas.

I kicked off my shoes in the entry hall. If I took a quick shower, I might be able to coordinate sneaking in some time with Cruz.

My bedroom door opened, and a tan hand attached to a muscular arm gripped my wrist, yanking me inside.

The door shut milliseconds before I found my back against it. Cruz hovered over me, pinning my hands above my head. Our eyes met in a war without words, stubbornness for stubbornness, both outmatched by the all-consuming desire that neither of us could escape.

His mouth found mine, and I opened for him, welcoming his kiss. He wasn't hard or commanding as I expected, but slow, sensual, utterly devastating in his thoroughness.

"Cruz," I moaned as his hands slid down my arms, brushing the outer curves of my breasts and ribs to frame my waist. The ability to say his name felt like the greatest privilege, freeing myself to voice the longing I felt for him every minute of the day—the same longing I had to keep secret in public.

My hands grazed the back of his head as I looped my arms around his neck, and he pulled me against him so our bodies were flush.

He kissed me a step past breathless, a moment longer than forever, until he had me arching in to him, everything forgotten but the slide of his tongue and the subtle caress of his hands.

Pulling away, he cupped my cheek with his hand. "You scared me. And before you get all defensive, I am well aware that you can handle yourself. I know that you are the best at what you do, and that your reputation is earned. Logically, I understand that you were fully in control. Common sense tells me that if anyone else had pulled what you did, I wouldn't be half as mad. But this—" He put my hand over his pounding heart. "This does not speak logic. This stopped working the minute you pulled the turn, and it didn't begin beating again until I saw you standing safely on the landing deck. This will not listen to reason, because it's too busy being terrified by how much of it you already own. Do you understand me?"

If I was a swooning kind of girl, I would have been on the floor. As it was, my knees definitely went a little unsteady. "I scared you."

"You scared me. You scare me every day. And after what almost happened to that Victor guy? Jesus, Penelope, that could have been you." His eyes went wild, and his grip on my waist tightened.

I ran a hand through his hair, back down his neck to rest it next to my other near his heart. "No, it couldn't have. You are right. I am the best at what I do. And yes, sometimes I get hurt. Sometimes I push the envelope too far, and things break—I break. But that's also how I learn. How I get stronger. A gust could have taken me, and I would have unhooked my rig before it dragged me across the deck, because I've been in situations where my chute's been caught. I started at baby steps, Cruz. I didn't just wake up one day and decide to run."

"You did with me," he said softly.

My cheeks warmed, and I ducked my head for a second. "Yeah, well, you seem to be the exception to every rule I've ever made for myself."

"There's a lot of that going around," he answered, wrapping his arms around me. I leaned in, resting my head between my hands on his chest, listening to his heartbeat. I didn't have to hold him, he held us tight enough for the both of us.

My chest filled with a sweet ache that was a step beyond infatuation and grew into a realm I wasn't ready to discuss. It was a feeling that made me ask myself questions like what were we going to do when the boat docked in Miami? Would he still want me when we got back to L.A.? When he left for his new job on the East Coast? Would he decide to be with a woman who didn't scare him? A woman who would let him protect her?

"IqueIque," he said, the sound a rumble in his chest.

"What about it?"

He rested his head on top of mine. "It's our next port."

"Right."

"We're there overnight, and I'd like you to spend that night with me," he said softly. "Off the ship, of course, but just the two of us. Like we're normal."

"Yes," I said without hesitation.

"That doesn't mean we have to have sex—"

"Yes," I repeated, pulling back with a grin on my face that was so wide it nearly hurt.

"—or do anything. I just want to take you out on a date with no jumping off shit, or parachutes, or hands-off, eyes-off rules."

"I already said yes!"

His dimples flashed before he kissed me, this kiss fast and hard.

The door to the suite closed. "Penna?"

I snapped back from Cruz, covering his mouth with my hand to keep him quiet. "I'm just getting in the shower. I'll be out in a bit," I called through the door.

Cruz sucked my ring finger between his lips, and then rolled his tongue around it. Holy shit, I felt that between my thighs.

He gave me a devilish grin, like he knew exactly what he was doing to me. Probably because he did.

"Sounds good," Rachel called. "I have to work on my thesis proposal for Dr. Delicious."

"Delicious?" he whispered.

I ran my hand down the length of his torso. "*Del*gado… *del*icious," I responded quietly.

His dimples made an appearance, and I nearly groaned.

"I thought you had it done," I called to Rachel.

"The asshole rejected my first one."

"It sucked," he whispered.

I put my hand back over his mouth and glared. This time he kissed my palm and then traced his tongue over my lifeline. The stroke sent little tendrils of electricity humming through my body, waking it with a need I knew only Cruz could sate.

Damn it, I wanted this man—everything he had to give.

"I'll help you out after I shower, Rach. How does that sound?"

Cruz stuck his ridiculously full lower lip out, and I leaned up, sucking it into my mouth. He groaned, both of his hands moving to my ass as he lifted me.

"Sounds good," Rachel answered, but the sound was muffled.

Cruz had carried me to the bathroom. He deposited me

on the cold granite counter, spread my thighs with one hand, and stepped between them. Then he kissed me until I couldn't remember my name.

My hands gripped his waist, then slid underneath his T-shirt to play with the rigid muscles beneath. Tension wound around me, through me, and there had never been anything—X Games medal or stunt—that I had ever wanted as much as I wanted this man, and not just for his body, or because he wanted me, but because he *saw* me. Me. Not just Rebel, or even Penna, but the me I was when no one was looking.

I slipped my fingers across his belt until I firmly grasped his hardness through his pants. "I want to touch."

"Fuck me, Penelope," he growled, his accent even more pronounced.

"Yes," I said, lightly nipping at his neck.

His hips rocked into my grip, and I loosened my fingers just enough to let him slide through, my thumbnail scratching lightly over the ridge that marked the head of his erection.

This time his kiss was openly carnal, his tongue thrusting at the same rhythm of his hips, his breaths becoming uneven. Then he jumped away from me and put his hands behind his head.

"Nope. Not here. Not like this. I want better for you."

"You do realize that you are way more concerned for my virginity than I am, right?" Damn it, my body was humming, electric, and he was still in complete control. How was that even fair?

He walked over to my shower and flipped the handle, turning on the water. "Shower. I'll see you in class tomorrow."

"Wait, how are you going to get down? The ship is moving."

He grinned at me on his way out the door. "You think you're the only one who can rappel in dangerous situations?

Guarantee I can kick even your ass at that, baby."

He winked, and my thighs clenched in reflex.

Then he shut the door and left me to shower away the day and imagine what our night together might be like. By the time I was clean, my Romeo had already climbed down the balcony.

Three days.

I could hardly freaking wait.

Chapter Twenty-Two

PENNA

IQUEIQUE

Chile was gorgeously warm. I'd left my hair down and put on a simple, curve-hugging dress that zipped the length of the front. The taxi left the port, only to pull over another block away, and Cruz slid in next to me.

"Hello, gorgeous," he said, kissing me lightly after he gave the driver an address.

"Hello yourself," I answered, slipping my hand into his. It was such a simple gesture, but it brought the sweetest feeling rushing through me.

"You ready for dinner? I figured we'd get checked in and then head out."

"Sounds good to me. I'm sorry I was so late. It took three showers to get the sand off me, and I'm pretty sure it's still in some pretty unmentionable places."

He laughed, those dimples making a much sought-after

appearance. "Me, too. I can't believe I let you talk me into strapping on one of those snowboards and sandboarding down the dunes this morning."

"Admit it, it was fun."

"Very fun," he agreed. "Landon is a beast on a board."

"Yeah, he's wicked talented with that thing."

The taxi pulled onto the seaside highway, and as Cruz stared out at the ocean, I studied him. His face was clean-shaven, and though I loved when he wore his close-cut beard, I loved this look, too. The angles of his face stood out without the beard, and I'd honestly never seen a more beautiful man. The sheer perfection of Cruz was overwhelming, and it wasn't just the chiseled face or the honed body. It was his mind, his heart, the way he protected and respected me at the same time, even when it cost him his own pride to watch me do the things I did.

"What are you thinking about?" he asked as the city sped by us on the left.

"You," I answered honestly. There were no games between us, no need to play coy.

"Good things, I hope." His fingers brushed across my knuckles, the sensation heightening the giant ball of anticipation in my stomach.

"All good things. Do you think we'll be safe where we're going?"

"I picked a place just outside the city. Most of the faculty was talking about the casinos, so I'm hopeful they'll stay away, but I have to be honest, unless we're locked behind a bedroom door, there's always a chance."

I leaned over, brushing my lips across his cheek as my hand shifted to his thigh. "I'm perfectly fine with a locked bedroom door."

Uncaring that the taxi driver was only a few feet away, Cruz kissed me, tilting my head for a better angle in the tight space. His hands stayed neutral and G-rated, but his tongue was clearly an R.

My fingers bit into the fabric of his pants, and my mind screamed one word: *closer. More.* Okay, that was two words, but they both centered around Cruz.

He gave me a soft, sipping kiss as he pulled away. "I told you there's no pressure—"

"I want you." I enunciated every word. "And that's not something I've said to any other man."

"How did I get so lucky?" he murmured, kissing my forehead.

"Vegas, baby," I teased.

The cab pulled up in front of a modern boutique hotel, and Cruz spoke with the driver in rapid-fire Spanish, handing over money before he stepped out. Then he offered me a hand, and I took it, sliding out of the taxi with my bag in the other hand.

My heels clicked on the marble floor as we made our way through the entrance, and my eyes caught on the fountain that decorated the chic lobby.

"Want to wait here while I check in?" Cruz offered.

"Sure," I agreed. He headed toward the reception desk, and I found myself at the end of the lobby, which opened to a wide patio.

We were right on the beach, only a thick strip of rock and gray sand between us and the Pacific Ocean. The sun made her descent in a riot of color, sinking into the water in a picture-worthy display. I didn't have my camera—I couldn't risk that someone would see a photo of Cruz and me together—so I memorized every detail. The waves crashed in a rhythm that hypnotized the beat of my heart, and a feeling of peace swept over me—of rightness.

I wasn't sure how long I stood out there, but the bare skin of my shoulders had a slight chill when Cruz found me.

"There you are," he said, his voice a low rumble in my ear as he wrapped his arms around me from behind.

"It's beautiful."

"You are beautiful," he whispered in my ear. "Do you want the good news?"

"Of course."

"There are no other Americans checked in—or checking in. Just you and me."

I turned in his arms. "How did you figure that out?"

"The receptionist was more than favorable to a little bribery," he answered with a grin.

My forehead puckered. Bribery meant he'd spent money, and by the looks of this place, our stay tonight wasn't going to be cheap.

"Penelope Carstairs, don't you dare even think about asking if I can afford this place," Cruz chastised softly, reading my mind.

"It's gorgeous—"

"And I'm fine. I've been working since I was fourteen years old. I'm well invested, and while I definitely don't own a cruise ship, my mortgage company thinks I'm pretty dependable."

It was on the tip of my tongue to offer to pay. The money meant nothing to me. I made more on a single commercial for Gremlin or anything Fox promoted. But that look in his eyes told me that was never going to happen, so I smiled instead and said the only thing I could think of. "Thank you."

His smile was more beautiful than the sunset.

"Don't worry, I'll let you sneak me away one night to make up for it when we're back in L.A."

I blinked, trying to ignore the swell of my heart that threatened to swallow my throat. "Back in L.A.?"

"Well, yeah. We do dock in seven weeks, right? I figured I'd be going home…and you'd be going there, too, right? With me?"

"You…you still want to be with me when this is over?" I asked softly, scared of the answer, because I wasn't sure if it would affect how badly I wanted him and subsequently what that would say about me.

"Penelope, do you really think I'd risk everything to be with you if I didn't see a future for us? You're not a fling. You're not someone to pass the time with. I'm in this way too deep and way too fast, but that doesn't change my feelings. Unless you don't feel the same?"

"How could I not feel the same? I just know that when we get home, you'll have your choice of any woman you want. I'm not stupid or blind. And that's not some insecure cue for you to reassure me—it's the truth. The same as I know I'll be hounded by guys on the circuit who all want to add me to their trophy cases. But I also know that I'm complicated, and kind of a pain in the ass—"

He stopped my word vomit with a soft kiss, gently running his tongue along the seam of my lips but not asking for entrance. "You are all that and more. You challenge every belief I've ever held about relationships, and I have a feeling you'll keep that up, which I am more than fine with. I'm not an easy man, and you're anything but an easy woman, but together we are effortless, because I can't imagine any other possibility."

Swoon alert: aisle three.

"Now, can I get us settled in our room so I can take you to dinner?"

I nodded, my powers of speech momentarily paralyzed by the utterly perfect words he'd said. We rode the elevator, our hands linked. Could this be what my life would look like in a few months? A few years?

Hotels in foreign countries after expos, Cruz at my side. Me cooking dinner while he graded papers, or him changing the bandages on whatever I'd managed to rip apart that week. I'd been so focused on getting him now, I'd been ignoring the possibility of what could happen in the future. And that future sounded really damn good.

With a *ding*, the elevator doors opened, and we found our suite.

"This is gorgeous," I said, seeing the comfortable living room, spacious bathroom, and plush bedroom. Our balcony looked out over the ocean, and the breeze gently ruffled the sheers.

"I figured if we were closed in here, it had better be someplace worth being closed in to. I don't know if we'll get another chance until Buenos Aires, and I wanted to make the most of it." He set our bags on the dresser. "Do you want to head down to dinner?"

I knew exactly what I wanted for dinner, and he was standing right in front of me. "I'd rather stay in," I said softly.

The air between us felt electric.

"Penelope," he whispered, those gorgeous brown eyes darkening as everything about his posture changed from relaxed to alert and ready.

I crossed the small distance between us, my heart rate picking up with every step I took until I stood in front of him, my hand on his chest. "I don't know how to seduce a man, Cruz. You're the only experience I have in that department. So pretend I've tossed my hair, or done some really erotic striptease or whatever it takes, and just know that I'd like to stay in."

His chest expanded with a swift intake of his breath, and one of his hands wove through my hair to grip lightly. "You are a walking, talking seduction. There is nothing you have to say for me to want you, nothing you have to do. You have been a fever I can't break since that first night in the bar, way before you ever asked me to jump with you. You want me?

Good, because I'm fucking desperate to get my hands on you. Just say the words."

My tongue swept out to wet my lips, and I looked him straight in the eyes. "I want you to make love to me. Those words good enough for you?"

"Yeah, those will do," he said a millisecond before his mouth met mine.

His kiss felt different from every other time—a little more wild, unrestrained, but still deliciously thorough. He kissed like a man who knew where this was going but wasn't in a rush to get there.

My fingers undid the buttons on his shirt. This time I'd explore him, touch and taste as much as I wanted. We weren't due back until the class excursion at noon tomorrow, and I planned to use every minute to my advantage.

By the time we left this room I would know every inch of Cruz.

He shrugged out of the shirt without breaking our kiss, his skin exposed and warm beneath my fingers. I'd always loved tattoos, and the one on his arm was a powerful reminder of his past—and a huge turn-on—but there was something to be said for yards of firm, untouched caramel skin draped over cords of strong muscle.

I broke our kiss to place one on his chest, running my mouth down the line of his pecs and flicking my tongue over one of his nipples.

He sucked in his breath, and I smiled. God, it was going to be so much fun to control him for once.

I pushed him backward, and he fell to the bed laughing, his feet hanging off the end. "This time you're naked first," I ordered as he grinned up at me, his weight braced on his elbows.

"Think you can break my control?"

I quirked an eyebrow at him as I slid the strap of his

belt free from its buckle. "Think I can't?" God, his abs were perfection, flexed in a perfect curve as he sat there. That line that drove me nuts ran in perfect symmetry down his sides, disappearing inside his boxers.

I followed them with my finger, savoring the way the muscles tensed under my touch.

"Oh, I'm well aware that you can, and if you had any idea of the fantasies that had played out in my head the last seven weeks, you wouldn't doubt it for a second."

My knees hit the floor after I slid off the bed, and I made quick work of his dress shoes and socks, listening to them fall to the floor with a satisfying thud. "Fantasies, huh?" I asked, hooking my fingers into the waist of his now-undone pants and taking his boxers for good measure.

Trying to steady my already-quick breaths, I tugged, keeping my eyes on his as I removed the last of his clothing, careful not to catch his erection.

"This would definitely be one of them." Our eyes locked as I stood at the foot of the bed. "You can look. God knows I'm going to do the same to you in a moment."

Biting my lower lip, I let my eyes drop over the smooth expanse of chest, to his washboard stomach, to—*holy shit* he was impressive. I tore my eyes away from his length and finished my open perusal of his strong thighs. The man definitely didn't skip leg day—I stared at his ass often enough to know.

"God, you're…you're…" I couldn't think of words that would do his body justice, and that didn't even include the perfection of his face.

"Yours. I'm yours."

He lay there so calmly that if I didn't see his fists in the covers, tightening over the fabric, I might have thought he was relaxed, almost unaffected.

Well, that and his giant, gorgeous erection. Could

erections be gorgeous? His was all smooth and strong, and…
My fingers found him, closing around the silken skin and
squeezing lightly. Oh yeah, so freaking hard.

"Penelope," he moaned my name, his head rolling back.

My hand ran up and down, watching his every reaction.
His hips rolled once, then stayed still, the look on his face
nearly painful. His eyes were closed, as if watching me would
be too much.

I let go, running my hands up the sides of his abs and
crawling onto the bed until my knees were between his
outstretched thighs. I kissed a path up his stomach, and as if it
was my own being caressed, my body temp rose, and a steady,
sweet ache grew between my thighs.

One of his hands massaged the back of my head as I
reached the strong cords of his neck.

"You about done playing?" he asked, his voice scratchy
and deep.

I pulled back enough to look into his eyes, which were
anything but playful. They were intense under the dark black
brows, as if I'd woken a beast who was trying his best to stay
caged.

"If I say no?" My leg ran up the inside of his thigh and
over until I straddled it.

"I'm trying, Penelope," he warned.

I kissed the smooth line of his jaw until his earlobe was
between my lips, and I ran my teeth along the flesh gently.
"Quit trying."

He flipped me over so fast I was shocked I didn't have
whiplash. With a quick motion, he lifted my weight with one
arm and settled my head on the pillow as he rose above me.
"My turn."

The sound of a zipper filled the quiet as he opened my
dress, his eyes growing darker, his breath deeper with every
inch of skin revealed. His gaze slid over my black lace bra, and

he muttered something in Spanish, then past the matching panties until my entire dress lay open on either side of me.

"Tell me you're certain," he begged as his hand ran from my throat, over the center of my bra, and down my stomach.

"Is this where you tell me that this is my last opportunity to say stop? That after this you won't be able to control yourself?" I half teased, half hoped he'd say yes.

Instead he placed a hot, wet kiss between my breasts, then peeled the straps of my dress from my arms, waiting for me to arch so he could get the dress off entirely.

"You read too many books." He laughed, then stopped, kissing my neck.

I groaned as he found my trigger point, wrapping one of my legs around his hips.

He pulled back, then slid his hands down my thighs, over my knees, past my calves, until he slipped my heels off, throwing them to the floor. Then he traced a path up my leg, punctuating his words with kisses. "You can say stop at any moment, and I'll listen. I'm never too far gone to do what's best for you. That being said, God, I hope you don't want me to stop."

He nipped gently at the skin of my inner thigh, and I whimpered as he soothed it with a kiss and a stroke of his tongue. My hips rolled, growing more restless with each passing moment.

I wasn't a prude; I'd thought about sex before. But this was nothing like the hurried, hard, union I'd pictured when I'd wondered what it would be like. I didn't even have words for what this was, but I knew I wanted—*needed*—more.

His breath blew over my panties a second before he placed a kiss to my lace-covered cleft, his nose lightly pushing so that the fabric brushed against my clit.

I gasped, my fingers fisting in his hair.

"Tell me you're certain," he repeated.

"I'm certain." I'd never been more certain about anything in my life.

He backed away and stood, which brought me up on my elbows. Before I could ask if I'd said something wrong, he crossed the room toward his bag, that magnificent ass flexing with every movement.

Suddenly the vision struck of me grasping onto that ass while he pushed inside me, and I nearly groaned from my own erotic thoughts.

He pulled something out of his bag and returned to me, tossing a condom on the nightstand.

"I'm on birth control, too," I told him. "So we're double protected." Nothing was worse for a girl than an unpredictable cycle on circuit.

"Good to know," he told me, settling back between my thighs. Before I could take a full breath, he'd drawn my panties to the side and ran his tongue through my folds, then spread me and sucked at my clit.

"Holy. Oh. My. *God*. Cruz!" I yelled, my hips bucking against him, seeking out his mouth. I smothered my yell, slamming my hand over my mouth.

Cruz leaned up over me, blocking everything from my vision but him. As he licked my taste off his lips, he pulled my hand away. "Scream as loud as you want. I don't give a fuck what the neighbors think."

He kissed me, long and hard, and by the time he pulled away, my legs moved restlessly against him. That sweet tension spiraled tight, the sensation its own desperate demand to be appeased.

I lifted my hips when he met my eyes and dragged my panties down my legs until they joined my shoes on the floor. Then his lips were between my thighs, licking, sucking, kissing, never ceasing.

My hips moved, riding against his mouth, chasing the high

I knew he'd bring me to. My skin flushed as pleasure whipped through my body, building and weaving into something impossibly, gloriously tight and tense.

His name was a plea on my lips as he worshipped me.

"You taste incredible. I could stay here all night. Tomorrow, too," he said, then continued his onslaught.

My whimpers grew to full-blown moans as I gave over to the feelings coursing through me. I became pure sensation, my entire being focused on the incredible way he made me feel—like I was lighter than air and could fly away at any second, all while being anchored to the ground by his hands, his mouth.

When his fingers entered me, stretched me, my hips changed their rhythm to meet him, relishing in the full pressure, the slight burn.

"God, you're so tight, Penelope. I can't wait to be inside you, to feel you ripple on my cock when you come."

Whether it was what he said or the way he stroked my inner walls, he had me mindless with the combination of overwhelming pleasure and stark need.

My muscles locked, then quaked as his perfect fingers sent me over the edge. I screamed his name as the orgasm took me, rocking through me in waves of bliss. When I came back down, I was limp, boneless, and I was sure my weak, sated smile had nothing on Cruz's. He looked like he'd swallowed the sun.

He kissed me, settling a portion of his weight on me, and as I arched under him at the contact of our skin, he slid a hand behind my back and undid my bra with a snap of his fingers.

A moment later I was finally as naked as he was.

His mouth worshipped my breasts, reigniting the fire I was sure he'd already put out. Each tug on my nipple, each stroke of his tongue brought that need back to the surface until it burned brighter than before.

His fingers stroked through my wetness, and I swore I saw him shake a little. "Perfection." Then he ripped the foil package open and covered himself. I'd never seen a more erotic sight—he was giving me so many firsts tonight.

His knees between my thighs, my muscles tensed as his hardness brushed my entrance. I closed my eyes, bracing for whatever came next. It shouldn't hurt, right? I'd done extreme sports my whole life, so it wasn't like I was about to bleed. And sure, he was huge, but it's not like he wasn't going to fit or some other absurd idea.

"Penelope," he called my name, and my eyes popped open to meet his. A ghost of a smile passed over his lips before he kissed me, long and deep.

Like he'd forgotten that his erection was *right there*, he thumbed my nipple, kissed my throat, and brought that fire right back to raging.

"Tell me you're certain," he ordered, rocking against me so that he slid through my folds. His eyes slowly shut as he hissed.

"We already had this portion of the conversation." My arms looped around his neck.

"I'm not kidding. I don't want you to have any regrets about what happens between us tonight." One of his thumbs brushed my cheekbone as his eyes searched my face for any sign of indecisiveness. "I've never done this before, you know, and I want it to be perfect for you."

"Sex? You've never had sex?"

He kissed my nose. "Been someone's first. Been *your* first."

"I guess we're both in virgin territory," I said with a grin, running my nails down his back lightly.

He groaned, arching into my touch. "Penelope," he said in half warning, half moan.

I waited until our gazes met and then kissed him, sucking

on his lower lip lightly. "I've never been more certain of anything in my life than I am at this moment."

He nodded, the muscles in his jaw flexing like he struggled for control.

"God, I'm crazy about you. Literally fucking insane," he told me. There was no chance to respond—not with his tongue licking into my mouth while his fingers stroked inside me with a smooth, hot push. He added a third, and I welcomed the sting, knowing he was way bigger than those three fingers.

I rocked with him, moving against his hand until I was just as desperate as I had been earlier and in complete wonder that he could bring those feelings on again with such intensity.

His fingers were replaced by the head of his erection, and while one of his hands gripped my thigh, the other was gentle on my face. "Tell me if you need me to stop," he whispered.

The earlier nervousness was gone, replaced by a feeling of not only need but adoration, and something much sweeter, so much more dangerous that I shoved it to the side and concentrated on our bodies.

Then he pushed inside, slowly and surely, never once looking away from me. I took a stuttered breath as he slid in farther, the burn present but not painful. Instead, I felt full, like every empty place in my body, my soul, my heart, had been consumed by Cruz. My eyes stung with the perfection of it, and I blinked back the tears as our bodies merged completely.

"Are you okay?" he asked, softly wiping away one I hadn't caught.

"More than okay," I assured him. I moved a fraction of an inch and was rewarded by a burst of deep pleasure that was unlike anything I'd ever felt. "God, that's amazing."

"Just wait," he promised, sweat dotting his forehead.

This man was huge, so strong, so powerful, and yet he was so completely tender and careful with me. I tilted my hips and then rocked them back as he slid within me, dragging through my most sensitive flesh.

"Penelope. God. Don't. Give yourself a second." His forehead puckered, and his eyes slid shut as he groaned.

The sound was gorgeous, and I wanted to hear it again immediately, so I rocked again, this time a little more forcefully. "I'm okay," I promised, knowing he held back on my account. I wanted all of him—no holding back, no pretending we weren't wild about each other. Just every raw ounce he had to give me.

"Promise?"

"Promise."

Watching me carefully, he pulled out until he was nearly unsheathed, then slid back in with a moan.

Holy shit, that felt good.

"You're so fucking tight. Perfect."

"More." It was the only word that came to mind. He felt so good that I could nearly taste the pleasure, sweet and heady.

Forehead braced on mine, he slowly pumped, starting an unhurried, sensual rhythm that made me gasp every time he left me and moan softly with every rejoining. "Faster," I begged. "God, please, Cruz."

"I don't want to hurt you." His breath was slightly unsteady, the muscles in his arms rigid.

"Don't hold back. We only have tonight here." Then we'd be on the ship—where we had to hide, had to sneak kisses. Had to cover our moans, or worse—stay away from each other.

His mouth consumed mine, the motions of his tongue in time with his thrusts, as the rhythm picked up—stronger, harder, but not faster. I brought my knees up to take him deeper, my cries echoing off the walls of our room.

God, this…this was worth everything. He was worth everything. Just the ability to hold him, to take him inside my body, to show him without words how I felt about him was worth every time I had to keep my eyes off him, every time I couldn't claim him.

Since I couldn't tell the world he was mine, I branded him with my body instead.

The man pushed me on and upward, his pace never slowing, never changing as my body coiled around his. My nails scored his back, and I braced my feet on the bed, rocking to meet him with every thrust.

"God, baby," he moaned. "My Penelope."

The hand that cradled my leg slid up the inside of my thigh, until he'd moved a thumb between us. He expertly stroked my clit, swirling and rubbing, taking every thought out of my head except the buildup of pressure in my belly that was slowly drawing me inward.

"Cruz," I whimpered, then yelled. How could he build me up like this again? Bring me to this edge so quickly?

"Right there. Can you feel it coming?"

"Yes!"

"Then let go." He pushed in, giving my body the exact pressure it needed to let go as he slammed home, and I saw stars. My vision faded, the edges going black as I came, too consumed to even scream.

"So fucking beautiful," he said softly as I drifted back down.

My breath came in giant gulps as his thrusts increased, our sweat-slick bodies sliding together as we met over and over again.

I locked my ankles and braced my hands against the headboard as his rhythm became frantic, his face taut with tension and wonder.

Then he pushed one more time, so deep that I gasped, and he shuddered above me with a deep groan. My arms cradled him, and I tried to take in every detail of this moment, from the pounding of my heart, the shortness of breath, to the way his weight stopped just short of crushing me.

He sucked in a shaky breath, and then rolled us to the side, brushing a damp tendril of my hair from my face.

We stayed like that for precious minutes, looking at each other while our breathing steadied, his hands lightly stroking my waist, my hip, my arm.

"Are you okay?" he asked.

"Better than. I'm just about perfect. *That* was perfect. Is it…is it always like that?" I hated asking, but I needed to know if it was as earth-shattering for him as it was for me, or if it was simply another time he'd had sex.

"It's never been like that for me," he answered softly, his thumb sliding across my lower lip. "Everything about you is a revelation."

I snuggled closer, tucking my head under his as his arms wrapped around me.

"You are the scariest, most addictive woman I've ever been around, and after that, Penelope, I'm not sure I'll ever get enough of you. Are you sore?"

I took stock of my body, noting the slight throb coming from between my thighs. "A little."

I winced as he slipped free.

"Wait here."

Rolling over, I openly admired his ass again as he made his way to the bathroom. A flush later, I heard running water.

"What are you doing?" I asked.

"Drawing you a bath. It should help with the soreness."

"You are a prince among men," I told him, stretching as he came back in, the water steadily flowing in the bathroom behind him.

He bit his lip, his eyes taking on that gleam I knew was desire as he looked over my body. "I wish I had pure intentions. I'm just hoping I can get you comfortable enough to take you again before we have to go back to the ship," he added with a wiggle of an eyebrow. "I wasn't kidding about not getting enough of you. How the hell are we going to keep this under wraps? I'm pretty sure my need for you is going to be impossible to hide."

"I guess we'd better make the most of our alone time," I suggested as he effortlessly lifted me into his arms.

Room service and two more orgasms later, I fell asleep curled in his arms, realizing that he'd ruined me for anyone else. I wasn't sure anyone could ever hold a candle to tonight—to Cruz.

When I woke a few hours later, it was to the *click* of our bedroom door as Cruz walked back in. I blinked, sleepy-drunk and trying to make sense of what was going on. "Is it time to go?"

He placed a thick envelope into his bag and started stripping.

"No, baby. I just needed a walk," he said softly, kissing me on the forehead.

He stripped, and I forgot all about his late-night need for fresh air as he replaced my breath with his, taking me slowly, sweetly, carefully, but with no less passion than before. I came apart under him, unraveling so completely that I wasn't sure I was me anymore as much as I was his.

Finally spent with bone-deep exhaustion, I tumbled into a deep sleep and, for once, my reality was even better than the dreams that waited for me.

Chapter Twenty-Three

PENNA

AT SEA

"Something is different," Rachel said the next evening as I studied at our dining room table.

I looked up from my calculus book and took a sip of my post-workout protein smoothie Landon was torturing me with. "With what?"

She sat down across from me, folded her arms, and narrowed her eyes. "With you."

I felt the sudden urge to swipe at my forehead just in case "Gave Up My V-Card" had been tattooed overnight. "I don't know what you mean."

"You're happy," she accused.

"Happy is a crime?"

"Happy is odd for you, lately."

I did a quick assessment. Physically I was sore in a way I'd never experienced before. *Because you've never had someone inside you before, duh.* Emotionally…huh. "I guess you're right. I'm kind of happy."

"Who is he?"

I scoffed and took a completely obvious sip of my disgusting smoothie. "What the hell does your boyfriend put in these?"

"The tears of my enemies. Now *who* is he?"

I shut my math book and stood. "I have no idea who you're talking about."

"Yeah, okay," she mocked. "Seriously. You didn't come home last night, you're all secretive in your room lately, and now you're all glowy and shit. I know one thing does that to a girl, and it's a guy, so who is he, Penna?"

"Maybe I'm happy because I aced last week's geography test. Maybe I'm happy because I've been getting enough sleep, or because I'm back in the gym. Exercise causes endorphins, you know."

"Uh-huh. So does sex."

I rolled my eyes at her and took my book to my room, dropping it on the stack that consumed my desk.

"You know I wouldn't tell the others, right?" she asked softly, leaning against my doorframe. "I owe you for so many things, and you were there for me when you most definitely didn't have to be, given our history. I just want to make sure that you're okay and that you know I'm here. Leah's here, too, just…you know…down the hall."

I smiled and hugged her to me, squeezing her tiny frame. "Yes, I know. And thank you. I promise that if it's something that needs to be talked about, I'll do the talking with you, okay?"

She pursed her lips and openly glared at me before softening when she realized she wasn't going to win this battle. "Yeah. Okay. Fine," she threw over her shoulder and left me in peace.

Rachel was right. I was happy. All the shit with Brooke, my parents' selfish defense of her dismissive cruelty, it all faded away with the thought of how simply, beautifully happy I was with Cruz. And that had been *before* the sex. Now I was just blissed-out on cloud nine.

Was this how Rachel felt about Landon when they cheated on Pax? How Pax felt about Leah when we told him it wasn't safe for him to fall for his tutor? If so, I finally understood why they had risked everything, their very souls at times, to be together—to keep this feeling.

I stared at myself in the mirror, wondering if I could see a physical change. Other than more muscle definition from my enforced gym time, I looked exactly the same. Except my eyes. Those were brighter. They weren't sunken in anymore, or shadowed. I looked like me again.

A blob of pink caught my eye, and I turned to see my lucky Fox bandana hanging off the corner of my bed frame. Before I lost the urge, I plucked it from its resting place and took off, barely remembering a key on my way out.

With single-minded focus, I ignored everything on my trip to the fourth deck, unwilling to let anything distract me in case I lost courage. Bursting through the door to the mechanic shop, I looked around at the team working. Every head turned to look at me, including Pax's.

"Everyone get out." My voice carried across the space, clear and decisive. "I'm not kidding, get the hell out!"

Pax's eyebrows shot toward the roof, but he cleared his throat. "You heard Rebel, get out."

One by one, the CTDs filed out. Pax never let a single Crash Test Dummy near a bike or any other piece of equipment until they knew how to destroy it and rebuild it from the ground up.

Pax walked over, camera crew in tow.

"You okay? Need me?"

I smiled and patted his arm. "Not this time. But if you could take them with you?"

"Your contract—" Victor started.

"Fuck my contract, or the next time I'll tell Doc to let you fly overboard, got it?" I snapped. There was zero chance I was letting this happen on camera. Not if there was even the slightest chance I couldn't do it.

"And that's your cue to leave," Pax said to Victor, slapping him on the back. The man took one more look at me and vacated the room.

"You too, Pax," I said softly.

"Look, whatever you're going through—"

"Isn't something you can help me with, otherwise I would have come to you after Dubai. You like to fix things. After being your best friend for the past, oh, seventeen years, I've caught on to your ways. I need to fix this myself."

His gaze dropped to where I had my bandana clutched in my hand. "Okay. You know I love you, right? There's nothing I wouldn't do for you."

"I know."

He swallowed and conceded the battle, closing the door on his way out. I knew what walking away cost him, and loved him all the more for it.

Alone in the mechanic shop, I walked toward where Elizabeth rested, held up by her travel stand Landon had made to safely house the bikes on the rough seas. I ran my hand over her smooth seat, across the gauge, and up to the handles, as if I was introducing myself again to her.

"I'm so sorry it's taken me this long," I said quietly. "It's not that I blamed you for what happened; I blamed my own choices. I thought if I returned to you that it meant everything that happened with Brooke meant nothing, like I was throwing my sister away if I went back to what I love. But that's not true, and the more I find myself, the more I know the biggest piece of me that's missing is you."

I swung my leg over Elizabeth and settled into the seat.

Home.

My hands flexed on her handles, and my eyes closed, my body finding the immediate balance and peace. I moved with the dips of the ship, and I knew it was time. This was where I belonged, and I couldn't let Brooke take this from me.

She'd taken enough already.

It didn't mean that I didn't love her, didn't worry about her. It simply meant that I couldn't live my life running from her fears. I hopped off Elizabeth's back and walked over to the supply section of Pax's shop, where everything was crated and carefully contained.

Then, with my thoughts on every pitch of the ship, I methodically changed her oil and performed some routine maintenance, losing myself in the actions I'd performed thousands of times.

When I was done, I washed my hands and opened the door to find Pax and Landon sitting with their backs against the wall in the middle of the hallway. They looked up with cautious optimism.

"Scared I was going to steal shit?" I asked with a grin.

Landon sighed in relief, then jumped to his feet, pulling me into a bear hug. "More scared we were going to hear the sounds of you beating the shit out of your bike."

"Nawh," I said, hugging him right back. "You guys want to come with me for a second? I think I have a plan."

They both nodded, then soundlessly followed me to my suite, knowing I'd only talk when I was good and damn ready. I brought my laptop out to our dining room and, filled with sheer jealousy, blatantly ignored Rachel sitting on Landon's lap.

Two months. Then you can go public.

A tiny skip of joy in my heart, I hacked into the ship's internet system, using precious bandwidth to connect to the net. Then I fired up Skype and hit Nick's name.

A few rings later, he picked up, those blond curls and

contagious smile filling the screen.

"Well, if it isn't my favorite Rebel. What can I do for you, girl?"

"You still there with Little John?"

"Yeah, he's working on some stuff with me. Miss him already?"

"Always. Look. I know you don't want to come down here. I know you're not ready to go public, and I'm about to ask you to chance it."

He leaned forward. "Penna, what's going on?"

"When Little John comes to Buenos Aires with my ramp, I need you to come, too. We'll need on-the-spot ramp modifications that only you will be able to accomplish."

Those eyes went dead serious, and I could all but feel Pax and Landon breathing down my neck behind me. "You have my attention."

"I know what I want to do for the Cuba open, and I might not be in shape yet, but I still have two months to get there and at least four ports, if you can move ramps that fast for practice."

He arched an eyebrow, waiting for me to drop the bomb.

"I'm going to be the first woman to complete a freestyle motocross double backflip."

"You're fucking kidding me," Pax growled.

I spun. "Seriously, Mr. Gotta-nail-the-triple-front?"

"The bike is too heavy. You know that. That's why it's never been done. It can kill you," he fired back.

"Then we drop as much weight as we can from the bike. Strip it to the barest of bones."

"No."

"You don't get to tell me *no*. You're not my dad, my boyfriend, or my sponsor. What you *are* is my best friend, and it's your job to shut the fuck up and support me just like we've *all* done for you."

His fists flexed on the back of the chair.

"Landon?" I asked, abandoning Pax to his temper tantrum.

He raked his hand over his hair and blew out his breath in a long sigh. "You're determined to do this?"

"I am," I said, not realizing just how badly until the words escaped.

"Okay. Well, you have a bigger shot at not killing yourself if we're all on board. You went to twenty-one thousand feet for me, and I'm ready to go to hell for you. I'm in. We'll get you stronger, but you have to be willing to put in the work."

Hope blossomed in my chest. It was one thing to make the choice, and another to know my family was ready to back me up.

"Nick?" I asked.

Out of all of us, Nick had lost the most in pursuit of a trick. If anyone had a reason to tell me no, it was him. But if anyone understood what it was like to chase the impossible… well, he had that spot, too.

"Maybe if we construct foam pits at each port until Cuba. I'll contact the FMX tracks there and see what they've got. It's going to cost us some money in material and crew to assemble at every port when there're only days between them, but it can be done. You have my support, even if I think you're a little nuts."

"I would totally hug you if you were here," I told him, wishing more than anything that he'd come with us, that the Originals were whole through more than a computer screen.

"Give me a few weeks and you can. I'll meet you in Buenos Aires in three weeks. Pax, can you keep the cameras the fuck away from me?"

We all turned to look at Pax, who'd backed against the bar that separated our dining room from our mini-kitchen, his arms folded across his chest.

"Hey, Wilder," Nick shouted. "You might be the leader of our little troop, but all four of us are the Originals. We have equal say, and when three go against four, the three win."

Pax's jaw ticked.

"So you don't have to agree with her, but you'd better damn well support her, because the last time we weren't fully there for one another I ended up in this goddamned chair."

Pax's head snapped up. "That's not fair."

"I'm not blaming you. I haven't in a long time. But I'm in here because I didn't wait for you. I competed against you, went on my own, and didn't have everyone there telling me when I'd pushed too far, or compensating for my idiocy. So you don't have to agree with Penna, but you will fucking support her, because that's what we do."

Pax looked at me, the weight of the world dimming his eyes. "What if you get hurt? What if you're the next one paralyzed?"

"What if I live every day with that fear and never get out of bed? Come on, Pax. I'm just like you. Just like Landon and Nick. You can't protect me from the same choices you'd make. You can't shield me from myself, from what we've made one another."

A long moment passed where it could have gone either way. Nick was right. We didn't need him, but I wanted him to be there for me the same way I'd always been for him.

"Okay, I'm with you."

My shoulders drooped with relief. The last thing I wanted on my mind at the same time I was trying to pull this off was infighting with my brothers. "Thank you."

"But I'm not the one who has to sign off on it."

"What?" Nick asked.

My eyes slid shut as my stomach hit the floor. "Fuck my life."

"She has to convince Dr. Delgado."

Chapter Twenty-Four

CRUZ

Three weeks. That's how long I'd had Penelope in my bed. They had been—without a doubt—the best and hardest three weeks of my life. The best because I had her curled into me at night, her soft moans in my ear, her body so sweetly encasing mine.

The hardest because it got more difficult every single day to keep my feelings—and our relationship—secret.

I'd gone surfing with her off the coast of Chile, sledded down the glaciers in Patagonia, made love to her as we passed through the Strait of Magellan, and when we'd passed through Cape Horn, the southernmost tip of our journey, I knew she would be what pointed me north when this was all over.

In a little over a month, we'd be able to go public. I could hold her hand, kiss her, claim her. Even though Penelope put off a don't-touch-me vibe, it didn't stop the guys from thinking they'd be the one to change her mind.

She still went to the bar as per her contract. Still danced, still smiled, still acted every bit the Rebel, and on nights when I chaperoned that little meat market, I sat like a tiny ball of rage, unable to tell each and every one of those asshats to fuck right off and leave my girlfriend alone.

Because they didn't know she was my girlfriend. No one did.

Every time she smiled at me, laughed with me, hell, even when she ignored me in public, I fell a little harder for her, gave a little more of myself over to her.

I gave her my everything. Except Elisa. I hadn't told Penelope my plan, yet. Not because I didn't trust her, but because there was no margin for error. Not even the smallest hitch could happen, or it would all go south.

Which I knew, when she eventually did find out, would sound like I didn't trust her. I just couldn't afford another cog in the clockwork, even if that cog was my very heart and soul right now.

Elisa was my sister, and every complication risked her life all the more.

The minute he caught wind of what we were up to, or so much as stumbled onto her acceptance papers from Harvard, she'd pay in ways that scared the shit out of me. Ways that had cost us our mother.

"You're sure these will work?" I asked the man in Spanish, thumbing through the documents. Elisa's face stared up at me, the same brown eyes I saw in the mirror every day. She looked so much like our mother now, but there was no lingering sadness or defeat about her the way there was about Mom the last time I'd seen her.

"Those will work," he promised.

"Thank you," I said, handing over a huge amount of pesos and leaving his seedy little shop. I grabbed the first cab I saw and told the driver the address of the port as the sun began to rise. If I got back in the next ten minutes, Penelope would never know I'd been missing.

As I got off on deck nine, Lindsay caught up with me. "Early riser?" she asked.

"I could say the same about you. What are you up to?"

"Went for a little walk. It's nice to get off the ship without the students sometimes, you know?"

"I do," I said, thinking that I'd be off the ship in a hotel with Penelope tonight. Alone for the first time since Chile, and I had zero intention of leaving our hotel room.

"What do you have planned today?"

"I'm with the Renegades today, and then I have a cultural excursion tomorrow. Hey, it includes a tango demonstration. You should come with if you don't already have one of your own."

Her eyes lit up, and I cursed inwardly. I'd meant it in a friendly fashion, but Lindsay still hadn't given up.

"I'd love to!"

"Great, I'll email you the details."

I made my excuses and got into my suite as quickly as possible, shutting my bedroom door. Penelope was already gone, no doubt at the gym with Landon. She'd been a maniac lately with twice-a-day workouts. Her body was perfect already, but she kept mumbling something about not being strong enough, and I'd lose her to the weight room. Not that I was arguing. I loved her body no matter what shape she was currently sporting.

I hid this set of documents with the others, my little treasure trove growing by the week. There was only one more piece I needed, and though it had to wait until right before we docked, I was going to need Penelope's help to get it.

But that was something I'd worry about closer to that date.

I checked the time and placed the call.

"Cruz!" Elisa called out.

"Hey! How are you?" I got that immediate shot of relief that nothing had happened to her since the last time I'd made contact.

"I'm great. Where are you now?"

"Argentina."

"That's amazing. Everything still okay?"

"I don't have a lot of time, but I wanted to tell you that I have it." I lowered my voice, as if there was a chance I'd be overheard on her end.

"You do? It's real?"

"As real as it gets until we get you a legal one."

"It's going to happen, isn't it? You're really coming?"

"You just hold on, Elisa. I'm on my way."

I was getting her the hell out of there, no matter what it cost me.

• • •

"So how exactly did you manage this?" I asked a couple hours later, staring at the biggest ramp I'd ever seen.

"I called in a few favors," a blond guy said, wheeling over. "I'm Nick. You must be Doc."

"So they tell me," I said, shaking his hand. "Penna talks about you a lot."

"Oh yeah? All I've heard about you is what a giant pain in the ass you are." He grinned, but he was completely blocked from my vision as Penelope came barreling past me, launching herself into his lap.

"Nick!"

"Man, it's a good thing I can't feel anything south of the border, because you're probably crushing me." He laughed as he hugged her back. "Damn it's good to see you, girl."

"You, too," she said, pulling back with a huge grin. "Thank you for coming all the way down here. You have no clue what it means to me."

"Yeah, I do." His hands felt up her biceps, and I did my best not to hit the kid. "Damn. You kept your word. Two-a-days?"

"I'm an asshole," Landon said, moving Penna out of the way so he could take her spot on Nick's lap. "Santa, for Christmas I would like—"

"Get off me, asshat." Nick laughed, and Landon hopped up only to be replaced by Pax leaning in to hug him.

"Good to see your face," Wilder said.

"Yours, too," Nick answered.

"Little John, my man!" Landon said as an enormous—

Holy shit.

"Penelope," I whispered so only she could hear me. "Is that?"

"I'll take care of it," she promised, not looking at me before she ran off to embrace the guy who had been our getaway driver after the High Roller BASE jump.

His eyes flew wide as he saw me—recognized me. "Hey, aren't you—"

Penelope got to him before he finished that sentence, dragging him away from the crowd. I watched their discussion, which was obviously heated, from the corner of my eye as the crew brought in the motorcycles. Among them were two minibikes.

"What are those for?" I asked Wilder.

"Practice," he answered.

"Practice for what?"

His eyes widened, and he glanced between Penelope and me before calling her name. She ran back over, a flush in her cheeks that had nothing to do with excitement, if I had to guess by the look she shot me.

"What's up?" she asked.

"Doc would like to know what the minibikes are for," Pax said with a false sweetness.

That flush of color deepened as she turned to me. "I'm learning a new trick today, and so is Zoe."

I'd signed off on FMX practice, so I wasn't surprised. "Okay, but you need baby bikes for it?"

Pax laughed and slapped her on the back lightly. "Oh God, this is too much fun."

"Shut up," she muttered toward him. "Currently I'm one of the only women in the world who can backflip a motocross bike."

"Right."

"Zoe would like to learn. So we brought in a minibike because she'll need to get the flip first before we can add in the weight of a full-sized bike. She's been working out, her muscles are building, and this is the first step. We have a foam pit to start with, so she won't come to any harm, and I'm the best person to teach her."

My eyes narrowed. "You've also been lifting weights and doing two-a-days, if I'm not mistaken. What exactly will you be doing that requires that kind of buildup?"

She sucked in a breath and raised her chin. Never a good sign when it came to this woman. "I'll be learning how to do a double backflip."

"A double backflip."

"Right."

This was when my lack of experience was glaringly obvious. Jump out of a plane? Got it. BASE jump? No problem. Anything with a parachute and I was golden, but motorcycles? Unless it involved driving it from point A to point B, I was pretty damn clueless. I'd simply trusted that this was their realm and given her the benefit of the doubt.

Obviously I'd fucked up.

"And how many women in the world have ever successfully completed a double backflip?" I asked.

From my peripheral, Pax looked like he was thoroughly enjoying himself, but I didn't take my eyes off Penelope.

"Well, I would be the first."

My jaw snapped closed so fast that my teeth clicked. I sucked in a deep breath and told myself to react as her advisor and not her boyfriend. The fact that this powerhouse of a woman carried my heart within her body couldn't play into this right now. Later…well, that was later.

"Why is it that a woman hasn't completed this trick?"

"Well, typically the bike is too heavy, and the girls can't get enough height or build up enough strength to get the bike around twice before they land," Nick answered, having appeared out of nowhere.

Or I'd just been too focused on Penelope to notice.

I looked up at the massive ramp and the foam pit that lay just beyond it. "And what happens if you can't pull the bike around for the second rotation?"

"She lands on her head and snaps her neck," Nick said with a shrug.

Holy fucking shit, I was going to be sick. I'd seen battle wounds, held one of my friends as he died, and still I'd never felt the gut-shaking nausea that gripped me when I pictured that happening to my Penelope.

"That's not going to happen," she snapped at Nick. "Stop trying to scare him. Dr. Delgado?"

I pulled my eyes from the ramp to hers, trying to remember that in this arena I had no claim on her, no right to shake the shit out of her or kiss the stupidity from her beautiful, brilliant head. "Miss Carstairs?" I said as formally as I could manage.

She winced, but not big enough for anyone else to notice. "That's why we have the minibikes. Strength won't be an issue today. Just the motion of the flip, and we have the nets and the pit to make sure we're okay. This is about as safe as we get."

"Today."

"That's all I'm asking you to sign off on right now. Today. Once you see that I can handle it, I'll bring you a proposal with the next step."

"What's going on?" Leah asked, looping her arm around Pax's waist.

"Penna just told Doc about the trick," Wilder answered.

"Oh? Ooooooh."

If we'd been in private, I would have let her have it. Would have let her into my head, where she was about to test the very limits of my sanity. But we were in public, so the best I could do was send a subtle glare in her direction.

"Right, so, if that's all, I'll go get warmed up," Penna said with a forced smile.

The others scattered, and, as Penelope passed me, I whispered, "This conversation is not over."

"I figured as much," she responded, then looked up at me. "But you have to trust me enough to know that this is my job. I know my limits. My friends know my limits. And yeah, I push them, but this is a safe environment, I promise."

"Yeah. Still not over."

"Noted," she said, and walked off to gear up.

I sank into the chair next to Little John, who was under a shaded canopy. The weather was steady in the high seventies, but the sun could still be brutal. "She told you?"

He shook his head and stared me down. "She told me enough for me to know that you shouldn't be doing whatever it is you're doing."

"Yeah, tell me about it."

"You're her *teacher*."

I looked around to make sure the cameras were nowhere near. Of course we were left alone. We were just the stagehands, and the cameras were on the stars. "I wasn't that night we met.

I was just a guy in a bar, and she…she's Penelope."

"You should have come clean to the school, to the other Renegades the moment you both realized it."

Thank you, Jiminy Cricket.

"Yep, but we didn't, and now we're here. I should have been stronger. I should have told her no, but like I said, she's Penelope." I watched my woman walk over to the bikes with Zoe, clad head to toe in protective gear. "And I am apparently a weak man. God, is she really going to be all right?"

Little John looked back and forth between us for a second before sighing. "Today she'll be fine. She's mostly refreshing and working on the mini. Don't stress. And as for being weak, well…I know what it's like to tell that girl no, and if what she wanted was you—*is* you—then you never stood a chance. I'm not sure Gandhi could resist Penna when she wants something. But I've never in my life seen her want a guy, which is why I haven't outed you to the others."

"Thank you," I said, loathing almost every choice I'd made. I hated being on the wrong side of any ethical issue, let alone one this big, but when it came to Penelope, there was no line I wouldn't cross, no evil I wouldn't commit to keep her.

Because I was in love with her.

Fuuuuuck. When had I let that happen? When I'd made love to her in Chile? When we'd fought in the classroom? When my anger at her was overcome by my sheer respect for her fearlessness? Even earlier, when she'd done dishes with me at Grandma's house? Maybe it was even before that, on her birthday when I'd realized I couldn't stay away from her, that she was a magnet and I was a compass, my north facing wherever she moved to.

Or maybe it was from the beginning, when I'd stepped out of that Ferris wheel. Little John was right: I'd never stood a chance.

"But I'll tell you this," he drawled on, and I tuned back in to the conversation. "If you ever hurt her, you won't have to worry about Pax and the boys, because I'll kill you with my bare hands." He cracked the top off a soda like he hadn't just threatened my life and started to drink.

"You won't ever have to worry about that. I'd move heaven and earth to keep that woman safe if she'd just let me."

Little John laughed. "And welcome to life with the Renegades."

. . .

The morning passed in white-knuckled nausea as I watched Penelope first take the ramp with her full-size bike she called Elizabeth. She performed trick after trick to the applause of her friends.

Every time she went airborne, my stomach dipped. Logically, I knew she was good—the best in the world in all actuality—but my heart wouldn't shut the hell up, screaming that she could kill herself at any moment.

This wasn't one stunt that had been meticulously planned and executed once. No, this was hours and hours of prolonged torture with a hundred opportunities for her to get hurt.

When she landed the single back flip perfectly, I split into two sides. The first swelled with pride that she was so fucking spectacular. The second screamed inwardly that she took such needless risks.

They moved the giant pit into place with the help of four forklifts as Penelope worked with Zoe.

"Why Zoe?" I asked as Leah took the chair next to me, the text I'd assigned for history in her lap.

"Because she asked," Leah answered. "Penna knows what it's like to be a woman in a sport that doesn't make a lot of room for them. So she puts the personal shit aside and helps."

"Personal shit?"

"Zoe ties her value to her vagina," Rachel answered standing next to me. "Penna doesn't put up with that, but she's willing to help her out of the hole she dug herself, so that says more about Penna's character than anything."

I slowly brought my gaze around to Rachel's, my eyes wide.

"What?" she shrugged. "That girl is a piece of work."

"Dr. Delgado, may I ask you a question?" Leah opened her book.

"Sure," I answered, my stomach clenching in paranoia. Had I looked at Penelope too long? Smiled too wide? Had Leah put it all together?

"Do you think that Eva Peron made Juan, or that it was more of a mutual rise?" Leah asked. "Sorry, I know it's not office hours, I was just wondering."

Relief flooded me. School questions, I could handle. I almost laughed at how these two women could not be any different, yet they were two of Penna's closest friends.

"Okay, first," I said to Rachel, "What? She's maybe a little flirty, but—"

"Rachel's just pissed that Zoe shacked up with Landon while they were broken up for a couple years. Give her a break, Rach. You won. She lost."

Holy shit, it was like I was back in college, except I'd gone to college through night classes and online courses while I was in the military full-time, so I'd never had this level of drama to contend with.

Completely ignoring everything that had just been said, I turned back to Leah. "Second, Eva Peron was a force of nature who I believe would have helped propel any man she wanted into office, but when coupled with Juan Peron's military experience and general charisma, they were pretty much the power couple of Argentinian politics." I looked back to where the woman I loved used her hands to explain something to Zoe as the three guys looked on. "But I will say that I don't think Juan would have had a chance without her. He was the lucky one in that relationship."

I folded my hands in my lap and bit my tongue, choking back the bile as Penna began to work with the minibike, under-rotating the flip again and again into the foam pit, only to be pulled out by the crane they'd brought over.

Leah looked up and glanced between where Penna failed another attempt and I held my face in my hands. "Don't worry. She'll get it. As for Zoe…" She sighed as Zoe landed on her back in the pit, the small bike on top of her. "She's never had the same dedication as Penna, and these tricks are all about commitment once you're in the air."

As the clock hit about three p.m., Penelope landed the first double rotation, hitting her tires into the pit. She came up with her fist raised, and the Originals rushed toward her, hugging and jumping.

She looked over at me, and I wanted nothing more than to do the same, to wrap her in my arms and tell her how very proud of her I was even though she continually scared the shit out of me.

The look that passed between us felt too intimate for public viewing, but I didn't break eye contact until she did, our smiles soft and saying what we couldn't.

Rachel noticed, lifting an eyebrow at me but saying nothing as she walked off.

Little John knew, and Rachel had suspected since the night of Penna's birthday. We had to be more careful. We had only six weeks left until we docked, and I couldn't afford to mess up now.

Elisa couldn't afford it.

• • •

"You haven't said a thing to me since this morning," Penelope said as she tossed her bag on the canopied bed of our beachfront bungalow.

We were thirty miles outside the city in the quietest, most exclusive resort I could find. Things needed to be said, and we couldn't chance ears or eyes. Plus, I wanted to hear her scream my name again.

Private bungalow it was.

"It's because there's so much to say that I really don't know where I could possibly start," I answered, dropping my bag next to my side of the bed.

"You're pissed about the trick." She crossed her arms under her magnificent breasts, making them rise above the neckline of her pink sundress. Her hair was loose down her back, and, if I didn't know that had been her under all that gear on the bike, I never would have guessed that Rebel was my Penelope.

But she was.

"I'm pissed that you didn't tell me. That you let me walk in blind like an asshole."

"You signed off on practice. You never asked what tricks we'd be doing."

"That's not fair."

"It's true. And you know what else? If you were just my advisor, you wouldn't be half as pissed. You're not pissed at Rebel for not telling you, you're mad at your girlfriend, and that's what's unfair."

"Hell yes, I'm pissed!" I growled, trying to keep my voice down. "How long have you been planning that?"

"About three weeks," she admitted, dropping my gaze.

"And in those three weeks, in *any* of our time together, it never occurred to you to say, 'hey, babe, I'm going to attempt something that might get me killed?' Or did that just slip your mind for twenty-one days?"

"I don't want to fight with you," she said softly.

"I don't really care. If this is the only time we have together to work this out, then we're going to stand here and fight it out."

She bit her lip, and damn I wanted to kiss it free. All day I'd been fighting every instinct in my body that screamed to get my hands on her. I needed to feel her heartbeat, hear her breathing, see her come apart, know that she was really unharmed. Was I going to feel like this after every freestyle session she had? Fuck my life. I'd never survive it.

"You cannot hide this shit from me," I said, trying to maintain some semblance of calm. "Not as your advisor, not as your boyfriend. I'm not going to like everything you do, but you can't blindside me like that."

"I'm sorry, but you don't get a say." She shook her head to emphasize her point.

"I don't what?"

"You. Do. Not. Get. A. Say. You can approve our stunts because of some stupid-ass legal deal, but you don't get a say in what I do with my body. That is my job, Cruz. That is what I've loved to do since I was seven years old, and you don't get to bust into my life and suddenly decide that you are ruler supreme or get mad when I'm doing exactly what I did before you showed up."

"For fuck's sake, Penelope! I'm not just mad, I'm terrified! How hard is that for you to understand? Do you have any idea what it's like to watch someone you love pull the shit that you do? To know that they are more than aware of the danger and that's *why* they didn't tell you? That's not partnership, that's treating me like I'm inferior. At least if I'd known what you were going to do, I could have resigned myself to it more than five minutes before you put on the gear."

"What did you say?" her voice was soft, incredulous.

I raked my hands through my hair, tugging in frustration.

"I said that you scare the ever-loving shit out of me, and you can't seem to understand that I'm having a hard time processing that."

Her mouth dropped open. "No, after that."

"That you don't trust me enough to tell me what the hell you're up to?" I flinched. Shit. I was the pot calling the kettle black here. I hadn't told her anything about Elisa. Not in all the time we'd had together.

Who had two thumbs and was a huge hypocrite? This guy.

But there wasn't a damn thing I could do about that. Telling her may have opened my careful plan up to mistakes, and the bottom line was that it put Penelope in real danger, and I wasn't willing to risk it. Even for Elisa.

"You know what? I'm going to step outside for a moment. I honestly think this argument has made its point. I'm pissed you didn't tell me. You don't think I have a say, and maybe you're right. We're kind of at an impasse, so let's just cool off."

I turned, kicked off my shoes and socks, and walked out of our bungalow through the sliding glass door. The area just outside was shaded by tropical trees, but once I stepped onto our private section of beach, the sand was perfectly warm between my toes. I walked a few yards away to a cave-like grouping of boulders and leaned against the sun-warmed stone.

I had to tell her about Elisa. I couldn't keep it from her anymore, but the risk...all of it was on me. I was the one who would get fired if we were caught. I was the one whose sister wouldn't get to college if I failed, or worse if my father found out what we were up to. I was the one who was in love with Penelope, not the other way around.

When it came to risk in life, Penna might be the one on the ramp, but I was the one without the helmet.

I watched the waves from the Atlantic Ocean come ashore in gentle pulses. The sound was soothing when my brain was such a fucked-up place to be. Closing my eyes, I let the rhythmic crash of the water fill my head, washing away everything else. When I opened them, Penelope stood in front of me.

"Hey." No matter how mad or how scared I'd been, I was ass over head in love with this woman.

"You love me?" she asked quietly, a slight lift to her voice at the end.

Had she just been in my head? "What?"

She licked her lips nervously and then raised her chin. "Inside, you said that I didn't know what it was like to watch someone I love pull the shit that I do. Did you mean it? Do you love me?"

Well, guess I let *that* slip. *Smooth, Cruz. Real romantic right there.*

"Yes," I answered. "I'm in love with you, Penelope. How could I not be? Look at you. You are everything. Beautiful, bold, brilliant, kind. Everything I've ever wanted."

She didn't respond, instead staring up at me with more than a touch of shock, or maybe wonder?

"Penelope?"

Silence was definitely not how I pictured this moment going. Not that I'd ever put much thought into it, but if I had, this was not on my list of desired outcomes. Damn, did I scare her off? Was she that skittish over the *L* word?

Slowly, she lifted her hands to my face and smiled so brightly she could have lit the world with her happiness. As if she'd flicked my "on" switch, I took my first deep breath since letting my feelings slip. That pit in my stomach disappeared, replaced by an emotion I was scared to call hope.

"I love you, Cruz." Her voice was soft but strong—just like she was.

"You don't have to say it just because—"

She shifted her hand so her thumb crossed both my lips.

"I'm not. I'm saying it because it's true. I tried to fight it; our relationship is already so complicated. But if there's one thing I've learned over this last year, it's that we have to say the things that demand to be said. Regret is its own heartbreak, and I refuse to regret a single thing about you— about us. So I'm saying it loudly. I am in love with you. Your honor, your determination, how you treat your family, but mostly I love you for the way you make me feel—cherished, like I'm something precious, protected, but still free. I love you because you're stubborn, and you push back when I'm wrong, but you're strong enough to step aside when I'm right. And yes, I'm glad you said it first, because I'm not sure I would have had the courage to."

I gently took her wrists in my hands, pausing to place a kiss on the inside of her palm before I freed my mouth from her hand. "So you love me."

She raised an eyebrow, and I nearly laughed. "Isn't that what I just said?"

My arms went around her waist, and I tugged her to me. "Yeah, but I'm not sure I'll ever get tired of hearing you say it." I'd never given enough of myself to a woman to love her, and I sure as hell hadn't had one love me.

She leaned up on her tiptoes and pressed a kiss to the outside of my mouth. "I love you," she said. Then placed another along my jaw. "I love you."

"Thank God, because I love you so much I'm not sure how to breathe around how monumental it feels."

I kissed her, sealing my words with my mouth. Before I could press her against the rocks, she backed *me* against the boulder. Her tongue slid into my mouth, all peppermint candy, tangling with mine until I groaned, my hands slipping from her waist to her ass. She kissed the same way she lived— with nothing held back. Was it any wonder that I was madly in love with her?

Her hands ran through my hair, her nails lightly scratching at my scalp, and the little whimpers she made in the back of her throat had me harder than the rock I leaned on. I'd never been so continuously turned on by a woman in my life. It didn't matter how many times I took her—how many ways. The sex got hotter every time we touched.

She stepped back, her breasts rising and falling rapidly. God, she was so beautiful every moment, but when she started to spin out of control? So fucking exquisite.

As if she'd come to some decision to a question I wasn't privy to, her eyes took on a gleam I couldn't discern before she was back, her mouth on my neck. I groaned, leaning my head against the rock.

She tugged at my shirt and I obliged, ripping it over my head.

"I will never get tired of looking at you," she said as her eyes raked over my body. "Or touching you," she whispered as her fingers trailed down the lines of my pecs to the outside of my abs. "Do you trust me?"

"With my life," I responded instantly.

She made me feel like every model and superhero rolled into one—someone who just might be worthy of loving her. Her kiss drove me mad, until I lost all care for where we were. My hands were in her hair, then on the straps of her dress, then under her hem, stroking up her sweet thighs. She was a fire I'd never be able to quench.

"Enough to give me control?"

It took conscious effort, but I paused, kissing her gently. "Do with me what you will."

Then she slipped from my hands, rained kisses down my chest and stomach, until she dropped to her knees in front of me.

"Penelope?" I asked.

"I've wanted to do this for forever." The heat in her eyes

was nearly my undoing.

Then she slid my board shorts down just low enough that my dick sprang free. My breath abandoned me when her hand closed around me and began to stroke up and down the length.

That. Felt. Amazing.

Then her tongue swirled around the tip, and my hips rocked forward once before I got control of myself. That tongue was pure fucking magic.

When the head disappeared into her gorgeous mouth, I nearly came at the image. She sucked me in deep, her mouth impossibly hot and wet, and I had to remember to breathe.

"Penelope," I moaned, my hands on her head.

She gripped my shaft with one hand and perfect pressure, then moved up and down with her mouth, swirling her tongue as she went. There were too many sensations to pinpoint one, so I quit trying. Quit thinking.

"Tell me how," she said.

"God, baby. If you do it any better, I'll be dead."

"Good," she said with a smile, and then took me inside, caressing me with the flat of her tongue while I slid toward the back of her throat.

So. Fucking. Perfect.

White-hot shots of pleasure ran through me, and my hips subtly thrust into her mouth. She moved with me, and when she moaned, the vibrations sent me nearly sky high.

I felt that tingle at the base of my spine, the tension that marked my approaching orgasm, and cursed. In control or not, I was not coming in her mouth right after I'd told her I loved her—after she'd told me she loved me. I wanted to be inside her, deep and hard. Wanted to hear that now-occupied mouth screaming my name.

I jerked my hips back, and she released me with a *pop*.

"What's wrong?" she asked, her eyes impossibly blue and

wide.

"Not a damn thing," I said, tucking my dick back into my shorts with a hiss. I threw my shirt over my shoulder, and then lifted her up under her arms.

I kissed her, nearly mindless, but not so far gone that I would miss out on this. Lifting her by her ass, I smiled as she wrapped her legs around my waist. Her sundress rode up until it was her bare skin in my hands.

All I had to do was slide her panties to the side and I could be inside her.

I walked us into the bungalow and sat back on the bed so she straddled me.

"I could have finished you," she said against my mouth.

"Oh, I'm well aware. You were just about there, Pen. But I'd rather finish *you*." I ran my thumb along her lower lip. "God, this mouth."

I tugged her soft lower lip with my teeth, and she whimpered. Giving in to her little demand, I kissed her thoroughly, until she was grinding down on me, her hips moving in a circular pattern that made me lose just about every thought in my brain.

Gripping the hem of her dress, I pulled it up and over her head, leaving her in just bra and panties. A snap later, the bra was gone, setting those glorious breasts free. Unable to help myself, I slipped one into my mouth, swirling my tongue around the pebbled tip until she moaned my name. Then I suckled, loving the sharp bite of her nails in my back.

Driving Penelope out of her mind was quickly becoming my favorite pastime.

She knocked me to my back and then stripped off my shorts, taking control again. I pushed up and pulled her panties over the flare of her hips, then pressed a hot kiss to her belly as I let them drop to the floor.

"I can't wait," she said, her breathing ragged as she

straddled me. "Please, Cruz."

One hand on her hip to steady her, I slipped my thumb along the seam of her core. She was drenched and ready, thank God.

"Please?" she asked again, angling her hips so her entrance was right at the tip of my straining erection.

Fuck, she was so wet, so hot as I slid through her folds.

Before I lost my mind, I reached over, pulling a condom from my bag and tearing it open with my teeth. A second later I was covered.

"You never have to beg me," I told her.

She responded by lowering herself inch by inch until I was buried in her to the hilt. She squeezed me tighter than a fist and hotter than the sun. Nothing compared to this. Nothing.

"I love you," she told me, her eyes open and bright.

Except that, I thought as she moved, her eyes locked with mine as she started to ride me.

"I love you," I swore, pulling her in for a kiss, open and deep, nothing slow or tame left in me.

After that scene on the beach, I wasn't sure how long I could last. Damn, the woman was perfect and so sexy. Her motions came faster with a deeper grind to her hips, and the tone of her moan told me she was climbing but not quite there.

Gripping her hair lightly, I tilted her head and set my mouth to the spot on her neck that drove her crazy. Then I concentrated on anything but the sweet glide of her body on mine, or that burning in the base of my balls that told me I was close.

Slipping my empty hand between us, I strummed her clit and felt the immediate tightening of her thighs around my hips.

"That's it, baby."

Then I swirled and pressed, using the combination I knew would send her flying. She tightened all around me, throwing her head back so that her hair brushed my knees.

"Cruz!" she screamed as her sex rippled around me, squeezed me so tight I had no choice but to join her as my orgasm overpowered. I emptied into her, as she collapsed against my chest.

"I love you," I whispered into her hair, just because I could.

She looked at me, her eyes hazy with release. "I love you, too. I just didn't know how much until you told me."

Cupping her face in my hands, I kissed her softly, sweetly, imagining that's how I'd kiss her good night every night for the rest of my life.

Because in that moment, I knew without a doubt that there was no one who could possibly compare to Penna Carstairs. She was it for me.

I just had to pray that I was strong enough to hold on to her, because I wasn't sure I'd survive losing her.

Chapter Twenty-Five

PENNA

"Again," Nick ordered.

"You know I love you, right?" I called out, sweat pouring down my back inside my gear. "But right now, I fucking hate your sadistic ass."

"My sadistic ass is going to keep you alive," he fired back.

I'd done at least twenty-five rounds on the minibike, landing every time, but he wanted another one. He was concerned about the height at which I started the flip, saying I wasn't going soon enough, and it would cause me to under-rotate when I moved to the big bike.

"He's right," Pax answered.

"Not in the mood, Wilder!" I shouted, more than aware that I was being obstinate.

"Penna." Landon waved me over, and I went, ripping off my helmet on the way and throwing the middle finger at Nick.

At this rate I was going to be too tired to move to the big bike, and we only had one more day in Rio before heading up north. The expo was less than a month away.

"What's up?" I asked, taking the bottle of water that Little John offered.

"Watch," he said, offering me his phone.

I glanced at Cruz while he cued up the footage. He'd been pacing nearly all morning, alternating between watching me and blatantly looking away.

The footage started, and I saw myself speeding toward the ramp. Good speed. Good angle. Good execution.

"Shit," I muttered, watching the flip start too late.

"Yeah."

"I can't pull the double with the full-size if I don't start back here," I said, rewinding to the point in the arc I'd need to begin the flip. "I won't have the time to pull her back around like I do the mini."

"Exactly."

I groaned in frustration but put on my helmet and headed back to the mini.

"How the hell did you get her to listen?" Nick asked. "Because it's not like she's paying attention to anything I have to say."

"She'll only listen to herself when she gets like this," Landon answered.

"Fuck you both!" I sang with a smile.

Cruz folded his arms and stood next to Landon, watching the same video and nodding.

He loved me. Really, truly loved me, and not like my parents—I wasn't a pretty trophy for him. No, he was content to love me in silence, to take every risk for me—his career and reputation both on the line—while I handed him nothing but my body and heart in return.

But a month from now, that would all change.

We'd be off the cruise, and I'd graduate. Then we could get back to L.A. and start living our actual lives out in the open. East Coast, West Coast…we'd figure it out, and I would love him so well that he'd never once question what I'd put him through keeping this secret.

"You see it, too, don't you?" I asked Cruz.

"Yeah," he called out. "You just have to find that sweet spot where you don't lose the height but can still pull the turn."

"Right," I said, loving that he understood the physics of it.

"Wait, so you'll listen to *him*?" Nick yelled as I took the bike back to the start of the track.

"He's not an asshole," I said, blowing him a kiss.

"What's she doing here?" Wilder asked as Miss Gibson walked onto the course.

"Nice to see you, Mr. Wilder," she said with a flat smile.

"She's here to replace me for the afternoon. I have a mandatory department meeting, so unless you guys want to call off your practice for the next few hours, she's me," Cruz explained.

"Great." Wilder pointed Miss Gibson to where Little John sat. "You'll need to sign some stuff with Little John."

"I'll take her over," Cruz said. He sent me one long look, and with a curt nod, I pretended his leaving didn't affect me, that we were just teacher/student, that I didn't love him.

Blatantly ignoring Miss Gibson's hand on his arm, I turned around. "I'm giving it another go," I told Nick.

"If we get it right this time, do you think he'll let us move to the big bikes?" Zoe asked as we walked back to the starting line.

I shrugged. "Not sure. But I know that I trust his judgment more than I do my hot head. You should do the same."

"I'm ready."

"You're barely landing it. You skidded out last time."

"So? I'm never going to know without going for it on the big bike, right?"

"True. Let's see if we land these, and then we'll have them move the pit in. Flipping a full-size is a whole different ball game, and you need to be ready."

"Okay," she said with a sigh.

I understood her frustration. When you were this close to something, to proving yourself, it was hard to take a step back and realize you had to go slower, that you weren't as ready as you thought you were.

That's why it was important to have Pax, Landon, and Nick on my side. Just like they had all day, they pulled me back before my ego wrote a check my ass couldn't cash.

I lined up to the ramp and then gunned it, speeding down the paved track. Gear by gear, I amped up to full speed until I was almost flying when I hit the ramp.

I flew up the arc, nearly vertical before I went airborne. I started the flip when I felt my momentum shift, and then brought the bike around once. Twice. The world spun around me, and I pulled the bike back under me, nearly over-rotating before I brought it down on the other side of the ramp, the landing smooth but not perfect.

"Yes!" Nick yelled out with a fist pump.

I threw both arms into the air as I rode off the ramp, shouting victoriously.

The guys all hugged me as Zoe took her turn, racing toward the ramp.

"But it wasn't…" Cruz shook his head.

"Perfect? Yeah, it's because I need to add the weight of the real bike now. I've got the timing down. Shit," I muttered as Zoe came down front-wheel heavy.

She landed it, but it wasn't pretty.

"She probably needs another month or so on the mini, and she's not going to want to hear it," I told Cruz as Zoe came off the ramp cursing.

"A stubborn Renegade? Huh. That's a new concept."

"I'll do better with my real bike," she argued. "I know the weight. I know the feel, the way she reacts. This is fucking useless," she tossed at Pax.

"This is the way it's done, Zo. Penna fought for you to get the chance, and we're happy to give it to you, but you have to follow the program."

Muttering something under her breath, she started off toward the line of bikes.

"Guess she's ready for a break," I said to Cruz.

"I'm not, but I have to head back. You're in good hands with Lindsay," he said, nodding to where Miss Gibson went over paperwork with Little John. No doubt Pax would have her sign the full gamut of NDAs and liability waivers. The stuff with Gabe really got to him.

"Lindsay, huh?" I stared at my hands, pulling off my gloves.

Cruz's laugh caught me completely off guard. "Don't even. I'll see you later."

"Later," I said to his retreating back. *I love you.* "Break for lunch?" I asked the guys.

They all agreed, and we headed toward the food truck. One thing Little John did even better than prepping for stunts was track down the best food in the area.

I got my lunch first and borrowed Landon's phone, heading back to the ramp to watch the footage again. He was right. Sometimes the only way I'd listen was when I actually watched my own fuckups.

Maybe that's what I needed to show Zoe, too.

Sinking into the camping chair, I dug into my lunch. The two-a-day workouts had turned me into an eating machine. Hitting play on the video, I watched my last jump, trying to reconcile my memories and feelings with what the tape showed.

A motor sounded at the end of the track, drawing my attention as I chewed my carnitas. Who the hell was down…?

Oh God.

I stood, my food falling to the dirt as Zoe sped toward the ramp at full speed, riding her full-size bike. My heart jumped into my throat.

This was going to go wrong, and there was nothing I could do to stop it.

I ran toward the ramp as fast as my legs could go. Her speed was good, her angle great, but she'd never pulled the kind of weight that two-hundred-and-twenty-pound bike was about to give her.

She hit the top and flew, throwing the bike back into the flip.

"Pull it!" I screamed, but it was too late.

She lost control of the bike, and her grip slipped. She was done.

Zoe fell from the highest possible point of her arc, and everything slowed for me on the ground. I couldn't get there fast enough. Couldn't freeze time. Couldn't catch her or stop the bike.

She crashed into the backside of the ramp with a sickening *thud* as I reached the platform. I slid onto the ramp, skidding toward her as the bike came down, slamming into her leg with an audible *crunch*.

She let out a blood-curdling scream and reached for her upper thigh.

Just like me. Flashes of Dubai raced through my brain. The bike. The break. The light. Landon hovering above me. The pain.

The bike came at me and made impact before I could dodge, its tires raking down my side in a skin-rending sideswipe. I yelled out in pain as the bike kept moving, finally coming to a stop at the bottom of the ramp.

I staggered to my feet while holding my side and scrambled the rest of the distance to Zoe. Her shinbone distorted the lay of her pants, and her upper thigh was soaked in blood that was traveling down her leg at an alarming rate.

"Cruz!" I yelled. He would know what to do. He had medic training, right? He knew our safety plan. *He isn't here.* "Landon! Pax!" I looked back to see the entire company of Renegades at a run toward us, a phone already at Little John's ear.

"I'm dead! I'm dead!" Zoe screamed, voice shrill, her gloved hands covered in blood that smeared down her white jacket. I took off her goggles to see her eyes were wide, her pupils dilated.

Shock.

"You're alive! Do you hear me? You're alive. You couldn't be screaming if you were dead!" I grabbed her hand with mine and her face with the other. I couldn't reach much through the helmet, but it was her only exposed skin that I could touch so she could feel the contact.

Where was she bleeding from? God, there was so much of it. My hands ran over her thigh, where the blood was darkest. "Where else are you hurt? Jesus, what got you?"

"It was in my leg!" she yelled, handing me a piece of sharp, blood-covered metal from the bike.

"Oh my God, you pulled it out?" I dropped it.

"Holy fuck!" Landon yelled.

Finally.

He yanked the bike off the ramp and then hoisted himself onto the platform, coming at us at a run. "Little John has the EMTs coming from the entrance to the park."

Thank God Cruz made us have them relatively on-site.

"Give me your knife." I held out my hand, and he obliged.

Careful not to get her skin, I made a clean cut through

the rough material from Zoe's upper thigh all the way to her ankle, careful to navigate the built-in pads. "That's an open fracture," I said, pointing to where the bones tore through the skin.

Don't vomit. You've seen worse.

I'd been worse. Wetness seeped through my pants, and I didn't need to look to know it was Zoe's blood.

More of the heavy liquid pulsed from a gash on her thigh.

"Take it!" Landon shoved a shirt at me, and I pushed it to the wound, applying all the pressure I could.

Zoe's back came off the ramp as she screamed.

"Try to stay still!" We didn't know what else was broken, and from the look of the red marks on her gear, she had other, smaller bleeds.

"Zoe!" Landon got in her face. "Zo! Listen to me!"

Her breath was haggard, but she stopped screaming.

"There you go. Look, you've got a nasty break and a really rough bleed, okay? But you're going to be fine. EMTs are almost here. Penna's got pressure on the wound, and you're going to be fine. Penna, you gotta put more pressure."

I pushed harder at the wound, blood already seeping through the shirt, and Zoe went limp. She'd blacked out.

Rapid Spanish echoed all around me, and I looked up to see several paramedics motioning for me to move.

"Penna, come on," Landon said, taking me by the shoulders. I brushed my hair out of my face, only to pull my hands back and see they were covered in blood.

Looking down, the rest of me was, too.

"Get her checked out!" Pax yelled at Landon, already climbing the ramp to help the paramedics lift Zoe's stretchered body down.

"I'm fine!" I yelled.

"Bullshit, I saw you take the hit!"

"This way, please," an EMT gently guided my elbow. I

started shaking, stumbling away from the scene.

"I'm fine," I repeated, even as they sat me on the picnic table.

"Oh my God!" Miss Gibson said, placing her hand over her mouth as she looked at me.

"Where does it hurt?" the EMT asked, his eyes wide and concerned.

"She got hit in the side," Landon said, motioning to my ribs.

"*She* can speak," I snapped. Glancing down, I saw that the bike had ripped the shirt to shreds under my arm. "Damn, and I liked this set, too." Not that I'd ever wear it again, anyway. I doubted the blood would come out. A hiss escaped as I started to take off my shirt, the fabric catching on the pads underneath.

"Can you lift your arms?" Landon asked softly.

I nodded, raising them above my head. He carefully stripped off the soft, long-sleeved shirt, leaving me in my protective jacket. It was one piece with sewn-in pads—not too bulky for movement.

"Out!" I snapped at a camera team that was filming a respectful three feet from my face.

"Rebel—"

"Get the fuck out," Nick snapped from behind them. "She's hurt, and you got that on film, but I'll be damned if you'll be filming my best friend in her bra so some perv can fill his spank-bank. She's never done underwear shoots, and you won't be the first—documentary or not, so get out."

Over Landon's shoulder, I saw Zoe being lifted into the ambulance.

Little John appeared next to Nick and then walked up to me and turned his back, crossing his arms in front of his gargantuan chest.

Rachel joined him, and I almost laughed. She was five-foot-nothing, so it was more symbolic, but I appreciated the gesture.

I unzipped my black and purple jacket and slid my arms out while Landon held it.

"Damn." His eyes were locked on my red, raw rib cage.

"See, nothing to worry about," I said. "Bad case of road rash...bike edition."

The paramedic gently examined the injury, and though it felt like my skin had caught fire, I'd been through a hell of a lot worse.

"Nothing's broken," he said. "Very badly bruised. This is the only injury?"

"Yeah. The blood isn't mine."

"You're very lucky," he said as he finished checking out the area around the tire tracks. "All surface damage. Of course you might want an x-ray."

"No, thank you. I know what broken ribs feel like, and mine are fine."

"Penna, you okay?" Pax asked, pushing through my barricade. His gaze went straight to my side, but he still managed to toss Landon a shirt, which he immediately put on.

"I'm fine. It's going to bloom into a gorgeous bruise, and my ribs are sore, but nothing's broken."

Unlike last time. God, what the hell was I doing?

"Why don't you let the EMT tell you that," Pax said.

"He just did. I'm fine."

"Wilder!" someone called out from the ambulance.

"Go," I told him. "Take Landon and go."

"You're sure? I don't want to leave until we know you're okay."

I loved them like the brothers they were, but they weren't the ones I wanted, anyway. I wanted Cruz, needed to feel his strong arms around me, hear his voice in my ear, and they weren't exactly capable of giving me that.

"I'm sure. I have Nick, and Rachel, and Leah—"

"And me!" Little John shouted, his eyes still facing the ramp.

"And him." I laughed, then hissed at the pain it caused.

"Go." *Go before I fall apart and you see what a wreck I really am.*

"I'll take her back to the boat," Miss Gibson offered from the other side of Little John.

"And we'll go with her," Leah told Pax.

I saw the war raging in his eyes, the need to be with me—his sister—versus going with Zoe, who was severely injured. "Go. Now, dammit," I instructed, taking the choice away.

His jaw flexed, but he finally agreed. "Just take care of yourself and rest. I'll come back to the ship, or send someone when there's news, but they think she'll be okay."

"Sounds good. I'll follow you guys as soon as I get cleaned up."

I wanted a shower—needed to scrub away the blood, the dirt, the memories of her screams, which mixed together with my screams in my head.

The EMT gave me some directions—nothing I hadn't heard before—and I slipped one of Little John's shirts over my head that came nearly to my knees. He drove us back to the ship in the SUV.

Adrenaline gone, my head started buzzing with the noise I tried hard to keep out. I shut my eyes against the barrage of images on endless repeat, but that only made them worse, so I focused on the road.

I could fall apart in private, but never here. Not with Miss Gibson in the car. Not where Leah and Rachel would tell Pax and Landon.

"Cruz is going to kill me," Miss Gibson said.

I flinched at the sound of his name, at her right to publicly use it when I couldn't.

"It wasn't your fault," Leah reassured her, because that's the kind of person she was.

Me? Not so much.

"He left me in charge for ten whole minutes, and look what happened," she said, putting her head in her hands like she was the one who'd just had a motorcycle dropped on her.

But she wasn't guilty, either.

"Stop. He's not going to be mad. He knows there's no contingency plan for stubborn and stupid," I said, my voice scratchy and raw. "In our line of work…things happen. There's no stopping someone else's bad decision. Zoe wanted something she wasn't ready for. This wasn't your fault. Or his."

Her eyes met mine in the rearview mirror, and I looked away, as if our secret was there on my forehead to be read.

"What are you thinking about?" Rachel asked Leah, who sat in the middle, softly shaking her head.

"Just…just something Brooke said when we were in Barcelona. It's nothing."

I tried to lock down every muscle, every reaction I could possibly have, but I still looked at her. "What did she say?"

Leah's soft brown eyes met mine. "She said that everyone wants to be a Renegade until they know what it costs."

Time, tears, broken bones, and broken hearts. She'd said it to me so many times, and I'd laughed her off, not realizing what she was trying to say.

Please quit.

Please walk away.

Please see what this does to the people around you.

But I didn't quit. I kept going. Pax and Landon kept going. Even Nick, who'd paid a steeper price than the rest of us, kept pushing it.

And then she pushed back.

"She's right," I said, breaking the heavy silence. "Because no one sees the price. We're so damn good at hiding it, even in the middle of a documentary."

Sure, they saw the lights, the cameras, the roar of the crowd. They saw the stunts, the flips, even the falls. But they didn't see the tears, self-doubt, scrutiny, and the months of rehab and recovery. They skipped that part until the comeback.

I didn't want to visit the infirmary, but my friends teamed up with Miss Gibson against me, and I gave in, knowing it would take ten times longer to argue with them. I held it together through the wait, counting the ceiling tiles to keep my mind busy and off what had just happened. After I'd been checked out and cleared by the ship's doctor, Miss Gibson finally left us, and we headed for the suite.

No doubt she was going straight to the dean now that she'd covered her ass and had me checked out again. Heads turned as Rachel, Leah, and I took the elevator, then walked down the hall. I kept my eyes on the floor, well aware that I looked like something out of *The Walking Dead*.

Rachel slid our key through the lock, and when the little light went green, my composure bit the dust. I stumbled through our hallway, only to lean back against the wall and slide to the floor.

"I'll take care of her," Rachel told Leah. "Maybe go pack a bag for Zoe? Hugo should know how to get into her room."

I drew my knees to my chest, uncaring that the skin on my side felt like it was being shredded as I moved.

With Leah gone, Rachel dropped down in front of me. "Hey, you okay?"

"I'm fine." The answer was automatic, rote, the same one I'd given time and again after the accident.

"You're not fine. What can I do?"

"I'm fine," I repeated.

There was a pounding at the door, and Rachel sighed, then left to answer it. "Hey, Doc. Yeah, she's here."

"Cruz?" I asked, my voice tiny.

He pushed past Rachel, his eyes wild, growing even more panicked when he saw me. "Penelope. Oh God." He hit his knees in front of me, brushing my hair back. "Lindsay said you got hit. We have to get you to the hospital."

"No, I'm fine. I got checked out. It's not mine…the blood."

"Which side?" he asked. Not that I could blame him. The blood was everywhere.

"This one." I motioned with my head.

"Okay."

My eyes slid shut, and I felt his arms surround, then lift me carefully, keeping my injured side in the clear. Just that small amount of contact and my muscles relaxed, as if they got the message that I was safe now, that he would somehow make everything better even though my ribs still screamed.

"It's okay, baby. I got you," he said, his lips against my forehead.

He kicked open my bedroom door.

"Ummm…" Rachel stepped forward.

"I've got her," he told her.

"Penna?"

"It's okay," I told her as he prepared to shut the door in her face.

"Apparently," she said softly, her eyes wide.

He set me down on the bed, then turned on the shower. Once the water was warm, he stripped me to my toes, cursing at the damage he found on my side.

"Tires," I muttered. "I just need to get it clean and gooped up with antibacterial ointment with some bandages. I've been through it before, I'll go through it again."

He gathered me in his arms and lifted me against his chest.

"I can walk," I said softly, but tucked my head onto his shoulder.

"I need to carry you. Please just let me."

I'd been hurt plenty of times in my life, but I'd never been taken care of like this, or rather never *let* anyone take care of me.

He carried me to the large shower, walking in fully clothed. The water cascaded down my body in red streams, and he gently washed my face, my hair, then my torso. When he got to the tire tracks, he couldn't have been more careful with me.

He turned off the water and then wrapped me in one of the giant, fluffy white towels, patting me dry. Then I slipped into my terry bathrobe while he put on a set of dry clothes he kept in my one of my drawers.

Then he peeled back my robe, lathered me with ointment, and joked that we were going to need the economy-size bottle.

I didn't bother to tell him that Landon's parents owned that company, so we wouldn't run out anytime soon. He applied gauze, wrapped my torso like a mummy, and put me to bed, tucking me into the curve of his body.

"Painkillers?" he asked.

"They offered. I declined. The pain isn't too bad compared to other injuries."

"You sure?"

"You know what happened?" I asked, changing the subject.

"Lindsay gave me the gist."

"I didn't know what she was doing until it was too late."

"I know."

"No one could have stopped her."

"Penelope, this isn't your fault. You know that, right?" He stroked my hair back from my face.

My eyes prickled, and I blinked quickly. "I should have seen what was going on. Should have known what she was thinking. I was right there with her. I said I'd help her after lunch, and then I turned my back for a second. How did I not see what she was going to do? Why didn't she tell me? She should have told me."

He gathered me tighter and kissed my forehead. "You had no way of knowing what she was thinking or what she would do."

"I should have. She's just like me, and when I want something, there's nothing I won't do to get it. Look at the position I've put you in, right now."

"I am exactly where I want to be," he assured me.

"Why didn't I see it? There were so many signs. If I had just taken the time and listened to her, or paid the slightest attention, I would have seen it. I should have known. Out of everyone, I'm the one who should have known."

Cruz rolled until he hovered above me. "You are not responsible for the choices other people make. This is not your fault. Dubai was not your fault. Zoe is not Brooke."

My throat tightened, and several moments passed before I could speak.

"I can't talk about her to them. Not after everything she did. It's like there's this giant portion of my heart that's slowly dying, all blackened and ugly, and they won't understand. I chose them. I always choose them. But there's this part of me that says I should have chosen my sister, and I can't even tell them that I miss her."

"You can tell me."

There it was. Pax, Landon, Leah, Rachel...they all belonged to one another. Coupled off, but still part of the whole. Cruz was mine only. His loyalty was to me, and not to the Renegades. It was mind-blowing to be someone's priority.

"She won't even talk to me," I whispered. "My best friend. I keep making all these excuses for her—for my parents letting her hide behind those walls like I'm some kind of threat to her recovery. I'm the one she nearly killed. I'm the one who spent months in that cast, and yet I'm the danger.

I'm the outcast because I drove her to what she did."

He lay next to me and reached for my hand. "You didn't."

"Didn't I? I'm the one who met Pax and Landon, eventually introduced her to Nick…and then Patrick. She should have been at ballet, or football games, or anywhere else. Instead she was at a skate park with me, or at Renegade Ranch."

"All her choices."

"Should I have left? When everything happened in Dubai? Should I have gone home? Helped her? Yelled at her? Maybe, but all I could think was that I wanted to be around family, and for me…they're all here."

"You made the choice that was right for you at the time, and doubting it now doesn't change the fact that it was right when you made it. You needed these guys."

"But I needed her, too," I whispered. My eyes blurred as a tear escaped, tracking to the pillow as I rolled to look at Cruz. "I couldn't tell them that, not after everything she'd done. Even after I almost died, after what happened to Pax, to Leah…I still miss her every day."

"She's your sister."

"She betrayed me. Betrayed us all."

"That doesn't mean that you don't still love her. You're allowed to love her, Penelope. It's one of the things I love most about you—your capacity for acceptance and forgiveness."

"But I don't forgive her." I whispered my darkest secret. "I love her. I miss her, but I don't forgive her. How can I when I don't understand, when she won't tell me?"

"That's a choice you're going to have to make now. That's what this all is: a sequence of choices. You have to step back and decide if you're going to let what your sister did change you—take away this sport you love so much."

"What if it already did?"

His smile was beautiful. "It didn't. I saw you up there.

The drive. The determination. The process of it all. You are a Renegade through and through. That need for adrenaline, to prove yourself, to be the best—it's all still there under that layer of doubt that you let Brooke put there, and that's your choice. Just like you decide right now if you'll let this incident with Zoe put another layer on, or if you'll see it for what it was—a stupid choice by an overly ambitious girl. Neither of their choices change who you are unless you let them, and you are still Rebel."

"How can you be so sure when I'm not?"

"That's why you have me—to show you the parts of yourself that you can no longer see."

God, I loved him. Wholehearted, full-soul, forever kind of love. I was completely wrong for him, not just in our five-year age difference but in my profession. Cruz was built to protect, to stand between his woman and any danger that might find her. I was the girl who frequently called danger to the playground and challenged it to a game of chicken. But that didn't stop me from loving him, from recognizing the gift he was.

"Are you sorry you fell in love with me?"

"There's nothing you could do that would ever make me sorry for loving you, Penelope. Now rest. We'll check on Zoe in a little bit."

"Rachel knows about us now." I burrowed closer to him until I could hear his heartbeat beneath my ear.

"Yeah, I would assume she does."

"What are we going to do?"

"Pray that you know her as well as you think you do," he said as I drifted off.

Chapter Twenty-Six

CRUZ

I closed the door softly, hoping Penelope would rest.

This afternoon had easily shaved a decade off my life. When Lindsay burst into the department meeting, crying and blubbering, it had taken me a good five minutes to calm her down enough to get the story out of her.

But nothing had prepared me for the sight of Penelope covered in blood, her clothes torn and messy, her shirt not even hers. I'd reacted in a primal way I'd never experienced before…and put us in a shit ton of danger because I couldn't control my emotions.

Speaking of which, Rachel sat at the dining room table, a Corona in hand while she studied.

"Beer?" she offered.

I walked the short distance to the table and gripped the back of one of the chairs. "I can't really drink with students."

"But you can fuck one?" she shot, her eyes devoid of emotion.

Ouch. "Let's keep the ethical lines I cross to the bare minimum, okay?"

She shook her head. "I knew something was up. The first time—back on her birthday. Shit, if I'd paid attention, probably in class. When did it start? Did you ask her to stay after class?"

Damn, and I thought Penelope was a handful. I in no way envied Landon.

"I don't owe you anything, Rachel. But I do owe Penelope everything, so I will tell you two things about us. The rest, you'll have to get from her. First, I met her in Vegas before we ever boarded the ship."

Her eyes flew wide, and I had to give myself a mental high-five for rendering her speechless.

"Not everything is as clean-cut as you think. Should I be with her? Absolutely not. But she is a force of nature that I can't…" I dropped my gaze to my hands while I struggled to find words that could do justice to Penelope. There were none. "Look. I won't ask you to lie for us. I don't drag other people into my shitstorms. But I will ask that you talk to Penelope first. I cleaned her up, and she's got fresh bandages. Now, if you'll excuse me, I need to make some calls and check on Zoe."

"She's in surgery," Rachel said. "Little John sent a message after he got to the hospital. She nicked the artery in her thigh, and they're repairing it. Broken leg, of course, and a few broken ribs, too, but she'll be okay."

My shoulders drooped with the rush of relief. "Good. Penelope is asleep, and she really needs her rest, so tell her to find me when she wakes up, please?"

"So now I'm your messenger?"

"No, you're her friend, and she's hurt," I snapped.

Guilt flashed in her eyes. "Yeah, you're right."

I was halfway out the door when she called my name. "Doc?"

"Rachel?"

"You said you'd tell me two things. That was only one."

I looked at the girl who had the power to destroy everything I'd been working ten years for, and gambled. Penelope trusted her, and I trusted Penelope.

"I love her. It's not a fling. She's not just a phase or something to pass the time. I would give everything for her." *I have given everything.* "So you can look at me like I'm the enemy, because maybe in some way I am, but I also know that there's no one in this world who can love her like I do."

I watched the debate play over her face. It would take one call to the dean and I'd be off the ship. I would never get another teaching job. Elisa would never go to Harvard—she'd eventually die just like our mother.

"You really love her?" she asked softly.

"More than my very life."

She sucked in a breath. "Gotcha."

I nodded and walked to the door. As I opened it to leave, Lindsay had her hand poised to knock.

"Cruz! Sorry, you surprised me." She looked back at the room number. "This is the girls' room, right? I'm not on the wrong deck?"

"Nope, this is their room," I said, trying to keep my smile loose. Guess I was about to find out if Rachel was going to out us or not.

"Oh, good. I was just stopping to check on Penna."

"I was doing the same. Come on in. She's sleeping, but you can talk to Rachel." I opened the door, and she came into the suite, glancing at Penna's closed door before reaching Rachel at the table.

Rachel glanced between us for a moment, and I waited

for her deliberation.

"Hey, Dr. Gibson. Beer? Dr. Delgado already turned me down."

Lindsay laughed. "No, no. Are you sure you should be…?" She gestured to the bottle.

"Well, I'm twenty-one, in my own room, and I've had a shit day, so I'm going to go ahead and say yes."

"Point taken. Penna's sleeping?"

God bless Rachel, she didn't bat an eye or look at me.

"Yep. She's okay. Cleaned up, bandaged, and resting like the doc ordered."

Lindsay nodded. "I wanted to tell her that I'm sorry. I was in charge—"

"No you weren't," Rachel said, leaning back in her chair. "You may have been in the advisor seat, but you weren't in charge. In that moment, Zoe was in charge of herself. Renegades tend to do what they want, when they want, and any illusion of control you have is just that. Landon, Pax"— she glanced at me—"even Penna. They all do stuff they're not supposed to do. That's how they made a name for themselves. So don't feel guilty. You had zero chance of stopping her."

She looked up at me.

"None of us had a chance of stopping her."

• • •

"She's fucking insane," Nick said as he parked next to me.

"Yeah," I agreed, sitting back on the picnic table. "Not sure why I thought she'd rest up for a week or so."

"I wasn't sure she'd get back out here."

I watched Penelope talk to Landon, already balanced on her full-size Elizabeth, nodding her head as Paxton joined in.

"I was. This is who she is."

He shot me a puzzled look, and I shrugged. *Stop fucking*

up all over the place, please. At this rate I may as well walk into the dean's office and tender my resignation.

But there was Elisa to consider.

"How the hell did you guys get this set up, by the way? These ramps don't exactly look easy to move."

"They're not." Nick laughed. "I called in some favors from the guys who own this park and the ones who owned the last one. Add to that the money Pax was willing to drop from the Renegade budget to get Rebel back on that bike, and here we are."

"What kind of favor?"

"The Renegade Open in Cuba. Usually you'd have to qualify to get in. I gave them each one guy from their organizations who could enter without qualifying." His eyes narrowed toward Penelope and the others. "What the hell are they telling her?" he mumbled and took off to join the conversation.

Rachel took a seat next to me on the table, and I inwardly cringed. It had only been twenty-four hours, but the girl felt like Robespierre, and I was at the guillotine.

"Heads up, these first few runs are going to be the hardest to watch," she said.

"There's a giant foam pit."

"Which doesn't protect her if the bike comes down on top of her. This isn't a mini. That's two hundred and twenty pounds of angry motorcycle. She'll be fine, it's nothing she hasn't gone through already, but unless you've sat through something like this before, it's kind of brutal."

"But she'll be okay?"

She studied my face for a moment before facing forward again. "As okay as she's ever going to be. You didn't exactly choose a tame one."

A quick glance told me the cameras were all busy capturing every aspect of Penelope, or what they could see of her under all that gear.

"She talked to you?" I asked quietly.

"If by talk you mean told me that it was none of my damn business. Oh, she also added that I'm sworn to secrecy because she kept my relationship with Landon a secret for so long. Excellent play of the guilt card by Miss Carstairs."

"You kept your relationship a secret, too?" What I wouldn't give to be out in the open with Penelope. A few more weeks, that was all we needed.

She shrugged. "Yeah, well, I was dating Wilder at the time, so…I guess you're not the only one to cross ethical lines around here."

"Jesus. You, Wilder, Landon, Brooke, and Nick—it's like an incestuous CW drama around here."

"Pretty much. Point is that I'll keep your secret, and not because you love her, but because *she* loves *you*, and I think you are the one responsible for bringing her back to the land of the living."

My relief was short-lived as Penelope started her bike and rode down to the end of the track. Knowing what would come next, my heart rate skyrocketed.

That goddamned ramp still had Zoe's blood on it.

"She just needed someone to listen."

"I would have listened," she mumbled.

I weighed my options and made a choice.

"Do you have siblings?"

"No. I'm an only child."

"Pax and Landon?"

"Landon is an only child, but Pax has an older brother."

"Then he might be the only one who can understand what she's going through. I have a sister whom I love so much that I'm willing to give up almost anything for her. Penelope is the same—and I think perhaps a few of you have forgotten that in the last few months."

"She misses Brooke," Rachel whispered, like it had never dawned on her.

"With the force of a thousand nuclear weapons."

"Oh God. We're so blind."

Penelope came barreling down the track, and I started rocking back and forth. She hit the ramp and flew impossibly high, pulling the bike into one turn, then a second— "Shit."

Midway through the second turn, she lost the bike and came crashing back to the earth. She landed in one end of the foam pit while her bike hit the other, and I heard her swearing from over here.

"She's fine," Rachel said.

"Yeah, glad *she* is. I was less nervous on house-to-house raids in Afghanistan."

"It's one thing to risk your life. Handing your heart to someone else and watching them toss it around in the air for fun? That's a whole different ball game."

I sighed and settled back on the table, trying to brace myself for about thirty upcoming heart attacks.

"What wouldn't you give up?" Rachel asked.

"I'm sorry?"

"You said you'd give up almost anything for your sister. What wouldn't you give up? Is there a measurement there?"

Penelope climbed out of the foam pit as her bike was lifted by the giant crane Little John piloted, and I grinned at how pissed she looked. I'd take pissed over crying any day.

"Yeah, there is. I'd give my own life for Elisa, but I wouldn't give up Penelope. She's the measurement of everything in my life."

Rachel nodded. "Good answer. I might just like you after all this."

I laughed, but it was short-lived.

Penelope ran that ramp again and again until she landed the bike in the pit. Landed, meaning she came down on the bike...just not necessarily with her wheels under her.

By lunch, I was ready to demolish the damn bike.

Penelope unsnapped her helmet, ripped off her pink bandana, and cursed fluently as she pulled her hair up high on her head.

"You've also got about a hundred pounds on me, Pax," she snapped, and I got the fuck out of her way as she walked by.

But she subtly brushed my hand, which sent bolts of lightning through me.

"How is your side?" I asked as she put her helmet on the table.

"Fine."

"Penelope?" I lowered my voice to a growl, noting that we had about twenty feet on the camera team.

"It fucking hurts, and that's not going to change."

Rachel's eyebrows shot up and she mouthed, "good luck," to me before hopping off the table.

"Oh no. You take her back to that little tent they set up and change her bandages," I ordered Rachel.

"I'm fine."

"You're one day post-accident and acting like nothing happened, so why don't we both cut the bullshit and agree that you're anything *but* fine, shall we?"

She turned to me, crossing her arms over her chest and leveling me with a glare. "Excuse me?"

"Oh, this should be good," Landon said, flanking Pax as they walked over to the table.

Paxton waved off the camera, and they backed away. *Probably got more than enough footage yesterday.*

"I said, go change your bandages." I picked up the kit Little John had put together and offered it to her.

"And I said I'm fine."

I handed the kit to Rachel. "Go with her, and get your

damn bandages changed, Penelope!"

"Or what?" she snapped.

I stalked forward until we were about twelve inches apart—barely outside the lines of propriety. "Or I cancel your practice for the rest of the day."

"You wouldn't."

Renegades tend to do what they want, when they want, and any illusion of control you have is just that. Rachel's words from yesterday ran through my head.

"After what happened yesterday, I most certainly would. Now you can be stubborn and fight with me right here for the rest of the afternoon, or you can go with Rachel, get your bandages changed, and go back to trying to kill yourself up there. It's absolutely your choice."

We stood there for what seemed like an eternity, waiting for the other to back down. I would win—I was far more patient, and she had more to lose.

"Who needs TV? This is awesome," Landon said.

At least six heads turned to glare at him, but Penna and I stood locked in a battle of control, concern, and compromise. She had to learn to give an inch, to trust me just a little, or we had zero shot at this thing once we were off the boat. I wasn't some pushover she could tread on, and while I'd never hold her back, I'd put my damn foot down when she was doing more harm than good.

"Ugh! Fine!" She stomped off, and Rachel followed.

"Damn," Pax said, slapping me on the back. "Glad we chose you, because she would have flipped us the bird and told us to fuck off."

"Yeah, well, she's just waiting for you to walk away before she does what she wants. Prove that you won't walk away, and she'll budge. It might be the slightest inch, but she'll give."

His eyebrows furrowed. "How would you—"

"Pax, I need to talk to you about the Cuba expo. We need

the finalized list of riders who qualified," Little John called out.

"Yeah, okay," Pax said, but he still shot me a look that told me I'd said way too much.

I wandered toward the food truck, only to get yanked to the side by a very small, very pissed girl. "Oh, you're not sending me into the lion's den. You created that beast, you soothe it," Rachel said, pulling me toward the tent.

Once she saw that no one was around to witness, she shoved me through the canvas flaps and then stood guard, her feet visible at the bottom of the box-shaped tent.

"Seriously?" Penelope barked. She sat on the small table they'd put in here, already stripped down to her protective jacket.

I walked up to her without pause and caged her in my arms. "I love you. That means that while I'll watch you pull idiotic shit, I'm not going to stand by and watch your wounds get infected. Got it?"

"You can't just act like you own me out there." She pointed in the direction of the ramp.

"And you can't act like you don't own *me*," I threw back. "Like I don't have a right to be concerned, to worry, to have a fucking opinion. You are the strongest woman I have ever met, but if you want this to work between us, you are going to have to let me care for you—care about you. I've watched you flinch and readjust that thing all day, and I would bet my life that you've ripped open a few scabs, which means you're sweating right into the wound. Has to sting like hell."

"A little," she acquiesced quietly.

I took her zipper between my fingers and arched an eyebrow at her.

"Yes," she said with a flirty smile.

Eyes locked, I unzipped her protective jacket, leaving her in nothing but a pink, zip-front sports bra that I desperately wanted to undo.

"Fuck. Is 'I told you so' appropriate?" I asked, pointing to where several splotches of blood showed through her bandages.

"Maybe. But you only get so many with me, so I wouldn't waste one on something this small. I'm bound to be far more stubborn down the line."

"I'm counting on it," I told her. Taking off her bandages, I hissed at the damage she'd done today. "You couldn't just let it heal?"

"Nope. No time for that."

"You don't think it affects your performance?"

"There's so much adrenaline in my system once I start toward the ramp that I'm sure I could lose a toe and not realize it."

I cleaned and dressed her side, hating how angry and red it was. But we'd be at sea for the next five days as we headed up the Brazilian coast. As long as she didn't tear herself all to hell, she could heal up before the next port.

"Thank you," she said softly. "I'm not used to someone watching so carefully."

"I will always watch you this carefully," I promised.

She grasped a handful of my T-shirt and pulled me toward her until I stood between her outstretched thighs. "Did you know that you cross your arms when you think a student is wrong in class but don't want them to stop talking?"

"What?"

"You sit back, fold your arms, and wait for them to finish. Then you ask questions until they explain themselves or realize they're wrong. When they're right, you flash your dimples once, then nod slowly. You only grade papers in blue pen, you can't stand ketchup, and you push yourself a tenth of a mile an hour faster on every run for about ten minutes."

I blinked at her, and she grinned up at me.

"I watch you just as carefully."

Uncaring that our only shield was a thin piece of green canvas, I leaned in and kissed her until she gripped my biceps like a vise. I changed the angle, taking it deeper, until I heard her whimper, felt her arch against me.

"I'm all sweaty," she said between kisses.

"You're all mine," I answered, then proceeded to kiss her until Rachel cleared her throat loudly outside the tent.

Penelope hopped off the table, zipped up her pads, and tugged her jersey over her head. "I'll head out first. You should probably wait to clear up that situation." She pointedly stared at my very hard dick. "Tell him to wait a few hours and I'll make sure my bike isn't the only thing I'm riding today. Now if you'll excuse me, my love, I have to get back to not killing myself."

I shook my head as she walked out, head high, 100 percent stubborn and beautiful and mine.

Chapter Twenty-Seven

VENEZUELA

"You sure about this?" Nick asked as we made our way onto the tarmac of the little, private airport.

"Sure we can do it? Absolutely. The question is if *you're* sure about it," I answered. "You know Pax will keep the cameras off you if that's why you're worried."

"It's not the cameras." He stopped close to the ramp that had been put up to the door of the small plane. "I just don't want to get my hopes up, to think it's something I can do only to find out he's wrong."

"I'm never wrong," Cruz said, coming up behind him.

I made the mistake of looking at him, and immediately lost my train of thought. He had on simple cargo shorts, a tight, mouthwatering black Under Armour T-shirt, and a backward baseball hat.

He looked every inch of my Cruz and none of Dr.

Delgado.

Six weeks together—almost three months since we'd met—and I couldn't imagine not having him in my life. Sure, I was annoyed to hell that I couldn't kiss him in public, that we had to watch our hands, our eyes, and our words, but in less than two weeks that would all be over.

Eleven days.

We could go public, and I couldn't wait.

"You sure?" Nick asked, rubbing the back of his neck.

"Absolutely. I've done the research, Little John ordered the gear, and we're going to do this. But only if you want. I'm not in the habit of throwing people off mountains who don't want to jump," Cruz told him.

"And you don't mind not wing-suiting with these nuts?" Nick motioned to where Pax and Landon handed over Rachel's and Leah's gear.

"I have hundreds of jumps under my belt, and I'm completely happy never looking like a flying squirrel. A man has to have some dignity. Besides, it would be my honor to jump next to you."

Nick sucked in a breath and looked around our small posse. It was an Originals-only trip, but with the cameras on board, Cruz was here in an official capacity. Unofficially, he'd found a way to light a fire in Nick I hadn't seen in the last year, and I was immeasurably thankful.

"Hey, can we do some tape real fast?" Bobby asked me, and I grimaced.

"Absolutely. Now seems like the perfect time, don't you think?" I quipped sarcastically.

"They're still loading the plane, and Pax told us that we'd be in the distance for most of this trip. We're only allowed to capture the jump from below the falls. GoPros only on top."

I could have kissed Pax. That gave Nick a sense of privacy for the moment he'd have to make the actual decision.

"Ask away," I told him.

"So we're here in Venezuela, and you're taking two days off the super ramp. This close to the open, when you haven't landed the double back, do you think that's the smartest course of action?"

And I was back to wanting to punch him.

I forced the Rebel smile. "I think we're in Venezuela. Angel Falls is a BASE jumper's dream, let alone with wingsuits. It's hard to pass that up."

"And the double backflip?"

"We still have the ramps in Aruba and the day before in Cuba. If I nail it, I'll use it in the Open."

"And if you don't?"

"Then I won't use it."

Bobby's face fell. Crashes had always brought more hits than successful jumps. Nothing like the promise of watching someone demolish his or her body to get the clicks.

"And now that Zoe's been sent back to the States, do you feel like you should reevaluate the training regimen? It's hard to lose another Renegade this close to the end."

"Zoe's injury was definitely unfortunate, but as Renegades, we're personally liable for our own safety and our own decisions. We wish her the best for recovery and can't wait to see her back in L.A. at the Renegade Ranch."

Bobby's gaze narrowed. "And how is the loss of another Renegade woman affecting you? It can't be easy being one of the only women in the company, and especially with the loss of your sister—"

"And we're done!" I gave Bobby a go-to-hell smile and turned on my heel to find Cruz waiting.

"You okay?" he asked.

"Fan-fucking-tastic," I answered, climbing up the stairs to the plane.

At some point I was going to have to answer the questions,

especially the ones I asked myself whenever Brooke came to mind.

· · ·

Four hours and another airport later, we lifted off with a fleet of three helicopters. The leafy green canopy fell away from us as we flew across the Canaima National Park toward the tabletop mountain.

Our helicopter was Originals-only. Nick, Pax, Landon, and me.

It felt like it had with every stunt before Nick had been injured—the four of us setting out to see what record we could break, what experience we could capture. Except we were in a foreign country, headed toward the tallest waterfall in the world, and one of us couldn't walk.

We weren't indestructible anymore, and we knew it, but we still had one another.

"How are you feeling?" I asked Nick through the headset.

"I haven't decided," he answered.

"Don't take this as a hallmark moment, but damn, it's nice to be back together," Landon said, looking at me over his shoulder.

"Yeah, it really is," I told him. My heart was full as we curved along the river, coming closer to the flat-topped mountain. The waterfall came into view, and my breath stalled in my chest. How was I so lucky that this was my life? "There she is."

"Whoa," Nick said, looking out the window.

"I'm glad you're here," I told him.

"Me, too."

"Hey," Bobby said through the headset. We'd left him on the ground with the rest of the production crew. "You know there's still time just in case you've chosen to let us tape this…" He sounded hopeful.

"Not a chance in hell," Pax said with a small laugh. "Whatever we record on the GoPros is fair game, but the rest is for us and us alone. Just this one time."

Bobby sighed. "Yeah, I figured it was going to be something like that."

"You've got guys on the ground?" Landon asked.

"Two crews. One at the landing site for the wingsuits, and one for the BASE jumpers. That BASE footage is just for you. Not the documentary. You know I'd kill to include it, but this is your private moment, and that footage is for your personal use."

"Thank you. I appreciate it," Nick said.

"Thank you for choosing me for this job in the first place. You guys enjoy your jump."

We landed before the others, giving Landon and Pax time to get Nick into his chair. We'd chosen the smoothest drop-off location, the one with the easiest path to get Nick to the edge.

The plateau was lush and green with trees and giant boulders, with no hint that the edge dropped off over three thousand feet to the bottom. I stepped out onto the rough gray stone and stood as close to the edge as I dared without a chute and looked over the view, trying to take in every detail. A few moments later, the helicopter took off, and the guys flanked me. I'd never felt so small and yet a part of something so big.

There were so many things about this trip I could do again if I wanted. Anytime I felt like it, I could hop a flight to Istanbul, or hike up to Everest base camp, or visit Machu Picchu. But this—standing on the top of Angel Falls with all of my best friends—this was a once-in-a-lifetime kind of moment and was all the more precious for it.

"Some life we have," Pax said.

"Not too bad," Nick added.

"Ever wonder why it is we find the best views, highest peaks, and then hurl ourselves off them?" Landon asked.

"Because it's fun," I answered with a shrug.

The guys laughed, and our moment passed as the next helicopter landed. Cruz got out, helping Rachel down.

As the chopper lifted off, it felt like it took a few hundred pounds of pressure with it. No production crew this time, just us. I glanced around at my friends, all working their gear, even Cruz latching Nick into the chair with the harness he designed, and I smiled.

This is more like it.

Here we weren't documentary stars. There was no pressure for ratings, for the perfect shot. We were just a group of friends with a few GoPros about to pull off something epic.

I picked the spot next to Pax and laid out my gear, winding the straps of the rig through my wingsuit.

"What are you thinking about?" Pax asked.

"We're about to hurl ourselves off a three-thousand-foot cliff."

"Right."

"With no parachute."

"True."

"Interesting day."

"Interesting life," he said with a grin.

Rachel motioned to me, and I walked up the hill to meet her. "What's up? You ready to jump with Cruz?" I asked. She'd be BASE jumping just ahead of Nick on Cruz's team.

"As ready as I'll ever be. He chose the best place with the sheerest drop for Nick, so there's almost no chance of…"

"Of him slamming into one of the outcroppings beneath?" I suggested.

"Yeah, that. I'll jump first, then Cruz is going to literally push our friend off the mountain. The plan is damn near flawless."

"Good."

"Oh, and he wants to see you," she said, motioning to the rock formation to my right, closer to the falls.

"Thank you. And thanks again for not telling anyone. I know it's above and beyond."

Her eyes darted to Landon. "I hate keeping something from him. You need to tell them soon."

"I'm scared they won't understand." Pax would think I'd been taken advantage of, and Landon would simply think I'd lost my mind.

"It's not their job to understand. It's their job to support and protect you, the same way you've done for them time and again. But you owe them the chance to be that for you."

She was right. We'd be at the Cuba Open in a week, and then Miami. I needed to tell them first as long as Cruz was okay with it. I'd promised to keep us a secret, and I would until he was in the clear. I thanked her for covering for me and raced over to the rock formation.

"I hate sneaking around like this," Cruz said, pulling me into his arms.

We were sheltered here, hidden from the others.

"We won't have to for much longer, right?"

He nodded, his chin resting on the top of my head. "Just a couple weeks. Then we'll be back in Miami, heading to L.A., and you'll no longer be my student."

"And we can be open?" There was still a part of me, as small as it was, that was terrified he'd change his mind—that I was nothing more than a ship fling with a touch of taboo for excitement.

"I'll change my Facebook relationship status and everything," he said, laughing.

I tilted my head up for a kiss, and he more than obliged. Our tongues tangled and danced to the symphony of rushing water behind us. That same energy took hold of me, all of my senses focusing on Cruz—his taste, scent, the feel of his hair in my fingers, the sound of my name on his lips. How did this get better every time?

"We should get back to the others," I said, reluctantly pulling myself from the kiss.

"True. Be careful, okay?" His thumbs stroked my cheekbones.

"Always. You, too."

Our eyes locked, and I leaned up on my toes, kissing him softly. "I love you."

"I love you more," he said, pressing a small, pink flower into my hand. "I found it near the edge of the cliff."

"Thank you," I told him, holding the flower as I walked away. It had narrow petals in the shape of a triangle with a smaller bud at the end. I'd never seen anything like it. It was an original, just like the man who gave it to me.

Careful with my footsteps, I made my way back down to the launch zone, tucking the flower into my breast pocket for safekeeping.

"Everything okay?" Landon asked.

"Perfect," I said with a smile, and meant it.

"Okay, then let's get to it," he ordered with a clap of his hands and a mile-wide grin.

A few moments later, I'd threaded myself through the harness straps and zipped up all but the leg portion of the suit. Helmet clasped, double checked, and nerves setting off fireworks in my belly, I walked to the edge of the outcropping we'd chosen. We were only a couple dozen feet from the falls, and I turned to look at the gorgeous cascade of water, glad my GoPro was on to capture the moment.

A quick look to our right saw Rachel, Cruz, and Nick ready to go on their ledge.

"You ready?" Nick shouted over the distance as I zipped up my leg panels and pulled the boot portion over my shoes.

Flying squirrel, indeed.

"You first!" Landon yelled back.

"You always were a chickenshit!" Nick answered. "Let me guess, you've made Pax go first in everything since I've been out, right?"

"I was just trying to be polite," Landon muttered as Paxton laughed uncontrollably. "Oh, just fuck off and go! No, not you, baby. You go when you're ready," Landon added when Rachel crossed her arms. "Love you!"

"Yeah, yeah. Love you, too," she answered.

She and Cruz shared a nod, and then she jumped. I noticed Landon didn't take a breath until her chute deployed, and then he rocked back on his heels with a huge sigh.

"We'll see you at the bottom!" I called out to Nick.

He gave us a thumbs-up, and then Cruz backed up about fifteen feet with Nick. They said something to each other—man, I wished we were closer—and then Cruz took off at a run, shoving Nick with all his might at the edge of the cliff before skidding back himself.

My heart lurched into my throat as the chair tumbled once, twice, and then the chute deployed, the sight allowing air into my lungs. "He did it."

"Hell yeah, he did," Pax said softly.

Cruz nodded to me—well, toward us, but I knew it was for me—and jumped off the cliff. He dove fast, and I found myself leaning way too far over the edge to watch him pass Nick and then pull his own chute.

"Ballsy to wait that long," Landon remarked.

"He wants to land before Nick so he can help him," I said.

"He's a good guy," Pax added.

"The best," I said before I thought.

They both looked at me, and I avoided eye contact. Rachel was right. It might get me bitten in the ass, but I was going to have to tell them. Keeping a secret like this from my best friends was wrong, no matter how much I loved Cruz.

"Shall we do this?" I asked, changing the subject.

"I'm going first," Landon said, and I smothered a laugh.

"Yes, you should do that."

"Same plan. Watch the curve of the canyon."

"Yes, Dad," Pax drawled.

"See you at the bottom!" Landon gave us a grin and then raced to the edge of the cliff and was gone.

"You're up," Pax told me. "And hey, random, but you know you can always talk to me, right?"

"Like, right now?" I eyed the drop-off.

"Well, no. I mean, yeah, if you wanted to."

I patted him on the shoulder. "I hear you, and I love you for it. But I was thinking I'd jump off this mountain right now, if you don't mind."

"After you," he said, sweeping his arm toward the cliff edge.

My heart galloped as I backed up, already feeling the rush of adrenaline through my veins. Restrained by the suit, I took as big of steps as I could and ran toward the edge of the cliff.

Then I flew.

No parachute. No engine. No sounds but the wind through my helmet and the rush of blood through my ears.

Arms and legs spread, with the webbing of nylon that turned me into my own sail, I glided through the air, careful to watch the curve of the canyon. A single mistake up here would be my last.

I flew past the falls, taking precious seconds to stare up at the sheer majesty of the breathtaking sight, and then focused fully on the flight, tracking Landon as he soared ahead of me. I dropped my right arm slightly to change course, avoiding the giant pillar of cliff that loomed, and headed toward the green vegetation that marked our planned landing zone. It was just beside the river, but treeless, so hopefully I wouldn't end up skewered in the middle of Venezuela.

Landon waved me down, having already landed, and I concentrated on my angle, speed, and descent as the field flew up rapidly to meet me. I ran through my landing, tripping on some of the foliage but catching myself before I ended up on a blooper reel.

The flight was beautiful, life-affirming, empowering, and over all too soon.

Landon *whooped* and gathered me into his arms, swinging me around. I was mid-swing when Pax landed, and we became a Penna-sandwich hug.

"Thank you for this," I told them as Bobby's Jeeps drove over.

"I'll admit, I thought you were nuts when you suggested it," Pax said as Bobby parked and the cameras rushed us. "But I should know better by now than to question your judgment."

A few quick interviews later, we were out of the wingsuits and headed to meet up with the BASE jumpers.

I smiled at Cruz, but the three of us walked straight to Nick, who grinned wider than when he'd medaled in the X Games a couple years ago.

"How do you feel?" I asked him.

He looked at each of us in turn and then laughed incredulously, his expression torn between wonder, joy, and a touch of confusion. "Like a Renegade."

Chapter Twenty-Eight

Venezuela

There was nothing better than kissing Penelope. Except maybe making love to her.

It was our last afternoon in Venezuela, and I was still high off yesterday's jump and the ultimate adventure of loving this woman.

She arched beneath me, her fingernails biting into the skin of my shoulders as I thrust inside her welcoming heat. Better. Hotter. All-consuming. Every time I took her, she took me somewhere I'd never been in a relationship—a place where the physical and the emotional met on some kind of ethereal plane that never ceased to amaze me.

God, she was perfection. There was nothing I would change about her. I thought about everything I wanted to share with her back in L.A. My favorite restaurants, her favorite coffeehouses. We had a whole life waiting for us as soon as we got off this boat in exactly ten days.

Until then, I'd keep her here as much as possible.

"Faster," she begged, her teeth on my earlobe.

So much for distracting myself to make this last longer.

I kissed her as I increased the pace, bringing her knees up so I could slide deeper. *Fuuuuuuck*, she was going to be the death of me in every way possible.

She writhed under me, seeking something I wasn't willing to give her yet.

"Tell me what you want," I ordered, locking gazes so I could see the moment she surrendered.

"You," she said, her neck arching, her head thrown back.

Her hair spilled out around her, and those pink lips were swollen from my kisses. She'd never looked so beautiful.

"You have me. What else do you want?" I asked, holding back just enough to keep her from hitting her edge.

"Deeper," she ordered. "Harder."

"Like this?" I asked, sliding in another fraction.

Her eyes snapped fire at me. "I love you, and I adore when you make love to me…"

"But?" I asked, watching her fight to say what she was really thinking. I halted my moves entirely, resting inside her. My dick throbbed, protesting, but my brain knew exactly what she needed and had no problem pushing her to it.

Penelope held back in zero places in her life. Our bed wasn't going to be the start.

"But?" I repeated.

She grasped both sides of my face and rocked her hips back into me, taking me deeper, and I groaned softly, unable to keep completely quiet when the jolt of pleasure hit me. "But I need you to fuck me right now."

God, yes. Yes to all.

I slid out of her, and she whimpered. "Not helping," she said.

Then I flipped her over, and she landed on her knees in front of me, that gorgeous ass in the air. "Grab the headboard."

"Why?" she asked.

"Do it, Penelope, so I can fulfill that little demand of yours."

A tremor raced through her as I ran my fingers down her spine. She crawled up my bed and grasped the headboard with both hands.

I moved between her knees, lined up my cock to her entrance, and thrust home.

She whispered my name as I slid deeper than I'd ever been within her. Then I set a rhythm that had her keening, whimpering, begging. Her body tensed beneath mine, her back arching.

I kissed her shoulder, gently raking my teeth across her skin at the same time I reached around her body to put pressure on her clit, and she bucked back. I felt the ragged intake of her breath, the clench of her body around mine, and I covered her mouth with my hand when she cried out, her orgasm taking her.

I followed immediately, surrendering to the mind-blowing ecstasy that only Penelope could give me.

Collapsing, I pulled her to my side. "When we get home to L.A., I'm keeping you in my bed for a week. Then I'm going to make you scream so loud your voice will go hoarse," I promised.

"Ten days," she said, smiling dreamily up at me. "Then we can go public."

"As public as skywriting." God, I couldn't wait to claim this woman as mine.

"I'm going to have to tell the guys, first. They deserve that much. I hate that I've kept it from them this long."

My stomach tied itself in knots, but I brushed her hair back from her face and forced a smile. "I trust you. If you think you need to tell them, then I will support you."

"Could you be any more perfect?" she asked.

"Sure, I could *not* be your professor."

"Eeew, you made it all porny again," she said, sitting up, her beautiful breasts swaying gently. "Mind if I use your shower? I have math in about an hour."

"Can I join you?"

A wicked gleam danced across her eyes. "Absolutely."

"Good." I glanced at the file on my desk and took a deep breath. "Can you get away tonight for a bit? I want to tell you some stuff about Cuba before we get there."

"Sure, I'd like that," she said.

Maybe not when you realize what I haven't told you.

She kissed me soundly and then headed for the shower, shutting the bathroom door behind her.

I cleaned up and headed to join her.

A knock at my door brought me up short.

"Who the fuck?" I muttered. "Just a second," I called out, and tossed on a pair of gym shorts. No point in traumatizing my super unsocial roommate.

I opened the door and blinked. "Lindsay?"

"Hey!" She smiled, way too chipper. "I'm so sorry to barge in on you, but I remembered you saying something about me joining your Cuba excursion that first day and I wanted to ask you a question. Am I keeping you from something?" she asked, looking over my shoulder at the closed bathroom door.

"Yeah, I was just getting in the shower," I said, trying to keep my voice even.

"Oh, of course. I'm sorry. I'll come back—"

I heard the door open behind me, and before I could slam this one in Lindsay's face, or get word to Penelope, I heard her voice. "Hey, I thought you were—"

Fuck me, Penelope was right behind me, wrapped—thank God—in a towel but nothing else.

I met her horrified eyes, her mouth slack, and turned slowly to see the same expression mirrored on Lindsay's face.

"Oh my God," Lindsay whispered.

"Lindsay, this—"

"Let me guess, this isn't what it looks like?" she shouted, backing into the entry hall of the suite. "You're not sleeping with a student?"

Fuck. Fuck. Fuuuuuck.

"She wasn't a student when we first met," I said, trying to explain, to say anything that would keep Lindsay from ruining everything when I was only days away from saving Elisa.

"And that makes it better? You…she…you can't. Oh my God."

"If you'll give us a second," I started.

"Oh, it looks like you've had more than a second," she said, eyeing Penelope. "Miss Carstairs, I'll see you in class. Cruz…Dr. Delgado, you'll hear from the dean."

She spun and left, slamming the door on the way out.

"What are we going to do?" Penna asked, her voice breaking.

I closed my door and turned, taking her into my arms and holding her against my chest. "This will be okay. It's all going to be fine."

"She's going to get you fired."

"Probably." My mind raced, but I couldn't think of any solution that would get us out of this. Holy shit, we'd been stupid. Complacent.

She jumped out of my arms and started throwing on her clothes. "Get dressed. Now."

"What are you doing?"

"We need help. Get dressed."

I grasped her shoulders after she tugged her shirt back over her breasts. "Penelope. We're in the wrong. *I'm* in the wrong. I took advantage of a student. I crossed the ethical and contractual line. I'm at fault here. Lindsay is the right one, and I'm the wrong one. There's no hiding from this."

"I am not going to stand by and watch them fire you! Ruin your reputation! Now put on a goddamned shirt so I can do something!" Tears brimmed in her eyes, turning the ocean-blue color crystalline, and I sighed. "Okay. Just give me a second."

I put on my shirt while she pulled herself together. She wiped her tears away, slipped on her sandals, and lifted her chin with a steadying breath.

She was the kind of woman you didn't let go, that you fought for until your dying breath—and that was my intention. No matter what happened in the next few hours, Penelope was worth it.

But then I thought of Elisa, and my heart shattered.

Chapter Twenty-Nine

VENEZUELA

I would save Cruz. I had to. I was the one who had pursued him in the bar, in the elevator, on the ship, everywhere. I was the instigator. I was to blame.

Me. Me. Me.

Pushing back the panic that threatened to overtake every ounce of logic in my body, I opened the door to Wilder's suite with my key and found the production team gathered around the dining room table. Cruz followed me in, the backpack he'd refused to leave behind slung over one shoulder.

"Get out," I said, my voice soft but deadly.

Bobby looked up at me, his eyebrows furrowed. "I'm sorry?"

"I need to talk to my brothers. Get out. Now."

Pax took one look at me, and Cruz standing behind me, and stood up from the table. "You heard her."

"We're allowed to be here by contract," Bobby started.

"If you use that contract word one more time I'm going to shove it up your ass," Landon said, standing next to Pax.

"Leave or stay, I don't care," Pax said to Bobby. "We'll just go to her suite where you're not allowed."

"Damn it," Bobby muttered. "Clear the room!"

"That means you, too," I told the other Renegades lounging in the living room.

Leah came down the stairs from Pax's room, Rachel in tow. "Everything okay?"

"They can stay," I told Pax.

The room cleared, and soon it was just Pax, Landon, Rachel, Leah, Nick, Cruz, and me gathered at the table, awaiting the confession they didn't know was coming.

"Maybe we should sit down," Pax suggested.

"No, I need to stand, but you might want to sit."

"Jesus, is it always like this? I should have come aboard earlier," Nick said.

I shot him a glare.

"I'm in trouble," I said, and the atmosphere of the room changed instantly.

"Okay. What do you need?" Pax asked. No questions or accusations. He didn't know if I'd cheated on a test or killed someone and needed help burying the body. He was in before I told him what I'd done, and I loved him for it.

"*I'm* in trouble," Cruz corrected, standing next to me.

"Okay, we're in trouble."

"Trouble. Got it," Pax said, leaning in.

"We're?" Landon's eyes narrowed.

"Here we go," Rachel mumbled.

"Remember when I got arrested in Vegas for jumping off the High Roller?" I gripped the back of the chair.

"Yes, as does every lawyer who represents our company," Pax drawled.

"Right. Did Brandon ever show you the paperwork? Tell you who I was with?"

Pax's eyebrows furrowed, and he shook his head. "No. We were busy, and I trusted that he took care of it."

"It was me," Cruz said.

Every head swung in his direction.

"What?" Landon snapped.

"I'm the guy from the bar in Vegas. I jumped off the Ferris wheel with her."

"You were the one found in bed with her?" Pax asked, his voice dangerously quiet.

"Pax…" I warned.

"Oh, Brandon filled me in on that bit, but I figured I sure as hell wasn't one to judge who you chose to…" He shook his head. "And since you've been on board?"

"We've been together," Cruz said.

"You have got to be fucking kidding me," Landon seethed.

"Seriously, Landon? You're the last person to lecture anyone about falling in love with someone you shouldn't. Even Leah was off-limits to Pax. I'm just following suit here."

"Leah was my *tutor*. Not my *teacher*," Pax corrected.

"Lay off her. I take full responsibility for our actions." Cruz subtly stepped in front of me.

I scoffed, moving to the side. "No. I'm an adult. I wanted him, went after him, convinced him, fell in love with him. Got it? Does anyone else need any other details or want to berate me for my choices? Because I've had a hell of a lot less sex than *any* of you three. Sorry, girls."

"No offense taken," Leah said, sitting back.

"God, this explains so much," Pax said, raking his hands over his face. "The way you knew things about him, how comfortable you are around each other, the way you've been sneaking off when we're in ports…"

"Yup, guilty and guilty. Anything else?"

Paxton's gaze flickered between Cruz and me before he finally sighed. "What do you need? What's happened, besides…the obvious?"

"Dr. Gibson just walked in on me coming out of Cruz's shower wearing nothing but a towel."

"Now that's an image I'm going to have to scrub out of my head," Nick chimed in.

"Fuck," Paxton seethed.

"Did you admit to anything?" Landon asked.

"She saw me practically naked," I threw back.

"Doesn't matter. Did you admit to anything?"

Cruz and I locked eyes for a second in silent conversation. Had we? She'd implied we were sleeping together, but he'd never agreed.

"No. I said that she wasn't a student when we met, but that was it."

"Okay, then the only evidence she has is a student in your bedroom, which…you know…is pretty damning, but it's your word against hers."

"I'm not calling her a liar," Cruz snapped. "Not to save myself."

"Not to save Penna's reputation? Because she's in the middle of this goddamned documentary, and your shit is about to hit the fan."

"I would never ask him to lie for me," I said. "He wouldn't be who I loved if he did. I can take whatever gets thrown at me."

"You shouldn't have to!" Pax yelled. "He should have protected you. Left you the hell alone until you were off this ship!" He turned to Cruz. "Is that what she is to you? Some fun while you're here? A little student fling to pass the time?"

"Pax," I warned.

"That's enough!" Cruz slammed his hands on the dining room table. "You love her, and because you do, I'll let you get away with that jackass comment. But don't you dare ever imply that she means less to me than Leah does to you. It won't end well for you."

"And this is why I didn't tell you in the first place," I said to the guys. "You're fine having me keep your secrets, clean up after your messes, but the moment I wind up in one of my own, you turn into judgmental nuns. I'm not here to ask for penance. I don't need your forgiveness, because I have nothing to apologize for, and neither does Cruz."

Paxton leaned back in his chair, Leah reaching for his hand.

"You really jumped off the High Roller with her? After knowing her what? Twenty minutes?" Nick asked.

"Yeah," Cruz answered.

"Why would you do that?"

"Because she needed me to, which is pretty much the answer to any question you could possibly have for me right now."

"You had me within weeks," Leah said softly to Pax. "We both knew we shouldn't, that it could jeopardize your entire documentary, and that didn't stop us."

"You seriously seduced me while I was dating your best friend," Rachel reminded Landon. "Not sure we should be casting stones, glass houses and whatnot."

"You're supposed to be the sensible one, Penna," Pax said, his shoulders slumping. "You have always made the sound choices."

"Well, love makes you do crazy things."

"Okay, well, we can't do anything until we know what Dr. Gibson is going to do. I own the ship, but not UCLA, so everyone sit tight. Landon's right. She has no other evidence besides what she saw."

The door opened, and we all turned to see Bobby walk in, red-faced and panting with Victor on his heels. "Those asswipes," he cursed.

"What's wrong?" Pax asked, standing.

"The dean just confiscated my entire editing room and all our tape."

"They can't—" Landon started.

"They can," Nick countered. "You guys signed an agreement that the university could preview all tape to ensure you weren't filming a *Girls Gone Wild—Study At Sea* edition."

"Okay, well, you guys were careful around the cameras, right?" Pax asked.

"Yeah. We were never together on set, or always super hidden," I told him.

"That's not entirely correct…" Victor said slowly.

"What?" Bobby snapped.

"Excuse me?" Cruz stepped forward, and Victor backed up.

"A couple of us knew she was sneaking off, and we wanted to make sure we had all the footage we could possibly need—not that we'd use it, of course. But…"

"But what?" I snapped.

"We followed you. In every port. Chile, Buenos Aires. All of it. Once we knew what you two were up to…well, there's some pretty damning footage in there."

Cruz's fist flew, slamming into Victor's face with a cracking sound that didn't bode well for Victor.

"Not everything about her life is up for grabs, asshole! You had no right. In fact, you violated about a dozen of *her* rights!"

"He told us to get the best possible footage!" Victor yelled, pointing at Bobby with one hand while he cupped his nose with the other.

"Of the stunts! The bar! The ship!" Bobby shouted back.

"You'd better go, Victor," Pax said softly, and the smaller man ran.

"It's only a matter of time before they know," Cruz told me, his face and posture strong but resigned.

"What do we do?"

Cruz picked up his backpack and slung it over his shoulder. "Come with me. We need to talk."

"Thanks, guys. I don't think there's anything else you can do," I told my friends. Over their protests, I took Cruz's hand. He led me out the sliding glass door onto the balcony that connected the backs of our suites and into my own.

I felt separate from my own body as he sat us gently on the living room couch, my hand resting in his. What was going to happen to him? What had I done to him?

"They're going to come for me as soon as they find the evidence."

"I know. I'm so sorry, Cruz. I should have stayed away from you."

"Stop," he said, cupping my face with his hands. "I am the one responsible."

"I ruined you," I whispered, my eyes prickling.

He kissed me lightly, as if it were the first time—or maybe the last.

"Never. All you've ever done is make me better. If anything, I wasn't careful enough. I failed you."

"But your job…"

"Penelope, there is nothing about you that I regret. No matter what happens, do you understand?"

I couldn't move—too terrified that the slightest motion would cause me to fracture into a thousand tiny pieces.

"I need to hear you tell me that you understand. I can't leave here thinking you don't know what you mean to me."

"I understand," I said because he needed me to. How could he still love me knowing what I was about to cost him?

"Good." He hoisted his backpack onto the coffee table. "I need to tell you something."

There was a knock at the door.

"Oh no," I said, looking toward the harbinger of our doom. *Too fast.* It was happening too fast.

"Don't answer that," he pleaded. "The backpack has all my—"

The knocking came again, this time as a pounding that seemed to last forever.

"Penelope," he called over the knocking, bringing my attention back to him.

"That has to be them!"

"Yes, I'm sure it is. Listen to me—the backpack. Please hide it for me. Keep it safe. Whatever you do, don't get caught with it. Throw it overboard if something happens, but don't let them find it."

"What do you mean if something happens? What's in it?"

"You can look, but it's best if you don't. It's nothing I'm ashamed of, but it is illegal, and there is such a thing as plausible deniability. Promise me you won't let anyone find it."

The knock at the door grew to a pounding, the voice on the other side calling my name. Cruz took my chin in his hand, gently guiding my attention back to him.

"Promise me, Penelope."

"I promise."

He kissed me softly. "This will be over before you know it. I'm sure they just want to talk to me, and then we'll figure out what we'll do, okay?"

"Okay," I agreed. Fear tightened my chest, making it nearly impossible to draw a full breath. "What if it's not okay?"

"It will be. No matter what's about to happen, we'll be in Miami soon."

The knocking ceased, only to be replaced by the swift *click* of the lock opening.

No. No, no, no.

"I love you," he whispered.

"I'll go with you," I said as the door opened.

"No. You stay as far away from this as possible. You have to."

"Dr. Delgado?" Dr. Paul, the dean of academics, called from the entry hall.

"Swear it. No matter what happens, you have to stay clear. Do not interfere. If I get the slightest idea you're trying to take any blame, I'll confess to things we never did."

"That's not fair." I shook my head. How was this happening? Why so fast? Why now?

"Dr. Delgado," Dr. Paul said with a sigh, standing in my dining room where he could clearly see us.

"I don't give a fuck about fair. Agree. Now."

He didn't look away, even with the dean just behind me.

"Okay," I said, knowing that even the nearly innocent picture we presented right now wasn't helping matters any.

"Dr. Paul," Cruz said, getting up.

"Dr. Delgado, if you'll come with me—with us—we need to speak privately."

There were two security guards posted in my entry, both eyeing Cruz like they had even a prayer of taking him down. Ignoring every instinct to the contrary, I kept my butt glued to the sofa, repeating my promise over and over in my head. I would not interfere. I would not take the blame.

"I understand," Cruz said with a nod.

Dr. Paul motioned toward the door, and Cruz walked out, never once looking back.

The *click* of the door shutting felt final, as if my life would now be divided into three categories: before I knew Cruz, while our love was a secret, and whatever was about to hit me next.

I didn't want the third phase to start, and the moment I

moved, it would. Right now was limbo, that gray area between two eras. Every fiber of my being screamed that limbo was better than whatever was coming.

Instead of accepting my new reality, I sat there on the couch, my legs curled under me, staring at the backpack he'd left behind. He'd come for me as soon as they were done with him, and then we'd deal with everything together. It would be okay because Cruz had said so.

A knock at the sliding glass door sounded, and I looked up to see Landon and Pax. I nodded once, and they came in to sit on either side of me on the sofa, each taking one of my hands.

"Nick's on the phone with the lawyers," Pax said, his voice soft. "He's trying to figure out if we can get them out of the editing room, but so far it doesn't sound good."

I nodded slowly.

"Dean Paul came to our room already," Landon said.

I kept nodding, the motion soothing.

"What can we do?"

"Just sit with me until they come back?" They'd take me for an interview, or let me know what had been decided; either way, I didn't want to be alone.

"We'll stay," Pax promised.

"Yeah, that's no problem," Landon agreed.

The door opened again, and Nick came in, parking on the other side of Landon. "There's nothing we can do. We signed those agreements."

"So it's just a matter of time."

"Yeah."

I glanced at the guys and felt a little stronger. They'd been at my side for countless challenges—some we didn't think we'd even manage to live through.

But we had.

And I would survive this, no matter what Dean Paul

decided to do.

Even if they fired Cruz, I'd find him in Miami, or back in L.A. in a few weeks, and it would be okay. We could hire him for the Renegades in some capacity, or something. It would be okay.

"I should have told you guys. I'm sorry that I hid it from you."

"It's okay," Pax said, squeezing my hand. "No matter how close we are, we all have things we just can't share."

"I really do love him."

"I know," Pax answered.

"And he loves you, Penna. It will be okay."

I nodded quickly, like my head had become capable of only making that motion. "He is so much more than you guys even know. He went with me to see Brooke."

Nick leaned forward. "You saw Brooke?"

I blinked quickly, shocked that I'd said it. But the cat was out of the bag, the horse out of the barn...whatever.

"I went to visit her when we were in L.A., but she wouldn't see me. She won't answer my letters, either. Or my phone calls. Apparently I'm a detriment to her recovery. After all, I'm still doing the very thing that caused her breakdown."

"Oh, damn. Penna, I'm so sorry." Nick rested his head on his hands.

I shrugged. "It's fine. Everything's fine."

"We all know that it's not," Landon said, pulling me under his arm.

"No. It's not," I admitted.

"Do you want to talk to us about it? We love Brooke, too. The shit that went down didn't change that."

For months I'd silenced it, bottled it, and kept it from the very people who knew the situation the best.

"Yeah...yeah, I think I do."

• • •

The sun streamed through the windows of the suite when I woke up, still lying on the couch in the same clothes I'd worn the night before.

The ship was moving, which meant we'd be in Aruba tomorrow.

I blinked the sleep out of my eyes and saw Pax crashed out on the floor, Nick laid out on the loveseat, and Landon lying across the two chairs like some kind of bendy bridge. A smile pulled at my lips until I remembered what had happened last night.

They never came for me.

I slipped on flip-flops and made my exit quietly. Once the door was shut, I ran for the elevators. Now that we'd been outed, it wasn't like I needed to climb down the balcony anymore.

There was a group of students in the elevator, but no one looked at me any weirder than normal or pinned a scarlet *A* to my chest, so the dean must have kept it quiet so far.

I walked as calmly as I could through deck nine, but I hurried as I saw Dr. Westwick coming out of the shared suite.

My footsteps didn't falter, but my heartbeat did as I made my way up to the door.

"Miss Carstairs," Dr. Westwick said, with a raised eyebrow. "May I help you?"

"I was looking for Dr. Delgado."

His eyes darted down the hall, which told me he was more than aware of what had happened last night. "That's something you'll need to talk to Dean Paul about. Now if you'll excuse me, I'm late for class."

He brushed by me without another word.

That pit in my stomach grew deeper, and a sickening sense of foreboding took over. I tried to push past it, but with every step I took toward Dean Paul's office, the feeling became heavier and more nauseating.

When I reached the administrative offices, I walked straight past Dean Paul's blustering secretary and into his office.

He looked up from his desk, startled for an instant, but then his face fell into something too condescending for words.

"It's fine, Peggy. I'll handle her," he told his secretary.

She nodded and left us, closing the door on her way out.

Dean Paul stood, and for the tiniest moment, I felt small, as though this man would crush me beneath the weight of his judgmental stare. *Hell no.* I wasn't just Penelope Carstairs; I was Rebel, the only woman to hold an X Games medal in an all-male category. I'd done things this man could never comprehend in his wildest dreams, and he could only make me feel small if I let him.

My chin rose a good two inches.

"I came to see about Dr. Delgado."

"Ah yes. I can see that you would. You'll be happy to know that you won't be expelled, though all your grades for his class will be reexamined by another professor who isn't… tied to you."

Expelled. It had never dawned on me that I would be kicked out of school, but for the moment, I just couldn't bring myself to care.

"And Dr. Delgado?"

"He's no longer with us."

My heart sank. I really had cost him everything. *No matter what happens, you have to stay clear. Do not interfere.* I'd promised him, and the least I could do was keep my mouth reasonably shut. "I understand. Is there any way you would allow me to speak with him now that he's not a member of the faculty?"

Dean Paul's eyes quickly widened, then narrowed.

"I think you misunderstood me. Dr. Delgado is no longer on the ship. He was removed from the campus last night while we were still in port."

And just like that, phase three hit me.

Cruz was gone.

Chapter Thirty

PENNA

AT SEA

"Hey, you okay?" Rachel asked from my doorway.

I looked up from where I sat cross-legged on my bed, Cruz's backpack in front of me.

She waited for a few heartbeats, and when I didn't respond, she walked in and sat on the edge of my bed. "You skipped class today."

"My grades can take it." My voice sounded raspy to my own ears.

"Yeah, well, everyone is going apeshit worrying about you."

"I'm fine." My mantra was back and stronger than ever.

"Yeah, you staring at this bag for the last six hours? Not fine. Not even partly fine."

"It's Cruz's."

"I figured. You open it?"

"No. He asked me to…" I sighed. Maybe if I'd told my friends about Cruz earlier, they could have helped me protect him. "He told me to keep it hidden."

She leaned back to look at it, but didn't touch it. "Is it ticking?"

"Very funny." A slight smile lifted the corners of my mouth. "You know what hurts the most? I have no way to get ahold of him. The university shut down his email, and I never thought to get his phone number. How funny is that? I've loved this man for months and don't know his phone number."

"This ship is like its own little universe. Phone numbers haven't exactly been needed."

"I sent him a Facebook message, though. At least I found him there, but I have no clue if he has internet access, or what he took with him, or if he can get out of Venezuela. I have no way to contact him."

"One, I firmly believe that Doc will be okay no matter where he is. Two, I also know that he'll find *you*. Third, just open it. Maybe there's a way to find him in there. Or it's a dead body."

"In a backpack?"

She shrugged. "Stranger things have happened."

"I'm going to need you to stop watching reruns of *Dexter*."

"Hey, on-ship entertainment is sparse. Now seriously. Open it. I can leave if you want privacy, but either open it or put it somewhere. Stop staring at it."

Right or wrong, curiosity and desperation to find something that might connect me to Cruz had my fingers unzipping before my conscience could battle back.

"Stay?" I asked Rachel as she stood to leave.

"Sure," she said, sitting back on the bed but not touching the bag.

I pulled out the single accordion file from the main

pocket, slipped the elastic over the front, and opened it. The first pocket contained the cruise itinerary.

The second held an envelope of pictures. I flipped through them. "They're all of his sister, but he's not in any of them."

"She's pretty," Rachel said, looking at the brown-haired, chocolate-eyed girl.

"She has the same eyes as Cruz," I said. She was daintier in her features, but those eyes were identical.

"Hey, can I see that?" Rachel asked, and I handed her a picture of Elisa standing in front of a stadium.

"She's in Cuba?"

"What? I don't think so. They immigrated right before she was born."

"No, this stadium…that's where we're having the Renegade Open. I just saw a bunch of pictures in Landon's suite. This is definitely it."

My forehead puckered, and I flipped through the other pictures, this time looking for the background details. The shops were all in Spanish, and the architecture definitely fit with what we'd studied about Havana.

I put the pictures in the envelope and went back to the file, hoping for an explanation.

What I found were two passports. Both with Elisa's picture, but only one with her name.

"What the hell?" I muttered.

"Hey, that's…"

"Dr. Messina's name," I said, running my thumb over the print like some other name would appear. "But Cruz replaced her."

"In more ways than one, it appears."

"But why would he…?" I shook my head and looked in the next compartment. There were dozens of military papers clipped together—pages and pages of forms with numbers and acronyms I didn't understand.

"He seriously travels with his military records?" Rachel asked.

I shrugged, unsure of what any of this was.

The next section held printed itineraries from Miami for Cruz and Elisa Delgado to L.A. Their flight was scheduled a few days after we arrived in port, just like mine. Another paper showed a printout of the stadium where we were hosting the Renegade Open in Havana. All the exits were marked, circled in red pen. Small *X*s adorned sections of the map, which was broken down floor by floor. The next page showed a receipt for a ticket purchased in Elisa's name.

Tingles ran up my forearms, followed closely by goose bumps as I put it together.

The last compartment held two ID badges just like the ones we all had to board the ship at every port. One held another picture of Elisa with Dr. Messina's name. The other was a picture of Cruz with Dr. Westwick's.

"You're right," I said to Rachel.

"About what?" She examined the map of the stadium.

"His sister is in Cuba. He was going to use the Renegade Open to get her out."

• • •

The sun beat down into my gear, and I sent a shot of water from my bottle down my back. Aruba was gorgeous, but I wish I was out with the rest of the Renegades playing on the flyboards. Instead, Nick and I were holed up at a makeshift supercross track nowhere near the beach.

"You sure you're ready to try again?" he asked from under his ball cap, the camera crew hovering so close I wanted to punch them. If not for this damn documentary, I would have still had Cruz. *If not for this documentary, you never would have met Cruz.*

"Yeah," I answered, putting my helmet back on. I'd consistently slid out on each of my dozen or so attempts this morning—failing to stick every landing. I knew I only had a few more runs in me before the heat and my own exhaustion took me out.

"This is getting painful to watch."

"I never asked you to stay."

He whistled. "Dull your edges there, Penna. I'm not out here to cut you."

I hung my head momentarily. "I know. You're right. The stuff with…you know…is still in my head."

"I get that. I really do. But if you'd like to live through this little stunt of yours, then you're going to have to block him out for a while. There's only room for one person on that bike, and he is weighing you down."

"Point taken." I gave him a nod and hopped onto Elizabeth. I rode back to the start of the track, giving myself those few moments to think about Cruz.

Where was he? How long had he been planning to get Elisa out of Cuba? How was she there to begin with? The questions hounded me at every moment, invading my peace and stealing my sanity whenever I did manage a quiet second.

I didn't mind the stares of other students or the rumor mill that had started the minute the European History professor took over Cruz's class and pointedly handed back an entire stack of my regraded work. Gone was the number system Cruz had used to protect us both, but I didn't smirk that I kept my *A*. I deserved that grade, and our relationship had never played into the classroom. I didn't mind that my teammates handled me like glass, or even Rachel's constant nagging that I should tell them what I found in the backpack.

What I did mind—the sharp, rending pain in my heart when I wondered if Cruz had planned this all around me. If he'd used me.

I wasn't stupid. He'd need me to hack into the database, just like I did every time I wanted to use the wifi, and he'd need me to add Dr. Messina back to the manifest so it wouldn't look odd when she boarded again. Unless Cruz had a computer science degree he wasn't telling me about, well, I was his best shot.

He wouldn't use you like that. My heart railed against my brain, demanding to give Cruz a chance to explain before I jumped to the obvious conclusion.

There's nothing he wouldn't do for his sister, my head countered.

I silenced them both as I pulled up to the start of the track. Taking a deep, steadying breath, I pictured my mind like a cluttered dry-erase board. Then I envisioned wiping it clean with big, powerful swipes of my mental eraser. Mind clear, I pictured the ramp, the jump, and the perfect landing.

A peaceful wave of serenity washed over me, and I felt it. This was the time I nailed it.

My eyes snapped open, and I hit the throttle. Palm and divi-divi trees blurred as I sped down the track. Gear by gear, I accelerated as the super-ramp loomed bigger and bigger.

I hit the ramp, going nearly vertical as I raced toward the sky. Then I flew.

Feeling the arc, I pulled the bike into the backflip. The ground and sky traded places once, and my muscles screamed as I urged Elizabeth around again, watching the kaleidoscope of the earth spinning around me.

As the ground rushed up to meet me, I righted the bike and braced for impact.

My back tire hit first, then the front. My body jarred, lurching forward, but I stayed seated as I brought the bike to a stop.

In the background, I heard Nick's whoop as I lifted off my helmet. I didn't cheer or even fist pump. I simply leaned my head back, accepting the sun's caress on my face. Then I laughed, loudly and joyously, ignoring the cameras.

I did it.

I was the first woman to ever successfully land a double backflip on a supercross ramp.

A small twinge of bitterness stole into my heart, twisting the taste of my victory. In that moment, it wasn't Nick's congratulations, or even Pax or Landon's that I wanted. All I wanted was Cruz.

· · ·

Nine. That was the number of times I landed the flip after the first completion. When Nick forced me to stop for the evening, he used the sunset as the excuse, but I knew it was because he saw the exhaustion stretched across every line of my body.

I had the trick, but I could still do some major damage to myself if I didn't stop while my muscles were capable.

I changed in the tent the crew had assembled while Nick handled settling up with the facility manager in the office. Bag packed, I slung it over my shoulder and walked out into the warm, humid evening.

"Penna!" Nick called from the office doorway, which sat about ten yards back from the track.

"What's up?"

"You have a phone call."

"Okay." My eyebrows shot skyward, but I crossed the distance, wondering if Pax or Landon needed something.

Nick held the door as I walked through it, his lips in a pressed line. "You'll want to take it in there," he said, motioning toward a small, private office.

I dropped my bag and headed for the phone, closing the door behind me before grabbing the receiver and hitting the flashing red light. "Hello?"

"Penelope."

His voice was a soft sigh that cut through me like the sharpest knife.

"Cruz? Where are you? Are you okay?" I sat on the edge of the desk, my knees immediately weak in a way that had nothing to do with the riding I'd done this afternoon.

"I'm in Santo Domingo."

I blinked. "In the Dominican Republic?"

"That's the one. I fly back to the States tomorrow."

"I looked in the backpack."

"Okay." His voice was annoyingly calm.

"That's all you have to say?"

"I assumed you would when I left. I needed you to hide it from Dean Paul and the ship's security, Penelope, not from yourself. I had no clue I wasn't coming back."

"What did you think I was going to do with it?" I snapped.

"I kind of hoped you'd throw it into the ocean." Ugh, I could practically see him shrug from here, like it didn't matter one bit to him.

"Really. You want me to get rid of fake passports, and maps, and ID badges that you obviously procured illegally and at some cost? Those passports look too good, Cruz. They must have cost you a shit ton."

"They did. And only one is fake."

"Oh, just one. That's the line you want to draw?"

"Throw it overboard, Penelope. If you get caught with it, you'll be arrested."

"No shit, Sherlock. But you obviously need it, otherwise you wouldn't have left it with me."

"That's one of the reasons I'm calling." His voice dropped in his I'm-getting-angry voice.

"And the other?" My heart paused its beats, as if it needed his response to push life through me.

"Because I love you, Penelope."

And just like that—I could breathe again.

"I needed to hear your voice," he explained. "When they interviewed me, they had some of the footage already, and it wasn't even the bad stuff. But I knew they'd find it. Dean Paul agreed that if I resigned immediately and didn't fight it, I'd lose my job but avoid any hit to your grades, your enrollment, or your reputation."

I rested my head in my open hand. "Oh God. You didn't have to. I'm the one who pursued you. I…I ruined you."

"You were the one who chased you into an office on your birthday, unable to bear the thought of another man's hands on you?"

"Well, no."

"Exactly. There is equal blame because we are equal partners in this relationship. And please don't think that because there are four hundred miles between us that we're broken up or something asinine like that."

I grinned. "So we're still together?"

"I just walked away from everything I've worked the last ten years for. If you're not waiting for me in Miami, then it was pretty much for nothing." There was a pause while I weighed his words against what I'd found in the bag. "Unless you've changed your mind?"

That small, nagging doubt edged its way in. "No, but I need to know if you used me. I found the receipt for the Open ticket, and you have to explain, because right now I know there are about fifty things you're not telling me."

He sighed, and I could picture his hand running over his hair. "Elisa is in Cuba."

"Figured that out."

"She went back with my mother. She was only a baby, and Mom couldn't leave her like she left me." He said it with such dispassion, as if his abandonment was simply a matter of fact.

"And when your mother died?"

"She stayed with my father. She had no choice, no way out, and she's been stuck there ever since, living with the man who killed our mother and won't ever see the inside of a cell for it."

My eyes slid shut, as Cruz's heartache took seed in my chest. "I'm so sorry."

"Me, too. I've tried to get her out before, but my father is high up in the Ministry of the Interior. Every time I booked a flight, I found myself detained at the airport before I could get on the plane."

"He has you on a watch list."

"Yes. So when Dr. Messina left for the cruise, and I was finishing up my dissertation, I asked if she would refer me to teach on board next year, knowing that they take professors from colleges all over the U.S., and Havana was one of the ports."

"But she left this year."

"And I took the opportunity. It was such short notice that I had to work on everything en route—the passports, the airline tickets…convincing you that Havana was the perfect place to host the Open."

I scoffed. "It took one suggestion. Apparently I'm pretty damn easy."

"You're anything but easy, Penelope. But I knew that with so many Americans coming in for the Open and the ship in port, it would have been the perfect time to get her out. She was supposed to find me at the Open—she knew I was with you guys and even that you call me Doc. That's how she was going to ask for me, not that it matters now. I would have signed her on board with Dr. Messina's badge—"

"That you faked," I said.

"Yes, but when they checked the manifest, they would have seen that she was listed and let her through."

"You mean after you asked me to remove you from the manifest so you could get into Cuba, and add her so she could get on. How were you planning to get off the ship? Posing as Dr. Westwick?"

"Yes."

"And when he tried to get off?"

"I figured you might be able to help me figure a work-around there."

"Unbelievable."

"Yes," he said softly, as if that was enough of an apology. "I was always going to tell you."

"But only when you needed me."

"I can't deny that. I put so much trust in you. My entire career was in your hands—my heart, my body, my future. But I didn't know how you'd feel about what I was doing, and quite frankly, I wasn't prepared to bet Elisa's life or risk that you'd get caught."

Logically, I understood. She was his sister.

I almost laughed, realizing that while Cruz was risking his very life to save his sister, mine couldn't even return a letter or be bothered to see me.

Elisa was innocent in all of this, and Cruz was genuinely worried for her safety.

"I'll do it," I said softly.

"Do what? Forgive me for not telling you?"

"Maybe, one day. But I'll get her out. I have everything, and I can do it. I need…" I took a steadying breath. "I'd like your permission to bring the others in. I'll need their help, and you can trust them."

It went against everything in my nature to ask someone to confide in my friends, but this wasn't my secret.

"No. You're not putting yourself in danger like that. You have no idea what the laws are there, or how watched she is. I don't give a fuck who you tell, because it won't work without me there, and I'm not putting you in the line of fire."

"She's your sister, Cruz."

"And I will find another way to get her out without risking you!" he shouted.

The air rushed from my lungs.

"I love Elisa, and I will get her out. I will get her to Harvard. But there is a line that I will not cross for her, and that line is *you*. Don't you dare put yourself in danger, Penelope. I can't bear the thought of it, and I will not live without you."

My chin trembled, and I did my best to force back every emotion that could cloud this decision. I had cost him his career; I would not be the reason he lost Elisa.

"I love you," I told him. "And you won't lose me."

"I love you even more." His voice pitched up, stressed. "Don't do anything. Throw the bag overboard, burn it. I don't care. There's another way."

"I am the other way. You just have to trust me."

"Penelope!"

"I love you, and I'll see you in Miami."

I hung up the phone before my resolve broke and then strode out of the office, Nick hot on my heels.

We were quiet on the drive back to the *Athena* as my mind raced with every possibility.

"Get everyone together," I ordered as we split ways in the hallway of the *Athena*.

"Please?" he openly teased me.

"Now," I said, with a smile and a nod.

I gathered the accordion file and everything that was in it and headed to Pax's suite, where the others made their way to the dining room table.

"Out!" I said to Bobby.

"For fuck's sake, Penna," he whined. "The contract—"

"After what you cost me, do you seriously think I'm going to give a rat's ass about the contract? Get out!"

He stomped like a toddler, but he took his crew with him.

"What's up?" Pax asked.

I spread the documents on the table and leaned forward on my palms.

"I want to pull off the biggest stunt of our lives, and I'm going to need your help."

Chapter Thirty-One

HAVANA

Little John led us through the crowd that had gathered outside the stadium. Estadio Panamericano was built to hold thirty-four thousand people, and we'd sold out, thanks to Nick's awesome marketing and inviting riders from all over the world.

We'd met with everyone last night, after we'd toured Havana all day, and I'd turned in my thesis to the professor who knew I'd been sleeping with Cruz. Awkward? Hell yes.

Havana was beautiful, the architecture reminding me so much of Old World class and elegance. I saw Cruz in every little boy who ran by, every young man crossing the street, and wished he could have been there to show me where he came from.

A hand reached out from the crowd, grabbing my shoulder, jarring me from my thoughts. Landon gripped the guy's wrist and shook his head at him as he pushed him back.

"Sorry, you looked distracted," he apologized.

"It's okay. I don't mind you treating me like a girl every once in a while," I said with a tight smile.

I was dressed every bit the part of Rebel today, my hair down and curled, my makeup flawless, my outfit sporty chic. Our plan required that I play my part to a *T*, and I was going to more than deliver.

We made our way into the building and through the small hallway to the closed room where our press conference would be held. Flashes went off the moment we walked in, and while Leah and Rachel headed to the seats Little John had saved for them, I took my spot on the dais between Pax and Landon.

Our names were called from every corner of the room, and Little John stepped up to run the conference, calling one reporter at a time. The questions were innocuous at first. How did we like Havana? What inspired us to host the first extreme sports event of this magnitude here?

"Rebel, can you tell us how you're feeling after your accident in Dubai?"

I gave him a billion megawatt smile. "I'm all recovered and ready to rock tomorrow. In fact, I have something new to show you guys that I promise you won't see anywhere else."

"And what about Nitro?" another asked, and I tensed. "Rumors are that he's here, but we don't see him with you."

"Nitro is with us, and he chose to keep his trip private. We'd really appreciate it if you guys would, too," I said before Pax flew off the handle. Nick was a line of inquiry he never took well.

We answered a few more questions, mostly about the tricks the guys had planned and the documentary, and got the hell out of there.

We walked down the guarded hall, concrete on both sides, as Nick joined us, his eyes wide. "Guys—"

"Wait one moment," a soldier in a green uniform said to us, stepping in our path. "Turn off the cameras."

Bobby nodded, and the crew did so, more than aware of the laws here about photographing police. We all traded glances as an armed entourage approached.

The guards parted, revealing a lightly bearded man in his fifties. His frame was strong, well-built, with a cocky smile and—oh God—those eyes.

They were the eyes I loved so much, but there was no softness there, only a diamond-like hardness to them.

"General Delgado," the guard introduced us.

Pax's hand reached for mine, and he stepped closer to my side.

"Ah, the Renegades. I was hoping I'd get to meet you. My daughter seems quite enamored of you."

"Your daughter?" Pax asked, smooth as butter.

"Yes, Elisa, come up here," he ordered, his voice turning harsh.

I squeezed Pax's hand as she stepped into view. Elisa was strikingly beautiful with thick, long brown hair and the same eyes that ran in the family. Her eyes darted up to ours.

"Hi there, Elisa," I said softly, trying to keep my heart from beating out of my chest like some kind of Poe story. What was he doing with her? She was supposed to come alone. I waited until she looked me in the eyes and then smiled. "I'm Penelope." *Please recognize my name.*

Her eyes widened. "Rebel?" *She did.* One small miracle on the day I needed a dozen of them.

"That's me. So you're a fan?"

She nodded.

"Of course she never told me," General Delgado said. "I found a ticket in her bedroom. Otherwise I never would have known." He clapped her on the shoulder, and she cringed.

"I just…wanted to see Doc," Elisa said softly.

I swallowed the lump in my throat. "I'm so sorry, but Doc couldn't make this show. But I know his routine, and I'm going to take his place tonight."

Her eyes widened, hope sparking in them, and I nodded with a shaky smile. It took every ounce of willpower in my body to not grab her and run. Screw the Open. Screw the documentary. She stood three feet in front of me, and I couldn't do shit. I'd never felt so powerless in my life. But she was a part of Cruz, and I couldn't—*wouldn't*—fail.

"Will you both be joining us for the show?" Pax asked, drawing the general's attention from me.

"We will," he answered. "I've taken out a box as a present to my Elisa."

Fuck. She wouldn't be in the seat we'd planned.

"We are honored to have you," Landon added. "You know, if you wanted the ultimate experience for your daughter, we'd love to include her in the Open."

I could have kissed him.

"For just a simple ride around the arena, of course," I said with a smile, hoping it came out innocent and naïve— something I was never good at portraying. "We'd have a helmet and everything for her, and she could ride with me. It would definitely be a day she wouldn't forget."

His forehead puckered.

"Of course, we'd also extend the offer to you, General," Pax offered. "Anything to show our host country how thankful we are for the hospitality."

His chest puffed. "No, no. I'm far too old for this. But I think Elisa would like that, wouldn't you?"

She nodded, her eyes locked on mine.

"It's settled then," Pax said. "If you'll please excuse us, we need to make sure everything is set up for the show."

"Of course. I'm needed elsewhere." The general dismissed us by turning on his heel and walking away with Elisa.

"Was that…?" Leah asked.

"Yep," I responded.

"Well, shit. Today just got a fuck-load more complicated," Nick noted.

"We never did like things easy. We're going to need a distraction. We can't just walk out with her anymore. We need something epic." I sighed.

"I think I have just the thing." Nick smiled.

• • •

The BMX and skateboarding portions of the show were over. Landon had won his event by a landslide, not that I was shocked.

"I'm a little nervous," I admitted to Pax as we stood in full gear with our bikes. The entrance to the arena was just ahead of us, the crowd roaring for whatever had just happened.

"I'm fucking terrified. Penna, if something happens to you…"

I took his gloved hand in mine. "Nothing is going to happen. It's been you and me in your backyard since we were five, Pax. We've pulled off the most ludicrous stunts we could think of. Isn't it about time we did something that will make an actual difference?"

"We're with you, Penna," Landon said, taking the other side.

"Make sure you go straight back to the ship. Rachel and Leah are already there, right?"

"Yeah. There was no chance I was letting Leah stay here with that general roaming the halls. They'll lock this place down the minute they realize what you've done."

"The ship is due to pull out a little after midnight, so we're cutting it close as it is," Landon noted.

Everything was timed to a *T*. General Delgado showing up had definitely thrown a huge wrench in our little machine, but this could work. As long as I could get Elisa on board before they found us, we'd be in the clear. After all, she wasn't on the manifest, Dr. Messina was, and that giant ship had tons of places to hide her.

Was it a bulletproof plan? No. But it was all we had.

"Nick is all set?"

"I'm ready. Maybe a little insane, but ready," Nick answered as he rolled up.

"I love you guys."

"Feeling's mutual," Landon promised.

Helmets on, we drove out into the arena. Pax rode, rocking the high score. He might win the title with that triple front flip of his, but I'd be the one in the record book today if I nailed this.

My name was announced to the crowd, the sound echoing around the stadium, and I took off. I pulled whips and a 360 on the smaller jumps before lining up for the super ramp.

My focus broke for only one thought—I wished Cruz were here.

Shoving that away, I locked the pain down tight. Now wasn't the time.

Instead, I gunned it toward the ramp, hit the perfect angle, the right arc. I pulled the bike twice around, the flashes around me going off like glitter bombs, and set the bike down perfectly.

The cheering around me filled my head as I was swept into Pax's hug, then sandwiched by Landon. "You did it!"

"And that's not the hardest thing about tonight," I said with a laugh.

"You sure about skipping the award ceremony?" he teased with more than a hint of worry in his eyes. "You might be able to podium with that trick."

"Might?" I smacked his chest.

"General Jackass will know the minute they call your

name, you don't show, and Elisa isn't in her seat. And that's if he doesn't see you ride out with her in the first place."

"I know. We'll be okay."

"We'll see you on board," Landon said, squeezing me tight.

I nodded, and we broke apart as Landon handed me an extra helmet.

It was time for the finale.

I rode around to the Delgados' box, where the general stood clapping, Elisa pale by his side. He frowned at my outstretched hand toward his daughter. "Unless you'd rather one of the guys take her? I'm sure she'd be happier to ride behind one of them."

His eyes flew to Elisa as he caught my meaning, and then he shook his head. "That was some trick, Miss Carstairs. I'm sure my daughter would be honored for your escort."

I smiled and handed her the helmet. She slid it on, and I worked the buckle underneath. "Ready?" I asked as she climbed over the barrier and onto the back of my bike.

"Yes."

"Let's go," I told her. "Hold on tight. Do you understand? No matter what, don't you dare let go."

She nodded, and I took off slowly, just as we'd planned. The finale commenced around us, motorcycles filling the stadium, flipping, turning, and wowing the crowd as I drove around the edge of the arena with Elisa tucked behind me.

Just as we reached the door that led to the closest exit, my trump card played.

Nick appeared on the smallest skateboarding ramp, raising his hands in the air as they called his name. The crowd went wild, and the guards who stood just inside the door came out to see what the ruckus was.

Then, helmet, pads, and all, Nick rode the ramp in his chair.

It was almost painful not to look, to watch him come back to life under those stadium lights, but I had Elisa and an open doorway.

I took it.

My motor echoed off the concrete hallway as we sped down the corridor. We passed guards, cameramen, and more than a few confused stadium workers.

The guards ahead of us had their radios up to their ears, and then they drew weapons.

"Hold on, it's about to get sporty!" I called out.

Elisa nodded, tucking her helmet in next to mine as she looked over my shoulder. Out of another gate, a forklift backed into the guards, forcing them into the closest supply closet.

Little John cheered us on from the driver's seat.

"Go! Awards are starting!" Bobby shouted, opening the garage-door-style gate that led outside. We raced through it, hitting the slight incline out of the stadium and going airborne for a second before landing. I turned only enough to see that he'd slammed the gate back down as guards raced toward us.

"The cars!" Elisa shouted as we raced into oncoming traffic.

I wove in and out of the stream of cars, focusing on nothing but keeping us alive. Then I heard the sirens.

We were busted.

Revving the engine, I tightened my thighs and settled in for a challenge. The police cars, tiny as they were, came up behind us about a block away. Then they came from the south, blocking the easiest route back to the ship.

Fuck. Shit. Fuck.

"Take the tunnel!" Elisa ordered.

"They'll come at us on the other end!"

"Maybe, but it's our only shot!"

I threw it into a higher gear and threaded the needle of two cars, speeding up the middle like it was my private lane, as we took the tunnel that ran beneath the entrance to the port of Havana.

A pickup truck pulled up next to us and honked as flashing sirens came into view, the lights bouncing off the edges of the end of the tunnel. Soon they'd see us. We'd be toast.

I spared a single look for the honking driver.

Then I did a double take.

"Cruz!" I screamed.

"Get in!" I read his lips, the sound lost in the noise volume of the tunnel.

"You have to get in the back, Elisa," I shouted, hoping she could hear me through the noise.

"What?"

"I'm pulling as close as I can, and then you have to jump!"

"Oh. Yeah. Okay. Right." She nodded, her motion at odds with the petrified tone of her voice.

The end of the tunnel was coming faster than I wanted. I pulled up to the truck so close that my leg rubbed against the metal of the bed. "Now!"

Elisa leveraged herself with my shoulders and then, with one foot on the seat, launched herself into the bed. She made it.

Keeping one hand on the throttle, I jumped, balancing both feet on Elizabeth's seat as the car next to me honked and yelled something I couldn't understand. I'd done this a thousand times before, just for fun, but never when my life depended on it.

I took one deep breath and simultaneously let go of the throttle while I hurled myself sideways, over the bed of the truck, landing next to Elisa on something soft.

My heart twisted for the loss of my bike as I saw her demolished under the SUV two cars back.

"Lose your helmet!" I ordered Elisa, Cruz falling in with traffic as if we hadn't just pulled off some Evel Knievel shit.

She unbuckled her helmet at the same time I stripped

mine, goggles and all, already mourning some of my favorite gear as I chucked it over the side. My jersey was next, leaving me in my close-fit protective jacket.

Cruz's hand was already extended through the back window of the truck, and I helped Elisa through. He reached back for me, and I gripped his hand quickly. We didn't have time for any kind of reunion. I spotted the blanket we'd landed on, and lay down, pulling it over me. My heart slammed in my chest, adrenaline heightening every sensation, every feeling—especially the fear—as we drove through the tunnel. The cops at the end gave us only a cursory look from the sound of it. After all, they were looking for an American girl on a motorcycle.

Cruz turned right, taking the road that ran level with the sea, and I flipped the blanket off, sucking in fresh air. The truck swerved in traffic, but I lay still, sliding back and forth in the bed.

"Hold on!" Cruz yelled, and I braced myself the best I could, hooking my hands onto the edge of the truck as we jumped the curb.

My legs slid to the other side of the bed, but I hung on as Cruz whipped the truck in a steep ninety-degree turn. "Now!" he shouted, offering his hand through the window.

I slid through feet first, landing on the bench seat between Elisa and Cruz.

"What were you thinking?" he shouted, his eyes glued to the road.

"That you weren't going to lose your chance at getting her out! Not because of me!" I fired back.

"Cop," Elisa said, pointing to the left.

"Shit!" Cruz yanked the wheel as we sped through a red light, cars blaring their horns. "That's the road to the port."

"How did you get here?" I asked as he passed another car.

"I chartered a boat, and then brought the life raft ashore," he said. "Basically I got here the same way I got out of here — illegally."

"Irony at its finest," Elisa remarked. "Guys, just leave me. He'll let you go if you leave me."

"No!" Cruz and I both shouted at the same time.

"I wasn't going to sit there and do nothing while you risked your life," Cruz growled, shooting me a death glare.

"Well, it's nice to see you?" I offered with a small cringe.

"Stubborn woman. Insane, reckless, impulsive…" He shook his head as he pulled another sharp left turn. "And I fucking love you."

"They found us." Elisa's voice was flat as the sirens took the turn behind us.

Dozens of blue flags flew on tall poles to the left as Cruz threw the truck in park, pulling me from the cab the moment he had the door open. He hauled me against his side as we raced around the truck to meet Elisa.

The doors to the cop cars flew open behind us.

This was most definitely not the ship. This was a towering building behind barbed wire…guarded by Marines. *The American Embassy.*

"We're American citizens!" Cruz shouted as we ran up the wide concrete steps.

As the doors slammed behind us, the Marines stepped forward, drawing their weapons on the Cuban police.

"Wait!" a stern voice rang out. "He lies!"

General Delgado.

The Marines looked from us to the Cubans as more armed guards came from inside the embassy.

Complete the first double backflip by a woman on a motocross bike? Check.

Start an international incident? Check.

"I have our passports," I told them, reaching in my back

pocket for both mine and Elisa's and waving them.

"But he is Cuban!" General Delgado shouted.

The guard checked our passports, waved only us girls through, and I pushed Elisa lightly. "Get in."

Her eyes flickered between us, and Cruz hugged her. "Go."

She ran, and my shoulders sagged in relief.

Cruz produced his passport, showing it to the guard.

"That paper means nothing! He was born in Cuba," General Delgado said as we turned hand-in-hand to face him. "And Cuba recognizes no other citizenship for her native-born sons. They cannot accept you over my jurisdiction."

General Delgado motioned with a hand, and four policemen ran up the steps toward us.

Cruz's eyes flew wide, and he grabbed my face, pressing a hard kiss to my lips. "I love you."

"Cruz!" Two Cuban officers ripped him from my arms, dragging him down the concrete steps at the same time the Marines stepped forward to flank me. "Do something!" I screamed at the Marines.

"Was he born in Cuba?" one of the Americans asked.

"Yes, but he's a veteran. He earned his U.S. citizenship!"

He grimaced but didn't take his eyes off the Cubans who moved up the stairs, training his weapon on one who got closer to me. "Then we can't help him. Cuba recognizes no other citizenship after theirs. They have every legal right to take him. The girl?"

"She was born in the States."

He nodded, and then they stepped in front of me, effectively blocking me from the Cuban officers. Other Marines joined them and backed me in through the gates until I was safe.

I'd saved Elisa.

But I'd lost Cruz.

Chapter Thirty-Two

CRUZ

HAVANA

I shook the blood back into my hands after the police uncuffed me, then stood guard at the door. The room I'd been brought into was straight out of every Cold War movie I'd ever seen. Concrete walls, a metal table, two metal chairs, and a two-way glass mirror.

I laughed, the sound ironic and ugly. I'd found myself handcuffed the first night I met Penelope, and now I was handcuffed on what was possibly the last night I'd ever see her.

She was so brave, so determined to save someone she'd never met. Every emotion I could possibly have coursed through me. Anger that she'd put herself in danger warred with the soul-searing gratitude that I loved a woman so fearless. Worry that I was about to spend the rest of my life conscripted into the Cuban army was at odds with the stark relief that Elisa would get out. Penelope would get her to Harvard. It hadn't all been in vain.

But the sorrow…God, that was ripping me apart, the gut-wrenching fear that I would never kiss Penelope again, never hold her, never see her rebelliousness echoed in our daughters or her intelligence shine through our sons. What the hell kind of life gave you your soul mate only to wrench her away?

The door creaked open, and my father walked in. Time had been good to the heartless bastard. He looked exactly the same as I remembered him, the decades only giving him salted hair and a meaner eye.

"Cruz," he said, kicking out the chair in front of me and sitting down.

"How did you figure that one out?"

"I found a few pictures of you with the ticket to the motorcycle show. I checked all the manifests for your name, and though I found it odd that you weren't on any of them, I brought in extra security."

"Well, she's gone. Elisa's safe."

He raised an eyebrow. "And yet, I have you. You look like your mother, Cruz."

"You look like her murderer."

His eyes narrowed. "Is that any way to speak to the father you haven't seen in almost twenty years?"

"That's the way I look at the piece of shit who attacked my mother, then me, then finally beat her to death when she foolishly returned to you."

"Her return was her choice. She could have stayed in the United States with you and I would see that her sister never saw the light of day again, or she could come home with my child. That was the agreement."

I leaned back in the chair, folding my arms across my chest. "You didn't know about Elisa. You thought she was bringing me."

"Yes. Your sister was quite a shock, but no matter how much I threatened your grandmother, she wouldn't send you to me. That stubborn woman moved you out of Miami and disappeared. How is she? Dead, I hope?"

"Happy. Thriving."

"God, you even sound American."

"I am American," I fired back.

"So this is what you do? Turn your back on your family? Your people?"

"I can love this country and still hate you."

He drummed his fingers on the surface of the desk. "And the blonde? Penelope? Is she yours?"

My jaw flexed. "She's mine and far beyond your reach."

"You sent a woman to do your work?"

"Penelope sent herself."

He laughed, the sound evil. "You always did hide behind a woman's skirts."

"You always were afraid of strong women. Or maybe you're just not strong enough to keep up with them."

His hands slammed onto the table, but I didn't flinch. "I am afraid of nothing!"

"And I'm not afraid of *you*. I'm not ten anymore, and quite frankly, I'd love for you to try to beat me now."

He sucked in a breath, and as he exhaled I swore I could smell the anger coming off him in pungent waves. "I don't need to beat you. I will break you."

"What could you possibly want from me?"

He smirked. "Absolutely nothing. You have no hope of escape, no life to return to. You will spend your days here with me. There is nothing your government or your pretty little blonde can do. You cost me my daughter, and you will pay with however many years you have left."

He stood, not bothering to push in his chair, and left,

taking the guards with him. The sound of the door shutting was final as it closed behind them.

This was my reality, and it would have to be okay.

Penelope and Elisa were safe, and that was all that could matter, and all I had to hold on to.

Chapter Thirty-Three

PENNA

LOS ANGELES

"It's been three goddamn months!" I shouted at our lawyers. "What do you mean you don't have anything?"

The three suits glanced at one another while Pax slid to my side, taking my hand in his. The length of this boardroom table wasn't sufficient to keep me from launching at them if they called us in here one more time to tell us they had nothing.

"Miss Carstairs." The oldest one looked down his glasses at me. "We've exhausted every resource. The Cubans won't let us speak to him, as is their right, and by law, he's a citizen of their country."

"But he's a citizen of ours, too," I snapped. "How many times can we meet here with you feeding me the same exact line?"

"This will be the last time," he said, his tone dropping.

Pax squeezed my hand.

"You're giving up."

"There's simply nowhere for us to go. We have no legal standing here."

"You have millions of dollars—my dollars—at your disposal, and you're telling me you can't get an American citizen out of a foreign country?"

He leaned forward, looking every bit of his sixty years. "I'm telling you I can't get a Cuban citizen out of Cuba. We have nothing that supersedes their jurisdiction in this matter."

I leaned back, sagging in my chair.

Pax rose and thanked the lawyers, and Brandon walked them out, leaving us alone on the seventy-fifth floor of the Wilder Enterprises high-rise.

I found my feet and walked over to the window where the city of L.A. spread out beneath us.

"Penna?" Pax asked, coming to stand next to me.

"I have all this money," I said, matter-of-fact. "Millions of dollars. Magazines, commercials, hell, my agent just got a movie offer yesterday."

"That's—"

"I have everything I could possibly want, but not the one person I *need*. I don't know how to give up on him, or how to reconcile the fact that everything I have is *worthless*."

He slipped his arm around my shoulders and pulled me to his side, resting his head on top of mine. "We will never give up. We just have to find a rule to bend."

But we both knew the truth: we were out of possibilities.

I drove to Grandma's house in silence, turning off the radio. Three months since we'd had a Marine escort to the *Athena*. Three months since Paxton declared that he owned the ship, and he'd invite anyone he wanted aboard. Three months since I walked Elisa onto U.S. soil, presented her passport, and realized Cruz's dream.

Two months since graduation.

A month until the premiere of our documentary.

The earth kept turning around me, while my heart lingered outside the U.S. Embassy in Cuba, kissing Cruz for the last time.

How different the world looked to me now that I'd tasted love and lost it. How much dimmer, how bland, how… depressing. It was as though my heartache had altered my vision as much as it had stripped me of every emotion except sorrow.

Well, anger was there, too.

I pulled my Range Rover into Grandma's driveway and got out, Cruz's voice in my head as I walked over the cobblestone path and up to the familiar porch.

"Penna!" Elisa called out, opening the door and hugging me.

"Hey," I answered, hugging the petite girl back. She was quiet, careful, but her mind was just as sharp as mine, and when she spoke, her words were all the more powerful for the care she took with them.

"Penelope!" Grandma hugged me even tighter, nearly squishing the air from my lungs.

"Grandma," I said, choking back a lump.

She drew away, her hands on my shoulders, her eyes deep wells of understanding and a lingering sadness. "Your meeting did not go well."

"No," I said, shaking my head as the first tears prickled. "There's nothing they can do. They've given up."

"Have you?" she asked.

I wiped away an errant tear and shook my head. "It took Cruz ten years to get Elisa out of Cuba. I think three months might be a little too soon to give up on him."

She smiled, holding my face in her hands. "Me, too."

• • •

Two days later, I pulled up in front of Oak Moss Grove,

parking next to my mother's Mercedes.

My hands flexed on the steering wheel while I pulled myself together. Then I sucked in a steadying breath, raised my chin, and got out of my car. I made my way up the steps that led to the rehabilitation center and opened the door, welcoming the icy blast of air conditioning.

Then I walked up to the reception desk with the biggest smile I could manage. "I'm so sorry, but I'm late!"

"Oh, that's okay, Miss…" The receptionist looked at me with wide blue eyes.

"Carstairs. I'm sure my parents already headed in to see Brooke, and I got caught in traffic. You know L.A. on a Friday."

"Boy, do I," she said, smiling at me. "Let me walk you back."

My heart thundered in my chest, at odds with my stomach that wanted to run the opposite direction, but I kept my pace steady as we made our way down the same hall Cruz and I had visited almost six months ago.

"Here we go," she said, opening the door.

"Thank you so much!" I said with a quick grin, getting in the door and shutting it behind me. I threw the lock and leaned back against it as I met the incredulous stares of my mother, father, and Brooke.

Brooke, who I loved more than myself.

Brooke…who met my eyes for one sharp, horrified second and then looked away.

"Penna!" Mom exclaimed, jumping up.

"Careful, Mom. I wouldn't want you to wrinkle your dress."

"I don't want her here," Brooke said in an all-too-small voice.

"Well, I don't give a flying fuck," I snapped.

"Penelope!" Dad hissed, but walked over to me slowly, kissing my cheek. "I'm glad to see you, but do you really think this is the best way to do this?"

"It's the *only* way to do this," I countered, "when your only sister, the other half of your heart, drops a fucking stadium light on you, watches you shatter your leg, and then refuses to speak to you."

"Penna, let's be nice," Mom cajoled, slipping over to the loveseat Brooke sat on in her designer tracksuit and wrapping her arm around her.

"I tried nice, Mom. I tried letters, and phone calls, and emails, and even a visit once. Nice got me nowhere, and I'm sick of being nice. Personally, I'm not sure how *you're* not sick of being nice. I'm the one she nearly killed, and yet she's the one you're comforting."

"She's delicate."

"She plotted against our friends and nearly killed several of us, Mom. I'd hardly call that *delicate*, right, Brooke?"

"I don't want to talk about it." Brooke wrung her hands.

"You don't get a say anymore."

Dad leaned against the door next to me, towering over me in height but never in attitude. He'd been the calm as I grew up, the blue sky to Mom's tornado.

"Richard..." Mom cajoled.

"I'm on Penna's side here. Brookie, I love you, but if you ever want to move forward, you're going to have to stop hiding and confront what you did and whom you've hurt."

It may quite possibly have been the most uncomfortable silence of my life as I watched Brooke struggle, then shake her head.

"I talked to Nick."

Her eyes flew to mine.

"He was with us for the last couple of months on the cruise. He actually pulled off some pretty amazing ramp work in that chair in Cuba."

Her brows furrowed.

"He also told me what you did to him. About Patrick."

She sucked in her breath.

"It wasn't your fault," I said. "That's the only thing I'll absolve you of. You cheating on Nick—that's on you. Everything he did after that, what put him in that chair? That's on him. He knows it. We all do. *That* was not your fault."

Her gaze dropped, and her mouth pressed into a thin line.

"The rest is on you," I said softly. "Everything you did to Pax, to Leah, to me. That's on you."

"You wouldn't stop," she whispered.

"I don't have to stop. You don't control me. What happened to Nick was a horrible accident that could have been prevented in so many ways. What you did was cause more, but you didn't rip us apart, if that's what you're wondering."

I waited for a response—hoped for one, but I'd stopped waiting for Brooke a while ago.

"I don't forgive you yet," I said, which got Mom's attention.

"Penna!"

"Be quiet, Claire," Dad snapped.

"I don't have to forgive you, and you sure as hell haven't so much as apologized or asked for forgiveness. Maybe one day I will, and that's my choice. I know now that waiting for some kind of closure or explanation from you only prolongs my hurt, when I have every right to heal from what you did to me."

"You didn't stop!" Brooke shouted, coming to her feet. "After everything, you went right back out there, flipping that goddamned motorcycle as if nothing mattered! As if I don't matter, only they do!"

"Of course you matter, and you were one of us!" I yelled. I sucked in a shaky breath; my eyes locked onto my sister for what I prayed would not be the last time.

"I was never one of you. Never reckless enough. Never willing to break myself over some stupid trick."

"But you were willing to break me."

"I never meant to hurt you, Penna. But you needed to stop. You all have to grow up and stop."

I stepped forward but left my fingers on the door handle. "Did you know that I pulled off the first double backflip ever performed by a woman?"

Her eyes widened. "No."

"Or that I fell in love with an incredible man who traded his life for mine? For his sister's? That there's an overwhelming chance that I will never see him again?"

Her shoulders sagged. "No."

"I know you're hurt. But your hurt does not trump mine. Somewhere along the way you forgot to write your own story. This one's mine, and you don't get a say in what's between these pages. I'll decide what my story is. I'm done feeling guilty over you. When you're ready, come find me. Until then…focus on what makes you happy, because I'll always want that for you, no matter what you did to me."

I turned around, kissed Dad on the cheek, and walked out of the room, concentrating on putting one foot in front of the other as I made my way down the hall.

The receptionist said something to me, but she sounded distant and easy to ignore. I pushed my way out the door and held my face up to the sun, feeling my heart break one last time over Brooke. Then I walked down the stairs, feeling like no matter how much it hurt now, I'd eventually stitch myself together. The hurt would come to an end.

"Penna!" Mom called, and I turned just before I reached my car.

"Go back inside, Mom. I'm sure Brooke needs you."

She tucked her bobbed blond hair behind her ears and cleared her throat. "You know that I love you, right? Just as much as I love your sister?"

"Sure."

"I do. But you… Penna, you're a force of nature. You

haven't needed me since you were three years old and you discovered how to apply your own Band-Aids. You shunned cotillion, every society event, and when you did show up, it was always with Paxton Wilder or Landon Rhodes. Nothing existed for you outside your troop of Lost Boys. I have always loved you, but Brooke has always needed to be protected in a way you never will."

"Maybe I needed you to side with me. She almost killed me, Mom, and you stand by her side like *I'm* going to hurt *her.* Like I'm the dangerous one in this situation."

She put her hand on my face, her perfectly formed smile slipping for the barest of seconds. "I knew you would be okay—you're so very loved by those boys of yours. But if I sided with you there was a very real chance I would lose Brooke to her demons, and I wouldn't be able to live with myself if I lost either of you."

"Well, the good news is that we're both alive. The bad news is you lost me anyway."

Mom straightened, dropping her hand. "Well, my conscience can live with that."

"I'm glad. Please tell Dad I'll see him for lunch like usual on Thursday. Good-bye, Mom."

I climbed into my Rover and shut the door. I made it to Grandma's house before I burst into tears and cried on the shoulder of a woman who had become more like family to me in the past few months than the mother I was born to.

. . .

Music blared through my speakers as I attacked my apartment with cleaning supplies. Yes, I had someone who cleaned for me, but after yesterday's fight with my mother and Brooke, I wanted to scrub everything dirty out of my life.

I threw open the door to my walk-in closet and started

on the pile of crap I'd let accumulate in the corner. Sorting dirty laundry, bags, and gear into piles, I paused when Cruz's backpack appeared.

I gathered it to me, hugging it against my chest like it was Cruz himself. God, it even smelled like him, or my nose tricked me. Either way, for that millisecond, he felt real instead of this nearly perfect man I'd made up.

I sat on the floor between the piles and pulled out the accordion file. Everything was exactly where I'd left it when I'd last looked at it in Miami. My fingers grazed his military paperwork, and I pulled out the paper-clipped stack.

None of it made any more sense than the first time I'd looked at it. I saw his discharge papers and read through the details of his service. Maybe it was a violation of his privacy, but I would have done anything to feel closer to him at that moment.

My forehead puckered when I found the next sheet, and my hands started to shake. *Could this…?*

Scared to get my hopes up, I read carefully. Cruz had gotten out of the military, but was there a chance this could be what I needed?

I whipped out my cell phone and called the only person I could think of—Brandon.

"What's up, Penna?"

"I think I know how to get Cruz back, but I'm going to need some help."

"What do you need? You know I'll help," he said after a moment of silence.

"I think I need to talk to the president."

"Of course you do."

Chapter Thirty-Four

CRUZ

HAVANA

"Let's go," the guard barked from the entrance to my cell.

I rubbed a hand over my beard, trying to wake myself. The thing about being kept in a solitary cell with no window was that I'd lost track of time, and not just hours in the day, but days in general.

I'd tried to mark every time they fed me, to delineate the time by what kind of food the guards brought, but I had a suspicion they were changing it up just to fuck with my head.

"Now," the guard urged.

I stumbled to my feet off the bare mattress of my bunk and followed him out of my cell. Another armed soldier trailed behind as we trudged through hallways and up a flight of stairs.

"What day is it?" I asked.

"Silence."

Super helpful.

We emerged on the first floor, and I covered my eyes from the blinding sunlight that poured in through the windows.

"Move!" the guard yelled, and I walked forward, my eyes prickling from the assault of brightness.

"Here," the one in front said, opening a door.

I walked through and was able to drop my hands from my eyes in the dimmer setting.

"Jesus Christ. What the hell have you done to him?" a man with a southern twang asked. I blinked as he came into focus. He was dressed in U.S. Army ACUs with full bird colonel rank on his chest and the name Ward.

"Treated him as any prisoner," my father answered.

"Have a seat, son," Colonel Ward said, pulling out a chair.

"He's *my* son," my father growled.

"Sure looks like you treated him like it," Ward drawled. "I asked for this meeting two weeks ago."

"I'm under no obligation to let you see this prisoner." My father shrugged.

"As a Cuban citizen, you're right. But as a member of the United States Army, you're dead wrong, and you will relinquish Sergeant Delgado to my custody, or you will risk direct consequences. The United States doesn't take kindly to foreign governments holding their soldiers."

I sat up straight, leaning forward. "What's going on?"

"How familiar are you with the Individual Ready Reserve?"

My mind floundered for an answer. "It's the four years you're on standby after you ETS."

"Bingo," he said, pointing to me. "Now for you non-Americans, I'll make it clear. Sergeant Delgado enlisted for three years when he was seventeen—"

"He's twenty-eight, so your point—"

"I'm talking now," Colonel Ward interrupted my father.

Guess I'd unknowingly spent a birthday in this hellhole, which meant it was at least August first. Jesus, I'd been here almost four months.

"Now," Colonel Ward said, turning back to me. "You enlisted at seventeen, served your three years as agreed, and then transferred to Individual Ready Reserve."

"Right," I agreed. Pieces clicked. IRR was automatic for anyone serving less than eight years. We were on the hook for eight and could be called back at the pleasure of the president, but it hadn't been done since Desert Storm in the nineties. It was a piece of paper I'd signed and never given a second thought to.

But my eight years was up when I was twenty-five.

"Turns out, you deferred that time while you got your doctorate, Dr. Delgado," Colonel Ward said with a smile.

"Deferred." A spark of hope lit in my chest, and even though I wanted to kill it, the damn thing started to glow brighter and brighter.

"Yes. I'm sorry to inform you that two weeks ago I received a call that you've been recalled to the Selected Reserve. Your reserve unit back in L.A. is expecting you."

A small, incredulous laugh slipped free.

"This is preposterous!" my father railed. "He is a criminal!"

"Accused of what?" Colonel Ward asked. "Kidnapping a willing eighteen-year-old adult and helping her get to the embassy for which she holds citizenship?"

My father's mouth dropped open and then snapped shut, the muscle of his jaw flexing. "We will not surrender custody."

The door opened and another Cuban general walked in.

"General Delgado."

"General Gutierrez."

Colonel Ward walked over to me and placed a hand on my shoulder. "As of this moment, I have custody of Sergeant

Delgado. With all our two countries have gone through to reestablish diplomatic ties, are you really willing to go to war over this? Because I am. I don't leave U.S. soldiers in enemy territory to be falsely imprisoned, and I have roughly five thousand soldiers about five hundred miles from here."

My father's fists slammed into the table, and he hung his head, his massive chest rising and falling rapidly. "No."

"Of course you may take your soldier, Colonel. Please do so now," General Gutierrez said with a smile.

"Pleasure meeting you, Generals Delgado and Gutierrez," Ward said with a nod at each. "Thank you."

He didn't need to tell me twice. I jumped out of my seat and followed him as he left the conference room as yelling erupted from behind us.

"Keep walking," he ordered. "Do not stop for any reason."

"Yes, sir."

We walked down the marble-floored hallway with its open arches into the Caribbean weather. Such a beautiful setting for ugliness.

We met up with a small group of armed U.S. soldiers, and I was led to a Humvee, which I immediately slid into. I sank into the seat as Ward took the front passenger seat.

"Is this really happening?" I asked, fully expecting to wake up in that solitary cell at any moment.

"It is. How are you? Hungry? Thirsty?" he asked as the convoy pulled out of the headquarters building.

"Yes to all," I said, my head hitting the seat behind me. I was really leaving, escaping, heading home. *Penelope.*

"Good. We'll need to debrief you, of course, and then we'll get you headed back to the States."

"Yes, sir. How did you know about me?" I asked.

"You have a hell of an insistent girlfriend, Sergeant."

That hope in my chest blew into a full-blown fire. I'd be back in L.A. soon. I could hold her, kiss her, fight with her until we had the best make-up sex of our lives, and then start all over again. "There's no one like her on the planet, sir."

"Doesn't take no for an answer, either."

I smiled—the first real one since I'd been taken away from her at the Embassy. "Yeah, well, there's a reason they call her Rebel."

Chapter Thirty-Five

PENNA

LOS ANGELES

"Rebel!" The reporters called out as I walked our little red carpet toward the premiere.

I paused, popping a hip in my strapless Vera Wang and smiling like I was the happiest girl on the planet. Truthfully, I was dying inside. My hair was shiny only because my hairdresser had spritzed me with God knows what, and all the makeup in the world couldn't hide the bags under my eyes.

It had been three weeks since I'd found the papers and started the slow-moving ball that was the U.S. Military on the hunt for Cruz.

I'd been denied any information as of two weeks ago and told that the situation was now classified. *Assholes.*

Fulfilling my duties, I stood and looked pretty until I felt they'd gotten enough pictures and moved on. As far as L.A. premieres went, ours was tiny, but the biggest stars in extreme sports were here, and even a few A-list Hollywood actors.

Turned out our little documentary was making quite a splash.

"Rebel, would you say that you and the Renegades are the new generation of Warren Miller?"

"The idea that anyone could replace Warren Miller is laughable," I answered. "Plus, I don't think I have it in me to do this every year."

I looked up the row to see Nick motioning me toward the door, and I made my excuses to the press.

"It's a zoo out there," I told him as we walked through the theater, headed toward the stage.

"We've got about ten minutes until speech time, and I didn't want you trapped in the melee."

"Thanks. The others?"

"Already waiting in the wings."

The theater staff parted the red velvet ropes that sectioned off the backstage area and let us through. We thanked them and headed for our designated meeting spot.

Landon and Pax waited just behind the curtain, and we met up center stage.

"Damn, you stand out like a red dress in the midst of tuxes," Landon joked.

"I thought about wearing a suit like you guys and then decided I'd never been afraid of being the only girl. You ready for this?" I asked Nick.

He nodded. "I pretty much came out in Cuba, so this is a piece of cake."

"Did you see Zoe?" Pax asked. "She's up and walking."

"Gabe is here, too. I banned his parents, though," Landon muttered at the end.

"Good call," Nick said.

We shot the breeze for the next few minutes, killing time until Bobby motioned from the wings and pointed to his watch.

"Looks like it's time," Pax said.

We lined up and faced the full theater, only separated by a layer of velvet.

"Sometimes it floors me that we actually did it," I said.

"It floors me every day," Landon answered.

The button on our mics flashed red, and we stopped talking. We were live.

Music blared through the sound system, and the curtain rose to the applause of our audience. The house was packed. I made out a few familiar faces in the crowd—Leah and Rachel sat next to our reserved seats. Little John wasn't far behind them.

"Thank you for coming," Paxton started. "I'm Wilder," he said with a wave.

"Rebel."

"Nova."

"And Nitro," Nick said, finishing up.

The applause was deafening, and I felt the heat rising to my cheeks.

"The Renegades started in my backyard as the four of us refusing to go in for dinner when we were called." Pax laughed. "We always wanted one more run, one more jump. I guess nothing much has changed."

"We got older, moved out of our parents' houses, thank God," Landon added to the enjoyment of the crowd. "We won a few X Games medals and earned a reputation for pulling off the stunts no one else was stupid enough to try."

"I was hurt," Nick said, and the crowd quieted. "And my friends stepped up with the idea for this documentary, hoping my stunt and ramp designs would keep me in the game. I found out in Cuba I'm still pretty ramp-worthy, too." The crowd whooped, and we all laughed.

"This documentary became more than sports," I said.

We'd practiced this a few times, but now that we were here, I was more than a little scared that I'd fuck up in front of the crowd. "Sure, we pull off some pretty amazing feats, but the stunts we do in this film are nothing compared to the experiences we had while traveling the world. Not just the places we saw, or the cultures we were able to witness, but how we grew together as friends."

"We pulled off firsts," Pax said.

"We failed others," Landon added. "And then we went back for a second try and nailed it," he said, smiling at Rachel. They'd spent three weeks in Nepal with the camera crew, and Landon had finally gotten his dream run.

"We pushed the boundaries of gender, logic, and gravity," I spoke my part.

"And as you'll see, we all fell in love." Pax grinned at Leah. "I fell for my tutor."

"I got back the one who initially got away." Landon winked at Rachel.

"I fell for the one I was never supposed to."

Grandma gave me a sad smile from where she sat with Elisa.

"I learned to love myself," Nick finished.

"We started our fair share of international incidents, but I think Rebel took the cake," Pax said with a laugh.

My gaze swung to him. Why the hell was he going off the script we'd agreed to?

Landon pulled me under his arm. "This girl was separated from the love of her life at the American Embassy in Cuba."

"Landon," I whispered, my mic down.

"Trust me," he whispered in my ear.

"When she got home to L.A., she didn't stop fighting," Nick said. "In true Rebel fashion, she kicked down every door she could find, trying to get him back to her. She went up against lawyers, the U.S. military, and pretty much the entire

Cuban government."

"And you know what? She finally kicked down the right door," Pax said, smiling at me like a lunatic.

"Pax…" I whispered, my voice breaking.

"Time to get your happy ending," he said off-mic.

My heart stopped as *Love Lifts Us Up* played through the sound system.

"Holy shit, it's like the eighties just came back," Nick mumbled.

Landon smacked the back of his head, and Pax walked behind to stand with them.

The spotlight hit the left side of the stage, and I stopped breathing, scared that if I so much as drew a tiny amount of air, the vision would disappear.

Cruz stood twenty feet away, dimples out, his smile so beautiful I knew I had to be imagining him—in full military dress blues. My mic hit the ground as my hands flew to my face, covering my mouth.

A sound like a whimper escaped me as he strode across the distance to the wild applause of the crowd. My arms fell away, like I'd lost all the strength in my muscles. He didn't say a word, simply took my face in his hands and kissed me as if we were alone—and as his lips moved over mine, his taste sweet, familiar, and oh, so Cruz, the crowd vanished, and we were the only people in the world.

My arms looped around his neck, and he lifted me off the ground and into his arms, tucking one hand beneath my knees in a bridal carry.

"All we're missing is someone shouting, 'Way to go, Paula!'" Cruz told me.

I laughed against his mouth, tears escaping down my cheeks. "You know *An Officer and a Gentleman* is the navy, right?"

How far we'd come since he'd said those words to me.

Those brown eyes locked onto mine, and I saw everything I needed there—strength, humor, home…love. "Shhhh. This is *my* grand gesture. My turn."

I grinned, recalling the time I'd told him exactly the same thing on the *Athena*, and threw my energy into kissing him.

He carried me offstage to the loudest applause I'd ever heard in my life, but it was background noise to the beat of my heart in rhythm with his.

"Now you just listen to me tell you that I love you," he said very seriously.

"And I love you," I answered.

"Good, because I don't want to live a day in my life where I don't wake up next to you and fall asleep with you in my arms. You're the only future I see, Penelope. And if that means I have to close my eyes while you pull off whatever harebrained stunt you've cooked up, I'll do it."

"Or you can do it with me. You've got some pretty good moves of your own."

"I have to keep up with my girl," he said against my lips, and we lost ourselves to another kiss that felt even more perfect than the last. "I would have called, but I only got back stateside this morning, and this just seemed…"

"Epic," I offered.

"Worthy of you," he answered with another kiss. Was there ever going to be a time when I grew tired of kissing him? I highly doubted it.

His cheeks were smooth under my fingers as I pulled back enough to look at him. "You're home? Really?"

"Thanks to you, I am."

A fresh set of tears tracked down my cheeks, as if my body finally gave itself permission to let go. "I missed you, and I was so scared I'd never see you again."

He tucked me in even closer and kissed my forehead. "Don't cry. I'm here, and I'm never leaving you. Well…" he trailed off, and a wave of fear replaced my euphoria.

"What? You'd better tell me!"

"I do have drill once a month now. I'm kind of in the Reserves for the next three years. But if you don't agree, I can always go back to Cuba."

I laughed, tears blurring my vision. "I think we can deal. Cruz?" I asked, my hands running over the hair that met the nape of his neck.

"Yeah, baby?"

All it took was that look, and my body caught fire, immediately ready for his. Months apart hadn't changed a single thing with our chemistry, or my soul-consuming love for him.

In those seconds, our future became so clear to me. We'd laugh, we'd fight, we'd push each other to the point of insanity, and we'd pull each other back from the brink. We'd love harder than any other couple in the history of the world.

"Take me home."

He smiled and kissed me softly. "Don't you want to see the movie?"

I shook my head. "I already know how it ends."

"Oh?" he asked, already headed out of the theater, still carrying me securely in his strong arms.

"Happily ever after."

Epilogue

PENNA

Five Years Later

"Aunt Penna?"

Melody's sweet voice startled me, and I put down my phone on the counter in Pax's kitchen. Funny how one phone call could change, well...everything.

I took a deep, shaking breath and tried to calm my emotions, which were currently on a roller coaster that didn't show any sign of stopping.

"What's up, Mel?" I asked the four-year-old, kneeling down at her level. She had Pax's blue eyes paired with Leah's serious nature, and was far more concerned with how motorcycles worked than ever getting on one.

"Are you ready to give Uncle Cruz his birthday present?"

My smile was instant, and I blinked away tears that had sprung from nowhere. This was a birthday my handsome husband would never forget.

"I think so," I told her, tucking a strand of hair behind her ear. "Want to help me?"

She nodded, her eyes lighting up.

"Okay, go grab your brother and Skye and meet me in the barn, okay?"

Another quick nod and she raced off, the kitchen door slamming home as she ran toward the ramps.

I followed, pausing on the giant porch Leah had demanded Pax add to their home a few years ago. It had transformed Renegade Ranch from our headquarters to their home and was the perfect place to sit with my friends and watch the sunset.

So much had changed in the last few years, but summer at the Renegade Ranch was still my favorite time of year. No matter where we'd all gone for the off-season, summer was sacred, and we came home.

"There you are," Landon said with a smile, meeting me at the bottom of the porch steps and slinging his arm around my shoulder.

"I sent Mel to grab Mason and Skye, if that's okay."

"If you can get Skye off that ramp, I'll be impressed. Both Rach and I have asked her four times if she's ready for a break." He laughed, pointing to where his three-year-old daughter hit the mini ramp on her tiny bike.

"Whoa, she got some air on that one."

"Takes after her aunt." He gave me a squeeze as Skye rode to where Nick sat ready to give her guidance as always. His girlfriend, Joy, was out of town this weekend on business, but they were never far apart for long.

"Lunch is about ready," Leah called out from the long, shaded picnic table, where she sat with Mason and Rachel. Right on cue, the two-year-old wiggled from his mama's lap and toddled toward his favorite person—Pax.

Pax lifted the little guy and headed for us. "It's all set up.

You ready?"

Before I could answer, Cruz came around the back of the largest ramp, wiping the grease off his hands as he laughed at something Little John said.

"We'll meet you in the barn," Pax said with muffled laughter when I couldn't peel my eyes from my husband.

My heart swelled, as if the happiness that flooded me couldn't be contained in something as small as my body. I felt as radiant as sunshine, all because that man had gifted me with the sun in more ways than one.

He grinned when he saw me, which effectively turned my stomach to mush just like always. Three years of marriage, but his effect on me never changed. Hell, it only got stronger.

My eyes didn't leave him as he crossed the distance to where I now stood alone. Did life get any better than this? Than being surrounded by your friends, your family, the man you love? I couldn't imagine anything better, but I knew we'd have "better" coming our way soon.

"Penelope," he said, his voice low as he looped his arms around my waist.

"Cruz," I answered, smiling up at him like an idiot. "Happy Birthday."

"You said that this morning when we woke up, and then an hour later once we got out of bed. Then again as we drove over," he reminded me, kissing my forehead.

"And I'll probably tell you another dozen times before it's over. If you can manage to tear Skye off the ramp, I have your present waiting in the barn."

He raised those dark brows, his eyes just as chocolate and melty as ever. "No one else can get her, huh?"

I shook my head. "Nope."

We walked toward the ramp, where Skye finished another run with even more air. She hopped off her tiny bike and ripped off her helmet, running for Cruz. "Uncle Cruz! Did you see me? Did you?"

"I did!" he said, swinging her into his arms. "You looked great! Are you having fun?"

"Yes!" she nodded, sending her chin-length black bob swinging. Then her eyes narrowed. "Melody didn't want to ride."

"That's okay. Melody doesn't have to ride for you to have fun," he told her as we headed toward the barn. Cruz was the one person Skye gravitated toward, which constantly melted me.

Nick caught up to us, squeezing my hand. "Thank you for the break. She's relentless."

"Wonder where she gets that from," I motioned to where her parents waited in the shade of the barn.

"Born a Renegade." He laughed.

I glanced over to Cruz and Skye. Cruz would make an amazing father. Not that we hadn't tried. We'd wanted to start a family as soon as we were married, to have our kids while we were young enough to run after them, to raise them with the new generation of Renegades, but that hadn't worked out for us the way we'd initially planned.

After the first year, we'd sought help and learned that I wasn't exactly a prime biological candidate for conventional motherhood. We'd had more than our share of heartbreak, specialists, injections, appointments, and failed IVFs in the last three years. It seemed the harder we tried, the worse it hurt, the more it mattered. It was a cycle we'd needed to step away from. Four months ago, we'd stopped fighting nature with science and decided to give ourselves a break.

"So what did you get me?" Cruz asked playfully as we made our way into the barn. He lowered Skye to the ground, and she ran over to her daddy, the very miniature of her mother.

"You'll see," I said, pulling him by the hand through our

small group of friends.

"Is that…?" His voice pitched upward.

"Pull off the tarp."

He shot me a look of pure excitement and lifted the cover off the exquisite dirt bike. The paint job mirrored my Elizabeth the Second's, only in blue. "Penelope! Is this…?"

"Next year's model! It's not even for sale yet!"

He ran his hand over the seat and then turned toward me, those dimples fully out. "It's amazing, thank you," he said, pulling me in for a quick kiss.

"Happy birthday!" I told him.

"What are you going to name him?" Pax asked with Melody tucked in between him and Leah and Mason on his arm.

Cruz's eyes narrowed in thought before he nodded to himself, as if he'd decided already. "Darcy."

"What?" Landon asked.

"You have Elizabeth the Second," Cruz said softly. "It's only fitting that I have Darcy."

Swoon.

"You have me to the toes of my *Pride and Prejudice* heart," I told him before he kissed me again.

"Okay, love birds, let's go. Lunch is waiting, and this new documentary won't plan itself," Pax said, leading his family out of the barn.

International Waters III had come out to rave reviews and a cult following, which gave us more than enough backing for the next installment, which we'd begin filming next year.

I tugged on Cruz's hand when he turned to leave, and he paused.

"You guys go ahead, we'll be there in a minute," I told Rachel when she looked back.

When the barn was empty, I looked up at my husband, memorizing every detail about this moment. I wanted to be able to replay it countless times for the rest of our lives.

"I think I'm going to have to pull out of the documentary this time," I told him, my lower lip near trembling. *Don't cry. Not yet. You have to tell him first!*

Concern immediately etched his face. "Okay, you know I'll support whatever decision you think you need to make, but if this is about me—"

Cruz had given up teaching in the formal sense—our affair had pretty much ruined his résumé, but he was happy tutoring the younger Renegades to make sure everyone had their high school diplomas or succeeded in getting their college degrees.

"It's not. I know you're happy wherever we're together. It's about me. Well, about us." My voice broke on the last word, and I blinked back the tears that had threatened since I'd taken that phone call.

"You're scaring me," he said, cupping my face in his hands.

Emotion closed my throat, and instead of speaking, I took one of his hands and slid it down my body until it rested on my lower abdomen. "It's about us," I repeated as the first tear escaped.

Then my beautiful, brilliant, articulate husband lost his ability to speak. His mouth opened and shut several times, his eyes jumping from my belly to my face. "Penelope?"

My smile was wide as more tears tracked down my cheeks. "Dr. Silverman just called. I'd gone to see him yesterday afternoon because I didn't want to think…to hope, but it had been months since…"

"You're pregnant?"

I nodded. "He thinks about eleven weeks from the labs and the dates, but he wants us in for an ultrasound first thing tomorrow morning to check."

He swept me into his arms, holding me tightly against his chest and burying his face in my neck. "Thank you, thank you, thank you," he repeated, and I didn't know if he was thanking me, or God, or fate, or Dr. Silverman. I didn't care, because I felt the same way.

"Happy birthday," I whispered, and he squeezed me lightly before putting me back on my feet. The kiss he gave me was dizzying—passionate and tender and so very Cruz.

Then he dropped to his knees in front of me, lifted up my tank top, and pressed a kiss to my belly. "Best day ever."

We eventually told the others, and Pax demanded we hold off filming for a year. He said that we filmed together or not at all, and we could all use the year to spend with our families.

So we all took it off.

Our daughter was born. Our perfect, seven pound, three ounce daughter who somehow had Cruz's dark hair and my blue eyes.

And in our delivery room, after Aria had been placed in my arms, the Renegades made their way in. I introduced our daughter to her family, including Cruz's grandma, who had no trouble elbowing Landon out of the way to get to her great-granddaughter.

While everyone chatted, I snuggled my daughter close and whispered, "Ride or don't ride. It will never matter to anyone in this room, and we'll never care as long as you're happy. This is where you belong. Where you'll always belong."

Cruz leaned down, gently kissing me before running his finger along the soft skin of Aria's cheek. "What are you thinking?" he asked.

"That my whole life I've been out chasing adrenaline, the rush of adventure, and yet I look at her, at you, and I know this is our greatest adventure."

"Living dangerously, Penelope." His smile was breathtaking as he echoed the first words he'd ever spoken to me.

"I wouldn't have it any other way."

"I wouldn't have *you* any other way."

His kiss was soft and full of every emotion we couldn't name. And I realized this was it.

This was the pinnacle of the jump, the moment at the podium.

"Best day ever," I whispered to our daughter.

"Best day ever," Cruz repeated.

And it was.

Acknowledgments

First and foremost, my thanks to my Heavenly Father, who blesses me with more than I could ever deserve.

Thank you, Jason, for your limitless love and understanding. Thank you for navigating the outside world and keeping me idealistic. You are the inspiration behind every book boyfriend, and I can only hope we raise our boys to be the man you are. Your unwavering faith in me is what pushes me through every book—especially this one. Thank you to our kids, for your smiles, hugs, and *I love you*s. You guys are my reason, my inspiration, my gorgeous chaos reminding me that our real life is the fairy tale. Thank you, Mom and Dad, for always believing in me and forgiving my deadline brain. Thank you, Kate, for coaching our kids in lacrosse, showing up when I need you, talking me off the proverbial ledge, and being my favorite (and only) sister. Thank you, Emily, for understanding that deadline months mean I go way too long without seeing my best friend.

Thank you to my awesome editor, Karen. Another series down!!! Thank you for pulling me out of a submission pile and giving me my dream job. None of this would be possible without your expertise, your refusal to let me settle for less than my best, or your friendship. You make my job so much fun! Huge thanks to the entire Entangled team, Liz, Melanie, Jessica, Holly, Brittany, Candy, and Curtis, you guys are simply amazing. Thank you, Alison, for running my group with such joy and enthusiasm. I am so blessed to have you! Thank you, Shelby, for walking into my burning house of a life and organizing it all. Thank you, Linda, squirrel-chaser extraordinaire, and the best table-partner EVER. Thanks to my phenomenal agent, Louise Fury, for your incredibly long hours and dedication to my career. I couldn't ask for a better partner in this crazy business.

Thank you to the incredible authors who are also some of my closest friends. Molly, you are and will always be everything. My work-wifeys, Cindi and Gina, the other two pillars of our unholy trinity, thank you for being my safe place and my motivation. Jay Crownover, my favorite neighbor, surrogate aunt to my kids…I have finally delivered the beach scene you demanded. Enjoy. There are so many other authors I owe every debt of gratitude to, but I will simply say, if you pick up a pen, I love you. Thank you for being the best coworkers ever. The bloggers who work so hard to promote, review, and support authors. You guys are my rock stars: Aestas, Natasha T., Natasha M., Wolfel, Kimberly, my love Jillian Stein, Jen, Reanell, Lisa, Angie, Beth and Ashley, and the countless others I can't fit here. If I've forgotten you, please forgive me and my overfull brain. Liz Berry, thank you for being a constant source of advice.

My Flygirls, you are my favorite place on the internet. Thank you for being so kind, supportive, and awesome to hang with!

Lastly, thank you again to my husband—my beginning and my end. Even as I type this, you're out grabbing dinner because I was too busy writing to cook. Thank you for feeding me, for choosing me, for simply loving me.

JOIN OUR SQUAD

CADETS, SIGN UP TO OUR
NEWSLETTER AND KEEP AN EYE
ON OUR SOCIAL CHANNELS FOR
OFFICIAL CORRESPONDENCE
FROM THE EMPYREAN

Need a new series to binge?

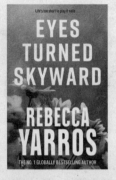